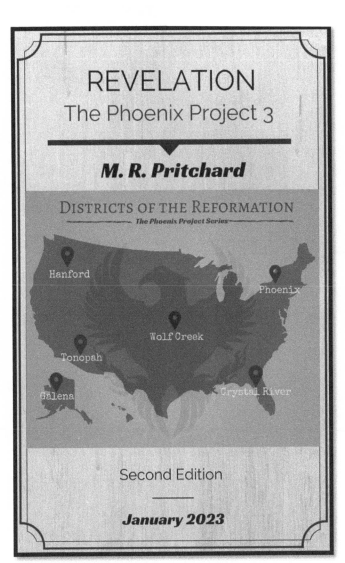

REVELATION
The Phoenix Project 3

M. R. Pritchard

DISTRICTS OF THE REFORMATION
The Phoenix Project Series

Hanford

Phoenix

Wolf Creek

Tonopah

Galena

Crystal River

Second Edition

January 2023

Copyright © 2023 M. R. Pritchard

ISBN: 978-1-957709-15-4

Second Edition January 2023
Midnight Ledger

CHAPTER ONE

He was given back to me. I didn't have to choose this time. My whole family was returned. We are back to being a complete unit. All it cost was Adam's life.

Now, *he* is down the hall in the small room I used for an office, sleeping in his bed. A single bed. Alone. Not where a married man usually sleeps. Not next to his wife as he should be.

I stretch my hand out, feeling the cool sheets of the empty half of the bed. I can hear the steady, even breaths of Raven sleeping in the crib that's pushed against the far wall. They're interrupted by the grinding squeak of the old spring mattress Ian sleeps on. Pulling my arm back, clutching it close to my body, I know he's not asleep. I know this for certain because these are the hours when he's more ghost-like than ever. I pull the sheets tighter around myself and hold my breath.

It is hard falling in love with a ghost.

His mattress springs grind again, followed by the soft thudding of his feet on the hardwood floors. I

1

know what comes next: the soft noise of his door opening further, his footsteps in the hallway. He stops outside my open door. Just like every night.

I could close the door, but I like to be able to hear what's going on in the house. I want to be ready, the first to hear if there is a problem so I can react. But nothing happens here at the Pasture. Except for Ian waking each night, walking the hall, and stopping at my door.

If there were a light on, his shadow might stretch into the room where I sleep. But being the middle of the night, it is pitch black here. I couldn't see my hand in front of my face if I tried. I can hear him though. He stops and holds his breath, just like I hold mine. I could speak. I could tell him to come here and talk to me. But I'm not ready for him. Not yet. Not feeling this mixture of emotions bombarding me at every second. Not knowing that Adam died to save us and his son sleeps just feet from me.

It's all too fresh.

Ian gives up, just like he has each night since he came back, his footsteps quiet as he walks down the hallway. What comes next is the same each night: he flicks on the kitchen light and shadows stretch down the hall, the dull light illuminating a portion of my room. He opens the refrigerator door. He closes the refrigerator door. He opens a cupboard. He closes the cupboard. He paces the kitchen, the floor creaking as he does. Then, he stops. And this is where he becomes a true ghost, slipping out of our lives each night almost as soundlessly as he did years ago when the Funding Entities took over. He walks across the kitchen to the hallway and out the front door. He's been doing this since he arrived.

Holding my breath, I wait to hear the soft click of the lock as he closes the door. Every night this is how it happens. This is the moment in which he leaves me just like I left him. The only difference is he comes back each morning. He doesn't abandon me for years. I'm not sure where he goes or what he does. All I know is that I fall asleep and in the morning, he walks down the hall and into the kitchen for breakfast as though he spent the night in his single bed, sleeping.

Whatever he does, wherever he goes, he somehow gets enough sleep to continue on with his duty of running the nuclear reactor. Crane wouldn't take kindly to his home life negatively impacting his work. After all, the reactor keeps the District safe, providing the fence with enough electricity to roast a chicken in thirty seconds. I'm sure if Crane caught wind of Ian functioning poorly, he'd take him away again. He would hide Ian back in whatever hole he had him in before and we'd never see him again. And since I am not allowed to raise fatherless children, I'd have to choose someone else. These are the rules described in the District Manifesto. These are the demands of the Phoenix District Entities.

Unsure of what keeps Ian awake at night, I do know that I can finally sleep. The nightmares stopped the day Crane told me Adam died. When his soul left the earth he must have taken them with him, all the dark, horrid images. I never had another one. I have never awoken in the still of the night covered in sweat, my heart racing, screaming things I can't remember. That's all done with. Now, I close my eyes at night and open them in the morning. There's nothing in between. No nightmares, no dreams, nothing. Just sleep and rest and peace.

Actually, I take that back. There is no peace while Burton Crane is still alive. This I know for certain, just as I know it's only a matter of time before he requests that I finish my tasks in Florida.

--

As the morning sun rises outside, I sit in a rocking chair feeding Raven. My eyes wander the room to the simple green bedspread, the whitewash walls, the thin white curtains hanging at each window, eventually stopping at the canvas bag at the foot of the bed. Even with all the sleep I still haven't found the energy to unpack my suitcase from that trip. *The tour*, the moments when it became glaringly clear that Crane had bigger plans for me and much less for my daughter. I stare at the suitcase. Perhaps it has nothing to do with energy and more to do with my emotions. It sits at the foot of my bed nothing more than a canvas headstone.

I look at Raven in my arms. My son. Adam's son. The son he never met and will never meet. Adam's dead.

Setting down Raven would free my arms and I could finally unpack. He probably won't even wake up and even if he does, he won't make a sound. He hasn't cried, he hasn't cooed. He has never made a sound since the day he was born.

Finally deciding to do something about the suitcase, I stand and set him in the bassinet. As I wrap his swaddling blanket a little tighter, he stirs but doesn't open his eyes.

Moving to the foot of the bed and kneeling, I tip the suitcase on its side. My hands tremble. Taking a clear breath and steadying my fingers, I unzip the suitcase. There's an assortment of clothes. Black slacks, dark colored blouses, a light sweater. My clothes. The same clothes I always wear. But there's something else. Something I wasn't prepared for. I can smell it before I see it. Lying on the top of my things is a T-shirt, a black T-shirt, Adam's T-shirt.

Never has a piece of cloth intimidated me so.

I fearfully stare at it, knowing what's going to happen if I touch it or smell it for more than just a slight whiff. I know how my brain will react, how it will remember. The olfactory receptors are part of the limbic system, and if I smell that shirt, that emotional part of my brain, the amygdala, it's going to remember. It's going to remember everything great and everything bad and every moment I ever had with him.

The amygdala is not my friend.

I've had to alter it in the Residents, shrink it down to the point where it can no longer think for itself, to the point where it will trust everyone and do what it's told. I've engineered it to curtail their emotions, but that's not what's going to happen to me. I am Sovereign. My amygdala is intact, fully operational, fully capable of absorbing all those neurotransmitters that are going to flood my brain as soon as I take a deep breath of that shirt that smells just like him.

The amygdala is definitely not my friend. It is nothing more than a drug dealer and I am about to take my first addictive hit.

In a desperate move, I reach for the shirt, moving faster than I have in weeks and I press it to my face, breathing in deep. The reaction is instantaneous. The breath pushes from my chest, my heart shudders, my head goes fuzzy. *Oh God*, they bombard me in one great wave: memories.

The rational part of my brain knows this isn't real, but when I open my eyes, it's almost as if he's standing in front of me. His image wavers. His hair is dark, his skin tanned, his eyes still the same pale blue. His hands are in his pockets and he seems to rock back on his heels. This is not real, just a wavering memory of him, his ghost. He's dead. Even though I know this, I still want him to kneel next to me and wrap his arms around me.

"Adam?" I whisper. His image seems to flutter and fade. I press the shirt to my face and breathe in deep. When I open my eyes, he's still there, his image a little brighter, a little stronger. "Adam?" I whisper again, wanting him to respond, wanting him to say something to me even though I know he's not real. Even though I remember what he told me on that train.

"This was a mistake. It's over," he says to me.

Yes, it's over. The memory before me seems to falter and fade and disappear. The hope that once filled my chest at seeing his memory is now replaced with an empty void. One cannot have an affair with a ghost. Yet, it seems I am married to a ghost most days.

"Andie?" I hear Ian's voice in the hallway.

I choke out a fresh breath and shove the shirt back into the suitcase, hiding it under my clothes. There's a knock on the bedroom door.

"Andie?" Ian asks.

"Come in." My voice sounds strained.

Ian walks into the room, stopping when he notices Raven sleeping in the bassinet. "Hey," he says, his voice hushed and completely nonchalant, as if we were just a normal married couple standing in a room together. He seems so tall in this old farmhouse.

"Hi." I look away from him.

"Unpacking finally?" he asks, motioning to the suitcase.

With the faint lingering smell of Adam's shirt and the memories still so fresh in my mind, I can barely look at Ian right now. "Yeah," I respond, my eyes fixed on the floor.

"I thought I heard you talking to someone." He gives me a worrisome gaze and looks around the room.

"Um, no." I press my fingertips to my forehead, trying to force the image of Adam from my mind. "I was just..." Unable to think of a good excuse I trail off and never complete the sentence.

An awkward five heartbeats pass between us before Ian breaks the silence, "I'm headed to the barn."

I nod. I don't look up at him. I know what I'll see if I do: the hopeful brown eyes, the creases around his mouth and locks of blonde hair falling across his forehead. I've become accustomed to this look upon his face and I can hear it in his voice right now. It's the only thing about him that makes me believe that he is truly real and not a ghost; you can't fake the concern that Ian exudes and there's no way a ghost could fill a room up like he does.

"I'll see you for dinner?" he asks.

"Okay." I finally look up and force a smile. I don't know why I smile, it doesn't help the discomfort of our current situation.

"Okay." He nods and closes the door as he leaves.

Staring at the lump of clothes in front of me, I try to control the urge to pull the shirt out again. My thoughts are interrupted by a voice outside my door as Ian's footsteps echo down the hall. Sam. I can hear them talking. Just a quick conversation and it's only a few moments before there is another knock on the

7

door.

"Sis?" I hear Sam's voice.

"Yeah?" I ask with a sigh.

He opens the door. "How are you doing?"

"Fine, Sam. I just… I wish everyone would stop asking me that."

He brushes a brown lock of hair out of his eyes and fidgets with his clothes. They're new, in the sense that Sam hasn't worn them before. There are worn patterns in the thighs of his jeans and the button-down shirt sleeves seem a little too short on him.

"New clothes?" I ask.

"Yeah." He smiles and presses his hand over the front of the blue shirt. "They finally found some hand-me-downs that fit me."

"Good."

Sam looks toward the bassinet where Raven sleeps and back to me, still kneeling on the floor in front of the open suitcase.

"What's wrong?" I ask him as I stand and move away from the suitcase.

"Crane wants to see me," he responds with a frown.

"And?"

"And I was hoping you would go with me." He raises his eyebrows, his face turning hopeful.

"What does he need to see you for?" I busy myself with folding a basket of Raven's laundry.

"He said it's something about my training."

"Why do you need me to go?" I ask.

Sam runs a hand across the back of his neck. "Truthfully, I thought you might like to get out of the house. You've been cooped up here for weeks."

Six weeks actually. I've been here for six weeks and I haven't left, not once. Dr. Akiyama, the District physician, has stopped in to check on me and the baby a few times, but I've never left.

Glancing around the room, my eyes stop on the suitcase. I am tired of being here. I am tired of sitting in this rocking chair and thinking about Adam's death. Part of me wants to hate him for not waiting for Hanford to show up and assist them. Maybe if he had, if he had waited for backup instead of rushing into that building, maybe he'd still be alive today. He could meet his son and I'd have more than just an old T-shirt to remind me of him. I hate him for risking his life to save mine. I just wish I could stop thinking about him.

Suddenly I feel claustrophobic. Maybe getting out of here is a good idea. "Sure Sam, just give me a few minutes to get ready."

"Meet you out front." He closes the door and I listen to his footsteps echo down the hall.

Looking at the clock, I find that it's nearly noon. I definitely have enough time to make it back before Lina gets done with her schooling. I head for my closet to find something to wear.

When I am dressed, I glance at myself in the mirror. I still look the same even after everything that's happened. Green eyes, pale skin, brown curly hair. Hair that's too long. Almost three years without a haircut has allowed it to grow down to the middle of my back, almost to my waist. It's too heavy, too tangled, and I don't want to deal with it when summer comes around. I twist it into a bun, telling myself to ask Blithe, or Ms. Black as the children know her, if she can cut it for me.

I give up with the mirror and take a khaki jacket from my closet, putting it on before wrapping Raven in an extra blanket and layering two hats on his head. I carry him into the living room where Sam stands.

"Bringing the baby?" Sam asks.

"Yeah." I look longingly out the window. It's still snowing. Thankfully, it's not as bad as last year when the drifts reached the second story of the house. That was when the ocean was seeded with iron by a rogue scientist—I stop that memory. I know where it leads, remembering what we did out there on the Tour. I don't want to remember that.

"The fresh air is good for him," I tell Sam.

"I'll go get the truck so you don't have to walk across the yard in this."

As Sam steps out, cold wind and snow blows into the house before he closes the door. Sam jogs to the SUV and drives it to the front of the house. I open the door and walk out onto the porch as Sam pulls up. When I open the passenger, door he looks at me then the baby.

"What?" I ask.

"Aren't we supposed to use a car seat or something?"

"I don't even know if those exist anymore." I sit in the passenger seat with Raven on my lap. "Just drive slow," I tell Sam as I buckle in and tuck Raven under the chest belt.

Sam drives down the ice-encrusted driveway, the heavy SUV breaking the thin ice and crunching the gravel of the driveway. There was a time when leaving the enclosure of the Pasture brought on a fear that I could barely control. Now it's different. I no longer fear Crane, or the Entities, or their plan here. I look forward to leaving the seclusion of the Pasture, for this moment at least.

As Sam drives down the long country roads that lead into town, he slows to a crawl when he comes across a snowdrift covering the road.

"Wish they'd run the plows," he says as he accelerates through almost a foot of snow. The tires of the SUV grip and push us through.

"Why don't they?" I ask him.

"Fuel is low. And we're the only ones out here. Crane doesn't see it as an acceptable use of the fuel."

"Figures."

I watch out the window as he pulls into town. It's the same. *Just like a Rockwell painting*, as Adam had described it. The houses are all painted white. Some have been demolished to make room for community gardens and greenhouses. Sam pulls up behind a bus. It stops at the corner. Residents unload. Some walk to the nearby houses while others, already equipped with shovels, begin shoveling the sidewalks. The factions are working just as diligently as they have always been. Some probably more, since Crane manufactured the vectors to alter their genetics and shrink their amygdalae. Their faces look placid–almost happy–as they work in the blustering snow. Just like Crane wants them to.

The bus turns the corner. Sam accelerates. We pass more houses, an empty gas station, the grocery store where the Sovereign can go to collect their rations, an old fast-food restaurant, an empty hotel, a few bars, the old town cinema with movie posters still hanging from before the Reformation. They're empty. All those buildings where people used to get together to eat or celebrate; they're empty and dusty and will probably never be filled again.

Sam takes the long way to Headquarters, avoiding the chemistry building where Crane once held me and Lina. He knows I don't like that place. He pulls up to the front of Headquarters. The Phoenix District flag whips in the harsh wind that blows in from the lake. Someone should tell them to take it down or it won't last. The brutal lakeside storms will ruin it.

There are Volker guards standing just inside the entrance. They hold the doors open as we walk through. I walk beside Sam as we take the familiar path to Crane's office. It's in the middle of the building now. He cleared the entire third floor of its furnishings.

As we step off the elevator there are tables with maps, stacks of papers, and a desk where he sits behind a computer.

"Ah, Andromeda," he begins, failing to greet Sam. "So good to see you outside the walls of the Pasture." He looks at Raven in my arms. "The good Doctor says the baby is well." I nod at him. "And you've fully recovered from your illness?"

"Yes." I may have recovered from being sick, but I'm not sure about recovering from causing two deaths. Because that's what I did. I shot a man and then I caused Adam's death. If it weren't for me, he would have never gone into that building without assistance from Hanford.

Now Crane stands before me, wearing his usual suit. Today it's a yellow tie with dark blue dots, a chipper choice considering the weather outside. His orange hair has been neatly trimmed closer to his head so he looks less like a clown and more like a leader. He looks fully rested, barely a wrinkle around his eye. He does not display the worrisome face of some leaders, like when President Berkley had to do that press conference and announce the dire straits of our country nearly six years ago. It seemed Berkley's hair grew a shade grayer with each question from the press.

That was before the Reformation. Crane doesn't even resemble a person who just lost his best Volker and nearly lost the District Matchmaker. He resembles a person who thinks he's fully in control, one with a plan.

I dislike Crane's arrogance very much.

Just as I am reminding myself how much I dislike him, his eyes seem to soften a bit as though his heart just started beating, as though he might be a real human with an ounce of compassion. And then he turns to Sam. "Thank you for meeting me, Sam." Crane reaches out and gives Sam a hearty handshake. "Let us sit." He guides Sam to a set of plush chairs near the window.

It's strange seeing them walk side-by-side, with Sam towering over Crane. They ignore me now and I don't mind. Rubbing Raven's back as he sleeps, I wander the large room, stopping at each table and looking at the maps he has set out. He has one of our county, complete with the fence. The occupied and unoccupied buildings are all marked. The roads that are in use are marked with a red line and the roads that have been left in disrepair marked in black. It seems he knows every inch of this town.

I stop and focus on Crane's conversation with Sam.

"Your test scores are very high in all areas of focus," Crane tells him.

"Yes," Sam replies. "Ms. Black told me this also."

"You had plans to join the air force before you were brought here?"

"Yes."

I hear rustling and turn to see Crane has a handful of papers. He flips through them, stopping on a few pages to read. "Very well then, I am assigning you to Volker training," Crane tells him.

I hold my breath. The last thing I want Sam training

for is to be a Volker. I don't want him responsible for defending the District, just like I didn't want him responsible for defending our country when he tried to join the air force.

Making a swift walk to where they are conversing, I interrupt. "I don't want him training for Volker," I tell Crane.

"Why, Andromeda." Crane smiles as he focuses on me. "Did you ever once ask Sam what he wanted to do or what training he prefers?"

"No," I tell him.

"Perhaps you should." Crane turns expectantly to Sam.

"I chose this, Andie," Sam says. "Actually... I requested it."

"What? Sam, don't do this. You don't know what you're getting into. You don't know what you will be responsible for."

"Yes," he says. "Yes, I do, Andie. I will be responsible for looking after the District and the Sovereign. For keeping the people I love safe. Just let me do this without an argument."

"And if there is ever a war or a breach at the gates you will be required to risk your life to save this place. I don't want that, Sam. I want better for you." I turn to Crane. "I don't want him finding the same fate as the last *Volker Sovereign*." They both know what I mean. I don't want Sam to die just like Adam did.

"You are no longer speaking about your brother's future," Crane notes the change in topic. He tips his head and smiles. He doesn't bother to redirect me back to the original issue.

I guess it's about time I confronted him about what happened.

"I don't understand why you took everyone out there to search for the medication," I tell Crane.

Sam stands.

"We had to," Crane replies, standing also.

"It doesn't make sense, Crane. You could have let nature take its course. After all, isn't that what you're trying to do here? You're letting Morris die. You restrict medications for the other Sovereign and Residents. Why was I the exception?"

"We had to." His face downturns, as though he regrets the trip or something about it.

"I don't believe you. You had to risk the lives of twenty Volker, the life of the Volker Sovereign. How many did you lose? Fifteen?"

"And it was worth it."

"My life was not worth the lives of fifteen other people, Crane." I point at Sam. "What if next time it's him?"

"Would you rather have the alternative? You would have preferred your children to go on with their lives without their mother?"

I stop, my heart screaming at the thought of dying and my children never knowing any more of me.

"Yes, you see, Andromeda," Crane continues, "you were worth the risk. You may not understand this now, but in time you shall."

"And now what?" I ask him, shifting the sleeping baby in my arms.

"Now you move on. You have work to do and so does your brother."

"I'm not ready to move on," I tell him with an unexpected surge of honesty. I immediately wish I had said nothing.

For some reason Crane seems kinder than he used

15

to be. Ever since he informed me of Adam's death, it's like he's been trying to make up for it. He hasn't threatened to take my children, he hasn't threatened to take Ian back, and he hasn't pushed me to get back to work with the pairings or reminded me of my future as an Entity. Perhaps he does have a drop of humanity left in him.

Crane tips his head in the opposite direction, like a robot changing its course. "Very well then, you may go," he dismisses us. "You will commence Volker training in the morning," he tells Sam as we leave.

I stop and turn toward Crane. "You should take that flag down in this weather. You know it's not going to last long with the wind and snow beating on it."

A pale red eyebrow rises. "That flag will never be lowered."

"Why not?" I ask.

"Because I don't want anyone in this District to forget who is in charge."

Newlyweds for fourteen weeks

and counting...

CHAPTER TWO

"Hello, Andie, how are things today?" Elvis asks, looking at Raven.

"Fine," I tell him.

"You sure?" Elvis eyes me suspiciously.

I think I am. I've never felt more calm and in control. So I must be fine. It's the only word I can think of to describe how I feel right now. Lina and Raven are safe. And Ian has been released to me. For fourteen weeks he's been a stranger in the house. Or maybe I've forgotten how he used to be. How he used to act. I'm sure I'm not like he remembers either.

"Never felt better," I tell Elvis, forcing a determined tone to my voice.

I look away from him and pull Raven's knit cap over his ears. It's blue with brown stripes. Someone made it for him, along with some of his other clothes. I'm not sure who. They just seem to show up every few weeks. Clothes, blankets, there was even one of those soft baby brushes. When I pulled it out of the bag, I brushed his dark baby-fine hair; parting it on the side, tucking the longer pieces behind his ears. He looked like a little man. He looked just like his father.

Elvis looks across the courtyard from which I've just walked. It's cold, the ground frozen and covered with a layer of hard-packed snow. "Isn't it too cold to have a baby out here?" Elvis asks me.

"Fresh air, it's good for him."

"Hmm." Elvis scratches his ear.

I've been working up the courage to ask Elvis this question. Here goes nothing. "I want a gravestone."

His eyes widen a bit at my request. "For what?" he asks.

"For Adam."

"We don't have a body."

"I don't care. I want a gravestone. It's been fourteen weeks since he died. Normal people would have had a service months ago. Normal people bury their dead and mourn," I say.

Elvis nods his head as though he agrees. "Where?"

"Out near the water tower, I think."

He presses his lips together. He's going to tell me no.

"Elvis, just do it."

After a long period of silence, he answers, "Yes, ma'am."

"And don't call me ma'am." As a passive threat, I mutter to him, "I know who you are." He is an Entity and soon—once Morris dies—I will join him and Crane and Alexander and whoever else is part of that group.

He nods and turns to open the door to his office.

"Elvis." I stop him. "There's one more thing."

"That is?"

"I want my own car." Elvis has been hiding his keys from me for months, ever since I took his SUV on tattooing day, and I dislike not having the freedom to go where I want when I want.

"I'm not so sure about that."

"Make me happy, Elvis. Either share your keys or get me my own."

He adjusts the brim of his hat. "I'll see what I can do."

"Thank you." I walk away, baby in tow, two Guardians following me. I'm not sure where I want to go or what I want to do. I just need to stretch my legs, to try and quell the unease in my gut from finally telling Elvis what I want. I feel Raven stir in my arms and, looking down, I see his eyes open.

"Want to meet the animals?" I ask him.

He blinks and sighs as though I've bored him. What more could I expect from a three month old baby?

Walking through the barn, I introduce Raven to the cows, the horses, the alpacas, the ponies, the chickens, the geese, and the handful of Guardians that roam the barn and the pens that we are walking by. This is enough to lull him into a deep sleep and I'm sure he has listened to none of my rambling. Soon I become bored with myself. Finding I have walked a full circle around the barn, I decide to make my way home.

I set Raven in his crib and turning around in the room, I stop when my eyes fall upon my dresser.

Damn you, amygdala.

As soon as I take that first step I know what I am about to do is wrong. But the memories propel me forward, they tell me to open that drawer, to lift up my old shirts and pull out the one that doesn't belong. The black one that smells just like Adam.

I sit on the edge of my bed, holding the shirt in my hands, rubbing my fingers over the soft fabric. This is so wrong. I shouldn't do this, not when I can't even hold a conversation with my husband. Still, I close my eyes and press the shirt to my face, taking a deep breath in.

In this moment I realize fully that I am an addict. All I need are the jittery hands and the sunken eyes and the look of despair to be complete. Even with the wrongness of this moment, I get to remember him, if only for a few minutes. I press my eyes harder together, letting his image form in my mind. It wavers and wanes. He gives a short smile, the corners of his eyes crinkling, before disappearing.

I open my eyes and look at the shirt in my hands. The guilt I'm now feeling is as fresh as the newly fallen snow. Cold, crisp, and heavy. I need to stop this. Folding the shirt into a small square, I walk it back to the dresser and hide it behind my clothes. Just as I'm closing the drawer, I hear the rapid running of small feet. Lina bursts in the bedroom, followed by Astrid and Stevie.

"Mom!" Lina starts as Stevie trots to where Raven sleeps and presses her nose between the crib slats.

Mouthing, "Quiet," I point at the crib, where Raven merely flutters his eyes open and then closes them again. Herding the girls out of the room and closing the door, I turn to find Lina ready to burst.

"What's wrong?" I ask.

"The mare, she's having her babies! Come watch with us."

"Okay, okay." Looking up and down the hall, my eyes fall on a sleeping Guardian. "Watch the baby," I tell the Guardian. It rises, dwarfing Stevie in its size, lumbers to the bedroom door and lies down, almost silently, in front of the door. "Come on girls." I take

Lina and Astrid's hands and head for the coat rack.

CHAPTER THREE

Morris hasn't been confined to the hospital. Yet. Instead, he has taken up his residence in one of the local Queen Anne historic homes. We sit in a walnut-paneled living room with an ornately carved fireplace. There's a tin ceiling, beveled glass windows, and an alabaster chandelier. A small fire warms the room. It's strange that he has a fire going, being almost spring now. But then, the weather hasn't exactly been cooperating. We've had blizzards followed by seventy degree days. It seems the earth is confused as to what seasons belong where.

"Are you ready for your lesson today?" Morris asks between bouts of coughing.

"If I said no would it matter, Morris?"

"No," he replies.

"Fine then. I'm ready."

He looks at Raven sleeping in my lap. "No babysitters available today?"

"He's a baby, Morris. He's not going to disclose your secrets. What's on the agenda for today?"

"Self-sufficiency," he replies with a weak voice.

"What do you mean?" I ask. "Here? We are already self-sufficient."

It's been a few months since we returned from the tour with a small amount of scavenged supplies. Other than that, with the farms and local workers, the District has been independent.

He shakes his head slowly. "The other countries." I wait as he takes a shaky breath, preparing himself for the lecture. "Remember what Crane told you? This is global. While you were gone, Canada was Reformed, as well as the South American countries."

I remember about Canada; George Crossbender from the Hanford District told us it was the reason for flying us in the helicopter to Alaska. That, and I am quite certain it was the starting point for chipping away at Adam's sanity.

He continues, "When this started, the Funding Entities built the Reformation on the idea that each country was to regain a sense of self-sufficiency. The loss of this is what some think helped with the downward spiral of civilization. People lost the knowledge to grow food and how to repair clothing with simple sewing techniques. Everything was imported; food, clothes, natural resources that already resided under our noses. And as each country developed their own main export, the other countries lost their ability to provide that resource for themselves. So we had food from the south, oil from the north and middle-east, mechanics and technologies from Asia. And when people could no longer buy what they needed, be it clothes or shoes or potatoes, they simply floundered without, unsure of what to do or where to start. And this is where the creation of the industrialized world went wrong. The new initiative: no trade, no swapping, no monetary exchanges. A District may bargain with another from their own continent, but never with another continent."

"I don't see how this would work, Morris. Self-sufficiency is hard enough to obtain let alone to have it happen overnight," I say.

"The gears have been turning for a while now. A process has been set up, just like here. Hanford wasn't built overnight, Andromeda. Each continent has its own District just like Hanford. Europe, Asia, Africa, and Australia are slated for Reformation in the upcoming weeks."

"You don't think they'll fight back, Morris? You don't think people will see what's going on over here and try to prevent it in the eastern countries?"

"They may, but the ones in power, the ones with the money and weapons, they are all on board. This is going to happen. This will happen. It's already happened here with success. Failure is not an option."

I think of the Residents, how they've worked to make the Phoenix District run as a well-oiled machine. There is order; everyone knows what is expected of them. And since I made that speech, the one to unite the District, to help gain the Resident's trust, they've been weaned off their mind-numbing medications. They are a bit too grateful for being alive, for being allowed to reside within these walls of safety. Still, there are all those people who died in the bombings and who will die in these bombings.

"So who's taking the responsibility for killing all those people?" I ask him. "The ones who die from the bombings? Who's going to take on that guilt?"

Morris sighs and looks at his hands, his eyes widen

slightly as though he could see the blood there. "We all will. Each Entity will live with this guilt. It will make them better."

I think back to my life, before all this. We had a garden, we grew our own vegetables. We were trying. We didn't deserve this. No one deserves this. To be plucked from the population, to serve and better mankind against your will. Or the alternative: to die, bettering the population through death. Neither option is one that I like.

Raven nudges his head into the crook of my arm.

"Does that mean they will be responsible for their own genetic pairings?" I ask.

Morris begins to cough, so much that he can't catch his breath. I reach for the oxygen tank at his side, pulling the mask to his face and turning the flow up. "Can't they give you some inhaled steroids to help?" I ask.

He shakes his head as the coughing slows. "I don't want them."

"Why?"

"This is how it is to be. Self-sufficiency in the District, in life, in health."

"But Crane went out and sought medication for me, to save me. He took some of our most important people. One who didn't come back." I argue. "Your self-sacrifice doesn't make sense, Morris. You are one of the original Funding Entities. Are you telling me your life is not important?"

"There are few exceptions, you were one of them. I am replaceable. You are not."

"You people keep saying this, but I find it hard to believe you can't find anyone else to do what I do. So what about the other countries, who does their genetic pairings?" I have to ask this. I want to know because my ability to do this job, to pair the Residents and their children, to help Crane create a race of passive, obedient humans, is the only thing keeping me and my family alive right now. I'm sure of it.

"That is a conversation for another day, Andromeda. I must rest now."

I stand, adjusting Raven in my arms.

"Andromeda?" Morris stops me.

"Yes?"

"Are you working things out with Ian?"

"That is none of your business, Morris."

He nods, sleepily. "Just remember, you are..." he falls asleep midsentence.

I watch him for a moment, holding my hand over his lips to make sure he is still breathing and didn't actually just die in front of me. Feeling the warm bursts of breath coming from his mouth, I leave Morris to rest and head home to the comfort and seclusion of the Pasture.

CHAPTER FOUR

Staring at the wall, ignoring Dr. Akiyama, for the first time I notice that there are no pictures here; no artwork, nothing but dull gray paint on the walls. I wonder how he can work in here with all of its lifelessness. A couch and chair have been added. The couch is small, simple, covered in a dark blue fabric. The chair Dr. Akiyama sits in is of a similar style, its fabric a deep burgundy. Besides the furniture we are currently sitting in, the dark cherry wooden desk is the only other piece of furniture providing color to this room.

"How are you, Andromeda?" Dr. Akiyama asks.

Crane has ordered me to come here. Morris confided in me that they think this will help me become more approachable toward Ian. They can't have *me* ruining the values of the District, one of their own Sovereign, imagine that. Either way, I've been coming here for weeks now, and it's done nothing to help.

"Andromeda?" Dr. Akiyama asks.

When I look at him, his face is placid and smooth,

his fine Asian characteristics a stark contrast to the now whiteness of his hair. *How am I feeling?* I cringe inwardly at the thought. I killed a man in cold blood, shot him in the head. I took a life out of this world, someone who was no threat to me. In my rush to get home, I didn't even give him a chance. I was selfish. A murderer. And then Adam died because of me. So in total I killed two people. So how do I feel? The only way I can: I hate myself.

I hate everything I've done and everything I've become. I went against everything I ever believed in; to do good and to preserve life. And I know if Ian knew this he would most certainly never look at me again. He would never trust me, and maybe he'd even take Lina away.

"How has the baby been?" Dr. Akiyama asks, changing the subject.

I nod at him, remembering his visits he made to see me after the baby was born. He would take my blood pressure, my temperature, and then he would turn to the baby, looking him over and judging his growth between visits. But Raven's not really a baby anymore.

"He doesn't ever seem to cry," Dr. Akiyama says.

"I know." I look at the child sleeping on the couch next to me. "How was my surgery?" I ask about the cesarean section he performed to deliver Raven.

"About the same as any," Dr. Akiyama responds his voice devoid of any tone which might make me think otherwise.

"It is very strange that I had this baby. I wasn't able to get pregnant before. Ian and I tried for years. So why this time?"

"You know I can't answer that, Andie. You were a nurse once, you know these things sometimes happen when they are least expected."

Being less than satisfied with his answer, I press on. "You didn't implant anything inside of me, did you? I know how Crane is with his transmitters and medications."

He seems to squirm a bit before replying with a firm, "No."

"I sure hope you're not lying to me."

"Andromeda," he says. "I take my position as District Physician very seriously. I have not harmed you, or anyone else, in any manner. Why are you asking me this? Is it because you feel different?"

I nod and turn back to the window, watching the snow flutter between the branches of the leafless trees. Of course I feel different.

"Andie?" he presses on. "I'm here to help and listen. I know you don't want to be here, but Crane demands this. You need to work toward coming here with..." he pauses as I turn to him, "with Ian."

"I don't want to do couples therapy, Dr. Akiyama. This isn't going to help us. I'm not sure if anything will."

"Maybe we need to think about some medication?" he asks, raising his thin white eyebrow. "You could be experiencing postpartum depression."

"What do you mean?" I ask, knowing full well that all non-essential mediations and medical procedures have been done away with. Crane let the cardiac and diabetic Residents die rather than continue them on with their medications. *To weed out the weak,* he had told me once. "There are no medications for mundane illness anymore. Besides, Raven is hardly a baby anymore."

"We have another medication." He dips his chin as

he looks at me. "The *Residents'* medication."

"No. That's the last thing I need, walking around all happy, not caring what happens or what people tell me to do."

He crosses his legs and adjusts the notebook on his lap, marking the paper as he does. "Just a small dose, you've experienced it before. How did it make you feel?"

"I don't remember any of it. And I don't care how it made me feel. I'm not taking that medication. I see what it does to those people." I point toward the window.

"They've never been happier."

"No. Never." The dose I received was an accident and no doubt the cause of my illness at the end of my pregnancy.

He takes a deep breath in, blinking slowly as he exhales. Dr. Akiyama never loses his cool. He's always level headed and I'm sure I'm annoying the crap out of him right now. "You have to do something. We can't let you go back to the way you were the first time you went to the Pasture. If you hadn't come out of that—"

"I don't want the medication." I tell him. "I don't want *any* medication."

"Then speak."

I glare at him for a long time before finally talking. "I don't know where to begin."

"Start at the beginning," he suggests.

"Will you tell it all to Crane?"

He shrugs a little. "He likes to be informed of everything."

"You owe me still," I tell him. "You were supposed to keep my pregnancy a secret and he found out before I could tell anyone else."

"It's hard to hide things from Burton Crane. He..." Dr. Akiyama grips the top of his pen between his front teeth for a moment as he forms the thought. "He likes to know all things that are going on with those he cares most about."

I snort out a laugh. "He doesn't care about me, only what I can do for him." I adjust myself on the couch, tucking a leg under myself. "So, will you tell him?"

"I'll do my best to keep this private."

"I'm sure patient doctor confidentiality doesn't matter anymore?"

"It never really did." He closes the notebook on his lap and uncrosses his legs. "Let's start at the beginning."

"There are too many beginnings."

"How about when you woke up after having the baby," he suggests, motioning to Raven who continues to sleep.

"Yes." I gaze at him, remembering the first time I met him. Raven had been two weeks old. The aftereffect of the seizures and the medication kept me in some state between a coma and a stupor during those two weeks. "I woke up and Sam and Lina came in the room with the baby."

"How did you feel?"

"Confused. A lot had happened before I delivered him and I felt foggy from the alcohol and the magnesium."

"Is that what you'd like to talk about?" he suggests.

"There's so much." I pull my sweater tighter around me and button it a little higher. "So much happened."

"What is the one thing that happened that keeps you from speaking with Ian?" he asks.

My heart rate picks up and feeling a sudden flush of

shame. I unbutton the sweater to its original state. "There's more than one thing," I admit.

"There's Adam?" he suggests.

I close my eyes when he says his name, flinching. "He's dead," I say. "He died."

"He died to save you."

"He died because of me. Because I am weak."

"No one could have guessed you would become sick during the pregnancy."

"It doesn't matter. I killed him." *And I killed an innocent man. I shot him in the head, without a thought.*

"You can't blame yourself for his death."

"I can blame myself for having an affair with him."

"Do you see your infant as a reminder of his death?"

"No," I answer quickly. I could never see Raven connected with his death. He is innocent, a child brought into this world by lust. He is just a reminder of my sins, not of Adam's death.

"How is your routine, with the children and your work at the Pasture? It's not overwhelming at all?"

"No." I shake my head. "I'm managing it all just fine."

"You? By yourself?" he asks. "Ian doesn't help you?"

"I've never asked him to. I haven't needed his help."

"You cannot bear the burdens of the entire household as well as your work as District Matchmaker on just your shoulders. You are a family, a workable unit. Ian is there as the father figure to help and support you."

"I've just..." I brush a lock of hair out of my face and tuck it into the bun holding my hair. "It's easier doing it myself. He's been through so much already."

"And you feel guilty about what he's been

34

through?"

"I feel guilty that I didn't fight to save him when this all started. I let Crane take him away and do whatever he did with him. And I moved on."

"You were under excessive circumstances and stress," Dr. Akiyama offers. "I'm sure Ian would understand, if not have compassion for all that you went through."

"No." I fumble with my sweater buttons. "No husband would have compassion for me, not after the things that I've done."

"Do you speak to him?"

"Sometimes."

Dr. Akiyama clears his throat. "When I say *speak*, I mean, do you produce full sentences and converse about things directly related to your life now?"

"Not really," I admit.

"Have you resumed relations with him?"

"That's none of your business." I look away, feeling the flush of red heading for my cheeks.

"You're well over eight weeks post-partum," he says. "There's no reason why you–"

"I know!" I interrupt him. "That's so personal and it's not a topic I want to discuss."

"He still has a separate room doesn't he?"

"You speak with him. I'm sure he's already told you this. Besides, I'm sure he wouldn't want me anyway, not after what I've done."

"I sense…" Dr. Akiyama leans forward, closer to me. "I sense you are speaking of something else, something other than this *affair* that worries you."

I simply stare at him. He must know. I'm sure all of the Funding Entities were informed of it. It was a test, after all. Every stop on that tour was a test, for both of us.

"Andie?"

He must know.

"What else is there?"

I pull the sweater tighter, pressing the edge of the button under my fingernail and the sharp pain focuses me. "I killed someone," I tell him. "I killed a man in cold-blood. I murdered him." Moving my hands to my face, I notice that they shake slightly.

"This bothers you immensely?"

"Wouldn't it you?"

"The world is different now."

"How different? Does it no longer matter if we kill each other?"

"The person you killed was meant to die."

"No," I argue. "No. We don't decide who dies. *I* don't decide who dies. I'm just supposed to sort genes, and pair the Residents up, and create these people for Crane."

"You will do more. I know this." He sets the notebook and pen on the table next to him and leans forward again, clasping his hands together. "Andie, sometimes… sometimes the higher we are in the pyramid of life, the harder the decisions we must make to better those below us."

"I wasn't brought up to believe that. I was brought up to believe that murder is wrong. What do I tell my children if they find out? That it's okay, sometimes? That it's okay if someone wants you to do it. They are supposed to look up to me. I am supposed to guide them through life. How can they believe anything I say to them, or suggest to them, when they know I performed the greatest sin of life? I killed someone. I shot him in the head. I took his life!"

Dr. Akiyama waves his hand in an arc in front of me. "There was another reason why you shot that man. You didn't just do it because someone told you that you had to. What is the other reason?"

I bite my lip, hard. I remember the look on his face. That lost, hopeless look as he passed the gun between his hands. And he had already killed one man on that trip, the one that seeded the ocean with iron. Or at least that is what they told us. The man that taunted Adam, the one from the Middle East. I did it for him. But I don't want to say his name. I don't want to hear it on my lips.

"Andie?"

"I did it so he didn't have to," I finally say.

"So who didn't have to?"

"Adam!" I almost shout. "I killed that man so Adam didn't have to."

"Why?"

"Because he had already been through so much. And I could see it on his face. It was killing him. Everything that happened to him came back the moment he looked at that helicopter as we prepared to leave for Galena." Remembering the look on his haunted face, I stand and start pacing the office as I speak. "I could see it in his eyes. The way he carried himself. He wouldn't talk to me anymore. They ruined him. They taunted him with that Chinook and that man from the Middle East, and then told him to kill again. I couldn't just watch him fall apart like that. Not after all he's done–did, after all he did." I stop, now standing behind the couch where I was sitting. I place my hands on the back of it. "I couldn't watch him fall apart like that. It was killing me." I take a deep breath and look up to see Dr. Akiyama lean back in his seat.

"There is something honorable in taking a life so someone you love doesn't have to. There is something honorable in settling that on your conscience, so someone you love doesn't have to suffer with that guilt for the rest of their lives. You did Adam a favor."

I push off the back of the couch and turn away from Dr. Akiyama, walking toward the window, my arms crossed tightly across my chest. "He's dead now. So I guess it doesn't matter," I mumble.

"He died to honor you. For all that you've done for him."

"I did nothing for him besides get him killed."

"You birthed his child. A firstborn son. Something I'm sure he was proud of."

I turn around to face him. "I wouldn't know. After he looked at that Chinook he never said another meaningful sentence to me about the baby. We didn't even pick out a name. Never once did he suggest anything."

Dr. Akiyama simply nods his head slowly and lifts his left leg, crossing it over the knee of his opposite leg. "Who else have you told this to?" he asks.

"Told what to?"

"That you killed a man and that this weighs heavily on your conscience."

"No one."

"Not even Ian?"

"No." I move to return to my seat on the couch, across from the doctor. "I can't tell Ian. He would definitely never speak to me again."

"Why is that?"

"You don't know him, his beliefs. He was raised in a strict Roman Catholic home. He's the reason why Lina went to Catholic School. Those were his beliefs

38

and I followed them with him because I loved him. He doesn't believe in capital punishment or death for a good cause. None of that. He believes if you kill someone then your soul will rot in hell for all of eternity."

"You don't like that he fears for your soul? That you may never ascend into heaven together when this life is over?"

"I don't like that this will cause him to think even less of me."

"What makes you think he would think less of you?"

"Because of everything I did."

"Andromeda, this conversation is going around in circles. You need to set forth a plan to put your relationship on the mend. Ian is your husband. You are both Sovereign. The first married Sovereign couple in this District. You need to set the stage for others to follow in your footsteps. You can't have a marriage that doesn't work, this will not be allowed."

"What do I do? Where am I supposed to start with him?"

"Talk to him."

"About what?"

"Anything, everything. Start with the day to day topics and then move on from there."

"And tell him what I did." I bite my lip in anticipation of his answer.

"If you mean tell him that you killed that man, then yes. There should be no secrets between you both."

"And if that means he never speaks to me again?"

"Then at least he knows the truth and you have nothing left to hide. What does it feel like right now? How would you describe the way you feel?"

"It feels like…" I swallow hard, trying to catch my breath; this is how it always is when I thinking of all of these things together. "It feels like I'm drowning."

"Have you been sleeping at night?"

"Yes." I turn to look directly at him so he knows I'm serious, telling the truth. "I sleep perfectly fine every night."

"No nightmares like you used to have?"

I shake my head. Only someone with a severe problem can kill a person and still sleep at night.

Newlyweds for fourteen
months,

and counting...

CHAPTER FIVE

Maybe the gravestone was a bad idea. I walk to it every day carrying Raven. I tell him stories, stories of our life before this. Fairytales, really. It all seems like fairytales now. He will never see the world as I once knew it. He will never know what it's like to go to the mall on Christmas, to play sports in school, to go to prom. My children will never know the life we had before.

I get the sense Lina may remember some of it, but not much.

I take one last look at the cold marble before heading to pick up Lina from the schoolhouse.

"Mommy?" she asks me as we walk to the alpaca pen to feed them. Stevie trots behind us, her tail wagging with excitement at seeing the animals. "Why did everything change?"

"What do you mean, Lina?"

"Everything is different now. I miss our old house and my old school."

"That was years ago, Lina. You still remember all of that?"

"Yes. Why did it all change?"

"Well, some people thought it would be a good way to keep our planet healthy."

"Why does our planet need to be healthy?" she asks and I wonder to myself if we really had sheltered her that much during her first five years of life.

"Because there were a lot of people and there was no one to teach them how to… Well, to control them, to stop them from polluting the earth." I search for the appropriate words to help an eight year old understand why Crane and his Entities did this.

"Maybe people don't want to be controlled. Maybe they want to be free."

"I'm sure you are right, honey."

"Do you still love Daddy?" She asks, staring intently with her green flecked eyes.

I stop dead in my tracks. I was not prepared for this. "Yes."

"Then why don't you hug him or kiss him like you used to?" she asks, tipping her head to the side, waiting, as I fight inside my brain for the best answer.

"Do you remember when he wasn't living with us?" I ask her.

"Yes."

"Well, when two people go through something like that, sometimes it's hard for them to remember how much they loved each other before."

She stares at me and reaches down for Raven's hand. "So if someone took me away, or baby Raven, you would forget that you loved us?"

My heart breaks in that instant, as she stares so intently at me, trying to make sense of what is happening to her parents.

"No, Lina," I kneel and pull them both close to me. "I would never forget how much I love you both. It is

44

impossible for a mother to no longer love her children."

And then I pull them so close, kissing them both on their cheeks.

"Mom," Lina continues. "Why didn't Adam ever come back?"

"There was an accident," I hold her away from me so I can look at her while I speak. "There was an accident when mommy was sick and in the hospital, and Adam was hurt really bad."

"And he died?"

"Yes." I nod at her.

"I miss him sometimes," she says with a quiver in her voice.

I pull her close again and I realize at this moment that this conversation is long overdue, about fourteen months overdue. "I miss him too," I whisper to her and squeeze my eyes closed, feeling the swell of tears behind them. I take a deep breath and open my eyes, feeling Raven's little hand resting on my cheek and his other hand resting on Lina's head.

--

Raven still doesn't cry. He doesn't speak. He doesn't even try to utter a sound. It's abnormal for a toddler. Dr. Akiyama worries that he suffered some in-utero damage, that he could be handicapped. I know he's not. He's just quiet. Observant. His eyes are inquisitive. I've watched him do things most toddlers don't. He started walking when he was eight months old. He's stopped using diapers. He listens, he understands. Raven is far from handicapped. But then, that's the same thing Baillie thought about me. He told me so,

45

when he hung me by my neck over the bridge.

I feel Raven rub his fingers over my face. He must be tired or bored.

"Say goodbye," I tell him.

Raven waves at the gravestone and then to the Guardians that watch us from the forest edge. I've never pointed out that the large dogs watch us from the forest edge, but somehow Raven knows they are there.

I walk back to our house, stopping when I see Ian's car parked near the barn. He should be at work for a few more hours. I get that tight feeling in my chest thinking about us being alone in the house as Lina finishes class and Raven sleeps. I'm still not ready for a real conversation with him. Instead of heading home, I walk to the barn and collect the SUV keys from Elvis's desk.

"Going somewhere?" Elvis asks from the doorway as I'm walking toward him.

"Just for a ride." I motion to Raven. "He's having trouble sleeping. I thought a quiet ride might help."

Raven scowls at me, or maybe at my lie.

"How long will you be gone?"

"I'll be back before the children are done with class." I walk out of the barn and toward the SUV that I share with Elvis.

"Should I tell Ian?" he asks as he follows me.

"You can tell Ian whatever you want," I reply loudly, a little too loudly. Instantly wishing I hadn't because I can see Ian's figure standing on the front porch of the house as I walk away.

I buckle Raven into an old car seat Sam found. One of the Guardians waits expectantly for me to move so it can jump into the vehicle. I get into the driver's seat

46

and drive away, my heart thudding in my chest the entire time. I don't know why I'm such a jerk to him, I don't know why I don't even try to make things better.

It's been fourteen months of us living together, never really saying much to each other. And each night he paces and then walks out the front door to places unknown. I can't bring myself to stand in the same room with him without the children there as a distraction, and I don't even know why. I wanted him back so badly and now I don't even know what to do with him.

It doesn't help that Crane has made Ian Sovereign and has spent the last few months teaching Ian everything he missed when he was under the same medication regimen as the Residents.

Sometimes when we are in Committee meetings and Ian doesn't understand something, creases form across his forehead and around his mouth. I'm sure he wants to ask me questions, maybe have deep conversations about what happened and how this place is being run, but I have no desire to speak of the Sovereign Committee meetings. I have no desire to speak of any of it.

I drive along the quiet country roads until I realize where I've brought myself; the county graveyard. I pull over to the side of the road and look out the window. Raven kicks my seat. He must be bored.

"Want to go for a walk?" I ask him. I know he's not going to answer, but I assume he'd say yes. I get out and release the Guardian. I pick up Raven and carry him up the overgrown, pebbled driveway.

There are scores of locals buried here, families that have lived in this area for centuries. My family as well;

my parents and grandparents. I look at Raven, wondering if he'd like to hear about his ancestors. I walk toward the family plot, someplace I haven't been in years, at least not since before I had Lina. I walk up the hill, taking the trail that leads to the left. I see the old mausoleum, and knowing that our family plot should be behind that area, I head in that direction.

We walk through the sea of stones. I stop when I come to the familiar granite stones adorned with small angels seated at the corners. The last time I was here, I had to bury my mother next to my father.

"Ah, here we are," I tell Raven as I set him down. He toddles over to the gravestone and places his hand on it.

"Those were your grandparents, your grandfather and grandmother," I tell him. "Your grandfather was lots of fun. He was a professor at the college, knew lots of crazy things about the Greeks. That's how I got my name, Andromeda; she was a Greek princess and when her parents declared that she was more beautiful than the sea nymphs, she was chained to a rock as a sacrifice to protect her land from a sea monster." Raven's eyes narrow on me as he judges the truthfulness of my story. "Perhaps this is a little much for you," I tell him. "Anyways, it means leader of men–" I stop short, digesting the information I've just told my son, information that I haven't thought about in a long time. Strange.

Raven runs his finger over the names etched in the stone. He moves to the stone next to it, placing his hand on the plain granite. This stone is much less adorned than the one my mother chose for herself and my father. "Those are your great-grandparents," I tell him. His fingers rove over the etchings. "Constance S.

Salk and Franklin E. Salk. Your great-grandmother was an orphan," I tell him. "She swore that she would keep the Salk name going as homage to the family that adopted her. Your great-grandfather Frank even changed his last name, something that was unheard of." Raven turns to stare at me. "Yes, our last name is Somers. I took your fath–… umm… Ian's last name when we married. I wanted to be a bit normal and Sam could carry on the Salk name. I wish they could have met you, Raven. I wish they could have been around, all of them, they would have loved you so much."

He looks at the gravestone of his great-grandparents and then down at the ground before he moves to the next gravestone. He sets his hand on the half-crumbled, lichen-consumed stone.

"No," I shake my head at him. The etching says *B. C. Bertrand*. "I don't know who that is–"

I hear a loud cawing from the other side of the graveyard and turn, looking across the hill. A large blackbird sits in a giant oak tree cawing toward us. For a second I think I see another person standing in the graveyard near where Adam's family is buried. I see a shadow, movement, an image of a man with dark hair. It seems to turn and stare at us. It wavers in the sunlight; a mirage, a ghost.

My breath catches in my throat, the feeling almost chokes me. It's not a mirage, it's a result of me sniffing his T-shirt like a crack addict. Seeing him out in the daylight like this is nothing but a bad acid trip.

"Raven," I reach out to pick him up and make our way back to the SUV by the road.

CHAPTER SIX

Staring at the empty seat across from me, Crane speaks and I do my best to ignore him. I've done my work. I've updated him. He's seen the data, the pairs, the families which will be made, the children they will have. I am bored now. I watch the children through the viewing glass that separates the committee room from the children's play area.

"Andromeda?" I hear Crane ask me. His voice has the edge of agitation. It won't be long before his ears turn as orange as his hair.

"Yes?" I ask.

"The Volker seat?"

I didn't hear them nominate anyone. Still, I tell him, "No."

For some reason I am also thoroughly agitated today. I'm not ready to have Adam's seat filled, not yet. I look across the table. Ian is giving me a face. He doesn't bother to wink at me anymore—not at a meeting, not like he did those other few times; as we left for the Tour and the day he showed up at the

Pasture. There were other times after that, but I put a stop to them. I said a full sentence to him once and asked him to stop.

"You've denied each and every prospect. It's been over a year. This can't go on any longer."

"What about Remington?" I ask.

Remington was our Runner, the one before Adam, the one who got caught divulging the secrets of the District to a woman at a bar while he was out getting supplies. That was before the Reformation.

"He's gone," Crane responds blandly, his features devoid of emotion. He doesn't even care that he ordered Remington's death. But Remington's not really dead.

Alexander shifts in his seat.

"I know he's still alive in the convict faction. You could bring him back."

A look of smooth irritation coats Crane's face. "You may be taking the place of Morris, but you're not there yet," Crane says. "I'm tired of waiting for a decision from you. Soon, I'm going to override your vote."

"Let's get things straight, Crane. You control the vote here. We all know that." I hear a rough gasp from Alexander. Ian closes his eyes. Morris, he's in the hospital, but I'm sure he'd be just as disappointed. "Are we done here?"

"No." A thin smile spreads across Crane's lips. I ready myself for the backlash. "Sam Salk will take the Volker Sovereign seat."

"No!" I stand in objection.

"Your vote has been overridden. He has excelled in his Volker training over the past months. His training to take the Sovereign seat will commence

51

immediately."

Crane ends the meeting. I don't even bother to look at Ian or Alexander to judge their responses.

"Andromeda," he interrupts my departure.

"What?"

"Sign your agenda."

Even though I don't want to, I reach down and press my fingertip on the screen. An image of my fingerprint shows up, signifying that I agree with the proceedings. I don't agree at all. Crane knows this already.

"Andromeda?"

"What?" I snap at him.

"I want you to remember this moment and the reason for my needing to force you to meet with Dr. Akiyama."

"For what reason?"

Two red brows rise on his face. "Your attitude. I can't have you involved in making decisions for the Residents when you are clearly out of control."

Turning, I find Ian and Alexander standing next to each other, watching us. "Fine," I mumble as I move to collect Raven from the play area and leave the building, headed for my own vehicle. I don't wait for Ian. He's been driving himself. We drove together once and it was extremely uncomfortable.

I drive home, probably faster than I should with a child in the car.

Parking next to the barn I take Raven inside and replace the keys. As I walk across the courtyard I can hear the sound of shots being fired, muffled by the thick barn exterior walls. Someone must be at the target range. It's probably Sam.

It was a complete surprise that Adam found Sam

and brought him back after the bombings, the last of my family that wasn't already here. But now, with Crane's nomination, it feels like he's being taken away from me.

As I walk through the courtyard, Lina runs out of the schoolhouse, toward me.

"Can we swing, mom?" Lina asks.

"Sure," I tell her.

She runs for the swing set in the courtyard. Elvis found it in someone's backyard. He disassembled it and brought it back here for the children to play on. Pushing Lina and Raven on the swings, Lina sings as I wait for the sound of the gunfire to cease. It's not long before Raven starts to rub his eyes.

"I'm going to bring Raven in for a nap," I tell Lina. "Stay here. I'll be right back."

"Okay, mom," she responds mid-song.

Opening the front door to the house, I release Stevie who races to the swing set where Lina is. I hear Lina giggle as Stevie jumps in the air, trying to nip at her feet.

I lay Raven down and on my way out the door, I notice the Guardian sleeping in the corner of the living room.

"What's wrong?" Sam asks as he pushes Lina on the swing. I walk toward him, unable to control the scowl on my face.

I motion for him to move away from Lina so she can't hear us. "They didn't tell you?" I ask.

"Oh, I've known. Aren't you happy for me?" Sam asks, flashing a smile of straight teeth. That's a smile he used to give the girls in high school, not his sister. Something's up.

"Why didn't you tell me, Sam?"

"I was instructed not to."

"Sam! Crane just made you Volker Sovereign, that's a huge deal. I can't believe he's having you keep secrets from me already." I cross my arms over my chest.

"Andie," Sam adjusts his uniform, "Can't you just be happy for me? I know this isn't the life we expected, but some good can come out of it. I still have a life to live."

"I'm scared for you," I tell him honestly.

"Why, Sis?"

"Because Crane always has another agenda. You becoming the Volker Sovereign is just another punishment for me because I am defiant and I was rude to him in today's committee meeting."

"Maybe this isn't about you." He scowls down at me. He's never looked at me like this before. It's intimidating. "Maybe I want more than just to be your little brother here. I don't need to be anchored to this place, to you. There are things that I can still do."

"It's not that cut and dry, Sam. These decisions aren't made with our best interest in mind. They are made with the best interests of the Districts in mind. Do you know what that means? We are nothing but pawns to them."

"You think I haven't realized that already?"

I take a deep breath. "Sam, things will get worse before they get better. You saw what they did to me before you arrived."

"Yeah, I did." He steps toward me; he's so tall that I have to look up to keep eye contact.

"If things were different, I'd be so happy for you right now. But to tell you the truth, I'm scared for you."

"I can take care of myself." He wraps his arm across my shoulders and squeezes me into his ribs.

I relish the contact, contact that I haven't had from him in quite some time since he's been training. My little brother is growing up. I glance up at him. Nope, I'm wrong, he *is* all grown up. "Sam."

"Yeah?"

"I am proud of you, really proud. I just don't want this for you. I wish the world were different, I wish it was years ago."

"We can't go back in time, Andie. All we have is now, all we have is each other, and I don't plan on sitting around and letting these people tell me what to do. We need to stick together, we're family. And now there are three of us on the committee. Now Crane's the odd man out." I feel the muscles twitch in his arm.

I still feel this overwhelming need to protect him, even if he is four times the size of me, he's my *little* brother after all. "Don't be naive, Sam. Crane has people all over, and for some reason they are afraid of him. So afraid they'll do whatever he asks."

"I'm not afraid of him." Sam releases his hold on me and steps back. "Where's Raven?" he asks, looking around.

"He's in the house." I point across the courtyard.

"You left him home alone?"

"He's not alone, there's a Guardian with him."

"Seriously?"

"What?"

"You left a dog as a babysitter." The boyish smirk I remember from our childhood returns to his face.

I shrug. "I trust them more than most people."

"Me too," he agrees.

"Mom?" I hear Lina's voice from behind me.

We both turn. "Hey, honey." Lina walks toward me, pulling a pink knit hat over her head. She's going to be nine soon and she's almost as tall as I am.

"Astrid wants to help me feed the horses today." She points to the schoolhouse where Blithe is releasing the rest of the children for an afternoon of fresh air.

"That's fine." I look across the courtyard toward the barns. Elvis waits with a bucket of oats and carrots.

"Can we go to the range after?" she asks as Astrid runs toward us.

And there goes my little girl, growing up, running off to do chores and spend time with the other Sovereign children. "Sure, Lina, just make sure you have an adult with you."

"I'll meet them there," Sam says. "I need to practice a little more."

I'm sure he doesn't. Sam has perfect aim.

--

In the evening, there is a fire in the courtyard and dinner to celebrate Sam's promotion. I bring a sweet pear bread, made with the last of the walnuts from my cupboards and ripe pears from the orchard. Elvis brings rabbits to roast over the fire. Blithe brings roasted squash.

As Elvis arranges the skinned rabbits on a skewer, I watch Ian pluck a few ears of corn from the field and submerge them in a bucket of water.

If we spoke much I might ask him what he is doing, but instead I just watch as he carries the bucket to the fire and places the wet corn, husks and all, onto the hot coals. The corn sizzles and smokes. The tassels burn away instantly, and after a few minutes Ian pulls the corn off to cool. The children huddle around him as he pulls the husks off, revealing a perfectly steamed cob

the time." She turns to look at me. "That's why I became a teacher."

"You're very good at what you do," I tell her.

"There was a time when I thought I might have children of my own." She stretches her legs out and twists her hands in her lap. "I'm not sure if I told you what I was doing in Japan?"

"You told me you were a teacher there, teaching at a private school for the children of U.S. Embassy personnel."

She nods her head slightly. "I followed my fiancé there." Blithe's eyes soften a bit and a sheen fills them, reflecting the orange glow of the fire.

"You're engaged?"

"*Was*. I *was* engaged. I spent my days teaching the lonely, well-traveled children of the Ambassadors. Do you know what it's like for those children, travelling the world, never having a chance to make real friends or moving each time they do?"

I shake my head. "The children are lucky to have you. What happened to your fiancé?" I ask.

"I lost him," she responds flatly.

"Oh, I'm so sorry."

"Don't be. I thought he was a good man, that's why I wanted to marry him. I had it all planned out—the wedding, the honeymoon. I wanted to have four children. But none of that transpired."

"What happened?"

"I came home to find him in bed with a beautiful Japanese woman." I try not to make a sound as my face flames with embarrassment. "They must have been quite satisfied, the two of them, they didn't even stir as I packed my bags. And as I was walking down the hall of our apartment building, I ran into a peculiar man who made me an offer I couldn't refuse at the time."

"You met Burton Crane in Japan?"

"Yes. And here I am now." She glances toward the men who continue their talking. Astrid runs up to Sam and taking his hand, she pulls him toward the fire to join the other children in their moonlight dancing. Blithe smiles a bit. "And now I have more children than I ever thought I could have. But still…" She trails off, never finishing her thought.

"There are plenty of men here, Blithe. You still might find someone."

She blinks slowly and as she does the clouds cover the moon so I cannot see her true expressions, only the shadows from the flames and the trees, spreading across the planes of her face. "Like you have?" she replies dryly.

Ouch. "I know," I tell her, and as though Ian were listening to our conversation, I notice him turn toward us. "I know what I did was wrong."

"As long as you know," she replies. And just as she stops speaking, one of the boys—Lex—runs toward us and taking Blithe's hand, he pulls her to join in the fire-dancing.

Lina runs toward Ian and Elvis, taking their hands and pulling them toward the fire. Cashel runs toward me, doing the same. We join hands, skipping in a circle as the flames die down, the children sing *Ring-around-the-Rosie*.

As the children skip, reveling in that possession by the moon and the fire, Marcus and Ira let go of their hands and switch places further down in the circle, followed by Astrid and Lex. I notice Lina smiling as she moves next to Ian, grasping his hand and shaking his arm to make him sing louder. With all the switching of places, it's not long before Blithe and Sam wind up next to each other, his large hand grasping her slender one, skipping along with the children. I feel Lina's familiar hand take mine.

"As fun as this is," Elvis starts and looking up, he moves his hands in front of him, pulling together Lex and Marcus—who were on either side of him—and connecting them to each other, closing the circle. Elvis salutes the lot of us. "I must go put the beasts to bed!" Elvis backs up, a wide smile spread across his face as he watches us skip, the children still singing, barely missing a beat as he leaves. Just as he gets far enough away that the fire no longer lights his face, I see his smile fade away to a look that can only be described as longing and melancholy. Then he turns and walks fastidiously toward the barn.

Skipping along with the children, listening to the laughter from Blithe and Sam as the children switch places with them again, the evening breeze blows my hair across my face and I feel Lina's grasp on my hand loosen. Turning, I see what is about to happen. Ian looks up as she lets go of both of our hands, skipping to the other side of Lex. It must be the look on my face, or maybe it's him, knowing that we'd have to hold hands. We both stop dead in our tracks. The children knock into Ian's back, causing him to lurch forward a bit. I take a step back. The fire flickers in his brown irises, and he doesn't even attempt to reach out and take my hand. There are moans and shouts from the children behind Ian, urging him to keep up with the song, but neither of us moves.

"Okay, wild beasts," Blithe answers the children's shouts. "I think it's time for bed!"

The night air is filled with, "*Aww*," and "*Already?*"

and "*But we were having fun,*" as she ushers the four boys into a line, leaving Lina and Astrid behind with us.

Ian looks toward the fire. "Sorry," he whispers as he turns abruptly, following Elvis's path toward the barn.

I gather up Lina and Astrid and bring them home for bed.

There is no pacing from Ian that night because he does not return. I lay in my bed, alone, awake, feeling the cold sheets next to me. I pull the spare pillow to my chest, trying to stop that empty feeling in there.

In the morning I hear Ian's steps as he walks down the hall toward the kitchen. I pretend to be occupied as he makes his coffee and drinks it. Turning, I watch as he pats each of the children atop their heads and walks out the door for work at the nuclear plant.

CHAPTER SEVEN

Ian

"She doesn't speak to me."

"Still nothing more than a few words?" Dr. Akiyama asks.

I shake my head at him. I think she's said one full sentence, and that was only four words: *Don't wink at me*. Yup, four words.

"She still refuses to come here with you."

I slouch down into the couch. I know this already. "I don't know what to do with her," I admit to him.

"What have you tried so far?"

"Just... I don't know. Normal things. I get the kids from the school if she has something to do. But she's always there, doing everything herself. She never leaves. I don't even know when she comes here." I assume it's while I'm at the plant, during those eight hours that I am away and the hours that Lina is in school that she has to visit Dr. Akiyama. But, she's never told me a day. I've never walked into the kitchen on Tuesday morning and had her tell me that she has to go to the doctor in the afternoon so don't worry if I come home and she's not here. She used to say things like that to me in the mornings. Now there's nothing but silence from her.

"Perhaps you should just do something for her, show her that you're there for her, to help. Maybe make dinner, fold the laundry?"

"No." I shake my head at him. "She doesn't like it when I do those things. It will just make her angry."

"Maybe not, she's changed."

"I know and I don't know who she is anymore."

Dr. Akiyama picks up a notebook from the table next to him and flips through it. "Do you still love her?"

"Yes," I tell him firmly. Of course I still love her. How could I not love the mother of my child? And after all I have done to get back to them? I wouldn't have starved myself half to death if I didn't still love Andie and Lina.

"After all that she has done? You can still love her despite the fact that she has lain with another man and bore his child?"

I think of Andie and Lina coming home from the hospital with the baby, *his* baby. Raven is what Lina named him. Over the past few weeks I've barely seen him, Andie keeps him to herself. I exhale a breath I didn't know I was holding. "I think I can learn to accept it."

"You are not angry with her?"

"No, not with her." I look away from him.

"With whom then?"

I don't answer. I don't trust any of these people.

"I see," Dr. Akiyama states softly as he writes

something in his notebook. "Has she told you what happened to her?"

Shaking my head, I reply, "She won't even tell me the time of day, let alone what happened to her."

"Perhaps with time then," he suggests.

"How much time? I've been waiting for… forever. How long am I supposed to wait?"

Dr. Akiyama exhales a long breath. "Ian, you do realize she loved two men and both of them died to her. Now, one has returned. That isn't easy for anyone. It does things to the mind and soul, things that take a while to mend together."

I nod to him, pressing my lips together, now is not the time to talk. But I want to tell him that I was never dead. I have never died. I have always been here. Alive, waiting.

"Is this problem impacting your work at all?"

"No," I answer, shaking my head. "That's the easy part. I've been doing that job for years. I could run that reactor with my eyes closed."

--

On my way back to the Pasture, I make a detour and swing by our old house.

Someone else has been taking care of it. The sidewalk is shoveled, the driveway too. It's strange staring at our old house and remembering everything we used to be. Dr. Akiyama wants to know who I'm angry with and it's not Andie. It's them and…me. I have to fix this.

Throwing the vehicle into park, I get out and head into the house. There's something I need to find here, something I've been looking for a long time now. They have to be here. There is no other place Andie could have left them.

--

Parking next to the barn, I sit in the SUV while the sun bakes the interior, warming this cold chill in my center as I listen to the snow fall from the barn roof, landing with heavy *plops* on the ground. It's strange, the weather we have now. Snowstorms and warm days, then it's back to blizzards again. I look at the dashboard clock and see that it's almost two. Today I promised to get the children from the school house so Andie could do some errand. She didn't give specifics. I wonder if she's going to see Dr. Akiyama. I wonder if he'll tell her what I've been telling him.

I walk across the courtyard and wait, leaning against the porch railing. Stevie is the first one to run out of the school house. The sound of her paws making hollow noises on the wood of the porch is followed by the door crashing against the porch railing and the sounds of the boys running and leaping off of the steps. Lina is last, holding onto Astrid's hand. Raven isn't here today. Andie took him with her wherever she went. She always takes him, it's like she's afraid to leave him with me.

I kneel to pet Stevie.

"Daddy!" Lina let's go of Astrid's hand and jumps on my back.

"Hey, sweetie!" I stand and adjust my arms to give her a piggyback ride.

"Where's mom?"

"She had some things to do." I spin her around. "So, what do you want to do until she gets home?"

66

"Let's feed the horses!" Lina wraps her arms around my neck. I pause, relishing that feeling. There was a time when I never thought I'd feel her arms around me or see her again. I make my way toward the barn. "Wait!" she shouts in my ear. "We forgot Astrid!"

Turning around, I search for the little girl with the short dark hair and find her standing on the porch holding Blithe's hand, her eyes wide and watery. "Astrid!" I release one of Lina's legs and hold my hand out to her. "Come on! The horses are hungry."

Blithe releases Astrid's hand, and nods with a smile.

Astrid runs, her little legs moving fast over the snowy yard. I hold my hand out, but at the last second, as she's reaching, she slips and starts to fall. A small noise escapes her throat. I move fast, two steps, and just before she lands on her hands and knees, I grasp her around the waist and lift her.

No tears today, not on my watch.

"Gotcha." I move to lift her up, settle her on my hip and notice the gleam in her eyes is more watery than it was before. "No flying today, Astrid." I skip a step and bump her in the air. "Only the birds can fly here."

This elicits a giggle from both of the girls, warming that dark chill in my center for just a few moments more.

After feeding the animals we arrive back at the house to find Andie. They're setting the table for dinner, Raven on her hip as usual.

I hang the girl's coats, arrange the shoes in a straight line by the door. The girls run into the kitchen, both of them rosy cheeked from the crisp air outside. I watch from the doorway as they both stop to hug Andie around her waist before dashing to their seats at the table.

I guess now is as good a time as any to offer to help like Dr. Akiyama suggested. I take three steps into the kitchen. Andie turns as soon as she sees me, faces the stove and reaches for a plate piled high with sandwiches.

"Can I help?" I ask.

She stops dead in her tracks, stares at me with wide eyes.

"Ah... sure." She hands me the plate of grilled cheese. I move to take it, hands shaking. I don't even know why, maybe it's her suddenly taking me up on an offer to help instead of telling me *no* or shaking her head. Maybe it's that necklace I can see hiding under her shirt. My nerves hit me like never before. I feel her hand release the plate, and with mine so nervously fumbling, the plate slides out of my fingers and onto the floor, shattering with a loud sound.

Lina and Astrid stop their schoolgirl chatter and turn to see what happened. Andie's mouth drops open and she mutters an apology. Don't know why she's apologizing. I'm the one who dropped the plate. I look up to find Raven staring at me, a scowl on his face, agreeing without words that I am every bit the klutz that I currently feel like.

Andie sets Raven down and grabs an empty plate off the counter before bending to pick dinner up off of the floor.

Raven glares, and for a moment I wonder if this stare he's giving me, if it's similar to a face his father would make. It has to be, he barely resembles Andie at all since he's all dark-as-night-hair and blue eyes. He looks down at his mother before returning his gaze to me with a *what-are-you-waiting-for* look on his face. He toddles away and climbs into his chair at the table.

I drop to a crouch, a little too late, and fumble to help pick up the sandwiches. Some have shards of ceramic plate embedded in them. Andie sets the salvageable sandwiches on the clean plate after brushing them off.

My hand runs into hers as we both reach for the last sandwich.

"I'm sorry," I tell her.

"It's fine." She throws two of the sandwiches in the pig bin, then cleans the broken plate off the floor with a dustpan. "Why don't you go clean up?"

I look down at my hands to find them coated with crumbs and small pieces of broken plate. I don't remember standing or walking away. But the next thing I know I'm standing in the bathroom, rubbing soap over my hands, wondering how I could botch a task as simple as carrying a plate to the table. Jesus, I wasn't even this nervous when I first met her or when I asked her to marry me.

By the time I return from the bathroom, Andie had filled the dinner bowls with homemade tomato soup and cut the remaining sandwiches into quarters. It was while I was eating my third piece of sandwich that I noticed she hadn't eaten any, and there was none left. After that she didn't even have to ask me to take out the garbage. I couldn't wait to get out of there. I grab the trash, the pig bin, and the compost bin and practically run out the door, feeling like an ass.

As I stalk across the courtyard I am interrupted by a low whistle.

"She got you trained good." Sam's familiar voice breaks the still night air.

I stop and wait for him to walk next to me, taking

note that he's coming from the direction of Blithe's house. "Guess so," I reply, looking down at the garbage bag and bins in my hands.

As we walk toward the barn, Sam asks. "How's married life? Again."

"Lot less talking than there was before." Sam chuckles. "Sam." I stop and turn. "I've never known her like this. I know you're her brother and you probably don't want to hear this personal stuff, but nothing is getting better. I don't know what to do with her."

"Don't know what to tell you, man." Sam slaps me hard on the shoulder. "She's gone through a lot. Hell, we all have. She's probably just waiting for Crane to pull another stunt, and he will. She still needs to go to Florida. There's unfinished business there."

"How long before she goes?"

Sam shrugs. "Don't know. Crane hasn't given me those details yet. But I'm sure it's going to be soon. Within the next few months. I think he's giving her time."

"Time?"

"With the kids. With Raven, because he's so young."

We walk around the back of the barn. I throw the garbage in the bin, the compost in the compost pile, and the ruined food in the pig pen. Stacking the two bins together, I carry them with one hand, listening as the pigs grunt over the toasted cheese sandwiches.

I turn to Sam. "So what are you? Crane's right hand man now?"

Sam laughs. "Not quite, but you know what they say, keep your friends close–"

"Yeah, and your enemies closer," I finish his

sentence for him.

"Don't trust for a minute that he won't slit your throat if you become less than useful."

"Jesus Christ, Sam. Are we seriously having war talk?" I take a step back and watch him in the moonlight. He's still the same Sam. Looks like Andie, just huge and intimidating, the total opposite of a *little* brother.

Sam frowns. That's unusual. He's always smiling. "Look, Ian, things are going to get tougher. I just need you to remember Andie has one agenda, she's always had just one agenda, and that's to keep those kids safe, to keep her family safe. That includes you and me." Sam pokes me in the chest. "I know you probably hate Adam for all that he was and all that he did, but if you had seen her like I did when I first got here..." Sam rubs his hands through his hair. "She was a total mess."

"I know—"

"No, Ian, you have no clue. They fucking broke her, man. They broke her to pieces and made her believe that Lina would be dust if she didn't do what they said. They told her that *you* would be dust. She knows she fucked up screwing around with Adam. And I can't say I wouldn't have done something similar if I had to consider my spouse dead. There was just something about him. Hell, I trusted him with my life within moments of meeting him. She may have done a hell of a lot of things wrong, but you know what she did do right? She aligned herself with one person that she could trust to get her and Lina out of here. And they almost made it."

"And left me behind in the process."

"No, man." He pokes my chest harder. "That's one thing about Adam, if she had asked him to go back and

71

get you out, he would have. He told me so. He didn't have to come pull my ass from the wreckage of the Reformation, but he did. He did it for her. He would do anything for her."

"But they didn't save me."

"He never got the chance."

I shove my hands in my pockets, chuckling a breath of defeat out of my lungs in the process.

"Hey, man. We're all on the same team now. We're all together."

"Yeah, we're all Sovereign. I just don't understand why. Out of all the people in the world, why us?"

"Don't know. But I'm going to find out."

"And what do I do about Andie in the mean time?"

Sam gives me a look, one of those *good-luck-with-that-buddy* looks. "That's your deal, man. Whatever you do, you need to get her head straight. It's going on two years since anything crazy happened. Something's coming. I can feel it. She probably can too."

"Great," I mutter.

"You should probably get some rest," Sam suggests. "Still sleeping alone?"

"Shut up."

Sam laughs.

I look toward Blithe's house, see her turn out the lights downstairs. Turning toward Sam, I ask, "What the hell are you doing coming from Blithe's house at this hour? Doesn't she have like seventeen kids to take care of?"

"Four. Douche. She has four." Sam turns suddenly serious. "And what I was doing in there is none of your damn business."

If I didn't know Sam, hearing him call me douche might have upset me. But that's Sam; sarcastic, funny,

72

easy going. Now I guess I'll have to add slightly-deceiving to that list.

He stops and turns as he's walking away. "Ian?"

"Yeah?"

"We're family. You and me."

"I know this."

He runs a hand over his head. "She cuts hair."

"Who?"

"Blithe. She's good with hair. And you could use a trim."

"Good to know, thanks."

Sam heads across the courtyard for his room above the library house, and I head for the home I share with Andie.

--

By the time I return to the house Andie is already tucking the kids into bed. Eager to avoid screwing up again, I duck into my room and close the door. It's not long before there is a soft knock and the sound of Lina's voice.

"Daddy?" she asks through the crack.

I stand and open the door. "Hey, Sweetie, you getting ready for bed?"

"Yeah," she replies with a yawn. "Mom said to tell you goodnight."

"Okay." I pulled her in for a hug. "Sleep tight, Lina. I'll see you in the morning."

She pulls away, stopping before she reaches the door. "Dad?"

"Yeah?"

"Mom said you were just a little nervous and that's why you dropped the plate." And then her little nose scrunches up in a thoughtful look. "I told her you can't be nervous. You've always been Daddy."

"Don't worry about it, Sweetie, this isn't kid stuff. Mom and me, we will get it right eventually."

I listen to her pad down the hallway to her room. Then the evening is filled with the clicking of doors being closed and lights being flicked off. When I hear Andie's soft footsteps in the hall as she heads to her room, I lie on the bed and do the same thing I do every night: try to figure out a way to fix this.

After a few hours have passed, I roll over and pull the dog-eared copy of the Manifesto out from under my bed—if you could even call this a bed, it's just a narrow twin mattress. At least this one has springs, even if they do squeak.

I flip to the page I've stared at for months. *Andromeda Somers, District Matchmaker.* As I stare at the photo of her I notice she looks different now, just slightly so. And looking up at the family photo I have on the dresser, I try and figure out what it is. I close my eyes, remembering what she looked like at dinner.

The only problem is Andie never looks directly at me. But she did tonight when I dropped that plate. I recall what she looks like from the side and as she faced me. She has almost the same profile as Lina, long lashes, green eyes, straight nose—I don't know why I didn't notice it before. I open my eyes and look at the two pictures in front of me then close my eyes and see her as I did tonight. Her nose is no longer straight. Instead, there's a slight bump in the middle like it's been broken.

Shit.

I toss the Manifesto under the bed and turn to lie on my back, my hands behind my head. This causes the mattress to squeal in protest to my movements. God I miss my old bed. It had one of those pillow tops, and it was King sized so my feet didn't hang off the end. And Andie was there.

I roll again, sitting up and dropping my feet to the floor. I can't wait any longer. I've wasted too much time staring at pictures and talking to the shrink. Standing, I push on my shoes and glance at the clock. It's nearly midnight; the chances of any of the children waking up now are slim. Grasping the door handle, I turn it just so, preventing it from making much of a noise. Usually that's impossible, almost every part of this old farmhouse groans and squeaks. When the door is open just far enough for me to fit through, I slide through, leaving it ajar for when I come back.

Walking down the hallway, I know just where to step, and just where to stop. Andie's door is open, just like it is every night. I wait, listening, making sure she's not awake. There's just stillness. I take two long steps and pass her door. Tonight, I don't bother stopping in the kitchen. I grab my jacket off the hook next to the door and slip out into the night.

I stand on the porch for a minute, pushing my arms into the jacket and zipping it. Two Guardians sleep on the far end of the porch. One of them raises its head to look at me. I glance at it before jogging down the steps and across the courtyard. When I reach the barn I slow down, there's no point in getting the animals all worked up with me running through, that will be sure to wake up everyone out here. I stop and knock on Elvis's office door, wait as I hear his boots as he walks across the room and pulls the door open.

"Early tonight, Ian," he says, rubbing his eyes, his Australian accent thicker than usual at the moment.

"Can't sleep." I shove my hands in my jacket pockets and follow him out of the barn, across the courtyard again, and to the smaller barn that is used as a firing range. I have to admit, I wasn't sure how I felt seeing Lina shoot a pistol for the first time. But seeing what happened here, and now realizing that something terrible happened to Andie, I'm glad she knows how to defend herself. But I don't come out here each night to play with guns.

"You ready?" Elvis turns to me once we're inside. He looks tired. I know he's been training Sam during the day. Staying up late with me is probably killing him.

I hold out my left hand as he secures the straps and ties them into place. "Yeah."

He looks up at me as he moves to secure my right hand. "I only have a few hours tonight, then the rest is up to you."

"Okay." I nod at him and flex my fingers.

"What do you think you're going to get out of this?" he asks as he walks to the cupboard on the wall and pulls out a pair of gloves.

"Does it matter?"

"A man who stays up all night doing this…" he tips his gloved hand at me. "Is preparing for something."

"And what do you think I'm preparing for?"

"Haven't figured it out yet."

I push my hair out of my face. "Is that a problem?" I stretch my arms across my chest, loosening the tight muscles.

"Not much of one. At least it keeps me in shape." He pats his stomach. "Not getting any younger."

I smile. I would guess he's in his early forties, maybe twelve years older than me. He still looks fit, tanned. His hair has yet to turn gray. "How old are you anyway,

76

Elvis?"

"Does it matter?" he asks with a glint of mischief in his eyes. "I'm still faster than you." And with that, his left arm jabs forward and he punches me in the gut.

Newlyweds for two years,

and counting...

CHAPTER EIGHT

Andie

"Mom?" Lina's sweet little voice breaks the silence of the morning.

"Yes, Lina."

"Are you going to kiss Daddy today?"

The plate that I'm washing slips out of my hands, landing with a loud *thunk* at the base of the wide sink basin. We had a similar conversation months ago, she had asked me why we don't sleep in the same bed like we used to.

I was hoping she would let the topic pass. "Do you remember our talk about appropriate conversations at the table?" I ask her softly.

I don't tell her that I'm afraid to push him back to being like that. And that right now he thinks I might still be a bit innocent, he might actually trust me. But I know all that will change if I tell him what I did. If he knew that I killed a man, I know he would never look at me again. I might actually lose him for good, for forever.

"I remember some things." She sips at her hot cocoa. "I remember that you used to love him, you used to kiss him. But you don't anymore."

"Yes, well…" I never expected the conversation to take this route, and I'm not sure what to say. As I stir my coffee, I move to sit at the table. I look across the table and Raven stares at me, toast in hand, lips pursed, awaiting my response. Astrid's all nervous eyes, waiting to hear what I say.

"And then everything changed and you loved Adam." Raven looks to Lina when he hears the name. "Do you think he went to heaven?" Lina continues as Raven's eyes flick toward the ceiling.

"Yes. I hope." I hear footsteps in the hall. Ian walks into the kitchen, buttoning the top button of his shirt as he walks toward the coffee maker. "Finish your breakfast, Lina. Today Raven goes to school with you."

Raven turns to me. Silent as usual. He bites at the toast in his hand and chews it thoughtfully.

Lina and Astrid finish their toast and cocoa. Then Lina takes the dishes to the sink. She returns to the table, standing by Raven's chair. "Come on, Raven, let's go brush our teeth." She holds her hand out and Raven places his chubby hand in hers. He slips down from the chair and follows the girls to the bathroom. Stevie follows closely behind them, dipping her head every few steps to pick up the toast crumbs that fall off of Raven's clothes as he walks.

"Is he ever going to speak?" Ian asks from behind me.

I stand and bring my mug to the sink. "I don't know," I tell him.

He stares at me, expectantly, like I might reach up

on my tip-toes and kiss him goodbye for the day. Like I used to years ago. I haven't brought myself back to that. I'm not sure if I can. It's been getting better. Two years later and we can speak in a few sentences at a time to each other, full sentences, without awkward pauses or abrupt endings.

I bring the children to the school house and return to make the beds, fold the clothes, and do the wifely things that women do. Normal things that normal women do, not the things that are expected of me, things like helping Crane run the world, like deciding on the future of the Residents.

I open my drawer, a pile of shirts in my hand. I stop before placing them inside. The black T-shirt is there. Adam's T-shirt. I reach in with my free hand, running my finger over it before pulling it out and placing my pile of clothes in its place. I stare at the shirt in my hands; the scent of it is starting to fade. It almost smells more like my own clothes than him. I know I shouldn't, but I press the shirt to my face. I breathe in deeply, smelling the last bit of him. And the memories, they're like a drug still.

I need to stop this.

"Andie?" Ian's voice interrupts me.

Remembering I left the bedroom door open, I turn quickly, hiding the shirt behind my back. "Yes?" I ask out of breath, as though I ran a mile... or twelve.

I didn't run though, I just relived two years of a life I had with another man in one breath, one man who was not my husband.

Ian looks around the room, taking in my bed, the crib, the rocking chair. He shouldn't be here right now. He should be at the nuclear plant, running the place, just like Crane wants. Ian walks to the crib, places his hand on the rail.

"We could rearrange," he says.

"What do you mean?" I stand still, clenching the shirt behind my back still.

"Put Raven in my room, give you more space in here."

"Then where would you sleep?"

"The master bedroom," he replies without looking at me.

I tense at his suggestion. *My room is the master bedroom.* "I don't think that's a good idea."

"Why?"

"Because, things have changed."

"We could learn to make it work," he pleads.

I know his eyes are searching my face. I just can't bring myself to look at him. Why? Because I was just sniffing the shirt of my dead lover, reliving all those memories, and that's just as bad as openly cheating. Which I kind of did already. Ian will see it all over my face. He probably does already.

"I'm not ready," I force out.

"When will you be ready?"

"I don't know."

"It's been two years, Andie. He's been dead for two years. Don't you think it's time to move on?"

That's it. "You know, that's the same thing Crane said to me about you, Ian, when I begged him to give you back to me. I don't need to be reminded of how long he's been dead for. I remember each time Raven has a birthday."

"Andie—"

"What, Ian? What do you want?"

"You've changed," he says, glancing at me from head to toe.

"We've both changed," I remind him.

He sighs, running his hand through his hair. He needs it cut. But I'm not going to tell him. I don't tell him much, besides *hello* and *goodbye* and *the garbage is full*. Unless he has a question. I usually answer his questions.

"Is that his shirt?"

"What?"

"Behind your back. Is that his shirt?"

Shit. "I just found it," I lie to him.

"Sure you did." He reaches to the side, tapping his fingers on the dresser near the door.

Seems I'm still a particularly bad liar.

I can't take this. "You know, Ian, I've spent so much time wishing things could go back to the way they were when it was just the three of us, before all of this. I never wanted this, Ian. I'm sorry. I'm sorry I hurt you. I'm sorry I haven't gotten over him yet, and I'm sorry I had to stand in that delivery room and help deliver your son as another woman gave birth to him. I'm sure you can see how hard this is for me. You're not helping right now."

"What do you need?" he asks. "We've been living like this for two years. What can I do to help you?" His face is tense, concerned.

"Space. I just need some time and some space. I just need everyone to stop pushing me."

"Fine."

I pull my arms in front of me, making it apparent that I was in fact reminiscing over an old shirt. "Thanks," I whisper.

"Andie?" Ian's face seems to waver between concern and annoyance, the furrow in his brow returning to smooth skin just a moment after it

85

appears.

"Yeah."

"Be careful."

"What do you mean?"

"I mean Crane. You keep stomping on his toes… he's not going to take it much longer. I'm surprised he's dealt with you this long."

I wasn't expecting that from him. "I know, Ian. Let me deal with Crane. I've dealt with him on my own for years."

"I know." I hear him tap his fingers one last time. "I've seen what he's done to you."

I don't want to talk about what he's done to me. I have other plans for this day. "Ian?" I ask.

"What?"

"Can you get the kids when they're done with class? There's something I have to do."

He eyes me warily. "Yeah. Sure. Anything you need."

"Thanks."

He leaves the room.

I stand still, waiting to hear him walk out the door before I head for the door myself, taking the shirt with me. Something catches my eye on the dresser as I pass it. I stop, looking at the top of the dresser which is usually bare. Except for now, right now, where Ian's hand was resting, is a gold ring. I reach out and touch it. It's my wedding band. I don't know where he found it. I only remember not having it anymore. I can't even remember when it went missing. I unclasp the necklace from around my neck and thread the chain through the ring. It makes a small clang as it falls against the owl charm Adam gave me. I re-clasp the necklace and straighten my shoulders.

Now I have one thing left to do: I have to end this affair with a T-shirt.

Leaving the room, shirt in hand, I head for the tool shed. As I get closer I can hear someone is in there shooting. I slip in the door, trying to be as quiet as possible. Sam stands at the far end of the building, his stance rigid as he demolishes the target in front of him. I reach for the wall, pulling a shovel from its resting place, then sneak out the door and head for the fields.

Standing in front of Adam's gravestone with the freshly disturbed earth at my feet, I think to myself that maybe I should have done this a long time ago. Maybe it would have made forgetting him easier. Still, I'm not sure if I want to forget him, all of him. I never even got to say goodbye, or thank you for saving my life, for giving me Raven. I pull his shirt from the waist of my jeans. I stare at it, wanting to press it to my face so badly even though I know it's not going to help. I know it will just keep things the way they are, with me unable to move on.

I toss the shirt in the shallow hole I just dug. "Goodbye, Adam." I tell the chiseled gray granite. With each shovel of dirt the shirt becomes less visible. The soft fabric wilts under the weight of the earth until I can see it no more.

Moving on should be easier, now that I've buried his T-shirt and the temptation to relive the short time I had with him.

CHAPTER NINE

"I don't want to meet you anymore," I tell Dr. Akiyama. I'm tired of these twice-weekly sessions.

He looks up at me, bored with my declaration. "And why is that, Andromeda?" he asks with a frown.

"I asked you to call me Andie."

"Okay, Andie, why don't you want to participate in these sessions any longer?"

"Because I have too much going on. Raven is two, Lina is carrying a heavier course load, I have Astrid living with us, and there are Residents that need to be paired. I don't have the time to drive here and meet with you."

"You must uphold the values of the District, of the Sovereign–"

"I know," I grumble at him. "I have."

"Crane suggests we meet until you've made progress."

"I have!" I practically shout at him.

He slaps his notebook closed. "Tell me about your progress." He folds his hands in his lap, his face takes on an open expression, his eyebrows raised just slightly so. "Well?"

"I…" I try to think about the progress we've made over the past two years.

"Do you speak to Ian?"

"Yes."

"In complete sentences?"

"Mostly."

"Are you letting him help you around the house?"

"Sometimes he gets the kids from school, when I need him to."

"Are you affectionate toward each other?"

I feel my body stiffen, it's almost an unconscious reaction.

"I see," Dr. Akiyama responds before I can say anything. "You still refuse to come here with him. How do you expect to make a real progress in your marriage? You can't live like this forever. Don't you think two years of living like this is enough? Perhaps it's time to move on."

"I know." I don't tell him that I buried my temptations in front of Adam's gravestone. At lease I have been able to let those memories go and move on with my life.

"There was a time," Dr. Akiyama gazes toward the ceiling as he speaks. I've seen him do this before, he's storytelling, "When this District was in its infancy and I remember a very brave young woman whom I had to stitch together on her dining room table." He pauses and looks directly at me. "And I remember there was a man at her side who held her hand, and changed her bandages—"

"Stop," I tell him. "I don't want to remember that. I don't want to remember Adam. He's dead. He's

89

buried. I'm done."

"What you fail to see is that you had two men in your life that cared very much for you and they've changed places. One has died and one remains alive. And the one who remains alive looks just like Adam did when he speaks of you and looks at you."

"Please, just stop, Doctor–"

"I will stop when you stop pushing away those who care deeply about you. This is not a path you can travel alone. Maybe you thought you could do it when it was just yourself and Lina, but you have two children now, and another little girl who is as close to being another child to you as any. Am I right?"

I nod at him.

"So, *Andie*, when you are done pushing your partner away and make an attempt–"

"I have–" I start, but he holds his palm up to silence me.

"More than just a few sentences, a real attempt at having a life together. He has been trying, you have not. Don't you worry that he's going to give up at some point, and then where will you be, living like this forever? It's been two years, which means it's time to hold a conversation, it's time to share duties, and it's time to move on. You know Crane won't wait forever for you, I'm surprised he's waited this long."

"Wait for what?" I feel my face twist in question.

"You will find out, soon enough."

I shake my head at the threat. "I have made some progress."

"What?"

"I buried his shirt."

"Who's shirt?"

"Adams. I had an old shirt of his that I was hanging

on to. It smelled like him. Anyway, I buried it at his gravesite."

Dr. Akiyama flips to a page in his notebook and jots something down.

CHAPTER TEN

Crane's office looks like the office of an accountant or an engineer, with the maps and the stacks of paper laid out on the tables, not a crazed man who's working on taking over the world. It's gray, and boring, everything neatly organized, chairs spaced perfectly apart. I'd like to move one, tip it to the side just-so, so he can see the indent in the carpet.

"You need to go to Crystal River," Crane says.

Startled, I focus back on him. "No. I don't think so." I shake my head at him.

"It's been two years. Morris won't last much longer. You need to finish."

I think of what happened. The tour he sent me on, all the *lessons* I had to learn. "And my children?"

"They will be safe with Ian."

"Who's bringing me?"

"Colonel Salk." Crane smiles.

"Are you sure he's ready?"

"He's ready. You should have more faith in your little brother."

"I have plenty of faith in Sam. You have no qualms with having a married couple in the Committee?" I ask him. I don't like what he's doing, that he's included so much of my family into this.

"Actually, it's perfect. What a better way to show the Residents what we are trying to create here. Why, you two are the perfect example. You work together, go home together, raise the next generation of Sovereign together. There's no space for a wandering eye, no space for secrets." He folds his hand on the desk in front of him.

"I don't like this."

"You don't like much of what is required of you."

I simply stare at him. He's wearing a red tie. I still hate the color red.

"You've changed, Andromeda." He's only the second person in a matter of days to tell me this.

"What do you mean?" I ask him.

"Well, your poor attitude is still the same, although it seems to come and go these days. You're different. I can't quite place my finger on it."

"What were you expecting, Crane? You think you could do what you've done to me and expect me to stay the same?"

"No. I'm sure you've figured it out that we've been grooming you for something more. But, something is off with you."

"I'm sure it is."

"Have you rekindled your relationship with your husband?"

"That is most certainly none of your business." I glare at him.

"Hmm," he responds, moving his hands to his chin.

"When do I leave?" I ask, trying to get as far away

from the subject of my relationship with Ian as possible.

"Two days."

I try to hide my gasp. Only two days. Two days to prepare myself and my family. I am suddenly filled with an overwhelming need to get the hell away from Crane.

"I'm going to see Morris," I tell him.

"That would be a good idea."

I practically run out of Crane's office. I take the stairs, afraid the elevator might take too long. I head for my vehicle, not taking a full breath until I've reached the safety inside. He always oversteps his boundaries, but asking if Ian and I have rekindled our relationship, that's just too much, it's too personal. Of course, it's been long enough, we should have rekindled something by now. I should at least be able to touch him, or hug him, or something, but I just can't bring myself to, and I'm not sure why. I thought burying the last bit of Adam, his old T-shirt, might help, but it just hasn't yet.

I start the SUV and drive to the hospital where Morris is now residing. When I reach his room, I pull a chair next to Morris's bedside. He's sleeping; his breaths slow, steady. I count them, making sure they are at a normal rate. I can hear him rasp with each inspiration. The skin around his lips is tinged blue. I reach forward and turn up his oxygen flow. When I sit back down his eyes are open.

"Morris?" I ask.

"Yes." He licks his lips. I hold a cup of water with a straw to his mouth. He drinks. "Much better," he says when he's done.

"How are you, Morris?"

"Old, ready to die."

I close my eyes. The thought of him dying, of being gone from this earth, just like Adam, just like half our population, it chills me. Whatever bad things he did, all the evil decisions he took part in making, it still hurts. I don't want him to be gone, he is my mentor here. He's saved me from Crane more than once, and I'm not sure I could save myself from the bullshit Crane pulls.

"Please don't say that." I tell Morris.

"It's going to happen. Soon, Andromeda. Are you prepared for my death?"

"What's that supposed to mean?"

He reaches out, laying his hand on mine. It feels cool, rubbery. Our conversations have gotten more morbid and dark since he was admitted to the hospital. It's the reason why I don't visit him as much. His teachings are done, and I can't take the death talk.

"You just need to be ready to take my place."

"I don't think I'll ever be ready for that."

He gives my hand a weak pat. "So, you're going to Florida?" he changes the subject.

"Yes, to finish my training I'm told."

"You will. Finish that is."

"I don't want to."

"We know."

I pull my hands away from him and set them in my lap. "You do?"

"Of course I do. Don't worry. Their problem is simple. I have faith that you will solve it quickly."

"That's a problem with you people."

"What," he asks.

"You have far too much faith in me."

He reaches out, placing his wrinkled, shaking hand over mine. He squeezes it, just a bit. "We have just the right amount of faith in you." He closes his eyes.

I wait in silence as he falls asleep before I remove his hand from mine and tuck it under his blanket.

--

Today I make my arrangements before I leave.

When I reach the kitchen I'm surprised to find Ian already awake. He smiles, and holding a cup of coffee out for me he says, "Good morning."

"Thanks," I tell him, turning to sit. I stop when I see what looks like a piece of round wood on the table where I usually sit. "What is that?" I ask.

"A gift." Ian walks up next to me, sipping at his cup of coffee, looking at the object on the table.

"For who?" I ask.

"You."

I reach forward, touching the piece of wood. It's a dark cherry wood. The width of a small tree trunk and about four inches tall, the growth rings are visible through the glossy finish. When I run my fingers over the smooth top it moves to the side, revealing a velvet lined space.

"It's a jewelry box," Ian says.

"Oh," I reply, picking it up and removing the lid.

"Do you know what today is?" he asks me.

I stop admiring the box as a flurry of dates rush through my memory. I'm hoping it's not something important, like our wedding anniversary...

Ian doesn't give me long to contemplate before he speaks again. "It's your birthday, Andie. Happy birthday."

"Is this from you?" I ask, setting the box down.

"Yeah, I made it." He sits next to me.

I run my fingers over the top again. "It's beautiful. But, I don't have much jewelry."

"You have some." He looks at the necklace around my neck which holds the owl charm from Adam and my wedding band that I still haven't been able to put back on my finger.

"Thank you," I tell him.

"You forgot. Didn't you?" he asks, leaning back in his chair.

Truthfully, I haven't thought about my birthday since this started. I never sat down and added the years. I was always too focused on keeping Lina safe and happy, and completing the tasks assigned to me. "I guess I did," I admit.

"It's kind of a big one, Andie. It's your thirtieth birthday."

Now the numbers add up. I was twenty-six when this all started, thinking I had a handle on my life, counting my accomplishments, doing my best to carve out a quiet life for my family. Now look at me, four years have flown by, our lives changed. No wonder I stopped keeping track.

"Thanks." He smiles and takes another sip of his coffee. "I have to leave tomorrow," I remind him.

He nods. "What will you do there, in Florida?"

I shake my head. "I'm not sure," I tell him. "It's kind of like a surprise, a test. They don't tell me until I get there and then there is usually some underlying problem I have to figure out on my own."

"And if you pass this test?"

I shrug my shoulders at him. I don't want to tell him the truth. "Then we'll be safe."

"That's it?" he asks. "We'll be safe."

"Let's just say my rank will be higher than

97

Sovereign."

"A Funding Entity then?"

"How do you know about that?" I ask. I turn and look into his dark brown eyes. Crane made it clear that we weren't allowed to speak of the Funding Entities or who they were.

"Crane mentioned them to me. Just, how do you become a Funding Entity?" he asks squinting his eyes in thought. "You have no money to fund anything. Actually, none of us have money anymore."

I tap the side of my head. "It's about more than money now. Intellectual property maybe."

"Because of what you do with the genetic information, the pairings."

"Yeah. Crane thinks that makes me special or something."

Ian spins his mug on the table, thinking. "But someone had to pay for all of this. You don't just take over entire countries without some financials."

"That's an answer few people know and they're not allowed to talk about it."

"You know, don't you?" he asks me.

"Don't," I warn him. "That's information I never wanted and I never want to relay to another person."

"You don't want to tell me?"

"Sure I do. I just can't. Not yet at least."

"Not yet? Then when?"

"When I die."

"Don't say that." He sets the coffee mug down on the table after taking a sip.

"It's the truth," I tell him. "These people have their own little laws and guidelines."

"You mean the Manifesto?"

I shake my head at him. "The Manifesto is for the

Residents and Sovereign. The other people who organized this, their rules seem to shift and change with the wind. But they all seem to have one thing in common."

"What's that?"

"They're all afraid of Burton Crane."

Our conversation is interrupted by the sound of the children padding down the hall, headed for the kitchen. I turn to make them breakfast, realizing that I just had a conversation with Ian. A real conversation. I said more than one full sentence to him. I did more than simply answer a few questions. I held a perfectly normal conversation.

Hearing him washing his mug in the sink, I turn to look at him. He smiles at me, probably with the same realization which I have just had.

"I'm headed to work," he says. "See you tonight."

As though I've used up my daily allowance worth of words for the day, I simply nod at him and watch as he pats the children on their heads and walks out the door.

"How would you like some honey in your milk?" I ask the children.

"No hot cocoa?" Lina asks.

"She said we used the last of it yesterday, remember?" Astrid asks Lina in her hushed voice.

I warned them that we were running out. And the way things are, with the last of our stock from the last run outside of the gates almost gone, I'm not sure when we will see cocoa again. I think Alexander was hiding the last of it just for us. Soon it will be the coffee.

"Honey then?" I ask, placing bread into the oven to toast it.

I warm the milk in a pan, adding a few spoons of the honey Elvis got from a beehive behind the barn.

Bringing the mugs to the table, I set them in front of the children and sit down with my coffee.

"Remember," I start, "how I told you I needed to go on a trip and that you were going to have to stay here?"

"Yes," Lina replies with a pout.

Astrid looks between us confused. Raven pouts his lips at me just like his sister.

"Well, tonight I have to go on a trip with Uncle Sam. I'll be leaving for a few days and then I will be back."

"Who will take care of us?" Astrid asks, her eyes widening with panic.

I reach out and squeeze her shoulder. "Ian will be here to take care of you all." The timer on the stove dings. I stand, pull the toast from the stove and spread blueberry jam on it. Then I return to the table and pass out the plates. The children eat.

"You won't forget about us, will you?" Lina asks, her mouth full of bread and crumbs falling out onto the floor for Stevie to clean up.

My breath catches in my throat. "Lina," I reply, forcing the air from my lungs. "I will never forget about you." I reach forward and brush her hair out of her face. "It's only for a few days. I'll be back before you know it. I won't forget any of you. I'll be back. I promise."

--

"Are you ready?" Sam asks.

We're standing in the hallway, by the front door. He's dressed in full Volker uniform. He looks authoritative. Much too authoritative to be my little brother.

"I'll never be ready," I tell him as my eyes drift to the pin on his shoulder. It's a small metallic bird; a phoenix. "Just a sec."

I rush down the hall, pushing open the door to my room. I walk to Raven's crib. He's sleeping, but I still lean in and kiss him. Next, I head to Lina's room. Stevie raises her head from the foot of the bed. I pet her as I pass. I kiss Lina and pull the covers up to her chin. I turn around to find Astrid mostly uncovered, her hair covering her face, her leg hanging off the bed. I move her legs and tuck her in, smooth her hair out of her face.

Stevie whines. I move to pat her head. "Stay with Lina," I tell her as I close the door and head for the hallway where Sam waits for me.

The last time I left, we at least had a backup plan to get Lina out of here. Sam was prepared and ready to run with her. Now things have changed. Sam is leaving with me, and I have two children and a husband. I don't think Ian realizes how bad Crane actually is.

Ian stands next to Sam as I walk toward them and I get the feeling I've interrupted.

"Ready now?" Sam asks.

"No, but let's go," I tell him. I don't want to leave. I'll never be ready to leave my children behind and run off on some horrid training crusade that Crane has planned. I guess it could be worse, he could be sending me to Tonopah. I could have to deal with that psychopath Sakima again.

Sam reaches for my bag. He looks expectantly at me and Ian, raising his eyebrows. "Watch over them, Ian." I tell him as Sam walks out the door.

"I will," Ian replies with a thick voice.

"No," I turn, "make sure Crane doesn't come near them. He's always lurking in the shadows waiting for me to be gone so he can pull some bullshit."

"I'll watch them," Ian promises.

"I'm serious, Ian. You don't know what I went through to get you all back. The things I had to do." *I killed a man in cold-blood and then Adam tried to save me and Raven, and died.* I don't tell him that though. I'm sure it's nothing he wants to hear right now. And to be truthful, I don't want him thinking any less of me right now.

He places his hand on my arm. I look down at it as though someone has thrown a meatball there. He hasn't touched me since he showed up here. He hasn't touched me in two years. Of course, I haven't touched him either. We just started having full conversations, can't rush this.

"Everything will be fine," he says in a smooth soft voice.

"I hope," I tell him. "I'm trusting you with them."

He steps forward, his tall frame bending down, and I feel my body stiffen as he wraps his arms around me. I know I should do something, maybe hug him back, but I can't move.

"See you in a few days," he says as he releases me.

I simply nod at him, then turn and run out of the house.

Sam is waiting in the driveway. I get in the passenger side of his vehicle.

"Wow," he says, smirking.

"What?"

"You know, you're not very nice to him. You could have at least given him a chaste kiss on the cheek. You two are married."

"Shut up, Sam."

Sam drives. Whoever has been training him has already shown him how to find the platform and how to run the train.

We load the train ourselves. Me, Sam, two Guardians, that's it. The train feels strange, empty. The Volker at the platform salute Sam. I listen as he gives them orders. It's strange to see my little brother taking Adam's place. When he's done, he steps on the train and starts it. I sit in one of the seats. There is no send-off from Crane or Alexander. No strange winks from Ian.

"Want to get some rest?" Sam asks me, motioning to the sleeping bunks.

There's no way I can go back there and remember everything, again. "I'm fine," I tell Sam.

"You sure? We'll be there by morning. You can rest. I've got this," he says confidently as he flips switches and checks gauges on the dash.

"I'm sure you do, Sam. But I'd rather die than step foot in those sleeping bunks."

He nods, giving me a look of understanding. I know he doesn't truly understand, but he saw what I was like when I came back from the tour: sick, seizing, exhausted from what Crane had put us through.

Now, here I am again, headed outside the gates of the Phoenix District. It's been two years. I doubt much has changed. The United States is still in ruins, *according to Crane*. The Survivors are still struggling, *according to Crane*. I find it odd that such a skeleton crew is being sent off, especially as this is Sam's first time out. But since I'm sure Crane no longer wants me dead, he must think Sam is competent to be sending us off alone. I rest my head against the wall of the engine car and close my eyes, forcing myself to sleep and not think about what awaits us in Crystal River.

--

Sam doesn't have to wake me up. The sultry Florida air does the job as it permeates the engine car. I stretch my neck, trying to work out the stiffness and move to stand next to Sam.

"Up already?" he asks.

"Yeah." I look around the engine car to find the Guardians sleeping in the corners. "How much do you know about Crystal River?" I ask Sam.

"Alexander debriefed me," he says.

"That was nice of him." No updates for me, though. This is nothing new, the Entities like to keep me in the dark.

"Sam," I warn him. "Don't eat the manatee."

"Who eats manatee?

"The Residents here do."

"Aren't they endangered?"

"I'm guessing not any longer."

I watch through the window as Sam slows the train. The fence opens and we pull up to the train platform. Two years ago was the last time I was here. And it was storming like nothing I've ever seen. Should have taken that as a sign.

Thankfully, we didn't come during hurricane season this time. Emanuel Torres and Colonel Ramirez meet us on the platform. They smile when they see me. I do my best to smile back.

"Welcome back," Torres says in his familiar thick Spanish accent, shaking my hand. Ramirez does the same.

"I'd like to introduce you to Colonel Salk," I tell them, holding my hand out toward Sam.

Torres and Ramirez greet him, both with hearty handshakes. Torres smiles, Ramirez does not.

I look around. The last time I was here the place was in shambles. Their population was low, they didn't even have their fence completed. Crystal River was the last District to be set up. And when we were here two years ago, it was a disaster. Their borders were not secure, their population was dwindling. And then I ate the manatee. I remember nothing else.

Now, I turn my head toward the chain-link fence, hearing the hum from the electricity that runs through it.

"How was your trip here?" Torres asks, eyeing Sam.

"Fast," I tell him. "Ramirez, perhaps you could show Colonel Salk around since this is his first visit."

Sam and Ramirez head off and I follow Torres into Headquarters. Everything looks the same as when I left. There's still a short building with the wide porch that's used for their Headquarters here. It still looks like an old town hall. There are still Volker guarding the door; they open it for us. The hallways are still sparse, empty. Torres opens the door to their Committee meeting room.

The rest of the Crystal River District Development Commission are there: Richard Ruiz, still looking like an overdressed banker, Mateo Pena and Javier Vega, still looking like they could be related with their tan skin and dark hair and eyes. I notice Javier's glasses are now being held together on the side with a piece of white tape.

"Thank you for coming back," Emanuel starts.

"You don't need to thank me," I tell him. "I didn't

come here willingly. I'm sure that's no surprise. So, Emanuel, tell me what your problem is here."

"Well." He scratches the back of his neck. "Colonel Waters helped us secure the boundaries when you were here last." He pauses, hesitant.

"Colonel Waters is no longer with us," I inform him.

"I am aware. Sorry," he says curtly.

"Cut to the chase, Emanuel. What's your problem here? Your boundaries are secure, you all look well fed, what's the issue?"

"You're right, we are well fed, and that's because our population has dwindled even lower."

"How many?" Last time there were only two hundred residents.

"Less than one hundred," he replies.

"Any children?"

"No."

I look to Richard, Mateo, and Javier. They watch me in anticipation. I know that a few of the other Districts are bursting at their seams, while this one is empty.

"What happened to them all?" I ask.

"Malaria, and…" he pauses. "Alligators."

I guess I deserved that pause. Last time I openly mocked him for losing so many people to alligators.

"Have you let any Survivors in?" I ask.

"No," Emanuel replies.

"Has anyone found your boundaries?"

"No," he replies again.

"And why is the malaria so rampant here?" I ask not so nicely.

Richard clears his throat. "We're no longer allowed to use pesticides," he says.

Emanuel nods in agreement.

"Is this some other rule from the Entities?" I ask.

"Yes," Emanuel says. "We are not to infringe on the wildlife, no matter how pestilent they may be."

"This is a problem," I mutter to myself.

The malaria is an ecological problem which I can do nothing about. But I can do one thing. Crystal River needs Residents and I know where to get them. From the same place the Tonopah District got them, from outside the gates. Let's get this over with quickly.

"Is your nuclear reactor up to full power?" I ask.

Emanuel tips his head. "Yes."

"Has all the power been diverted to your fence?"

"Yes. Why do you ask?"

"Because, Emanuel, we're going outside the gates. We're going to find you some new Residents."

He smiles. I don't like his crooked smile just now. I don't trust it. It's like I just told him exactly what he wanted to hear. "You think it's worth the risk, to go out there and find people to bring back?"

"What other option do you have, Emanuel?"

"Crane won't want you outside the gates with the feral Survivors, you're too important to him. He's already lost one important member of his team."

"Well, we're out of choices for this place. What's the motto? *Failure is not an option.*"

Just then the door opens. Sam and Ramirez walk in.

"Failure isn't an option," Emanuel responds. "But bringing in new Residents, going out to find new Residents, it's risky."

"Where do you expect to get them from?" I ask.

I know there are other Districts that are flooded with Residents, already assimilated Residents. But I'm not about to contact Crane and ask him to send people.

Sam raises his hand to interrupt. "What happens

when you bring these new people back here? What then? What if they don't cooperate?" Sam asks.

"They will be medicated," Emanuel answers.

"Still, we go out there," Ramirez starts. "We risk our people, what little people we have left, and when we get them back here we risk an uprising."

"That won't happen," I assure him.

"How can you be sure?"

"Because if there's one thing I learned in Tonopah, the medication combined with the strong desire to survive at all costs overrides everything. A speech to unite the new Residents won't be necessary, they will trust anyone."

The room is silent, each man contemplating this plan in his heads.

"Do you have one of those magical lists?" I ask Emanuel.

"Yes," he replies, giving me a hard look.

It's the list of people they didn't have time to pull from society before the bombings. Each District has one. They use it to find new Sovereign, who will enrich their population. We aren't to speak of the list.

"What's the plan?" Ramirez asks.

"Let's start today. Get supplies ready, houses in order, what's left of your medical team."

"How will you know where to look?" Javier asks, adjusting his glasses. "Are you just planning on searching the woods, the abandoned cities, the swamps?"

"They don't need to," Emanuel tells us as he makes way for the computer. He sits and types a few things into the laptop. "Come here. All of you."

We walk to where Emanuel sits. Standing behind him, I look at the computer screen and see an image of

North America. As Emanuel scrolls with the computer controls, the screen zooms in over Florida to give a bird's-eye view. He moves the screen to the West, stopping over a cleared area. I make out the train instantly.

"Is this live?" I ask.

"Yes," he responds.

"How?" Javier asks, placing his hand on the table and leaning closer to the desk.

"The satellites still circle the earth," he tells us. "They are still live, they still run, and some of us still have access to them."

I glimpse at Sam, whose forehead is currently wrinkled in thought. Emanuel just relayed a potent piece of information. With his revelation, and his deceptiveness to his own people, he must be an Entity. Who else would have this ability and keep it from the Sovereign for years?

Javier walks to a filing cabinet and pulls out a large map. He rolls it out on the table. Emanuel spins the laptop around, so we can all see the screen. Ramirez pulls the top off a red marker.

"I guess the first decision is whether to go by train or by foot?" Ramirez asks.

"By train we are limited to the direction we can go," Sam speaks up. "The tracks only connect the Districts. They don't meander around the states."

"Even if we tried to use the old tracks," Mateo speaks up, "we run the risk of getting stuck if the tracks were damaged in the bombings."

"We could use the train, and scour a radius around the tracks, that would make it easier to get people back here," Sam suggests.

"Let's see what we can see," Emanuel tells us. He

moves the screen north along the tracks, he scrolls out so we can see a twenty-mile radius. There's nothing. No houses, no trails, no movement. Just nothing.

"Make the radius larger," Ramirez urges.

Emanuel scrolls out to a forty-mile radius. We watch the screen for anything.

"What's that?" Javier asks, pointing at the corner of the screen.

It looks to be a cleared area with a dark figure walking. Emanuel follows the figure. The person walks further north, through tall brush and grass. He zooms in. It's a man; young, with tan skin, dark hair, a backpack, two dead squirrels hanging off a line attached to his bag, and a knife attached to his belt.

The image is crystal clear. Disturbingly clear. Deceptively clear.

"So," I ask, on a hunch. "Which one of you worked for NASA? Or was it government intelligence?" Mateo and Javier turn to look at me. "Just you two?" I ask, pointing at them. Emanuel taps his finger on the table. I'll take that as a yes also.

So, here we have a town Sheriff, three NASA scientists, maybe, and Richard Ruiz, whose background I have yet to figure out, running Crystal River.

I turn my attention back to the computer screen. The man we are following walks across a small stream and slows when he comes to a fence. He climbs, swinging his legs over the short wooden fence. He walks across an overgrown lawn and up to a house. Emanuel scrolls out. We can see what was a small housing development, a cul-de-sac with five houses. We wait and watch as people trickle in and out of the homes. Some seem to stand guard at the opening to the street. There are small gardens and what looks like chickens in a fenced area.

"How many do you think are there?" Ramirez asks.

"Not enough," I reply.

"It's a place to start," Sam says.

"We need more than a few people. We need a few hundred," I say, watching as Ramirez marks the map where we spotted these people.

Emanuel scrolls in and out, moving to the east. There looks to be a large cluster of people at an old shopping mall. We can see people moving by the glass windows, and milling about in the parking lot.

In another area to the south there's a camp near a small pond with six tents. He continues searching. Each time we find a cluster of Survivors, Ramirez marks the map. By the time we are done there are just over a dozen marks on the map, the furthest point is almost ninety miles to the south.

"We could use the train to go north," Ramirez points out.

"Yeah, but what about to the east and south?" Javier asks.

"You have Volker SUV's here, we could use those," I suggest.

"What happens if we run out of gas, or get a flat tire?" Sam points out. "Then we're sitting ducks, drawing attention."

"And safety?" Richard asks. "What happens if the Survivors don't want to come, what if they attack, or…"

"We have guns," I say. "They've been picking through the ruins for four years. I doubt they have many weapons."

"We'll have to go by foot to pick up people from

the east and south," Sam says.

"That's a long trek," Ramirez points out.

"Don't they have helicopters in the Hanford District?" Richard asks.

"What are you planning on doing? Dropping flyers, Richard? They won't send a helicopter, and even if they did, we couldn't use it. That would draw too much attention," I dismiss his suggestion.

"You think they'll come with us?" Sam asks.

"What Survivor wouldn't want a hot shower, a clean house, fresh food? From what I saw in Tonopah, the Survivors were begging to get in their gates," I tell them.

"So when do we leave?" Ramirez asks.

"How long to get some weapons together and a few supplies?" I ask.

"It's too late," Emanuel interrupts. "It's late afternoon. By the time we get out, even if we get the train to the north, we won't get to those Survivors until evening or later. I think starting in the morning would be best."

"I don't see why we can't start now. What easier time to make a decision like this when the Survivors are settling down for the night, stomachs empty, fearful for what the night might bring? For what tomorrow might bring?" I respond. The truth is, I'm pushing it. I don't want to be here any longer than I have to.

"Say we go tonight; bring back a few Survivors, then what?" Ramirez asks.

"They get fed, assigned houses, test them in the morning when the medication has taken its full effect."

"Don't you think we're moving kind of fast?" Emanuel asks.

"I don't want to be gone from home any longer

than I have to, the sooner we get started the better." I tell them, all of them. I even make eye contact.

"Okay," Emanuel agrees, "let's get moving."

Ramirez and Sam leave to collect weapons and a crew of Volker.

Javier rolls up the map and leaves the room with Mateo on his heels. I start to follow, but Emanuel stops me, holding his hand out.

"What?" I ask him.

"You're not going with them," he says, shaking his head.

"Why not?" I argue. "I'm not going to just sit around here and wait. I need to do something."

"There's plenty for you to do here."

"Why are you telling me I can't go? We're pretty much equals now." Well, almost–Morris hasn't died. I haven't taken his place. If anything I am acting as his apprentice.

"Not yet, Andie, and I won't have Crane lunging for my neck if anything happens to you. So you stay here and wait for the men to bring back the Survivors."

"So what do I do, pace at the gate?"

"No, you get ready for an influx of Survivors to categorize and sample. You're going to have to analyze their genetic data and pair them when you get home. And you still have a problem to solve here."

"I'm solving it for you," I tell him.

"If you think that the lack of Residents is the problem, I'll give you a hint: it's not."

I stare at him. I know their problem is the population. But malaria is also a problem here. But without pesticides I can't do much about that. Perhaps it's a combination of the two. I need a bit longer to think. Maybe staying behind is a good idea.

"I think I know what this District's problem is," I tell Emanuel. "And it's not something that can be solved overnight."

"Then you had better get working on solving it if you want to go home," he says.

--

"You're not going?" Sam asks me.

"No," I tell him.

"Good. I didn't want you to go."

I focus on the sweat dripping down his neck and into his collar.

"That's not very nice."

"I didn't mean it like that, Andie. If we run into trouble I don't want you getting hurt."

"I don't want you getting hurt either, Sam."

I brush at the sweat dripping down my own neck from the Florida heat. Sam squeezes my shoulder, a brotherly gesture. I turn and watch Ramirez and a crew of ten Volker load the train with a few bottles of water, and some food and weapons.

"What do you think about the ethical impact of what we are about to do?" Sam asks.

I step back. "Are we in Sociology or something, Sam? You do realize that all ethics flew out the door when a clandestine group of scientists and world leaders decided they were going to restart the human race? I can't worry about ethics. I can only worry about my family and how I can keep them safe. I worried about ethics once and all it got me was trouble. These are new times, we must adapt, survival of the fittest has been reenacted. And by *the fittest* the Entities mean the least ethical, so God help me because I let my ethical

114

concerns fly out the window a long time ago."

"That was quite a speech." He raises his eyebrow and shoves his hands in his pockets.

"Take your hands out of your pockets, Sam."

"What?" he asks.

"You are the Volker Sovereign. You don't raise your hand in Committee meetings, you don't look at the floor, and you definitely don't put your hands in your pockets. If you don't know what to do with your arms, cross them over your chest. You're six-foot-five for Christ's sake. It will make you look intimidating. You need people to listen to you. You need to be authoritative. You need to be an asshole."

"You don't need to be such a jerk," he takes a step toward me, scowling.

"Sam, do you really see what's going on here? What these people are doing? They think they are making everything better, but they are just sending society into the dark ages. Women, men; we are no longer equals. Crane's project to create genetically submissive humans, that's no better than slavery."

"Yeah," he replies. "I've been thinking the same thing." I look up as he towers over me. My hulking, angry brother. "You need to check the attitude, Andie," he warns. "I want to get out of here too. But pissing everyone off isn't going to get us anywhere."

I shrug at him and step back to regain my personal space. "I think you should take one of the Guardians with you," I tell Sam, changing the subject and watching the two we brought with us as they wander the train platform.

"I'm not sure that's a good idea."

"Sam, they're better guards than the Volker. One already tried to save your life." I remind him of the incident when he first showed up and tried to protect the children at the Pasture from being tattooed.

"Yeah." He begins to run his hand through his hair, stopping partway through and crossing his arms. "Maybe you're right."

Ramirez steps off the train and waves. "Ready?" he shouts.

Sam waves back. "That's my cue, Sis. See you in a few hours."

"Hurry back," I tell him as he jogs for the engine car. One of the Guardians trots protectively behind him. "I'm sorry I was a bitch," I mumble under my breath as the train leaves the platform.

"What's that?" I hear the voice of Richard Ruiz ask from behind me.

"Nothing." I wave my hand at him, hoping he didn't hear my pathetic apology. "We need to get the manatee ready and make sure it's saturated with a full dose of the medication," I tell him.

"Done," he says, pointing across the parking lot.

I see smoke and people gathered around large-barrel grills. Within moments the scent of grilled manatee makes its way to us. It smells like a delicious bacon hamburger. My mouth waters.

"Don't eat it this time," Richard warns.

I narrow my eyes at him. Richard looks at his diamond-studded watch. "Well, looks like we should get you ready to greet the Survivors," he says.

"I don't need to get ready."

"We need to get your supplies and your list. You know, the magical list, as you called it." He winks at me.

Richard Ruiz is a Funding Entity. He has to be.

"Don't wink at me," I warn him. "It's creepy."

Richard throws his head back and laughs into the afternoon sun. He unbuttons the top three buttons of his dress shirt and removes his tie as he catches his breath. "Crane keeps warning us that you have a bad attitude." He uses the tie to wipe at his eyes. "But I really just think he doesn't get your humor."

I cross my arms over my chest just like I told Sam he should do. But at my height it does nothing to make me look intimidating. It barely gets Richard to stop laughing.

"Okay, okay, let's get going. We have to get the list and swabs for your samples." He starts walking toward Headquarters, waving for me to follow him.

--

It's well past evening when Richard opens the door to the committee room. "Train's coming," he says.

I pick up the box of swabs, the list and notebook, the cooler with the snap-freeze ice packs, and follow Richard out of Headquarters. Three Guardians tag along. We follow the tracks past the platform, spanning the few hundred yards until we make it to the cement wall. The air is saturated with the scent of grilled manatee. My stomach growls. Richard pulls out a set of keys and unlocks the gate leading to the open area between the cement wall and the electrified fence.

"No electronic touch pad?" I ask him. That's what we have in the Phoenix District, a touch pad with a code to open it.

"Too humid down here," he says. "Corrodes the electronics."

"So who gets the key to the outside?" I ask.

"Those who are chosen," he answers nonchalantly,

as if it weren't a problem that everyone is locked inside. But that's what it's like in all the Districts; no one in, no one out. Unless there are special circumstances, like a lack of Residents or a Sovereign who needs to learn a few lessons.

"They're not bringing the Survivors to the platform?" I ask.

"No, it's easier to be out here if something happens, if they rebel. Easier to contain them near the perimeter of the district," he says. "And force them back out."

I stand next to Richard and watch as the train pulls up. My stomach fills with an uneasy feeling. I'm nervous, afraid of whom they've brought back. If they've brought back anyone at all.

My thoughts drift back in time to Tonopah, when Sakima showed me his assembly of Sovereign who sit at their gates all day to judge who will enter and who will be thrown back out. I didn't want to see it then. And I definitely don't want to take part in it now. But I don't really have a choice now, do I? This job Crane wants me to do, these tasks I have to perform, I don't do them willingly. I do them to keep my children safe, to keep the ones I love safe. I play Crane's twisted game because I know that Morris will die and then I might have a tiny chance at changing something. Still, I'd like nothing more than to retreat home and raise my children in peace. To grow old and gray and help them become better people. Better than what I have turned into.

Sam and Ramirez jump down from the engine car. They head to the rear cargo areas, sliding them open. A Volker stands near each door helping the Survivors get down. There are three train cars with people that don't seem to be full. But still, it seems like many more than we planned on finding tonight.

The Survivors trail out of the train, with their gaunt faces, their tattered clothes, the children with their bellies distended in hunger. They look tired, hungry, and desperate. They look like they came from some third world country. But then, that's what our Great Nation has been reduced to. I remember the commercials on the television, when we had television: *Just a penny a day could feed one child…*

We have no money, no currency. We get paid with protection, food, and clothes in exchange for doing a job, whatever job has been assigned to us.

Third-world countries. With all their poverty and disease and social injustices. That sparks an idea. I remember a tiny morsel of information about those third world countries. A great majority of the African and South American population developed a way to survive malaria infections, or at least their bodies did. They had a genetic blood disorder in which their blood cells became malformed, sickle-shaped. It was those people who carried the trait, instead of affliction with the full disease, who were less susceptible to the disease of malaria. Those people survived.

My focus shifts. I gaze at the Survivors, searching for skin color, features, accents, anything to tell me that these Survivors might have African or South American ancestry. The Volker line the Survivors up. A single line. I take their name, their previous occupation, swab their cheek, label the sample, and place it in the cooler.

As they pass through the gate a Volker leads them to the parking lot where workers are handing out plates heaped with manatee. I glance once and then turn away, not wanting to see what Sakima told me was his favorite part of assimilating the Survivors.

"It's quite impressive. The chosen get cleaned, provided with clothing, tested, assigned duties and living quarters. They get their first meal also. It's very interesting to watch. The transformation these people go through, the look in their eyes when they are handed a plate of warm food, and how the food changes them, returns them to civility." That's what he told me.

Their first meal, their first dose of Halcyon, it will permeate their brain, it will make them cooperate. I continue with my task, trying to numb that part of my brain and my soul that's screaming at me how wrong this is.

--

It's our second day of scouting for new Residents.

Today the men went out on foot headed east. Sam and Ramirez lead the way with a Guardian and two other Volker. They are headed toward the shopping mall and the small camp near the pond.

I keep myself busy and try not to spend too much time thinking of home. I categorize the new Residents samples, preparing them for travel back to Phoenix where Kira, my lab manager, can analyze them. Then it will be simple, searching the data for the sickle-cell gene and breeding it throughout the new population. That should solve their problem. Of course, I will also have to work the subordinate gene into the Resident population.

Emanuel and Richard leave me alone in the committee room to do my work. I stare at the computer, wanting to call home. Until finally, I do. I select the Phoenix icon and wait. Not long after the screen lights up and the image of Burton Crane comes into focus.

"Ah, Andromeda." He smiles at me. "What a pleasant surprise. How are things in the sunny Crystal River District?"

"Great," I reply as sarcastically as possible.

"To what do I owe this call?"

I force a breath, preparing myself for one of those moments where I let my guard down and tell Crane exactly what I want. "I'm calling to check on my family."

"You miss them already?" he asks with his smug smile.

"You know I do."

"Why it's barely been a full day."

"Just tell me how they are. That's all I want. I need to know."

"They are fine. I even gave your husband the next few days off from his duties at the nuclear plant until you return." He overemphasizes the term *your husband*.

I nod at him, forcing out the words, "Thank you."

"I believe you have never said those two words to me before." He raises his right eyebrow and tips his head to the side.

"Don't get used to it," I mumble.

There is a moment of silence as I stare at the wall behind Crane's head, and I'm sure he's looking at me. "Are you solving their problems?" he asks.

"I think so." I tell him. "A team went out last night and today to search for Survivors."

"So that is your plan?" he asks. "Simply repopulate the District?"

"No," I tell him. "Since the malaria is so rampant down here I think it would be a good idea to breed the sickle cell trait throughout the District." I watch as Crane smiles at my plan.

"Make them good and hearty," he says. "That's what we want, healthy Residents." I hold my mouth closed, wanting so badly to say something back to him about how he just referred to these people as though they were a stew we were cooking for dinner. Thick in the head and hearty in the health. I shudder a little. "Will I hear from you again, Andromeda?"

"I'm not sure," I tell him, pressing my lips together in slight disgust. "Goodbye," I tell him suddenly and turn the video feed off, no longer able to look at his speckled face.

--

On the third day the men return.

I hear a whistle from outside Headquarters, followed by the rush of running footsteps. Emanuel raises his head; he's sitting across the Committee room table from me. We both get up. I collect my box of supplies and we exit the building.

The Volker are making their way toward the gate. We follow them. I skip a few steps, trying to keep up, eager to see Sam, hoping that he has returned safely.

I run up behind Richard, who is at the gate sorting keys. As I stand a few yards away, trying to catch my breath, I look past him. Sam and Ramirez look tired and dirty. The Survivors that stand behind them look even worse. Desperate people, following a pied piper with hopes and dreams of a better life, a better future.

But isn't that how our country first started out? Seems we've gone full-circle in this attempt to re-vamp humanity. I wonder if Crane's realized this yet. I wonder if the other Entities have realized this.

"Name?" I ask the father of the family of five that stands in front of me.

"Jackson," he answers.

"Ages and previous occupation," I ask, flipping through my list of missing and desired Sovereign. I stop when I find their surname. They're on the list, they are predetermined Sovereign.

"Pediatrician, forty-two. My wife is forty. She was an endocrinologist." I raise my head and stop writing. This family is an easy in. I scan their faces, noting their dark skin. Perfect. "We have two daughters, ages ten and fourteen. And three sons, age sixteen, eight and two."

I look at the family standing in front of me, realizing that I only count four children. Two boys and two girls.

"Where's your other child?" I ask.

The mother reaches behind her back and leads a toddler out. I smile at him. He smiles back. His eyes squinting, his cheeks plump. It's when he stops smiling I notice that his ears are too low, his eyes spaced a little too far apart, his tongue pushes against his teeth, a little too large for his mouth. This child has Down's syndrome. *Shit.* This family is exactly what Crystal River needs, two doctors, a healthy family that probably carries the sickle cell trait. But Crane's rules ring in my ears. No genetic defects.

"Has anyone in the family had sickle-cell disease?" I ask them. The father hesitates. "It's a good thing," I say.

"My grandmother did," the mother speaks up, solidifying my speculation.

I focus on the child. "Downs?" I ask softly. The

parents nod in agreement. I look at the father, unable to hide the remorse on my face. "We can't take you," I tell him. He nods, as though he was expecting my reply. "I know you're not going to leave your child, but we have to follow the rules."

"It's just one extra chromosome," he pleads with me. "He's not going to pass that on. He has a heart defect. He may not even live long enough to make it to puberty." I notice the mother reach out and pull the child to her. I shake my head, angered at myself for enforcing these rules that I hate so much. "If he were your child you wouldn't leave him behind," the father says.

I remember the speculations from Dr. Akiyama about Raven and his quietness. "No, I never would," I tell him with utmost truth.

They turn to leave, all of their heads hanging. They will not dine on manatee steak, or be given a home, or fresh clothes, or the safety of the fence. I watch them collect their things, the dirt-stained bags, tattered clothes, empty water bottles. They are going back to whatever hole they crawled out of. They will dine on whatever scraps they can find and that father, with his teenage sons, will do whatever he can to protect his family in the desolate world Crane and the other Entities have created.

I feel horrible. And that's an understatement. Something clicks as I watch them. I am going to join the ranks of Entity soon and perhaps this could be the first change I make. Not splitting up a family.

"Wait," I call the father back to me. "You are going to have to hide him or something. These people, they won't bend the rules. But we need you. We need your family here in this District."

He nods.

As I hand him a pass, I catch Ramirez out of the corner of my eye, watching me, his hand resting on the assault rifle that's slung over his shoulder. I wave the family through the line and watch as they walk through the gate to receive their meal. As they pass me with smiles on their faces, my thoughts continue to drift to Tonopah. No wonder the Sovereign are medicated there. I might be able to tolerate the decisions I just made if I were also. But I did a tiny bit of redeeming: I let that child inside. That child with Down's syndrome. An outlawed child in the eyes of Crane. I'm not sure who will face the worst punishment for him being within the gates: the family, Emanuel, or me? I let them pass after all. I could argue that failure was not an option. We need these people. Perhaps their dedication to their new District will negate their son's genetic inequality. Not that any of them could have done anything about it. Not that he is less of a person. He smiled at me. And I think it was the first smile I've seen from a Survivor.

The rest of the Survivors pass by me in a blur until the last man in line walks toward me. I observe him as he walks to where I am sitting. He's sweating profusely. More than necessary for this heat and humidity. There's a tattoo on his neck with long calligraphy letters and the writing continues down onto his arms. I can't make out what any of it says.

More Volker move to stand behind me, where Ramirez has been standing guard.

"Name and previous occupation?" I ask the man.

"Rico, Rico Smith. I was a mechanic," he says.

I sift through my sheets. There's a long list of Smith's, just none matching the first name of Rico.

"Where are you from?" I hear Ramirez ask the man. He's walking up behind me, closer than he has for any of the other Survivors.

The man named Rico looks toward Ramirez. "South Florida," he says, looking down as one of our Guardians makes its way toward us.

"What are you doing up here?" Ramirez asks.

"You know, escaping the heat, the bugs. Trying to get away from the Everglades. You wouldn't believe how bad things are down there," Rico tells us.

"You sure you were a mechanic?" Ramirez asks.

"No reason to lie, brotha'," Rico responds.

"You done time?" Ramirez asks.

"That matter?" Rico's eyes flit between the Volker flanking me.

"Yeah, it does," Ramirez answers.

Before I have a chance to process what's occurring, I feel one of the Volker pull on my shoulders, pulling me away as the others rush toward Rico. He doesn't seem to be intimidated with the onslaught of armed men. Instead, he runs forward, toward the gate in the cement wall. A last ditch attempt to make it in, as though he'd be safe once he got inside. The Volker tackle him, pulling him to the ground with an array of grunts and groans.

"District rules," Ramirez tells Rico. "No convicts, no history of jail time. We made that clear."

The Volker pull him up by his shoulders and walk him toward the gate at the electrified fence. They force him outside, back into the wilderness.

"Let go of me!" I shake off the Volker who held me back and walk toward Ramirez.

"It's time for you to go back," Ramirez tells Rico.

"I got nowhere to go, man," Rico says. "You saw

what it's like out there." He points behind him into the overgrown southern forest.

"We can't help you here," Ramirez tells him.

"No one can help me now," Rico says. He has a look about him, a look that warns me he keeps secrets. He knows something.

"What's going on out there?" I ask him.

Rico smiles with just the one corner of his thin lips. "You ain't seen it yet? None of 'em told you yet?"

"No," I tell him as I walk closer. Ramirez puts his hand out, blocking me from walking too close. I push it away. I know how close I can get before the hum makes my nose bleed. "Do you have something you'd like to tell us?" I ask Rico.

"What are you going to do for me?" Rico asks. "You tossed me out. You want to offer me a warm bed, dinner, a new wife now?"

"We can't offer you those things, you don't qualify," I tell him.

"And the other District, that one in Arizona, will they take me?" he asks.

"None will take you," I reply.

"So there are more than just these two?" he asks.

"What are you getting at?" Ramirez asks, his tone getting increasingly annoyed.

"Things are happening out here. Bad things. Been going on for years. People been dying, doing crazy things, hunting other people. We've got a leader out here too, someone to make decisions," Rico says.

My stomach rolls in unease. "What are you saying?" I ask.

"He'll come for you. He'll try to take over. He's ruthless."

"Rico, if that's your real name, I assure you there is

127

no one more ruthless than the people running these Districts," I tell him. "Who is *he*?"

He smiles, a crazed smile, and reaches toward the fence. It hums loudly. "Don't touch that!" I warn him, reaching out only to be blocked by Ramirez's arm.

Rico's chest quakes with a strange laugh. "Don't matter. Can't go back there. I'm a dead man either way."

I watch in horror as he grasps the chain-link fence. There's an odd gurgling in his throat as the electricity ripples through his body. And the smell is almost worse than the sight as the air fills with the wretched stench of scalding human tissue. I watch as his hand bubbles and blisters. Smoke seems to rise from his singed hair. He drops to the ground, his body still convulsing from the voltage of the fence.

I hear a rustling in the forest. The Volker must hear it too. They walk closer, trying to block me. Someone swings down from a thick tree branch, a young boy. At least he looks like a young boy. Another steps out from behind a tree trunk, this one a young man. And then a third, another young man, stands from under a short bush. They run to Rico's charred body, grabbing his stained shirt and under his arms, dragging his crisp body off behind the thick row of trees.

We all stand there in a moment of silence. "What the hell just happened?" I ask. "Who were they, the lost boys or something?"

"Don't know." Ramirez moves his assault weapon between his hands, readying himself for someone else to come out of the forest.

"Do you think there are more?" I ask. "What if they want in?"

Ramirez never answers because something terrible

happens. The humming of the fence lessens and stutters a few times before it goes completely out. There are a few arcs of electricity snapping and stretching across the metal weave of the chain-link fence as the power glitches on and off.

"What happened?" I shout to Ramirez, trying to ignore the hairs rising on my arms.

"Reactor trouble," he replies with a questioning tone.

Then the sirens start, just like they did when the reactors were running half-power in Phoenix.

CHAPTER ELEVEN

Sam comes running toward me, weapon drawn, eyes scanning the forest beyond the fence.

"What happened?" I ask him.

"Power's down. I have to get you out of here."

"Where?"

"Headquarters. Let's move. Now!"

"Guard the gate!" I yell to the Volker and Ramirez as I turn and run toward Headquarters with Sam at my side and our two Guardians following closely behind us.

I push my way through the new Residents that stand in the parking lot. They hold their plates, chew their manatee, the medication already having its effect. The sirens blaring do not interrupt their current state.

"Emanuel!" I call as I pull open the door to Headquarters.

He steps into the hallway, beckoning me to the Committee room. "Reactor trouble," he says as soon as we make it through the doorway, confirming my fears.

As Sam and I enter the Committee room, the other members of the Crystal River Sovereign are seated at the table as though they were doing nothing but waiting for us to arrive.

"What are you all doing?" I ask. "Why is the power on in here but not out there?"

"We have a small generator," Emanuel replies.

"Well, what are you all doing, just sitting around?" I ask.

"We were waiting for you," Javier responds.

"Yeah, and I'm here. Get the power back on, get the gates back up!" I yell at them. "There are Survivors at the gates. Who's running your reactor?"

"We don't have any operators," Emanuel says. "Just technicians to monitor the radiation."

"Who runs your plant then?"

"There's a crew in Hanford. They do it remotely."

"Then get them on the phone," Sam tells them urgently.

"We did," Emanuel replies. "They're looking into it."

"What?" I ask. "We can't wait for them to look into it. They need to fix this. Now!" I walk toward the computer on the table, pushing Emanuel to the side as I pass him.

"What are you doing?" he asks.

"Calling Crane." I select the Phoenix icon and wait as the image comes into focus. Crane is there, sitting at his desk.

"Andromeda?" he asks, not in the least bit surprised.

This is a test.

"The reactor is down," I tell him in a hurried rush of words. "Power is off to the perimeter and we've got

131

Survivors at the gates."

"Hmm," Crane starts. "Survivors at the gates... Did your plan of acquiring new Residents backfire?"

"No, Crane. This is something completely different. We've already acquired the new Residents. Except one of them lied and had to be removed from the premises. He touched the fence and fried to a crisp."

Crane doesn't answer, his eyes seem to be focused away from the computer screen on something else in his office.

"We can't wait for Hanford to fix this."

"I think Hanford is quite capable."

"Have they ever had their reactor power down?" I ask. "Because if they haven't, I'm not waiting for them to figure this out."

"Well then," Crane says, the corners of his lips starting to upturn. "What would you like to do then?"

I know before the words come out of my mouth. There is one person who fixed our reactor trouble the last time I heard the sirens and that was Ian. "Get Ian."

Crane smiles. "Your wish is my command. I will send someone for him."

An unexpected pang of fear hits me the way he says it. "Make sure he brings my children with him," I warn just before Crane ends the video feed. I turn to Sam, unable to say anything more.

"So we just wait?" Javier asks as he inspects the tape around his glasses.

"Where's Ramirez?" Emanuel asks.

"He's at the fence with the other Volker," Sam tells him.

"He should be here." Emanuel glances toward the door.

"He's doing his job," Sam tells him. "Leading the

Volker, defending this District."

"He can't monitor the entire border by himself, we don't have enough people out there," Emanuel protests.

"Pull up your satellite images then," I tell him. "We can check the borders while we wait for Crane."

Emanuel moves toward the computer and pulls up the program he used to find the Survivors. We wait as the images clear and Emanuel scrolls to the District. He moves in, focusing on the Volker at the fence line we just came from. There is a line of Volker, guns pointed toward the thick forest where we watched the lost boys emerge from and run away with Rico's charred body. Ramirez paces behind the men, his mouth moving with orders we cannot hear.

"Follow the border," I tell Emanuel.

He moves the screen, following the metallic gleam of the fence, stopping when there is a shiver from the tree line. As we watch in those areas it seems to be nothing more than animals and the wind.

Sam leans toward the screen. "Looks clear," he says. "Whoever is out there seems to be focused on the gate that we came through."

A new window pops up on the computer screen, hiding the satellite view of the District. Crane's image comes into view. I pause for a moment, taking in the image of Ian sitting next to Crane. Raven is sitting on his lap and Lina is leaning on his shoulder.

"Hi, Mom!" Lina blurts out.

"Hi," I tell her, almost forgetting the reason for the communication.

"Andromeda," Crane interrupts.

The words come tumbling out of my mouth. "Ian, the reactor has powered down, there are Survivors at the gates, and somehow Hanford is working on the problem remotely but we need this fixed now."

I watch as Ian lifts Raven and turns to Lina, whispering something to her. Lina leaves my view. "How long has it been down for?" Ian asks, the familiar creases of concern appearing on his face.

"I don't know." I look at Sam. "Maybe ten minutes." Sam nods in agreement.

"What happened?" he asks.

"I'm not sure. One of the Survivors touched the fence and a few minutes later it just all shut down," I tell him.

"Okay," he says. "Just give me a minute." He turns to Crane, but because he isn't speaking directly into the computer I can only catch a few words of what he says.

"Ian?" I ask as he turns back to the computer. His eyes and shoulders move as though he's looking at something on the screen and typing.

"Just give me a little bit," he says, the creases in his face intensifying. "I'm accessing their programs from here. Why don't they have operators and engineers there?" he asks as he works.

I look at Emanuel, who stands as still as a statue, refusing to answer that question. "I'm not sure. Perhaps we could put in an order for some to arrive here from Hanford. What do you think, *Crane*?"

I hear his voice from somewhere near Ian. "If that is what you think that District needs, Andromeda. As you know the resources of the Districts are spread thin."

"This is kind of important," I tell him. "At least have a few operators and engineers visit here every so often to check on this place."

Ian continues with his typing and his looks of

concentration. "Check the perimeter again," I tell Emanuel.

He switches the screen and zooms in, toward the fence where the Volker stand, still fixing their weapons on the forest. Now the three lost boys who dragged away Rico's body stand in a line in front of the Volker.

"Scroll out," I tell Emanuel.

He does and we can see movement from not far away. The trees tilt and quiver in a trail. "Someone's coming," I warn.

The other Sovereign move to stand behind us and watch. I grip the side of the table, watching as the movement gets closer to the boys and the gate. Sam moves closer, pressing me against Emanuel's chair.

"Okay!" I hear Ian's voice.

"Switch back," Sam urges.

Emanuel clicks away from the satellite image and back to Ian and Crane.

"Are you there?" Ian asks.

"Yeah," I say.

"It's fixed."

"How long before it's up to full power?"

"A bit," he replies.

"How long is a bit?"

"Maybe... twenty minutes."

"We don't have twenty minutes," I tell him. "There are more Survivors on their way here."

"What are you going to do?" he asks, his eyes wide.

I turn to Sam, my heart beating fast, knowing what I'm about to say. I can't let this District fail. That would only show the Entities that I am, in turn, a failure. And that puts the ones I care about at risk. "I guess we're going to help defend this District until the fence powers up." I turn away from the computer and take

Sam's arm. "Let's go." We run for the door and down the hallway.

"Andie!" Ian's voice shouts from the computer as we run. He shouts my name one last time before Emanuel begins speaking to him. We cross the threshold to the room and then we are running down the brown haze-lit hallway and out into the heat.

We run hard, the humid air so thick it seems choking. I notice Sam at my side. "Go," I yell to him. I know he's over a foot taller than me, his stride longer, he's a faster runner. "Don't wait for me, Sam. I'll catch up."

"I'll save a weapon for you," he says as he takes off at full speed. It's not long before he's almost out of my sight, passing the gate in the cement wall, the first barrier to the District. I follow the direction he went, my breaths heavy in my chest. I can't remember the last time I ran, let alone trained to do something physical. That seemed to stop when Adam died. I pass the wall and then it's just through the grassy field I have left to scale. The thick southern grass brushes against my legs. Seeing the line of Volker in front of me, I slow to a trot, trying to catch my breath before I get to where Sam and Ramirez stand.

"Sam," I choke out.

He turns and hands me a handgun. His hair is matted to the back of his neck from the oppressive heat. "No extra magazines," he says shortly. "Use those bullets wisely."

"Has there been more movement?" I ask them, surveying the scene in front of me. The lost boys are closer to the fence. One of them actually has his hand on it, as if to test its strength.

"I said back away!" Ramirez yells to the boy with

his hand on the fence. The boy smiles a wicked grin that doesn't belong on a person who looks to be so young.

The boy looks between us, his eyes stopping at me. "Bonswa," he says in a low voice with a flick of his chin.

I look away nervously, pretending to flick the safety on the handgun I'm holding. "What did he just say?" I ask Ramirez. "That wasn't in English."

"It means good evening, or good night, in Creole," Ramirez replies. "Seems these boys here traveled along the gulf. Probably from Louisiana."

"Great," Sam mutters. "Just what we need, a bunch of backwoods rednecks who fight alligators."

"There's more of them coming, Ramirez," I tell him. "We saw it on the satellite."

"How many?" he asks as he scans the row of Volker in front of him.

"Don't know," Sam replies.

The boy turns to speak something unintelligible to his companions and then, turning back to the fence, places a booted foot on the chain-links. "Mo manje," he says with a fierce look in his eyes.

"Get down," Ramirez yells.

"What did he say?" I ask, moving forward so we are standing in line with the Volker.

"He's hungry," Ramirez replies.

"Great," Sam mutters.

The Volker aim their weapons at the boy on the fence. "Not going to like yourself when that fence lights back up, boy!" Ramirez shouts.

The boy smirks and continues to climb. It's while he stretches and pulls himself up that I notice the long machete attached to his belt. There is a loud whistle from the forest. The boy stops.

"They're close," Sam says. "Get ready."

This time, I do flick the safety off. I place my body in the stance I once saved for the firing range. The position seems odd now, stretching muscles I haven't used since Raven was born. *I should have been practicing all this time*, I think to myself.

There is the sound of deep male voices getting closer. The boy stops climbing, staying where he is like a cat on its perch, ready to pounce.

"You ready?" Sam asks.

I swallow, my throat feeling suddenly dry. "Yeah," I lie to him.

We aim, all of us, as the men step into the clearing on the other side of the fence. I'm not sure what I was expecting them to look like, but I feel myself gasp in surprise at the five men, at their long greasy hair, the mud caked to their clothing and exposed skin. They each held some type of weapon, be it another machete, an ax, or a strange sword-like apparatus.

"Go back to where you came from," Ramirez shouts to the men.

They don't speak. Their eyes, black and hollow and fiery, are fixed on us. And even though there is only eight of them and fifteen of us, their threatening glares are enough to make me feel outnumbered.

One of the five men step forward and, looking up to the boy perched on the fence, he grasps the chain-link. His dark hair hits his shoulders and he has a scar from his left eye to the corner of his mouth. "Sa tchob byen," he says with a sneer and a flick of his chin, just like the boy. I control the shudder from their threats.

"Go back," Sam shouts to them in a deep, commanding voice I've never heard from him before.

"We will shoot you."

The man shakes the fence, and looking up, he begins to climb.

Ramirez fires a shot. It hits the machete hanging off of the man's waist and pings off into the forest. "Go back," Ramirez commands. "That was a warning. The next one will be in your skull."

Far off in the distance, I can hear the heavy hum of electricity making its way across the fence.

"That electricity is on its way," Ramirez warns the boy and the man on the fence. "You're not going to like yourself once it hits. It'll fry you up like it did to Rico."

The man jumps down and the boy gives one last smile before releasing himself, jumping backward off the fence with an inhuman ease. And then it happens fast; the hum, the shiver, the spark, the arch of current. We step back, feeling the thickness in the air and the taste of blood in the backs of our throats.

The group backs away, slithering into the forest, their eyes on us the entire time. The man with the scar mouths something, but with the hum from the fence, we can't hear what he says.

"Holy fuck!" Sam exclaims once they are out of our sight, dropping his arms in relief. "Those were some creeps."

"We've gotten a few here before the changes," Ramirez tells us. "That's how they breed them in the depths of Louisiana. Creepy bastards."

I click the safety on the handgun and pass it back to Sam. "I guess we should go tell them that the power's back on," he says.

"Yeah," I say with a shaky breath. "I think so."

"Go," Ramirez tells us. "We'll stand guard until

they're gone."

We walk back to the Committee room, weaving between the crowd of new Residents in the parking lot, who stand oblivious to everything that just happened. Emanuel is still on the computer conversing with Crane and Ian. He looks up at me as I walk in the door.

"She's back," Emanuel tells them.

As I walk toward the computer, I see Crane standing behind Ian. "The electricity's back on," I tell them.

Ian stands and walks away from the screen without a word. I catch a glimpse of the look on his face, he's not happy.

"Good, Andromeda," Crane says. "I'm guessing you're ready to come home then?"

"Yes," I tell him.

Emanuel closes the top of the computer. "Congratulations," he says.

"For what?" I ask.

"For completing your task."

I control the urge to shrug at him, as though it's just another day, just another task, just another excuse to control me.

"Can we go now?" I ask.

"One last thing," he says.

I watch as Emanuel walks toward a desk in the corner. He pulls out a metal instrument. I've seen this before, I recognize its gleam. I also recognize the stick of numbing agent in Emanuel's other hand. He's so kind.

"Figures," I mutter.

He nods.

Pulling the shoulder of my shirt down, I expose the bare skin which already holds the long healed marks of the other Districts. It's been a few years since I earned one of these. Of course, I got my others in sequential order. This was my last task. It just took me two years to get down here and complete it. I smell the familiar scent of burning skin, similar to when Rico committed suicide by grabbing the fence, just not as strong.

"Andie?" I hear the door open. Sam steps into the room. "What the hell!" With a few quick strides he's at my side, his arms out, ready to shove Emanuel.

"Stop," I warn him, my hands pressing against his chest.

"What the hell is going on here?" he asks.

"I'm just finishing the job," I tell him.

Soon the room fills with the slight smell of burnt skin and the skin of my back itches and tightens. Emanuel removes the instrument, leaving the Crystal River District brand discoloring my skin right next to the others.

"You're free to go," Emanuel says.

"Goodbye, Emanuel." I pick up the box of Resident samples and head for the door, pulling Sam's sleeve. He staggers, glaring at Emanuel. "Let's go, Sam."

As I push open the door to Headquarters and walk outside, the humid air seems to gulp at my body. Being outside of the cool Headquarters, I'm sweating instantly.

Sam stops me. "You have all those marks, those brands. Worse than the children. More than me." He holds out his right wrist, revealing the Phoenix district emblem. "Why didn't you tell me?"

"I don't need to, Sam," I say.

"It would make things easier. I almost killed Emanuel in there."

"Sam, I make things easier by not telling you this, by not telling Ian this, by not telling the children this. I protect you all by not telling you what Crane makes me do and what he does to me. This is how I keep you all safe. This is how I keep you all alive. I keep the focus on me."

"You're wrong."

"Maybe I am. But this is how it's going to happen."

"You're keeping more from me," Sam pushes. "I deserve to know. I am the Volker Sovereign."

"Don't push it, Sam." I shake my head at him. "I told someone everything once. And you know what it got him? Death. He died. I'll be buried long before I let those secrets kill you too."

--

The trip home is made in silence, with Sam on edge from what he has just learned. His mood seems to lighten by the time we make it to the Phoenix District gates. As we step out of the train onto the platform, one of the Volker informs Sam of our instructions to meet Crane at Headquarters.

Sam drives us to the Chemistry building first so I can put the Crystal River Resident samples in the freezer, then we drive to Headquarters to debrief.

The building is dark and even though I can smell early summer in the air, it feels awkwardly cold here compared to the heat we just experienced. Sam walks me to Crane's office. As the elevator doors open to the floor he uses as an office, we immediately see Crane standing in the middle of the room with Alexander.

"Congratulations," Crane says as he walks toward me. He slaps me on the back, as though I was his pal,

142

an old friend come to visit. I might have smiled, maybe slapped him back like comrades do in the movies. But truthfully, I just wanted to punch him in the face. He slapped my right shoulder, the one with the fresh Crystal River brand, and the numbing agent wore off hours ago. I don't flinch. I wouldn't want to give him the satisfaction.

"That was fast. Faster than your other tasks. I must admit, Andromeda, I was afraid, after everything, that maybe you wouldn't be able to perform as well." He smiles, beaming.

Looks like I made him proud. "Can I go home now?" I ask.

"Not yet, we still have one last matter."

"What?"

Crane glances to Alexander, who clears his throat before telling me, "Morris has passed."

"What?" I hold my breath.

"Morris, you know how sick he was, he's passed on." Crane waits for me to digest his news. "He's dead," he finally says the words.

His eyes tell me everything. I am now a Funding Entity. I've just taken the place of Morris.

Worst. Promotion. Ever.

"I want to see him," I tell Crane.

"Yes, well, I guess you could go down to the morgue, but do you really want to see a dead man?"

"More than anything." I have to make sure he's dead. That this isn't another one of Crane's tricks he pulled while I was gone.

"Just, before you leave," he turns, pulling something out of his drawer. "Colonel Salk, I need you to step out."

I nod to Sam, letting him know that everything is

fine. Sam waits for the elevator, and as the doors close, I turn to face Crane. "What do you want?" I ask, looking to Alexander, whose face remains placid as he says nothing.

"I need your arm, Andromeda."

I hesitate. "Why?"

"Think of this as your induction as an Entity." I look to his hand and see that he holds a syringe with a large-bore needle.

"What's that?"

"Your transmitter."

"Is that like the one you gave the Runner?"

We used to have a Runner, who would go out and get supplies, when there were supplies to get, before the Reformation. Crane injected him with a transmitter, one which contained a lethal dose of potassium.

"No, we wouldn't be so careless as to allow such a simple way to kill one of the Entities. This is just a tracking device. So we never lose you."

I roll up my sleeve. He presses the needle into my forearm. I don't flinch, I don't fight it, and for the first time I simply accept it. I feel the sharp pinch as the foreign object is inserted under my skin. Crane sets the syringe down and places a bandage over the injection site. I pull away from him and replace my sleeve.

"Are we done here?" I ask.

"Yes, and welcome, you are one of us now."

I control the shudder that's trying to run through my body. The last thing I'll ever want to be is someone like Crane. I turn to leave, but just as I reach for the elevator button Crane stops me. "Oh, Andromeda." I turn. "Don't cut this one out. I'd hate to see another scar on your body." Somehow, he figured out that I cut out Adam's transmitter. Probably after Adam broke it to pieces with a hammer.

"Why?" I ask Crane at his suggestion. "I find it hard to believe you care much about me." *Especially since my body is currently riddled with scars*, I think to myself. All of them received since I became a part of this Phoenix Project.

"Just don't," he warns. "And I, *we*," he swipes his hand to include Alexander, "care a great deal for you. You're important."

It seems these people think I am worth more than I do. And I don't understand it. I don't see it. Just because I helped Crane play with the human genome, it doesn't make me anything special. I'm sure they could have figured it out on their own in time. If they had that kind of time.

I leave, collecting Sam at the front doors of Headquarters. We head for the hospital so I can verify that Morris is truly dead.

--

"This couldn't wait until morning?" Dr. Akiyama complains as he escorts us to the morgue. Even though we've only been gone a few days, I notice his hair is whiter now, much too white for a man his age. Must be the toll this place has taken on him.

"Sorry, Doc, but no," I tell him. "This can't wait."

He unlocks the metal doors with a set of keys. As we enter the room, he flicks on the lights. Instantly, I see my breath in front of me. The sterile room is freezing.

And then I feel a large, warm body behind me. "Are you afraid of ghosts?" Sam whispers directly into my ear, his breath tickling the tiny hairs of my ear canal. It causes a hard shiver to run through me. He's laughing, barely able to contain it; he thinks he's funny.

I elbow him in the gut. "Can you act like you are the Volker Sovereign for five minutes, Sam?"

Sam coughs hard. "You need to loosen up," Sam chokes out, holding his stomach.

Dr. Akiyama flips through a chart as he walks toward a gurney, waving for us to follow him. He unzips a black body bag and pulls the dark plastic back so we can see what's inside.

It's Morris. His face limp, pale, eyes closed. I will never see him smile ever again.

"What will you do with him?" I ask.

"Not sure, no orders."

"Send him to the Pasture. He can be buried next to Adam." Dr. Akiyama jerks his head toward me as though I've said something wrong.

"You buried Adam?" he asks.

"Well, no, we just have a gravestone. I don't see why we can't bury Morris out there."

"Oh," he settles a bit.

"I'll have Elvis set it up," I tell the doctor. "Goodnight."

"Goodnight," he says as he zips the body bag closed.

I take Sam's arm as we walk out of the morgue, into the night, and back to his vehicle.

CHAPTER TWELVE

There are flowers on the table, a small cup with a handful of crocus, their stems immersed in water. A note beside the cup reads *Welcome back*, in Lina's handwriting and then Astrid's, repeated with Ian's and then a scribble, which must be Raven's. I smile at their thoughtfulness.

Sam is right, I should be nicer. I should at least try. Walking through the dark house, I make my way to Lina's bedroom. Stevie licks my hand as I walk by the bed, welcoming me home. Lina and Astrid are both sound asleep. I pull their blankets over them, then walk to my room to check on Raven. He opens his eyes, as though he senses my presence, as I walk to the side of the crib. I pick him up and squeeze him close to me.

"I missed you, baby Raven," I tell him. He reaches out, pressing his chubby fingers to my cheek. Silent as always. I lay him down and pull the blanket over him. He closes his eyes and goes back to sleep as though I had never left and he never feared I wouldn't come back for him.

Stepping into the hallway, I notice Ian's door is open. I walk toward it. His room is empty. Panic floods me. I know that he wanders at night but I was hoping that would end with me gone and him in charge of the children. I make my way through the small house, searching the bedrooms, the bathroom, the kitchen. I find him in the living room sleeping on the couch, one of the Guardians stretched out on the floor below him. I must have walked right past him when I got home and never noticed.

I watch for a moment as he sleeps so peacefully. His face is relaxed, his blonde hair askew. Walking toward him, I pull the spare blanket off the back of the couch and lay it across him, and just as I set the edge of the blanket across his shoulders his hand grabs my wrist in one quick motion. I look up to see him awake and looking at me. I take a step back, flustered at his quick reaction.

"You're back," he says, his voice merely a whisper as he loosens his grasp on my wrist.

"Yes," I tell him.

"I didn't mean to scare you." He lets go of me and moves to sit, rubbing a hand across his face. "You shouldn't have done that."

"What?"

"Risked your life for those people."

"I didn't risk my life for *them*. I risked it for the children and… you."

He just stares at me in the dim light of the living room, not saying another word, his lips pressed tightly together as though he wants to say something else.

I back away from him, hands raised in defeat to avoid any argument. "Okay." I try to control the quiver in my voice. "Goodnight," I tell him as I turn and head toward my room. I wasn't expecting that. Ian was never one to wake so suddenly or react so quickly.

I shower, rinsing the last of the dried Florida sweat off of my body. Dressing in a pair of old sweats and a tank top, I crawl into bed. An empty bed. And touching the cold pillow next to mine, I wonder if I will always be alone here. Ian has expressed his desire to truly live as husband and wife, but I just can't bring myself to that. I'm not ready. I'm not sure when I'll be ready.

Hearing the familiar sound of Ian's quiet footsteps in the hall, I hold my breath. As usual, he stops outside my room and then after a few moments, he paces to the kitchen before leaving. I pull the blanket up to my chin and curling onto my side, fall asleep to the sound of Raven's breaths as he sleeps in his crib.

--

I stare at the phone on my desk which was moved to the living room when Ian arrived. Morris will never call me on it again. Neither will Adam. I think about unplugging it and throwing it out into the forest for the Guardians to play fetch with.

"Mom?" I hear Lina's voice from the hallway.

I stand and close the wall cupboard that holds my computer as Lina walks into the living room.

"You're home."

I lift her onto my lap and wrap my arms around her. She snuggles into my chest. "I missed you, Lina." I kiss the top of her head. The Guardian by the door raises its head and I hear the shuffle of little feet in the hall. "Raven?" He turns the corner and walks toward us. "How did you get out of your crib?" I ask him as he wanders toward us, hands midair, expecting to be picked up.

"I think he climbed out," Lina says. "He kept sneaking into my bed while you were gone."

"Did you put him back in his crib?"

"Daddy did, but he just got back out."

Raven closes his eyes and leans into me.

"I think it's time for him to get a big boy bed," Lina says.

Ian walks by the living room. He merely glances in at us and nods before walking toward the kitchen. I hear him start the coffee maker.

A big-boy bed. There is no room for another bed in my bedroom. That means one thing, Raven could take Ian's room, and we'd have to share, or one of us could take the couch.

I pat Lina on the back. "Let's get moving. We need to wake up Astrid and get you all ready for school."

"Okay, Mom." She slides off my lap and runs to her room.

I stand and carry Raven into the kitchen. "What do you want for breakfast?" I ask him. He raises his head off my shoulder and stares at the side of my face. "Are you ever going to talk to me, Raven?" I turn and look at him, so close in front of my face. He looks just like Adam, his eyes such a pale blue I can see my reflection in them. I push his dark hair across his forehead and he shakes his head from side-to-side. An effective *no*. "Someday, Raven, you'll need to speak." He lays his head back down on my shoulder.

Ian is making his breakfast. He pulls down two mugs from the cupboard, setting them on the counter as the coffee machine spits out fresh coffee. Reaching for the bag of bread, I place four pieces in the oven before filling a pan with water and heating it on the stove for hot cocoa. Then I remember there is no hot cocoa.

Turning the stove off, I walk to the fridge to warm some milk for the children's breakfast. As I pass by Ian, he reaches out and ruffles Raven's hair. Raven lifts his head off of my shoulder and leans to the side toward Ian, reaching for Ian to take him. I lean, passing Raven into Ian's arms, giving him a look of shock. Ian shrugs. Raven has never gone to Ian. Not that I ever forced him to, or that Ian ever pushed the issue. Raven has always been in my arms, in his crib, or toddling around the house.

I watch as Raven lays his head on Ian's shoulder, his little arm settles across Ian's back. I reach for the breakfast plates and Ian turns to finish his task, now with just one free arm.

Unable to stop myself, I glance at them out of the corner of my eye. It's been so long since I saw Ian carry a child. The last time was Lina. This is something that I never expected. It's comforting, seeing him bond with Raven, since he is the only father Raven will know. He will never know his real father, his real father is dead.

I set out the plates and the mugs, just as the girls run into the kitchen, dashing to their seats dressed and ready for the day. Ian sits at the table in Raven's seat, Raven on his lap. I look around, never expecting to be sitting at a table with three children and Ian, albeit, it's a mishmash of ours, mine, and someone else's.

Stevie nudges my elbow; I pass her a piece of toast.

We eat our breakfast with the girls chatting about which goat is their favorite and the foals that are about to be born. Raven observes, eating his toast in silence.

As the children wander off to brush their teeth and get their shoes on, I stand to collect their plates. I catch Ian watching me. I guess I could start trying to be a little nicer, now.

"Thanks for the flowers," I tell him.

"The girls picked them."

I look out the window at the melting fields of the Pasture; a few spots of snow still litter the fields. "Where did you find them?" I ask. I hadn't seen any near the houses or the courtyard.

"Out near the water tower," he says.

I stop. That's where the grave is. "What were you doing out there?"

"Don't you bring Raven there every day?"

I didn't think anyone noticed. "Yes."

"I brought him there," he stands and collects his dishes, "while you were gone."

"You didn't have to do that, Ian."

"Yes, I did," he says firmly.

I guess now I understand why Raven is suddenly so smitten with Ian. Ian is the first person to put forth some effort in trying to understand him.

--

We walk to the schoolhouse. Raven walks on his own now, holding Ian's hand. I suddenly feel naked, not having Raven on my hip or holding onto me. Not having the comfort of the last tiny bit of Adam close to me.

Blithe is waiting on the porch. Sam stands near her and they talk as the boys run in the open grass of the courtyard. Lina and Astrid run to Sam, throwing their arms around him, greeting him for the day. Raven lets go of Ian's hand to walk toward me as Ian heads for Sam. I pick up Raven and set him on the porch next to Blithe.

She bends down. "Good morning, Raven," she says, smiling.

Raven just stares at her.

"Can you say good morning?" I ask him.

He looks between us, saying nothing, his chubby cheeked face placid. A crease appears between Blithe's brows. I know what she's thinking; he doesn't even try to speak. He makes no attempt. I kiss Raven on the cheek. "I'll see you in a few hours," I tell him.

His expression changes. I think he's mad–no, that's an understatement: he's pissed.

Blithe herds the children into the schoolhouse. Lina runs to me for a hug. Astrid runs to Sam for a hug. We leave them at the schoolhouse to learn all the things Crane thinks are important. I'm sure he wouldn't be happy to hear about the things I teach her, when school is out, after dinner. I tell her things, about how the world used to work. Things he probably doesn't want her to know.

"Shouldn't you be at Headquarters?" I ask Sam.

"Headed there now, just needed to speak with Elvis first."

I remember I need to talk with him too. I need to arrange a burial for Morris. We walk to the barn together, and Ian follows, veering off toward his vehicle with a short *goodbye* as he leaves for the plant. Sam knocks on Elvis's office door.

"Come in!" Elvis shouts. We both enter. "What can I help you with?" Elvis asks.

If he was sad about Morris's passing, he hides it well. Since he is one of the Entities I would expect for him to feel something in the death of one of his cohorts. Instead, I don't see a wrinkle of caring on his tanned face.

Sam gestures for me to go first.

"I want a grave for Morris. Out near the water tower," I tell Elvis.

"Figured you would," he replies. "Have someone working on the granite now."

"How long should it take?"

"Few days, once the ground thaws fully we can dig. Give him a proper burial."

"Good," I tell him.

We stand in silence for a moment. Sam looks at me expectantly.

"What?" I ask. Then I remember Sam needs to speak with Elvis also. Must be he doesn't want me around for it. "Bye," I tell them, turning to leave.

I guess these people have already stressed the importance of secrets to my brother. I guess it's expected of him now. It was how Adam had that job; his ability to keep secrets, to find out information. I'm sure Elvis is training him now. Teaching him how to keep his face placid, how to be deceiving. This is not what I want to see Sam turn into. This is what I worked so hard to protect him from.

--

"Committee meeting today," Ian says.

"How do you know?"

"Crane called while you were bringing the kids to the schoolhouse."

"Okay, just give me a sec." Leaving Ian standing on the porch, I head into the house, grab a sweater from my room and pull my hair up into a bun. When I get back to the porch Ian is still standing there, waiting.

"Want to ride together?" he asks.

"Uh, sure."

I follow him to his car, one of the Volker SUV's. It kind of perturbs me that he was designated a vehicle before me. But then, Ian follows the rules here so I guess he's earned it.

He steps in front of me and opens the passenger door. "You look nice," he says, smiling.

I feel my eyes widen, a bit shocked. I'm wearing nothing more than what I always wear; slacks, boots, blouse. Maybe it's the sweater, because it hides the necklace Adam gave me, the one I've been unable to remove from around my neck.

"Uh, thanks." I slide into the passenger seat. Ian closes the door and makes his way to the driver's seat. As he drives, I try to interrupt the awkward silence. "No work today?" I ask him.

"Got the day off." He smiles as he drives the poorly kept country roads into town.

Nobody gets a day off in the Phoenix District. "What are you up to?" I ask him.

He shrugs. "Nothing. Just headed to a meeting with you." He smiles. I remember this, this playful banter we used to have. It seems strange right now, forced. But, I'm not sure how to interact anymore. I just sit, staring out the window, watching the order of the District as we drive. I notice Ian takes a turn toward the lake, a detour from our usual route.

"Where are you going?" I ask him, sitting up straighter.

"Just need to make a quick stop."

"A quick stop? Out here?" The view of the lake

emerges as Ian crests a hill. There is a length of green grass and then an endless dark blue body of water.

He stops in front of the lake at an open park. He gets out and opens my door. "Come with me." He tips his head toward the open park, his mouth upturned in a boyish half smile.

I follow him, not sure of what he has planned. I don't like surprises, not anymore. "Crane will be mad if we're late," I warn him.

"We've got time," he says with confidence.

We walk side-by-side across the great expanse of lawn. The asphalt sidewalk has been replaced with a cobblestone one. It looks nice, quaint. Ian stops at the wooden fence at the edge of the park. There is a straight drop down to the lake. There used to be boats here. A marina and docks. It's all been removed; the break-wall has been extended, heightened. I can see the gleam of the chain link fence which has been added to the break-wall. I haven't been out here in years. I haven't seen the changes and just how different it is.

Tugging the neck of my sweater up, I try to ward off the cold lake breeze.

"Andie," Ian turns to me. "Do you remember this place?"

My eyes wander to the surrounding maple trees. Of course I do. This is where he proposed to me, so many years ago. It wasn't springtime, though, it was fall. My favorite season. He paid Sam one-hundred dollars to collect every last orange leaf in town. And he brought me to this spot. I close my eyes, remembering. We had just gotten over a horrible fight. I had accused him of not spending enough time with me, that he had been ignoring me. In all seriousness he had every right to. He was in his last semester working hard on defending his thesis on the sustainability of nuclear energy, during a time when everyone wanted the nuclear plants closed down. Some feared a nuclear emergency, that our water and soil was already contaminated. Little did they know what was to come, and that the nuclear reactors would one day be responsible for their safety.

But that day, that day it was beautiful with the orange and the green and the blue of the lake. It smelled like apples and freshly sharpened pencils. And he was so handsome with his blonde hair and brown eyes and fair skin. Ian wore dark jeans, a blue dress shirt and a khaki jacket. He got down on one knee and proposed. And I accepted, practically ripping the ring away from him. It was simple ring, small and perfect. I remember I hugged him, and I kissed him, and I laughed, and I cried. He smelled like lemons and mint.

He still smells like lemons and mint.

I sniff the air, tilt my head, it's more like lemons today. I open my eyes to find Ian standing directly in front of me. His face softened, poignant. He must remember too. He must remember everything we were and everything we are having such a hard time returning to. He just doesn't have the memories in between. The ones I have that are so hard to forget, the ones where he was taken away from me and I was forced to move on as though he were the one that was dead. But he's alive, standing here in front of me now. I have him back, I just don't know what to do with him anymore.

"I know it's hard," he says, almost whispering. "But I want you to try." I stare back at him, at his familiar face. "We were great once. Really, really great."

"I know," I say.

"Can you try?" he asks. "Can't you try just a little bit

harder?" he steps back, drops to one knee, holds something up to me.

My eyes focus on his hand and I see he's holding my engagement ring. I haven't seen it since... since before all of this. I left it at home because we weren't allowed to wear jewelry at the hospital where I worked.

I stand there, silent. I could try. I should try. I should try and do something. I should make some effort. I raise my hand to accept the ring. But instead of dropping it in the palm of my hand, Ian grasps my fingers, turns my hand, and pushes the engagement ring onto my ring finger.

This time I don't laugh, I don't cry, I'm actually not sure what to do. And then Ian moves so quickly, before I even have a chance to react. Standing, stepping toward me, reaching for me, his hand brushes across my cheek, pulls the pin from my hair, releasing it into the afternoon breeze. His fingers sink into my hair as he presses his lips to mine. He inhales through his nose, breathing me in, pressing his lips harder, hungry, like he's been starved to do this for years. He *has* been starved for years. And still, here I am, continuing to starve him.

He softens.

I stiffen, trying to remember how to do this with him.

He stops. "Aren't you going to kiss me back?" he asks, breathless.

"I just did."

"No, you didn't." He kisses my cheek, buries his face in my hair.

I want to tell him something, a reason, an excuse. But I'm sure he won't believe me. He wants a fairytale when our new reality is that we are living in what seems like some alternate universe.

I'm afraid to go back to the way things were. Because it's been two years that Crane has left me in peace. It won't be long now; something is going to happen, soon. Going to Crystal River was just the beginning. Crane will continue on with his twisted games, endangering the lives of everyone I love while he tries to create his perfect world and uses me to help him do it.

"Let's go." Ian gives up. He takes my hand and leads me back to his vehicle so we can continue on to the committee meeting.

--

Morris's seat has been removed from the table. And now Sam sits across from me in Adam's old seat. There's just an empty space there, now that I have taken his place. Perhaps I should feel different, more powerful, more in-control of the future. Instead, I feel a little numb. Between Ian's advances, the decisions I made in Crystal River, and the genetically defunct child that I let into that District, it's all making me feel a little off kilter, more than usual. Now sitting here, next to the orange-haired dictator, I have to keep reminding myself to pay attention.

Crane starts the meeting.

"Welcome, Sovereign. We have one topic on the agenda today and that is the Sovereign children, one in particular." He pauses to look at me. "Raven Somers."

The topic pops up on my computer screen as each of the Sovereign look to theirs.

"What are you talking about?" I ask, glancing at the report in front of me. It's a copy of a record, his medical record, a report of his milestones. I've never seen this before.

"Well, Andromeda, I'm sure you've noticed he's not normal. There's something wrong with him."

"He's fine. He's just a quiet baby," I argue. "I would know if there was something wrong with him. He's *my* child, Crane!"

"If he doesn't start meeting milestones then we have to make other arrangements for him."

"What do you mean *other arrangements?*"

"We don't have the means to care for children, or adults for that matter, that are... *handicapped.* None of the Districts do. This is the reason for your pairings, to prevent such occurrences, to ensure the genetic diversity and robustness of all Residents and Sovereign."

I don't bother telling him that Adam and I were a perfect match. I reviewed our data when I was pregnant. There is no way in hell Raven has any handicaps, if anything he is more intelligent than most of the people in this room. Unless, perhaps he was without oxygen at delivery for an extended period of time. But that would have been noticeable. There is absolutely no way.

"And what would you plan on doing with them?" I ask.

"Send them away or..." He smirks, his stupid smirk. "Euthanize them."

My blood boils. "How do you think you know so much about my child? You've never met him. You've never spent one second of your life with him!"

He smiles, adjusts his tie. It's green today. I'd like to strangle him with it. "There are still many things you are not privy to."

So quickly Crane returns to his usual ways. I thought that Adam's death might have changed him, since he was being so nice before. But now I see that I was wrong.

"Leave the children alone, Crane," I warn him.

Crane leans toward me, drops his voice so only I can hear him. "You shouldn't have let that child into Crystal River."

--

I slam the door to Ian's vehicle just as Ian gets in the driver's seat. He doesn't start the car.

"You see?" I practically scream. "You see what happens? It was only a matter of time before he started in again."

"I wasn't expecting him to pull that," Ian admits, reaching in slow motion to put the key in the ignition.

"This is your first lesson, Ian. This is what Crane does. He likes to dangle shiny things on fishing wire."

"What do we do?" He stares straight ahead as he asks.

"What I've always done." I buckle the seat belt. "Everything in my power to protect my children. We need to get back to the Pasture, now."

Ian doesn't wait for me to give orders. He starts the truck and speeds out of town.

I almost forgot what this feeling was like. My heart beating so fast I can't keep myself still. I want to leap from the SUV and run the rest of the way to the Pasture, as though I could run as fast as Ian is driving. I can't run that fast. This knowledge doesn't stop the adrenaline from pumping through my veins. It's overwhelming.

"I'm sure they're fine," Ian says as he drives.

"I wouldn't be sure about anything when Crane's involved," I tell him.

"You think he'd harm Raven?"

"I wouldn't put it past him."

"I mean, I know Crane is fucked in the head, but he wouldn't hurt a child. Raven's nothing but a baby."

I remember how much Ian has missed. "You know what he did last time? When Crane decided that all the Sovereign needed to be tattooed, so that their rank would be easily identifiable?" I hold out my wrist and pull up my sleeve so he can see the mark burned into my skin.

Merely glancing at the mark, Ian slows the SUV considerably, preparing to pull into the hidden driveway of the Pasture as I continue. "He beckoned me to the hospital with some bull-crap excuse of needing my help. And while I was gone the Volker stormed the Pasture and tattooed the children." Ian shifts in his seat. "I know you saw the mark on Lina's wrist. Sam tried to stop them. That's when he was new here, before he learned how Crane runs things and how the rules seem to change to accommodate his agenda."

"What happened when Sam tried to stop them?" Ian asks.

"They sedated him. But that didn't stop one of the Guardians from killing the Volker that stabbed Sam in the neck with the needle."

"Hmm," he responds thoughtfully. "Hang on." Ian gets out of the vehicle and punches in the code to open the gates to the Pasture. He returns to the driver's seat. "So these Guardians, I thought they were pretty innocent. Now you tell me that they are capable of killing?" he asks.

"I've only seen it happen once," I tell him.

"What are they?" he asks, gripping the steering wheel tightly as he drives down the gravel road of the Pasture. "I mean, what are they really? I've never seen any dog like them before."

"Crane told me once that he created them. So I can only assume that they are some genetically engineered species."

Ian nods as he processes the information. He pulls up next to the barn that holds Elvis's office. "Seems Crane has a thing with manipulating nature," he finally responds.

We both get out of the SUV and look around the courtyard. Everything seems to be in order.

Elvis walks out of the barn.

"Welcome back," he tells us, walking toward us.

"Elvis, did we have any visitors today?" I ask.

"No one has come through here," he says. "Why do you ask?"

I shake my head at him. I'm still not fully trusting Elvis. He is an Entity. Morris told me for certain. "I'm going to get my children," I tell him. I start walking toward the schoolhouse, expecting Ian to follow me but he doesn't. I turn to find him speaking with Elvis. I'm sure they are talking about what just happened in the meeting. I have to let Ian know that Elvis is not one to trust. None of the Entities are. And I guess that means that he can't even trust me.

--

It's been days since Crane threatened Raven's life. I've been working away like a good little Sovereign, waiting for the children to wake up. Hoping that my compliance with Crane's terms will distract him from Raven.

"Andie?" Ian asks.

Turning, I find him standing in the doorway. I save my work and take a break from assigning the Residents into pairs. "Yeah." I shut down the computer.

"We need to talk."

"About what."

"Something important." He looks around the room before walking toward me. "Meet me outside. At the ruins."

"For what?" I ask. I haven't been to the ruins since before Raven was born. They are just some broken down old buildings out in the forest.

"Just meet me there. After the children are in school."

"Why, Ian? What's this about?"

"Andie, just come. Trust me." He gives me a look, a pleading, *trust me* look.

"Okay." I agree, watching as he walks out the door. Great. I don't know what he's planning, but meeting in the overgrown ruins in the woods is not my version of a hot date. He's up to something.

I get the children ready for school. And as we walk to the schoolhouse, I pass Ian in the courtyard. He stops to hug Lina and Raven.

"Fifteen minutes," he whispers to me.

I nod at him, still unsure of what he's planning. He smiles, and gives me that look. I've seen it before, the one that says he's thinking of other things. He nods. My fingertips tingle. I'm not ready for whatever he's planning. I don't want a date in the woods. I want to formulate a plan to keep my children safe and get rid of Crane for good.

After leaving the children with Blithe, I head for the south fields and the ruins. I zip my jacket to my chin to ward off the morning spring chill. The walking should warm me up. I notice the Guardians of the forest as I pass. They watch me. Only one follows behind me, they know I'm on my best behavior.

I pass the small lake and before long I can see the dilapidated buildings ahead of me. I follow Ian's tracks, the disturbed leaves and footprints in the spring mud.

"Ian?" I ask as I come upon the first house. Stepping up onto the sagging porch and looking inside, I see nothing.

I move on to the next one. The roof is gone, the cavity inside filled with small trees and thick moss. A bird flutters as I walk by. The door is open on the third house. This one still has a roof. I peer inside and see a glow coming from under the floorboards. I remember this one; this is the house with the hollow floor, the one the Guardians wouldn't let me explore. I take a deep breath. A date in a musty basement, still not my idea of fun. As I walk closer, the floorboards groan under me.

"Andie?" I hear Ian's voice.

"Yeah," I respond.

"Come down here." He holds out an old oil lantern, illuminating the aged stairs that lead into the ground.

"Ian?" I ask as I take his hand when I reach the last few steps. "What are we doing down here?"

I let my eyes adjust to the darkness, taking in the sight before me. There's a table, chairs, lanterns. Sam and Elvis are here, seated and waiting.

This is not a date, this is some secret meeting.

"What are you all doing down here?" I ask.

"Formulating a plan," Ian answers. "We can't risk

Blithe seeing us. She answers directly to Crane."

I look to Sam, he nods.

I look to Elvis, he nods.

"A plan for what?" I ask.

"To overthrow Crane," Ian says.

I look to Elvis. "You can't be here," I tell him, pointing so everyone in the room knows exactly who I'm talking to.

"It's alright, Andie," he tries to soothe me.

"No, Elvis, you can't be here. I know who you are, who you really are. And you know what I am now. You can't be here. They don't know about you, who you really are. You're not just a rancher out here watching the farm." I don't say that he is a Funding Entity. I don't say that I am now either, it is forbidden. I turn to Ian and Sam. "You're worried about Blithe seeing us? You need to be worried about him."

"I'm on board, Andie," Elvis says. "I went to Ian and Sam first."

"It's true," Ian speaks up.

"What do you think will come of this?" I ask Elvis. "When Crane finds out, this is just what he needs."

"We want Burton Crane gone. A lot of us have wanted Crane gone for a long time now."

"Why didn't you come to me then? Instead you go behind my back and involve my family!"

"You were in Crystal River. I approached Ian in case anything happened."

I look to Ian, who nods in agreement.

"Crane has a lot of friends," I tell them.

"Crane has a lot of enemies," Elvis retorts. "A lot of people, powerful people, who are afraid of him, who would like to see him gone."

"What does he have on them?" I ask.

166

"He knows their secrets, all of their secrets," Elvis replies.

"Their secrets mean nothing to me," I tell Elvis. "I don't care about their secrets. I just want him out of my life for good."

"So do many other people."

"And then what happens?" I ask. "What happens to this new society; the Sovereign, the Residents, the Survivors?"

"It is all set up. The Districts are running smoothly. There's not much else to do but continue on."

I turn to Sam and Ian. "You two realize what you're getting into?"

"I think we've known for a long time, Andie," Sam replies.

I don't think they really know. I don't think they understand what I've gone through to get them all back, to have peace, just a tiny bit of peace.

"Who else is involved?" I ask Elvis.

"No one else is on board yet, officially."

"And how do you intend to get them on board?"

They all stare at me.

I get that dropping, free-falling feeling in my gut. "Are you kidding me?"

"What?" Ian asks.

"Me?"

"You've been to all the Districts," Elvis says. "You've met *all* the other Sovereign. Some of them trust you. Some of them trust you a lot. Like the ones with weapons."

He's talking about Hanford, the District that's bursting at the seams with weapons and technologies we don't have here.

"There are others too," I respond. "There are other

Sovereign who are just as much a psychopath as Crane, like Sakima in Tonopah," I remind Elvis. "Sakima will never be on board, he's brutal, and there are more Residents there than anywhere else. He has thousands of medicated minions. I'm sure you know, Elvis, because you are privy to these details. Sakima refuses to take any of his Sovereign off of the medication. We wouldn't stand a chance against them. We don't have the population."

"We aren't talking war here, Andie," Elvis says. "We're talking about taking one orange-haired denominator out of the equation. The rest of the pieces are already set into place."

I don't like this. But then again, I dislike following Crane's orders more. "Fine," I tell them angrily. "I only ask one thing."

"What?" Elvis asks.

"Tell them how your family died."

He told me a few years ago, his wife and daughter died in a car accident. But that's an easy excuse and it sounds like something I've heard before. Adam's family died in a car accident and he didn't think it was really an accident. I don't think it was for Elvis either.

"Why?" he tips his head.

"Tell them one of your secrets. The real reason why you want Crane out. What happened to your wife and daughter, Elvis? What truly happened?"

He gives me a hard look, presses his lips together. Ian and Sam watch him. "Crane killed them."

I turn to Sam and Ian. "You see what you have to look forward to? If we don't succeed in getting him out, we have a lot to lose."

"You're on board then?" Elvis asks, not giving them a chance to answer my question.

I look to Sam and Ian. "I have no choice now," I tell him.

"There will be plenty of choices, and some you will get to make. Let's break for now. We'll meet again soon." Elvis points to Sam and Ian. "Separate paths back home," he reminds them. "We don't want to be spotted exiting the forest together."

They blow out the lanterns. Sam and Elvis head aboveground first. Ian and I wait a few minutes.

"Ready?" Ian asks me.

"Sure."

Ian takes my hand, leading me up the stairs. He stops to close the opening to the cellar, letting the floorboards drop and cover the open space. We walk toward the fields.

"I bet you didn't think I had it in me," Ian says proudly as we step out from under the protection of the forest.

"What's that, Ian?

"Back there." He thumbs toward the ruins.

"No, Ian, it never crossed my mind that you were suicidal."

"What?" he asks incredulously.

"That's all this plan is going to get us. It's suicide. Someone will die or all of us may die. Crane is not one to be played with, he doesn't play nice."

Ian places his hand on my arm, stopping me. "I'm not suicidal."

"Then what is this? What are you trying to prove?"

"I'll never forgive myself for not protecting the both of you. I sat by for two years and waited, Andie. Crane used me as his tool and he still is. You think I don't know that he's using me?"

I let out a sigh. This is something I've wanted to

hear for years, an apology from him for not protecting Lina. But now, after everything, it sounds wrong. Deep in my heart I know he's not truly at fault. "You can't take the blame. There's no one here to blame but these people who planned this. Crane is using all of us."

"You mean that?" He steps closer to me.

I look into his eyes. They're hopeful, waiting for my response. "Yes."

He reaches for me, pulling me into his arms. And for the first time in ages, it seems, I wrap my arms around his neck and let him press our bodies together. I don't do it because I feel like I should; I do it because I want to, because for the first time we are on the same page, we are in this together, finally.

Somehow we manage let go of each other and immediately I miss the familiar warmth of him being so close. "Come on." I take Ian's hand and head for the water tower.

As we come to a stop, Ian admires its height and rustiness. "What's up with this?" he asks.

"Climb," I tell him as I begin to scale the ladder.

The water tower creaks and groans.

"Do you think this is safe?" Ian asks from below me.

I don't answer. I just keep climbing and pull myself to the enclosed walking platform that surrounds the top of the water tower. Ian follows and soon he is standing next to me taking in the view.

We can see all of the Pasture from this height; the cooling towers for the nuclear reactors, the lake, the forest that separates us from the surrounding cities and towns. The tree branches are swollen with spring buds and soon the forest will once again become dense and green, enclosing us in a barrier, protecting us from

170

what is outside.

"Why are we here?" Ian asks me.

"This is where I used to come to think," I tell him.

"Hmm," he nods and continues to appreciate the view.

I watch him from the corner of my eye as he closes his eyes and takes a deep breath in. The breeze tugs at his hair, shifting the shaggy blond strands. I sit, my back against the chain-link barrier of the enclosed walking platform. Ian sits next to me, cross-legged.

"I spoke with Dr. Akiyama," he breaks the silence.

I tense. "About what?"

"Us." Ian stares at my face, his features softening.

"What did he say?"

"He said that we need to talk. Really talk about everything that's happened."

I look away from him, trying to hide the shamed flush that I know is shading my cheeks. A lot has happened in four years, a lot that he doesn't know and that I'm too ashamed to tell him. My stomach twists with nausea at the thought of everything; how I've betrayed him and our marriage.

"Andie?" Ian asks, pulling me from my thoughts.

"Yeah?"

"Dr. Akiyama said we could try this game, that it might help, you know, us." I look at him and his face looks so hopeful with the idea that we might be able to regain what we've lost, what we once had.

"Fine," I tell him. "What do we do?"

"We just say, '*Do you remember when*,' and then we tell each other a memory, from before... before all of this." He waves his hand in the air, gesturing to the Pasture below us and toward the demolished city to the south.

I'm not sure I want to relive any of my memories. I've pushed so many of them to the dark recesses of my brain that I can't think of much now. I just know that I want to stand and climb down the ladder and run away to escape his hopeful gaze. I don't want to remember our life before. I know we can't go back to that and I don't want to remember what's happened over the past four years, all the changes, because of the things I've done and the things Crane required from me. I don't feel like the person I once was. And truthfully, I'm afraid Ian will see that and he will be just as disgusted with me as I am.

"So, what do you think?" he asks.

My mouth is suddenly dry. "Sure."

"Okay. I'll start," he says, his face turning serious.

I nod at him, preparing myself.

"Do you remember when I met you for the first time at that campus party?"

"We actually met in Biology class the day before," I remind him.

"Oh, yeah. Well, I offered to get you a drink and you told me no and then we got paired up for Chemistry lab the next day."

I adjust my legs, fidgeting as nervously as I did that day we were paired up. I knew who he was, and his reputation, but I was quite sure he had no idea who I was. "Yeah," I tell him quietly. "I remember that."

"Okay, your turn."

I stare out at the spring forest. I can't pull one memory. "Can I skip?"

"Just this time." He continues, "Do you remember when we went to that Japanese restaurant and I forgot to tell you I was allergic to shellfish? I swelled all up and we spent the night in the emergency room."

"Yeah," I giggle lightheartedly. "I remember that." His face was swollen and red and I threatened to take a picture and send it to all of his friends.

"Okay," he says. "Your turn."

"Do you remember when…" It's still so hard to pull a good memory of us to the forefront.

"Andie, come on, just try," he urges.

"I am." I stare out at the forest again. Finally, I think of one of the most important aspects of my life, what I did all of this for, what I risked everything for. Lina. "Do you remember when Catalina was a baby, and we brought her home and she was so small she barely fit in any of her baby clothes?"

Ian smiles. "Yeah, I remember that. Never expected her life to change so drastically."

"She's going to be ten soon," I warn him.

"Can't believe that." He runs his hand through his hair.

"Me either. This wasn't the plan I had for her future."

"It was right, you were right, choosing her," he stares into my face. "You had to choose her."

"I'll still never forgive myself."

"Forgive yourself." He reaches forward, brushing the hair off of my face.

"Your turn," I tell him, trying to take his focus off of me.

He stares at me, thinking, and then a sly smile spreads across his lips. "Do you remember that summer I taught you how to swim?"

Oh, I remember that well. "Don't you mean our first summer together when you tried everything possible to get me in my underwear or see me naked?"

"Well it worked, didn't it?" He smiles widely,

showing a faint dimple and a row of perfectly straight white teeth.

"Not as fast as you had hoped."

"Okay, your turn," Ian says.

"Do you remember Lina's first word?"

The memory comes to me easily, all of us sitting at the dinner table, Ian discussing his day, me half-asleep from staying awake after working a night shift. As Ian went on about the interns, he paused to say, "*Can you believe that shit?*" and like a little parrot Lina set her spoon down and chirped out, "*Shit!*" with a huge smile on her face and her two bottom teeth jutting out.

Ian tips his head back, laughing into the spring breeze. "I'm glad no one heard that besides us."

"Your turn," I tell him.

He looks out over the Pasture, his expression becoming a little more somber. "Do you remember all those times you showed up at my work to bring me to lunch?" He gives a half-hearted smile.

I glare at him. No, I don't. And I wouldn't, because he always begged me to meet him for lunch and I never did. I always told him I was too busy, that I didn't have time. I can't believe that he would bring this up now. That he would choose a moment that would make me feel like this. Guilty. Because I am guilty. Of being a bad wife, a horrible wife who would abandon her husband and move on with a new man. I guess that's the problem with memories, we don't all remember everything the same way. It's subjective. This is where Akiyama's plan backfires.

I am filled with hot anger. "Do you remember," I spit out at him, "that time when I was getting ready for work and the house was a mess and Lina had on the same pajamas for two days and her hair hadn't been combed and you wanted to know what was for dinner as you sat in front of the television? Do you remember that night I left? Because I do every single day! I remember coming home to look for you both and all the shit I went through that day, Ian. I had to walk home. Forty miles! Did Crane or anyone else tell you that? Did they tell you what I went through to find you and when I got here all I found was that our daughter was gone and you weren't the same?" I try to control the rapid beating of my heart and the shaking of my hands, but I can't.

The blood drains from Ian's face.

Yeah, this little game definitely backfired. And I feel like an ass. I just told him not so long ago that I forgave him for not protecting Lina and now here I am, yelling at him about the same situation. It seems my heart and my brain are at a disconnect. I know I can't blame him, but I can't seem to get rid of those feelings from that day. I stand, ready to walk around the other side of the platform, to get away from him and climb down the ladder. Ian stands faster than I move. Gripping my shoulders, he stops me from dodging him.

"Andie—"

"I don't think this little game is going to help us, Ian." I can't even look up at his face as I speak. Instead I stare at his shoulder, watching the muscle twitch as he squeezes my arm.

"You just have to give it time," his deep voice becomes so soft.

"We don't have enough time."

"Yes, we have all the time we want now."

"No, Ian, I thought we had time. I thought we had a normal life when it was just our little family, then everything changed. And I get the horrible feeling it's going to change again soon. We don't have all the time in the world to fix this."

"That's why you need to stop thinking about time and live in these moments, Andie, you need to be here now. Not somewhere in the future, trying to plan and worry. Be here now. For Lina and Raven and... me." I move my eyes to his, as his hand moves to my face. "Do you remember–"

"I don't want to play anymore," I tell him.

He grips my chin, forcing me to make eye contact with him. "Be here, Andie. Do you remember when it was the Fourth of July and we were standing in the park watching the fireworks?" I nod at him, remembering those carefree summer days. "Do you remember that when they were done I turned to you and asked you if you would be my girlfriend?" I nod, my chin trembling. "Do you remember what you said?" I shake my head, my brain too scattered at the moment to remember every absolute detail. "You said *maybe*."

His words make me remember. I did say maybe, because Ian had a reputation back then; he was a player and I didn't want to be another name on his list of conquered girls.

"You said maybe," he continues. "Not yes, or hell yes, or dear God yes, or anything. You said maybe and you smiled that little quiet smile you used to do and the summer park music played. You know what I was like back then, a college guy looking for one thing. You know what I would have done if you were just another girl, Andie. I would have walked away. But I didn't give up on you then and I'm not going to give up on you now. I loved you from the first time I saw you and I love you now. You are my wife and I'm not going to give up so easily."

"But I've done things," I confess to him, looking away. "I've done bad things and I hurt you. There's Raven–"

"I don't care," he says, his expressions seeming to vibrate between soft and cold. "I don't care what you've done. I could be angry. I could be sad. God knows I've felt a combination of those feelings since Crane woke me up. But those feelings aren't going to get me anywhere. What happened here is unbelievable, but we are still alive, we still have each other. If Crane hadn't chosen you to do what you do, it could be worse, we could all be dead." I barely contain my sharp intake of breath. There was a point when I thought I might have died, or that Crane might have killed me. I'm sure Ian can see it flash on my face. "Do you want to tell me about the other things?" he asks. "I know that there is a lot I don't know about."

I've only told one other person everything that has happened and now he's dead, his makeshift gravestone solidly set in the ground just a few yards from the water tower ladder.

"You want to hear everything?" I ask. "What they did for two years while you were medicated?" He nods yes to me, dropping his hands from my shoulders. I raise my hand, self-consciously rubbing my finger over the now permanent bump in my nose from when Baillie broke it.

I sit and talk.

When I'm done spouting my memories, I finally look up to Ian. With his digestion of everything, the look on his face is the same as Adams was: cold and angered. His mood shifts as he notices me watching him, his features soften.

"Do you remember when," he starts, "we were just

married and had landed in Hawaii for our honeymoon?" I stare at him. "And we spent a whole week alone? It was just us and the beach."

I'm not sure if it's a smart thing for him to do, tethering one horrible memory with such a good one. For the moment it works. Those images of Baillie are replaced with ones of our honeymoon, with the beach and the sun and the hot nights in our rented bungalow. I get that clenching sensation in my stomach, the familiar one I used to get when we were young and in the early stages of our relationship.

He leans toward me. I wait, anticipating the pressure of his lips on mine and the familiar smell of him. Fueled by the memories of our honeymoon, it all comes flooding back, those feelings. This time I kiss him back and it all returns in a spark, an instant. The feelings. Every single one I've ever had for him. They flood me. A giant swelling wave so strong it's ready to burst from my chest. I should stop. I shouldn't let it go further. I should wait for us to heal, to weave and mend together like the roots of the old forest oak trees, deep and strong and unshakable. But I am weak. I can't stop. This time I lean forward and wrap my arms around his shoulders.

--

"Mom!" I hear Lina's voice as we near the courtyard. "Mom! Dad! Where are you?" she shouts.

Ian and I break into a sprint, running toward her voice. We find her at the edge of the courtyard looking thoroughly distraught; hair escaping from her ponytail, the ends tangled and curled, her eyes huge and watery.

"What's wrong?" I ask, out of breath when we

finally reach her.

"Stevie's missing," she says, her voice wavering, her face twisted with concern. Stevie usually spends her days lying on the floor of the schoolhouse, but she can leave as she pleases, thanks to the dog door Elvis installed.

"What do you mean?" I look around the empty courtyard. There is no Stevie and none of the Guardians are present.

"She never came back this morning," Lina says. "She went outside and never came back. I've been waiting for her for hours."

Ian's brow wrinkles as he walks behind the schoolhouse, searching. We couldn't have been gone more than a few hours.

"Okay, Lina." I kneel down and hug her. "We'll look for her. Come on, let's get Raven first."

I take Lina back to the schoolhouse. Blithe opens the door before we reach the porch. "Lina," she starts, "you can't just leave the schoolhouse. I can't leave all the children here to look for you."

I squeeze Lina's hand. "Stevie's missing," I tell Blithe.

"Oh!" She steps back, allowing Lina to walk past her and take her jacket off the coat hook.

"We're going to look for her," I say as Lina passes between us again and sits on the porch steps.

Blithe turns and looks to the children in the classroom. "Okay," she says. "We'll help."

"You don't need to."

"We do. The children love Stevie. She is as much a part of the classroom as one of the children." Blithe reaches for the coat rack and, taking a canvas jacket off of one of the hooks, she pushes her arms through it.

"Let me just get the children ready."

I pick up Raven and, zipping his jacket up to his chin, I step off the porch. Lina sits on the steps, her hands cradling her cheeks. I squeeze her shoulder. "Come on, Lina, let's start in the field."

As we make our way behind the houses, Ian appears with Elvis at his side. "How long she been missing?" Elvis asks.

"I'm not sure," I tell him. "Lina said that she went outside this morning and never came back."

"Well, it's nearly afternoon." Elvis tips his hat and looks toward the sun. "We had better split up if we want to find her by dark."

"Why don't you stay with Blithe and the children?" Ian suggests.

"Sure," I tell him as I hear Blithe close the school house door, walking with the other children in tow. I adjust Raven on my hip, waiting for them to catch up with us. Then we set off to search for Stevie.

We walk across the spring field, the wild iris and lavender brushing against our legs, the soles of our shoes caked with mud. The children shout for Stevie. A few of them bark, trying their best to make her appear or make a noise. The Guardians at the edge of the forest watch us. It seems they've multiplied again. I stop counting how many there are when I get to fifty.

When we reach the edge of the field, we turn to the west, headed for the acres of gardens. As the afternoon sun starts to dip in the sky, I get that panicked feeling that we might not find her. Lina becomes so upset that she begins to cry.

Blithe gives me a worried look as we walk between the rows of corn seedlings. "It's past dinner time," she says.

"Let's head back," I suggest.

We turn, leading the children back toward the courtyard as they continue to call for our missing dog. I leave Blithe at her house and tell the boys goodbye.

"We'll never find her in the dark," Lina says, her voice soft and distressed.

"Let's get you something to eat, Lina. Daddy and Elvis will keep looking for her. I'll call Sam to come help."

"Okay," she says, her head hung, dragging her feet.

Astrid takes Lina's hand, trying to give her friend just a little bit of comfort. "It will be alright," Astrid tells her in a quiet voice.

I cook a small dinner and try to keep the conversation off of Stevie as I rush them through the meal and into the bathtub. Just as I lay Raven down to sleep there is a knock at the door. I hear Lina's footsteps as she runs to answer it, and as I make my way down the hall, I can tell from the scene before me that the news isn't good. Ian stands on the porch, Elvis is a few feet away. He's carrying what looks like a burlap sack over both of his arms.

Ian kneels in front of Lina. "I'm so sorry, baby," he tells her.

Lina cries. She howls and screams and sobs as though she's lost her best friend. She *did* just lose her best friend. Ian wraps his arms around her, pulling her close to his chest, muffling her sobs.

I walk down the steps and over to Elvis.

"What happened to her?" I ask. Taking a deep breath, I try to calm myself.

"Not sure. Found her at the back of the grazing lands lying by the far fence, edge of the property. There's no wounds. Seems to be natural causes."

I turn and see Astrid standing in the doorway, her eyes wide, chin trembling. I rush over to her and pick her up. Ian picks up Lina. We carry them both inside, doing our best to soothe their broken hearts. Ian rocks Lina and I sit with Astrid on her bed. We wait as they fall asleep, tucking them into bed when the sobs stop wracking their small bodies.

Together we leave the room and the sadness hits me as I close the door and don't see Stevie lying at the foot of Lina's bed. Stevie was my dog before she was Lina's. And even though she slept each night at the foot of Lina's bed, I would pat her head on my way out of the room and inform Stevie of what I was doing. She was always there, for all of us.

Trying not to wake the girls, I choke back the tears but it must have been loud enough for Ian to hear. When I turn around he is there, wrapping his arms around me, and just like our daughter did, I cry into his chest, soaking his shirt with my tears. He rubs my back, his warm hand moving in slow circles over the thin fabric of my shirt, slowing slightly when he feels the scars that are there, scars he doesn't know about.

While part of me wants to stay in the hallway with his warm arms wrapped around me, the rest of me wants to hide and privately deal with the losses that have been dealt to us in such a short time. Adam, Morris, and Stevie. They are all dead. While Morris's death was expected, the others weren't. There was no time for goodbye. No planning for the grief. We will never enjoy another day with them in our lives.

The next day brings a spring thunderstorm, which just adds to the somberness of the house. I keep the children from school to mourn, spoiling them with warm milk and honey, cookies, and books filled with fairytales. Elvis visits, bringing Stevie's collar and telling us that we can bury her the next day. We had already planned to bury Morris the next day. Just a simple act while the children were in class, with no more than Elvis and myself standing at the gravesite. I never thought we would be burying Morris and Stevie together.

The next day the girls pick handfuls of wildflowers. I show them how to wrap the stems with twine so they resemble bouquets.

When we are done and the dirt has been replaced, and small homemade bouquets rest on the mounds of fresh soil, there is an uncomfortable silence. As my eyes focus on Adam's gravestone, Ian shifts on his feet. Raven wiggles in my arms. I set him down. He toddles to Adam's gravestone. And staring in a quiet observation he reaches out with his chubby fingers and touches the cold granite. He stands like that for a moment as Lina and Astrid become consumed with picking the surrounding wildflowers and setting them on Stevie's grave, which does not have a stone yet, just a perfect rectangle of overturned soil. And then, as though Raven has come to a conclusion, he turns from Adam's gravestone and walks toward Ian, raising his arms, signaling he wants to be picked up. Ian lifts Raven into his arms, who rests his head on Ian's shoulder and closes his eyes.

When Ian's eyes finally meet mine I give him a small smile.

CHAPTER THIRTEEN

There is something about death that creates this strange urge to find comfort in the arms of someone else. Maybe it's because we are looking for a reminder that we are alive, a celebration that our souls remain on this earth as our loved ones ascend into the heavens. I'm not certain what it is. All I know is that I want to be alive, for just a few minutes. I don't want to feel like I have felt lately: lost and alone, even though I'm surrounded by family.

As the children sleep and Ian goes to the barn with the excuse of helping Elvis with farm work, I work on the Residents pairings. Of course, now it includes many more Residents, the new ones from Crystal River and a few in Wolf Creek, the District that lies on the eastern edge of Kansas. I scan the data, noting the Residents who have been preselected to get the injection with the DNA altering vectors, the ones which will forever alter these people, turning them into the subordinate humans that Crane so desires. He plans to start with a few hundred Residents from

Phoenix, before subjecting the rest of the District Residents to the same therapy.

I immerse myself in the data for what must be a few hours until, feeling a soft prickle on the back of my neck, I look up and turn. Ian is standing quietly on the other side of the room.

"When did you start wearing glasses?" he asks me, his hair damp and curling from the heavy night air. He sounds slightly out of breath, like he just got done running.

I reach up, pulling the dark frames off of my face. "I just started," I tell him. "I guess I'm getting old. All the computer work and reading has been making my eyes tired." I glance at him as he kicks off a pair of muddy boots onto the mat near the door. "What are you doing?" I ask, replacing the frames and turning to save my work. I shut the computer down and leave the glasses on the small desk. Turning to receive Ian's answer, I find him standing right next to me.

"Watching you work," he says with an odd smile. I've seen this look on his face before: a mixture of sadness and tease. And I remember the last time I saw him look like this. It was after his parents died, and each anniversary after their deaths. He must be experiencing the same effects of the recent deaths as I am.

"Why?" I ask, standing.

"Because I like to," his smile grows, but it's odd, upturned on one end, and downturned on the other. A lock of light hair falls over his face and I want to reach up and swipe it away like I used to.

"Kind of like a creepy stalker?" I ask, trying to inject the sort of playful banter that we used to have into the conversation.

"Something like that."

He searches my face and I watch as that look of remembering death melts away and a new one replaces it, still, a look I've seen before. He had it when we were married, and before we were married, the one that says he wants to kiss me and more. I realize in this moment I can be who I am supposed to be–his wife–or I can freeze and push him away just as I have been doing for so long. I weigh my options as he steps closer and that look in his brown eyes grows more intense.

He said that he wasn't giving up on us. He begged me to try harder with us. And now with the recent deaths fresh in my memories, I find it hard to shy away from him as I've done for the past two years since he was released to me. This time, when he reaches out, cupping my cheek in his right hand and his left moving to my hip to pull me close, I don't stop him. I don't step away. Ian bends, pressing his lips to mine and I can smell the scent of lemons mixed with the night air. And with that kiss a million things seem to run through my mind. I can't stop them. I can't focus on him or the moment. I know I should be enjoying this. I used to enjoy this, a lot. And as though Ian senses my reluctance, his grip on my hip loosens, his hand leaves my cheek with a brush of his thumb across my jaw sending a sharp tingle down my neck.

Stop, I tell myself, *stop thinking*. Ian is here now. He is alive and well and his feelings for me are blatantly apparent, even after all that I've done. I let the guilt evaporate off of my conscience. I let my mind stop churning and simply enjoy. I wrap my arms around his shoulders and press myself to him. Again, as though he senses my resolve, his arms squeeze me tighter as though he's afraid he might lose me. Soon the kiss turns into much more than a kiss. It's an unquenchable angst. And in my unthinking state I barely notice that he is directing the both of us down the hall, toward his bedroom.

"Wait," I tell him, trying to catch my breath as the back of my knees hit his bed frame. But he doesn't wait. He pulls his shirt off and I stare, my words at a loss. This is not the body of my husband, or at least, not the one I remember. Ian has never been heavy by any means, nothing more than a few comfortable extra inches to him, but he has never been like this; firm and taut, all angles and planes. His pants hang low on his waist and I can see the hip bone there jutting out like never before, catching the waistline of his jeans. A chording of muscle stretches across his flank, and it continues, the perfectly smooth skin stretched across more muscle, muscle that was never there before. Ian's chest and abdomen are now taut, and contract with each motion he makes. When he reaches out to pull me to him I notice his arm like I never have before: the now narrow wrist, the webbing of blue veins visible under his too pale skin. Pulling me to him now, I feel those jutting bones press into me. I was aware that he had lost weight since this began, but this, this was not the Ian I have known through years of marriage. This is not my fair-haired, soft-mannered Ian. And I worry Crane may be changing him into someone else. Or maybe I have. Maybe it's the years of worry and change that have done this to him, that have turned him into this changed man.

"Have you been…" I choke out an awkward cough, "working out?" I ask, hoping it doesn't sound like a stupid pick up line but a true question.

"Yeah," he smiles, his eyes hooded and glazed.

"Why?" I lay my palms on his warm shoulders.

"Because I have a family to protect," he replies in a mere hurried whisper.

And then he is back to kissing me, securing his hand in my hair, demanding more, tipping my mouth to meet his. I put my hands on his chest ready to push him away but my arms don't seem to obey. They stay there intact with his warm skin, savoring the heat and feel of him. His hand untangles from my hair as he reaches for my shirt and begins unbuttoning it.

The gravity of our current situation hits me. "Wait," I tell him, placing my hands over his and closing my eyes, trying to focus, breathing much faster than I should be.

"I'm tired of waiting," he says, shaking my hands off of his.

I shake my head at him, reaching to cover his hands again. "It's not like I don't want to go further, we just... we just can't."

"Why?" he asks, his question pained. "Why not, Andie? I've been waiting for so long. Too long."

I feel the flare of embarrassment rise in my cheeks. "There are risks to doing this without... without birth control."

"We always wanted more kids," he offers as his hands roam down my sides, grasping my shirt at the hem.

"Not now." I shake my head at him and cover his hands again, holding the shirt in place. "Not like this." I think to step away from him, but I'm trapped between the bed and his body so close to me.

"What's wrong with this?" His hands make a quick return to my shirt buttons.

"The world is a disaster." I grip my shirt closed,

afraid for him to see what's underneath, the scars from all of this. "I never want to bring another child into this world. Not the way it is now. Not with Crane or any of the Entities or what I have to do."

"You might change your mind," he says as he dips his head and resumes his onslaught, kissing my neck, his hands roaming to my back, pressing me to him. "After all," he whispers in my ear, "I am your pair. It is expected of us now."

Dear God, he must have been reading the Manifesto. Or Crane mentioned this to him. "I'm serious, Ian." I push him away, hard, the thought of Crane ruining the moment and causing me to remember the trouble I've already gotten myself into. "I don't want any more children. None. End of story. You have to know this. You can't tell me that you don't feel the same way."

"So is this strictly platonic then?" he asks, dropping his hands at his sides.

"If it has to be," I reply. He gives me a look of agitation and defeat. "I'm sorry. I… I don't know what to do."

"Sure," he replies as he reaches for his discarded shirt at the end of the bed, still trapping me in his room.

"You don't understand, Ian. Whoever I let close, Crane will use against me to get what he wants."

"What does he want?"

"I'm still trying to figure that out." He looks at me one last time before turning swiftly on his heel and walking out of the bedroom. "Where are you going?" I ask after him.

He doesn't reply, he doesn't turn around. And I watch as he walks toward the front door, steps into his muddy shoes, and pulls the door open with an angered force before closing it quietly behind him. He leaves, just like he does each night. Although, I've only ever heard him, I've never watched him walk away like this with my own eyes. It seems I have pushed him away again and I worry that one of these times I'm going to push him so far that he may give up and never return.

This is not a step in the right direction. Dr. Akiyama will be quite dissatisfied.

CHAPTER FOURTEEN

"Good morning, Raven," Blithe tells my son. "Are you going to speak today?"

He stares at her, twisting his cherub face before looking at me.

Something doesn't seem right here. And it seems like Raven might actually be trying to tell me this. I remember what Crane said about him needing to meet his milestones; there is no other person to let on to Crane that there is anything wrong with Raven.

"Blithe," I stop her as she leads the children indoors. "Do you have a second?" I ask her.

"Sure." She closes the door and walks toward me.

"Do you know anything about Crane receiving reports on the children's progress?"

She pauses, pondering whether or not she's going to tell me the truth.

"Blithe?" I ask her.

She leans back to view the children through the window and turning back to me, she says, "I write reports on all the children and their progress. Those go directly to Crane."

"You never thought to tell me?"

"I was instructed *not* to tell you," she whispers to me.

"Why did you put in there that he isn't meeting his milestones?"

"Because he isn't. He's almost two and a half and he doesn't speak." She says it so matter-of-factly, without the inclination that she used a bit of emotion in the report; it was just redacted facts about the children.

"He's quiet, Blithe. He understands, he communicates in other ways."

She opens her mouth as though she's about to say something, but stops herself. This is not the Blithe I've known. She's always been approachable, confident. Of course, I've never questioned her work before.

"I want you to change his report." I demand before she says anything.

Blithe crosses her arms. "You want me to falsify his documents, the documents that sway Crane's decision on the next generation of Sovereign?" In the moment of silence between us the spring breeze pulls loose a few locks of her blonde hair.

"I've trusted you, Blithe. What happened? You used to protect these children."

"I have a job, like you have a job, and that is what ensures my safety here. And there have been other things on my mind." Her eyes flick across the courtyard toward the barn.

"You know what Crane will do to Raven. He's just a baby. He suggested euthanizing him or sending him outside the gates. I can't let that happen. *You* can't let that happen."

Her eyes widen, then narrow the tiniest bit as she realizes the rocks I am stuck between. "Let's make a deal," she offers.

"What kind of deal?"

"I'm not getting any younger, Andie. I want a family."

"A family? But you have all these children. The boys are your family now, and if more children come you will be responsible for them also."

"No." She shakes her head slightly. "A real family. A husband, children of my own."

"What are you proposing?"

"You're the District Matchmaker–"

"What are you getting at?" I interrupt.

"I want Sam."

"What?" I reach out and grasp the post of the porch.

"You heard me." She smiles and I have a hard time telling if it's one of slight embarrassment or slyness. "I want Sam. I want us matched together."

"I... I can't do that."

"You want Raven's reports altered. I want Sam."

"You are both Sovereign. I don't decide for the Sovereign. You can choose whoever you want."

"That's what you think." She leans back, checking on the children through the window again. "Make the data work, Andie. Make it gleam and glow. Make it match perfectly. Just like yours and Adam's did. Then Crane will have no worries about the arrangement."

I step back. "How do you know anything about our data?"

"Crane has a close eye on everything you do. I've managed to find a few things out."

"I didn't alter our data!" I snap at her.

"Sure, maybe you didn't, but you *could*. You think Crane would allow anything but perfection from the Sovereign? If it doesn't work, he won't allow it. He'll put an end to it, just like he wants to put an end to your son."

"When did you turn into this?" I ask.

"This is just a side of me you've never seen. Crane, sometimes he brings out the best in us or the worst. Take it as whatever you want."

Her eyes flick away for just the tiniest fraction of a second. And it's in that movement I know she's not telling me something.

"Blithe."

"Andie."

"There's more. You're hiding something. Tell me."

She sighs while maintaining her tall, unwavering stature. "While Crane threatens your child's existence, he threatens me for not adding to the Sovereign children's gene pool."

"Are you saying he wants you to have children?"

She nods stiffly.

"What did you tell him?"

"Nothing, Andie. I looked at my prospects here. We have Alexander, Crane, and Elvis. I'd die long before selecting any of them. Sam's my only choice."

"He's my brother. No," I shake my head, "I can't do this."

"If he ships me out, Andie, just think of who could replace me. We know each other. We've been here since the beginning. I am willing to lie to Crane to save your son's life."

I take a deep breath as my options run through my head. Really, though, I have no options.

"And Sam," I ask Blithe, "Does he even want you?

194

I'm not forcing my little brother into a relationship he doesn't want."

"He'll want me. I'll make sure of that."

"And you'll alter Raven's reports?"

"Yes."

I give her a hard look before I respond. "Deal."

"Thank you," she says, letting out a breath of relief just before turning and walking into the schoolhouse.

I look after her, realizing what I've done: I just traded my brother for my son.

--

I stare at the three graves: Morris, Adam, and Stevie. I begin to realize that I may never enjoy the comforting knowledge that I could grow old, retire, mingle with the old bitties in the nursing home, sipping on my wine and slapping the asses of the young male nurses. No, I will most likely never make it to that age. I'm sure it won't be long before Lina and Raven stand in this same place, staring at five headstones, mine and Ian's added, maybe even Sam.

I sigh. I shouldn't have come here. This is depressing.

A cluster of tall grass sways in the breeze in front of Adam's stone. I've forgotten. I can barely remember what he looked like, the sound of his voice, the delicious way he smelled. I want to tear the grass up and find his shirt I buried there. I want to press it to my face and take a deep breath and remember. Even though I know it's wrong and I need to move on, I don't want to forget him. For some strange reason the heated evening with Ian just made me want to remember. I don't know why, it seems so wrong, and if Ian knew what I was about to do, he'd be pissed. But I just can't stop myself, even with all that has improved between me and Ian, the progress we've made in our relationship. We can hold conversations now; we've even kissed a few times.

Turning away from the graves, I run, the sound of the Guardians paws striking the ground as they follow me is the only thing I can hear. They know I'm going to do something stupid. Somehow they can sense it.

I take Elvis's keys and drive, speeding toward town. The Guardians that pushed their way into the vehicle before I could close the door growl from the backseat. I drive past my old street, Grenadier Street. Adam told me his parents lived not far from my house. I circle the blocks, driving slow and reading the mailboxes.

Most of the Residents are working now. I pass some as they sweep the sidewalks and tend to their spring gardens, turning the soil, getting the dirt ready for planting. The factions have been instructed to ensure all the houses look tidy, even the empty ones, which we have a lot of here. A mother walks by with her children; two identical boys, the twins. I know them, the first twins born in the District. They should be almost four now. I drive the next block, stopping sharply when I see it, the mailbox with *Waters* written on it.

I park the SUV in the street. The Guardians follow me when I get out, headed for the front door. Through the windows I can see it's dark inside, and I can tell from the layers of dust on the windowsills that no one lives here. I reach for the door handle, turning it; to my amazement it's unlocked. I push my way inside.

There are coats by the door, shoes along the wall. I walk down the hallway, turning into the living room. I look at the pictures on the walls, in the living room and the dining room. There is a mother, father and daughter. No son. I scan the walls, the display cabinets, the shelves. I make my way to the kitchen, the floorboards creaking under my feet. There are dishes drying in the sink. They should be plenty dry for the years they've sat there. One of the bowls is bleached from the sun. There is a small table next to me, keys in a bowl, a wallet, mail. I pick up one of the letters. Mail, something we haven't had here in so long. It's addressed to Mr. and Mrs. Waters. I flip open the wallet. There is a driver's license for James Waters. This has to be the right house. I wander, searching each wall for any indication of a son. I climb the stairs, a Guardian at my heels. This is eerie, walking through the house of people long dead, seeing their memories, their belongings.

I find two rooms, one glaringly obvious that it is a teenage girl's room, painted a light purple color with pictures and magazine pages taped to the wall. There is a foam cutout of the high school mascot, the Phoenix Firebird, resting next to a pair of red and white pom-poms.

Making my way across the hall I find another bedroom that is sparsely decorated, just a simple green quilt covering the bed. This must be the master bedroom. There is one last door at the end of the hallway. I walk to it, my footsteps muffled by the shag carpet. The Guardians watch me from the stairs. I pray that when I open the door, I will get a glimpse of his life before this. Maybe there will be pictures, something that smells like him, a T-shirt I can steal. I twist the door handle and push the door open. It's empty. There is no furniture, no pictures, nothing. I stand in the room, alone. There is no indication of these people having a son. Maybe I'm at the wrong house? Or maybe they were just so distraught by their son's death that they got rid of everything. Maybe they couldn't stand another moment living with all of his memories so they got rid of them.

I walk down the stairs in defeat. When I make it to the living room, I circle it, stopping at the fireplace. Something catches my eye, a dark yellow envelope behind one of the pictures. I push the picture of a smiling girl aside. There is an envelope, with *Andie* written across the front of it.

But no one I actually know lived here and since I can find no trace of him, I can't even be certain that this was Adam's family. I pull the envelope down, holding it in my hand. There's something inside, something solid, bulky. I open the clasp and peer inside. There's no letter, just a cellular flip-phone and a charging cord.

A phone… This is Adam's cell phone! The one he got off his contact, just before the bombings. The one I used to call Sam while we were on tour. It has to be. I open the phone, press the power button. Nothing happens. It must need to be charged.

I'm interrupted by the sound of sirens blaring. The same sirens I've heard here, the same sirens I heard in Crystal River, which means the power to the fence is down or off or there's some other problem. *Oh God, no.*

I run out of the empty house, slamming the door behind me, the Guardians at my heels as I run to the SUV. I rush through the town streets, making my way back to the Pasture as the Residents continue on with their daily activities and duties, as though the sirens weren't whistling through the air.

--

Elvis and Ian are leaving the Pasture just as I arrive. I pull over, park and run to their vehicle. Elvis rolls his window down.

"What's going on?" I ask, out of breath.

"Survivor at the gates," Elvis says. "Get in."

Ian reaches behind him and opens the back door of the SUV.

"Where's Sam?" I ask.

"Probably already there," Elvis replies.

"What about the kids?" I ask, worried about Lina and Raven.

"They'll be fine here," Elvis says as he drives down the driveway. "This place is safe. Ms. Black and the Guardians will keep them safe."

The forest blurs by as Elvis speeds in the direction of where they keep the train. The rocks of the gravel parking area grind under the tires as Elvis brakes hard. We all get out and make our way for the Gateway. As I follow Elvis and Ian, Ian reaches back and grasps my hand, pulling me along at a faster pace. We walk parallel to the train tracks, past the cement wall and toward the electrified fence.

What I see is too familiar to what we took part in not that long ago in Crystal River: a row of Volker stand a few yards from the fence. I notice Sam's tall frame as we get closer. Elvis jogs ahead of us. I skip a few steps to keep up with Ian's pace.

"Who's out there?" Elvis asks.

"They said they saw a figure. Weren't sure who," Sam replies as we walk up next to him.

And then the figure appears, silently, without the rustle of the underbrush. Just like a ghost. It's a girl, a mere teenager with an oversized New York Yankees sweatshirt and mud brushed jeans. She's wearing a pair of boots that reach to her knees.

"Can I help you?" Sam asks the girl loudly.

"You could," she replies with a soft smile, an innocent voice.

"Do we let her in?" I whisper to Elvis.

He shakes his head. "Just wait and see what else happens."

"You could help me," the Survivor girl continues pushing her inky black hair out of her face. "You could let me in and keep me *safe*." She suggests, her face turning devilish. "Mo swaf," she tells us with the same thick Creole accent of the Survivors outside of Crystal River.

I reach out and grab the back of Sam's shirt as he raises his firearm and aims it on the girl.

"What did she just say?" Ian asks.

"She's speaking Creole," I tell him, "like the Survivors that tried to break in at Crystal River."

"What does she want?" Ian asks.

"To get shot in the head," Sam replies.

"Get out of here!" Elvis orders the girl loudly, waving her away.

She walks closer to the fence, tipping her chin in the same manner as the boy and man did in Crystal River. But this time, our fence is at full power and it's not long before she gets close enough for the electric hum of the fence to affect her. She reaches up, brushes her sleeve across her nose, leaving a streak of bright red blood across her face. And then there is a sharp triple whistle from somewhere behind her. Just like the men

200

and boys in Crystal River, she slithers back into the forest, silently.

"Swamp people," Elvis starts. "Like cockroaches. They'll survive anything."

As Sam's radio receives the transmission that we are to go directly to Headquarters, I'm stuck with the realization that I brought the Survivors back, showed them where we lived. I did this, this is my fault. I just put my entire family at risk. Elvis is right, I need to go get the others on board and collect troops and supplies. We need to be ready in case the swamp people come back, in case they bring more of their kind.

--

"We've been found," Crane announces to the Committee. "The Survivors have found our gates and now we need to make preparations to defend this District."

Crane has summoned Elvis to this meeting. And for the first time, it seems Crane isn't directing the meeting, he's genuinely asking for help in deciding what to do.

"We need to prepare," Elvis tells Crane. "The Survivors could still outnumber us. And if they get in, if they breach our walls, everything we have worked for here could be over."

Crane nods his head. "We need weapons, more than what we already have, and troops."

"Hanford has weapons," Alexander offers.

"Tonopah has more than enough troops," Elvis says.

I shudder at the thought of Tonopah. I look at Sam. He has yet to offer any ideas. But he is young and inexperienced, much too young for this position he was put in.

"Who will we send?" Crane asks.

"I'll go," Sam offers.

I throw him a glaring look. He's not ready for this.

Crane agrees immediately. "Good," he replies as he types into the computer in front of him. "I want a full inventory of our weapons," Crane tells Sam. "This meeting is dismissed. Be ready to act," he warns us as we stand to leave.

"Give me your keys," I tell Ian as we descend in the elevator. He tips his head, questioningly. "Just... Ride with Elvis. I need to talk to Crane."

"Andie–" His eyes search my face.

"Just trust me, Ian. Give me your keys."

He drops the key into my open palm. As I wait for the others to leave I sit in the Headquarters vestibule, contemplating long and hard on what I'm about to do. I don't want to do it, I don't want to leave, but I have to do this to keep us safe, to make sure my children stay safe. The Volker at the doors pretend not to watch me, but I know they are, this is their job.

Returning to the elevator and pressing the button to Crane's floor, I make my way to Crane's office, alone, determined, and fully aware of the situation I'm about to put myself in.

Crane's face brightens as the elevator doors open, seeing me there. "Ah, Andromeda, to what do I owe this visit?" he asks. "It's as though I just saw you ten minutes ago."

I think he just told a joke. Of all the inappropriate moments to choose. "We need to talk," I tell him.

He walks across the room and sits behind his desk. "What would you like to talk about?" he asks, raising

202

his finger to his chin.

I lean against his desk, arms and feet crossed. I have to lie. I suck at lying. I have to do my best acting. I have to make Crane believe that I need to go there. "I want to be the one to go with Sam to collect supplies and troops."

"Why, Andromeda, you hate leaving the Phoenix District. Why would you willingly take off and leave your children behind?"

"This is different," I tell him.

"How do you think?"

"Sam isn't ready to go out there. He isn't ready to meet those people alone."

"What's wrong with *those people*?" Crane asks innocently.

I shake my head at him. "You know what I mean. You sent me out there before with Adam. I know what they're all like and I won't even begin discussions about Sakima. You can't let them sharpen their teeth on Sam, not now, not with those Survivors lurking at our gates."

Crane smiles, fully aware that Sakima is a psychopath, just like him. "He's been fully trained. I assure you, Andromeda. I wouldn't send Sam if I didn't believe he was ready."

I shake my head. "I don't believe you, Crane."

"Fine," he sets his palms on his desk. "You can go. But first, we call to warn them."

"About me?"

"No," he laughs lightly. "They need no warnings about you. We warn them about the Survivors, or at least this particular group of Swamp-people Survivors."

"Most of the other Districts have seen Survivors

already," I tell him.

"Yes," he smiles condescendingly at me. "But this is the first time we've had an incident. Usually they are scraping and begging to be let in, they have never delivered a direct threat to us."

"This doesn't make sense. Why these people? You obliterated this country. How did they survive?" I ask.

"We didn't bomb the wetlands," Crane replies.

"Why?"

"Too rich with wildlife. The wetlands and swamps are the heart of nature. We couldn't damage those. It would go against everything we are trying to accomplish."

For a moment I am at a loss for words and simply blink at him.

"No need to stress over it. You just mull that around in your brain for a bit, Andromeda."

I stand by as he dials each of the other Districts and informs them of the Survivors and the need to prepare in case they attack.

"Now," Crane closes the open tab on his computer screen after ending his last call with Sakima. "You go and prepare, you leave in the morning."

I walk to the door, ready to leave, but something nags at me and I don't have the sense to stop myself from asking.

"Why are they so afraid of you, Crane?"

He smiles. "I know their secrets. And they know what I am capable of. Also, I have something that they all would like to have."

"Secrets don't keep people that afraid of someone."

"Perhaps if you knew their secrets, then you would understand. Would you like to know them?" he offers.

"No," I tell him. The less I know the better. Then I

think to ask, "Who are you afraid of, Crane?"

"Me?"

"There has to be someone above you. You can't be the mastermind of this all by yourself." He gives a wicked smile. "So who are you afraid of? I know that the Entities work as a whole to keep you under control, there has to be one of them that you are afraid of."

"Why, Andromeda, there is only one person on this earth whom I fear." He gives an annoying pause. "You."

I step back. "Me?"

"Yes, you."

"Why would you fear me?"

"Do you ever wonder why I keep tabs on you, why I keep such control over you? Because I fear you and what you are capable of and what you will become."

He's playing mind games again. "You didn't need to lie to me, Crane. No answer would have been better than that half-assed response."

He simply smiles back at me. "You think I would let the other Sovereign speak to me like that?" he asks, pointing one long, freckled finger at me.

"I don't much care right now. I have to go pack."

"I'll meet you at the tracks in the morning," he says as I walk out of his office.

--

As I drive, I think of how I can do this again. Leaving the District, entrusting the safety of Lina and Raven to others. At least I have the phone Adam left for me. I think back to his house, where I was early this morning, searching for some sign of who he was, searching for some memory.

Maybe I didn't have time to fully think about the lack of evidence that Adam was a part of the Waters family. But then, I didn't see one trace of his existence in that house. Something doesn't make sense.

I turn sharp, changing my direction from headed to the Pasture to the graveyard.

A sea of gray gravestones spreads out before me. There was once a gravel road here, weaving between the grave plots. Now it's overgrown with shrubs and tall grass. I park on the side of the road. Walking between the graves I search for the headstones marked *Waters*.

The task seems overwhelming. And so do the memories from the last time I was out here alone, making my way home. It's too easy to remember watching Adam fall to his knees and grieve for his family. Of course, now I'm wondering if that was even his family. I wander up the hill, finding the large oak tree I sat under waiting for him. I turn toward the south. Seeing the large stone wall that I watched our Residents build that day and for weeks after, effectively keeping everyone out of here.

I continue my walk, meandering between the granite jutting from the ground, searching for the stones, until I find them. They are the same as the day we were here, except for now there are overgrown dandelions flanking the sides of the stone.

Jim Waters
Margaret Waters
Samantha Waters

Their dates of death are the same. The soft dirt now replaced with a fine summer grass. I hear the distant caw of the crows in the oak tree. I wish I knew what I was looking for. And then a crow flutters down from the tree, landing a few yards away on the top of a gravestone. It stares at me, blinking its beady eyes, cocking its head to the side as though it's waiting for me to speak. I imitate its movement, tipping my head, wondering what it's doing here, staring at me. It caws loudly before flapping its large black wings and rising into the air. I look at the stone it was perched on, walking toward it. Stopping, I back up and look at the dates of death from the Waters gravestones and back to the stone that the crow was resting on. And it hits me with a shock and a realization that I've been lied to once again, because the dates of death are the same. And of course, these names are different and there is only one gravestone.

Mr. and Mrs. Whitmarsh

Looking to the surrounding gravestones, there are none for a child, a sister or daughter with the same last name or dates of death. I walk back to the Waters gravestones, and kneeling just where I remember Adam did that day. And then, looking forward, I see that I have the perfect view of the Whitmarsh gravestones.

The awareness hits me stronger than I might have guessed. Maybe it was because I trusted him, because I thought we were close, because I was pregnant with his child—of all things—and stupidly I thought that might make him trust me more. He lied to me about his identity. Perhaps the crow was his last hint, now that he is dead. Maybe he's trying to send a message from the afterlife or a clue for me to figure this out.

It seems Adam was a particularly good actor.

How could I not sense that he was sent here under an alias, with what he told me he was doing, this mission he was on? All this time I've been telling Raven stories about his father and now I realize that they were all lies. I have no idea who Adam really was and neither will his son.

Rubbing my arms in the darkening day, my palm runs over the small bump from the transmitter Crane injected under my skin. The skin now healed a light pink color. And I remember the day I found that Adam had one, and I cut it from his skin when he returned from a run for supplies. I look around me, all the bodies resting under my feet, their memories now encased within the cold gray rock. Perhaps Adam got the best part of the deal; the end, no longer here to play in the Phoenix District games.

I think that he got the easy way out.

I turn my back on the stones and walk the overgrown path out of the graveyard. I make my way to the SUV I left at the roadside. The tree of crows begins cawing at my back, shrieking and squawking. A deep shiver runs up my spine. I glance back at the dark tree, and, intimidated by the birds, afraid that they might take flight and peck me to death, I run the rest of the way to the SUV.

--

The children are asleep, even after telling them that I was leaving in the morning. I hope this is the last time, the last trip I'll ever have to make out of here. Now I have to focus on the task at hand; collecting supplies, preparing for an attack. But what I'll really be doing is rallying the District leaders against Crane in an effort to overthrow him. I just have to gather the other Sovereign and then we will be set free of Crane. We will be set to defend ourselves against the Survivors. And I will finally have peace with my children. And I can watch them grow and all I will be responsible for are the pairings.

We wait until Blithe has turned all of her lights off. This time we meet in the dark courtyard.

"Who do you think will be the easiest to get on board?" Elvis asks me.

"Torres should be simple," I tell him. "I'm not so sure about Ruiz, there's something about him that I just don't trust."

"It's the fancy watch," Elvis says with a smirk. "No one should still be wearing a watch like that."

"Maybe." I catch Ian watching me closely as I speak of these people he has never met, The Entities. "Crossbender will be an easy in. John Blackmore from Wolf Creek might take some convincing. I haven't met any of the other Sovereign from those two Districts."

Elvis nods his head. "What about Berkley in Galena?" he asks.

"No. I'm not going to Alaska on this trip. There's not enough time."

"Alaska's not on the agenda," Sam agrees with me. "Besides, Berkley has nothing to help us."

"Berkley is scared shitless of Crane. So when it comes down to it, I doubt he'll go against our plan," I say.

"So what does that leave?" Ian asks.

"Tonopah," I say wearily.

"What do you think of them?" Sam asks.

I catch Elvis shaking his head from side-to-side. He

knows what I'm going to say, before I say it. "Tonopah is no good. The Entity ruling there is Sakima. He runs an... interesting ship."

"How so?" Sam asks.

"There are ten Sovereign who are all on the Halcyon protocol."

"Wait," Ian interrupts me. "What's Halcyon?"

"That's the medication they give the Residents."

"So why is he giving it to the Sovereign?"

I take a deep breath, not wanting to waste my time with these details, but then I remember that Ian doesn't know this. "Sakima wants control over them all. His committee members sit at the gates all day and decide who will be let in from the Survivors to work in the District and keep it running. There is no weaning off the medication. Even their Volker are on a low dose of it. And everyone who visits."

"Didn't you go there?" Ian asks.

"Yeah."

"Did you take the medication?"

"No. I figured out what he was doing ahead of time. The rest of our crew wasn't so lucky."

"Where was it?"

"In the food. This is why we don't eat food from other Districts, especially from Tonopah."

The sound of soft footsteps causes me to stop talking.

"It's okay," Elvis tells us as he moves to the side and turns.

Ian and Sam look at each other in a silent preparation to deal with trouble. I watch as a shadowed figure walks up next to Elvis. I take a few steps back, ready to hide behind the men. Then, I notice, it's Alexander.

"What is he doing here?" I ask Elvis through clenched teeth.

Alexander holds up his hand. "It's okay, Andie."

"No. I don't trust you." I point at him.

"You don't trust anyone," Alexander responds with cool confidence.

"What are you doing here?"

"I'm in. I'm joining your Resistance, under one condition."

"What?"

"When this is over, when Crane is out, I'm going back to Hanford. I'm not getting any younger and my family is there. I want to spend time with them before I die."

"You're not dying." I tell him.

"We are all dying, Andromeda. And to answer your earlier question, Crossbender is in. And I suggest spending as little time in Tonopah as possible. You could probably skip that stop."

"Crane wants us to get troops from Tonopah," I tell him.

"Do you really think troops from Tonopah are a good idea? Think about it," Alexander suggests. "Morris was expected to explain this to you before he died. Maybe he was too sick to remember, but let me tell you now: those are Sakima's people. Those people answer to Sakima and only Sakima. You bring them here then you will be running into the same problem we had when our own Residents were uprising. They won't listen to us, they won't trust us. Get the horses from Wolf Creek and the weapons from Hanford. Skip Tonopah. And Galena is no good. Crane has old President Berkley running at a minimum and we can buy his membership into this little club easily. So, take the guns and the horses, swing by Crystal River. Emanuel Torres will be easy to get on board. Just be careful of Ruiz, he's greasy. Buy them with weapons and horses. They've had Survivors at their gates threatening them also. Seems to be a band of them running communications up and down the east coast. When that's done make your way home."

"I don't think I've ever heard you speak so much at once, Alexander," I point out.

"I've never had much to say. But this," he waves an arm toward the town. "This is important. And I'd like to see Crane out. He's nothing but a crazed worm rotting our apple."

"And when Crane is out, what happens to us?" I ask.

"We continue as we are, just without Crane."

"So there will still be Districts, we will still be turning the Residents into docile humans."

"It's already been set in action," Alexander says. "There's no reason to stop it. We don't want things to go back to the way they were. We will be safe. The Districts are running perfectly. This is exactly what the original Entities were looking for. A better society. A healthy planet. This was the original plan. We needed Crane's help and now we no longer need his help."

"That sounds like something Crane would say," I tell Alexander.

He shrugs, neither admitting nor denying it.

--

"I can't believe you're leaving in the morning again," Ian says as we stand in the living room. "That it's finally starting and we are one step closer to being free from

Crane."

"I'm not sure if we'll ever truly be free, Ian."

"Why do you have to do that?"

"What?"

"Twist everything around. Be so negative."

"Because I've seen what these people do. They just want Crane out of the picture. We will still be treated the same, our futures will remain as they are. Sometimes I wonder, with Crane being as crazed as he is, he might actually be protecting us, our family, against the others."

"Okay." He nods his head, looking around the living room at the few bags I have packed and set near the couch.

"I'm leaving you with the children."

"I know," he replies firmly.

I hold back the warning I want to give him about the last time I left Lina in his care.

He must sense my apprehension. "I won't let anything happen to them, Andie," he promises me.

"I know," I tell him, trying to convince myself.

"When you went to Florida, nothing happened. It won't this time either."

"I'm going to be gone longer this time," I tell him. "And I'm taking Sam. You need a plan. If the Survivors get in, if Crane pulls something, you need to be ready to run with Lina and Raven."

"Elvis says we'll be fine."

"Don't put all your trust in Elvis."

"Why?"

"I can't tell you the reason. I can only warn you."

"Alexander was right. You don't trust anyone."

"You shouldn't either. Do you have a plan?"

"Yes. I have a plan to get the children away from

here."

"Guns, supplies," I remind him. "Lina is like a walking map, Ian." I start to pace the living room.

"I know," he says proudly.

"I think we should meet up in Hanford if there's a problem."

"That's across the country." He shakes his head. "We'd never make it that far. Not with two kids in tow."

One of the Guardians shifts in its sleep in the hallway. "The Guardians will follow you. They'll keep you safe."

"You put a lot of trust in those dogs."

"I trust them more than most people."

"Okay, so Hanford."

"You'll be safe there. We can trust them. If you have to, stop at Wolf Creek. I wasn't there long enough to get a good understanding of Blackmore. Still, if I get him on board he's not going to shun my family."

"Okay," Ian agrees.

"I should get some rest," I tell Ian, hanging my jacket on the hook next to the door. Ian does the same, following behind me as I walk down the hallway, headed for my bedroom. But just as I reach for my door handle, Ian grasps my arm.

"What are you doing?" I ask him, turning to see that he is standing close and I can smell the scent from the burning embers in the courtyard fire.

He smiles, his hand moving up my arm and tugging me away from my bedroom door. "Making sure you don't forget me while you're gone."

"I won't forget you," I tell him as he pulls me toward his room.

"I just want to make sure." He leans in for a deep

kiss. "I was afraid you forgot me before."

I pull back, seeing everything on his face that he told me he forgave me for. "I never forgot you, Ian. You were on my mind every day, every minute."

I let him lead me to his bed, grateful to be off my feet since it seems my legs have become wobbly, no doubt as a direct effect of his mouth and his hands. And before long I can tell what's happening. I remember the familiar feelings, the way his body reacts, the way mine does. I stifle a moan when he nibbles on the sensitive skin of my neck. He's getting too intense. I know where this goes next. And I already told him why I can't.

"Ian, stop." I press my hands against his chest.

"Shhh, it's ok." He tugs at my shirt. His fingertips brush against my abdomen, making it quiver.

"No it's not, we can't risk—"

"I found something to help," he interrupts, turning around and reaching into a drawer.

"What?" I ask out of breath.

He holds up a box... a box of condoms!

Covering my face with both hands, I let out a groan. This is so embarrassing. I feel like a teenager, my own husband begging me to sleep with him, scouring the town for the last box of condoms so I don't get pregnant.

"What do you think?" He kisses my neck in that tender spot again.

"I don't know, Ian." I look at the box and then back to his face. "It's been a while. A long while. I may have forgotten what to do."

"Don't worry, I'll show you what to do," he says with a wicked grin.

The Collection of Sovereign and Supplies

CHAPTER FIFTEEN

Just like our recent trip to Crystal River, Crane is sending us out sparsely equipped. It's just me, Sam and four Guardians. This time the train has been equipped with extra cars for the horses and weapons.

There are only Crane and the Volker crew that watch the gateway out of here to send us off as Sam and I load our respective bags onto the engine car.

"Godspeed," Crane tells Sam as he shakes his hand. Sam nods.

Crane turns to me. "You will hurry back won't you?" Crane asks me. It's a strange question since he knows just how much I dislike leaving the comforts and familiarity of my home and children.

"Of course I will." I give him a short smile.

We board the train and Crane waves from the platform as we pull away.

--

"This is nice," Sam says as we pull into the Wolf Creek District. He admires the view from the elevated train tracks which branch out over the fields.

As we pull up to the platform we see a man waiting for us. It's John Blackmore, their District Moderator. I forgot how much John reminds me of Elvis, tanned and rugged with his sandy-brown hair and wide smile.

"It's been a long time," John shakes my hand. "You're looking well."

"Thanks," I tell him, remembering how sick and pregnant I was the last time I was here. "John, meet Sam Salk, the Phoenix District Volker Sovereign."

"Nice to meet you." John gives Sam a hearty handshake and claps him on the shoulder. "What happened to Colonel Waters?" he asks me.

"He died." Sam gives me a look, like I might break or cry, but I don't. I already told Adam's grave what I think of him. "Just over two years ago," I tell John. "You didn't hear?"

"Don't have much time for gossiping out here." He replaces his hat, an old baseball cap which the embroidery has been pulled out of, removing whatever team it represented. "My condolences." He tips the hat at us. "I hear the Survivors are getting antsy up in the northeast."

"We've had a few threats in Phoenix and at Crystal River," I tell him.

"Have you had any here?" Sam asks.

"None so far. I imagine most didn't make it though. Or they went further south to escape the worsening winters, seek refuge in South America."

"But South America was slated for Reformation," I

say.

"Survivors didn't know that," John replies.

I feel terrible for those people. Living through the destruction here only to seek refuge in another country and relive it all over again.

"So you think you'll use the horses for transportation?" John asks.

"That's the plan," Sam tells John. "The roads are mostly overgrown outside the District walls. We think the horses will give us better mobility in an attack from the Survivors."

"Hmm." He scratches his sideburns. "I don't know much about fighting, but I guess that would work."

We stand in a moment of silence, watching a herd of buffalo run in the nearby field. The ground vibrates under our feet as the beasts thunder across the plains.

"So, the horses," John waves us along to follow him. "This change of events isn't what we've been planning for out here. As you know," he motions toward me. "This District was set up for reintegrating the domesticated animals into the wild. I was surprised by Crane's orders. Usually he doesn't budge much on the rules." He heads down a gravel walkway toward a large red barn. "We've had to change our operating procedure because of this. These horses were slated for release into the wild. We had to gentle and train them. Since we didn't have much time I'm afraid a few are still a little wild. That's why I have to send them with a handler. We're hoping they'll be ready for riding not long after you arrive back in Phoenix."

"We weren't planning on bringing another person back with us," Sam tells John.

"I know. I cleared it with Crane already. We didn't have much time to get them ready."

We continue into the barn and unlike the last time I was here the individual stalls have been removed and what remains is a large gated open space. There are horses with gleaming coats of all different colors and patterns. They take one look at us as we approach and a few gallop away, others seem to stand and stare at us. A cowboy-looking man walks around the fence, making his way toward us.

"This is Tim Johnson, he'll be looking after the horses," John tells us.

Tim looks young, as though he's in his mid-thirties. He has dark hair, a faint beard and a cowboy hat on.

He tips his hat at us. "Howdy," he says with a smile, reaching out to shake our hands.

"Tim, this is Andie Somers and Sam Salk. They're the people from the Phoenix District that I told you about."

"Pleasure," is all he replies with before he turns back to the horses.

John starts walking again, circling around the gated area until we reach an open door. Inside there is an office space with rows of filing cabinets and a desk.

"Just need you to sign for the horses, their food, and handler," John tells us.

"Sign?" I ask.

"Yes. I keep records here. How much livestock comes in, what's bred here, and what's released back to the wild." He holds a pen out to me and flattens a piece of printed paper on his desk. "Just in case there are any problems or issues with their genetic vitality. Don't want a repeat of what happened here before."

"Sure," I tell him, taking the pen from his hand. I scan the piece of paper. It's an invoice listing fifty horses which all seem to have identification numbers, there's barrels of food and water, bales of hay, and of course a note stating that Tim Johnson is leaving with the horses. I sign my name at the bottom and hand his pen back.

"I have something to speak with you about, John."

"What's that?"

"We need to go outside, where it's private."

"Sure."

We make our way out of the barn into the Midwestern afternoon sun. Sam looks about, ensuring we are alone and that there are no prying eyes.

"What's going on, Andie?" he asks.

"I'm not sure how to say this, John, but we're planning something, something that will change the Districts for good."

"And what's that?" He crosses his arms over his chest.

"We want Burton Crane out of the picture," I tell him.

"Are you serious?" he asks. "Did you learn nothing from the last time you were here and everything that's happened?"

"I know," I hold out my hand, trying to get him to listen. "I know, John, just give me a chance. There are a lot of people on board."

"Who?" he asks.

"All of the Phoenix Sovereign, Hanford, and I'd bet money on Crystal River."

"What do you plan on doing?"

"I'm not sure yet. We–"

"Well you can't well be planning a revolution without a plan!"

"I'm just getting people on board. And then the original Funding Entities will be in control. They won't have to worry about Crane."

"What are you going to do with him?" he squints at me as though he can see right through me. I know he's one of the original Entities.

"Maybe imprison him or banish him. We just want to make sure everyone is on the same page once he's out."

"Hmm," John grumbles and looks around.

I stand still, waiting for his decision. He can either join or turn me in right now. And I'm sure turning me in would mean certain death for all of us.

"It would be much easier with him gone. A little more," he circles his fingers in the air searching for the right word, "*democratic* without him."

"So you're in?" Sam asks. I had almost forgotten he was behind me.

"Yes. I'm in."

"And the rest of your people here?"

"Andie, we deal with animals here, we don't have many people."

"But what about your other Sovereign?"

"There's just a few of us. I'll get the others on board," he promises me.

I let out the breath I've been holding, relieved.

"Well, now that that's taken care of, I have someone who's been waiting for your arrival. He asked to see you."

"Who?"

"Dr. Belamy Drake."

"So you found him? After all of that?" When I was here last there was a man impersonating Dr. Drake. And I shot him in the head, adding another tick to my list of bad things I've done since The Reformation took over.

"Yeah," John replies.

We walk to a nearby barn, a smaller one this time. I recognize it immediately; it's the one which held their genetics laboratory. This time when John opens the door there is not a handful of workers milling about. There is just one man in a white lab coat. He turns as the door opens. It's Dr. Drake, with the same paunch belly, same yellowed eyes, same white tufts of hair around his balding head.

"Mrs. Somers," he smiles as he crosses the room. "Of all the people I would expect to see I have to say you are the last."

"Was that a compliment?" Sam asks under his breath.

I don't answer. I just keep my eyes on the man who made me decide to leave the genetics field so long ago.

"I'm so glad you came." He stops in front of me. "I wanted to thank you personally."

"For what?"

"If you hadn't identified my imposter they would have never sent another team out to find me. And well, you saw what was happening here, all those horrid creatures that were being created."

He's talking about the mutated animals. The ones they sent me here to fix, but when I got here I had figured out their true problem. The person running the lab was not qualified, it was not Dr. Drake. Just an imposter, a plumber.

"Well," Dr. Drake continues. "It's a good thing you came here. We didn't need any more tinkering with the genome. We are getting things back in order here, back to nature, breeding strong animals, sending them out to repopulate in the wild like God intended." He smiles at me.

"Good for you," I tell him. "I'm glad to see you're doing a great job."

"Yes, well, I've heard you've been busy yourself. *District Matchmaker*," rolls off of his tongue like a curse word. "That's quite impressive, Mrs. Somers."

"We'll go get the horses loaded up," John interrupts. As they wander away from us I hear John mention something to Sam about the horses and grain.

Dr. Drake looks toward them and as soon as they are out of earshot, he leans toward me and says under his breath, "Put me on your team."

"Why would I do that?"

"I'm sure you need someone to check your work. Make sure you know what you're doing."

"I don't think so," I tell him. "Besides, I don't have a team. I work alone."

"Yes, you always did. I remember what you were like. It was years ago but I still remember that we could never replicate your work. What are you going to do when what you're doing doesn't work out? When these Residents turn into some horrible creatures."

"I know what I'm doing! The data doesn't lie, Dr. Drake. I don't need your help. I didn't need it when I worked for you and I don't need it now."

"You are still so cocky. Think of how they will make you suffer when this doesn't work. You know what they did to my imposter?"

Of course I know. I'm the one who shot him. I stare at him, reliving those moments in my head.

"They killed him," Dr. Drake spits the words from between gritted teeth.

I can see what he's trying to do. He did the same thing when I worked for him. He's trying to put uncertainty in my mind. He's trying to make me doubt my work. "This conversation is over. I'm done talking to you."

"I heard you abandoned all of those babies the day they took over your town."

"You don't know anything," I tell him.

"I know some things."

"No, you don't. I had to find my family and there were more than enough nurses on the unit when I left."

"The Residents here have received their injections. The ones that will alter their DNA and shrink their amygdala and then they will be the perfect docile humans Crane desired. I couldn't have done it better myself."

"You couldn't have done it yourself," I mutter.

"Well, I don't have to, thanks to you."

"What?"

"You're the one who made this possible."

"I didn't have a choice—"

"Are you sure?"

"What do you mean *am I sure*? Crane was holding my family. He... He told me I had to."

"And you never said no. You just did it."

"He forced me!"

"Did he hold a gun to your head?"

"He threatened my family!"

"He threatens everyone's family!" Dr. Drake's face turns a bright purple as he yells.

I quake with anger, trying to decide whether to walk away or scream at Dr. Drake.

"Do you believe in coincidences?" he asks.

"No. Not when it comes to Crane. Nothing is a coincidence with him. He has some twisted plan. He always has a plan."

"And if I told you there was someone higher than

Crane?"

"Why should I believe you? You have been a member of this District for what? All of five minutes? You don't know what's been going on. You have no clue who these people are and what they are capable of."

"Why should you believe anyone?"

"This conversation is just going in circles. I don't know what you want from me." I wave my hand at him and start to walk away.

Dr. Drake grabs my arm. "Protection!" He glances behind me at the Guardian that has been following me around ever since we arrived. "I want protection."

"From what?"

"Changes."

"I can't protect you. You know better than that."

"Yes, you can."

"What makes you think that? What does Crane have over you?" I ask. "What is he dangling over your head that's got you so scared?"

"The future. It's all about the future. I can't go back out there with the Survivors. It's bad."

"There will be more changes in the future. I can't help you. And I don't need you on my team. I don't need your help so don't ask me again." I wretch my arm out of his grasp.

He leans forward, his face flexed in seriousness. "This is why they chose you. Not because you were smart or strong. They chose you because you are weak and selfish and malleable," he says in a perfectly hurtful manner. "You're really not so different from the Residents. What's to stop them from altering your genes?"

"I'm done listening to you." I tell him. "Goodbye,

Dr. Drake. I hope this time I truly never see you again."

He chuckles lightly as I walk away.

I move as fast as I can without running to the train. Sam and John are standing near it talking and I can see the District Volker and Tim leading horses onto the rear cars, as well as bins and troughs.

"What's got you running like that?" Sam asks as I approach.

I shake my head at him. "Nothing," I reply, almost out of breath.

"Don't let him get to you," John says.

"Who?" I ask.

"That old crank Drake. He's been unpleasant since the day we pulled his sorry ass out of the slum he was holed up in."

"Shouldn't he be a little more grateful?" Sam asks.

"Most are. But Dr. Drake," John points toward the barn I just exited. "He has to make himself worthy here or he'll be out. We have plenty in Hanford who can take his place."

"I never saw him set foot in the lab when I worked for him," I admit to John.

"Seems the type."

"If there are others in Hanford who will work here then why go looking for Dr. Drake?" I ask.

John gives me a look. One that signifies I just asked a question that I should have been able to figure out on my own. I guess I know why he was here. Who better to make me doubt my work than my old boss asking to double-check everything that I've worked so hard on? If I had said yes that would have done nothing but show everyone that I don't have confidence in the vectors we created or the pairings. Maybe Dr. Drake already realized his job here was done. It was complete the moment he asked to be on my team. And now that this District has done so well reintegrating the livestock back to the wild, I wonder if Drake is on his way out already.

We make small talk as the horses are done being loaded on the train. Then I turn to John with one question I need to ask. "John, if this doesn't work, if Crane does something before we make it back to Phoenix, will you give my family refuge?"

"Your family is in Phoenix, what would they be doing out here?" he asks with a blank face.

"I told my husband to escape with the children. Crane has threatened them before and I just want to be prepared in case something happens and I'm not there."

"Yes, Andie, they are welcome here."

"Thanks, John. I was worried there would be no place for us to go if this doesn't work out."

"We won't shut you out here," he nods at me sincerely. "We've been looking out for you this entire time."

"Thanks, John." I give him a short smile and feeling the cell phone in my pocket, I'm antsy to call home and let Ian know that if he has to leave he can find refuge in Wolf Creek.

Tim reluctantly rides in the engine car with us. He was adamant about staying in the rear cars so he could monitor the horses but when Sam told him how fast the ride to Hanford would be, he decided to sit in the front with us.

As the train starts moving, I leave Sam and Tim, headed to the sleeping bunks to find my bags. I search the pockets for the cell phone I hid. My fingers grasp the cool plastic and I pull it out. Closing the door to

230

the sleeping bunk, I turn on the phone. The battery is still at full power from when I charged it. Now if I can only get a signal. I wait as the train moves and the icon on the phone circles until it pauses, flickers, and connects. Three bars of service.

Punching in the phone number to home, my heart beats fast, afraid that I might lose the signal before anyone answers. It rings one, two, three times.

"Hello?" I hear Ian's voice on the other end.

"Ian?"

"Andie, are you okay?"

"Yes, Ian I just wanted to check in."

"Where are you?"

"Just leaving Wolf Creek."

"And—"the other line crackles and statics.

"Ian!" I move the phone and see that there are only two bars of signal. "Ian!"

Between the static I hear his faint voice. "A... Andie?"

"Are the children safe?" I ask, afraid that I'm about to lose him and might have to finish this trip without knowing.

"They're," he replies between the static, "fine. Everything's fine."

Before I can answer the line goes dead. I check the phone. There's no bars, no signal.

CHAPTER SIXTEEN

Hanford

As we enter the Hanford District the sign comes into view. It's still rusted, the blue and white, sun-bleached lettering states that this is a Restricted Government Area, property of the United States Department of Energy. And then there's the abandoned high school that holds the elevator to the underground District floors.

There is one person waiting on the train platform for us. I recognize him right away, George Crossbender. He's dressed in the same khaki pants and a red button down shirt as the last time I met him. The summer breeze blows at his bangs, covering up the thick glasses perched on the end of his nose. He takes the glasses off, cleaning them on his shirt as we prepare to step off the train.

It's so nice to see a kind face and as I step off the train, I have to control the urge to hug him. Since I haven't spoken to him since the last time I was here, it would be an inappropriate gesture.

"Welcome, Andie!" He grips my hand hard and shakes it.

"So great to see you, George," I tell him.

"And this must be Colonel Salk?" He looks Sam up and down. "You're tall," he says and then looks to me. "He's your brother isn't he?"

"Don't you already know that?" I ask him.

"Nope, didn't know that. But it's easy to see. Who else do you have here?" he asks as Tim steps off the train.

"Oh, George, this is Tim Johnson from Wolf Creek. He's the handler for the horses." Tim walks forward and shakes George's hand.

"Howdy," Tim tells George with the tip of his hat. The horses whinny and stomp from the rear train cars. "If y'all don't mind, I'm goin' to stay here with the horses. Check on 'em, water 'em."

"Sure," I say.

"Well, if that's the case we had better hurry," George tells us. "We don't want the horses getting too stressed."

As Tim walks toward the back of the train to check on the horses, George leads us off the train platform toward a truck.

"We aren't taking the *secret elevator*?" I ask, pointing toward the abandoned High School.

"No, this will be much faster. We can cross the grounds and go directly to the Artillery Research Unit and get you what you need."

There is an old Jeep Wrangler waiting for us, the doors and roof removed. Sam looks at me expectantly. He can't sit in the back, his legs are too long. I give him an exaggerated huff before I climb into the back of the vehicle.

George gets in the driver's seat and starts the engine. He takes off with a heavy foot, speeding across the grounds. As he drives, I hear a strange noise coming from the tires, and when I look over the side I can see it's the sound of the Jeep speeding over the transparent roofing of the underground levels of Hanford. The thin layer of sand swirls and blows around the Jeep. And being able to see the drop of the multiple underground levels makes my stomach lurch. I lean back and focus ahead at the buildings coming into view. George stops just as we reach the first building and as we get out of the Jeep I recognize a few of the buildings. As we pass the building labeled *Natural Birthing Center* I notice that the building is dark and there is a board over the door.

"Whatever you told them last time you were here," George says as I stare at the empty building. "It worked well. Not a single birth in almost two years."

"Great," I tell him. All I did was threaten them with the loss of their children. I threatened that Crane would break up their families.

We follow George and as I take in the view of the buildings and people milling around us, my thoughts are interrupted by the sound of soft footsteps behind me. I turn to find two of the Guardians following us, panting. Strange.

George takes us to the building that leads us to the underground Artillery Research Unit. It's still massive, the rocky walls lined with the familiar green vines from the last time I was here. The ceiling is the same as before, thick glass with a thin coating of sand. Bright sunlight that filters through lights most of the space. The unit is filled with workers.

He collects a few of the workers, Sovereign, identified by the images burned into their wrists, just like most of the people that live here, the intellectually elite. Someone brings a large flat cart as we walk toward a small door in the rock wall.

"This," George informs us, "is storage. I like to call it the *Gun Safe*."

He pushes the gray metal door open and fluorescent lights illuminate the space in a long tunnel. There are boxes piled to the ceiling, and rows of neatly stacked weapons and supplies. Enough for three armies it seems.

"What do you think you might need to protect yourselves from the Survivors and Crane?" He gives me a soft wink

I don't like it when people wink at me. I look down the room at the rows of strange guns, weapons I've never seen before.

"I don't know much about these," I turn to Sam. "I'm not sure what to take back."

"I'll get this." He walks around me and down the room, the person with the cart follows him. I watch as Sam selects an assortment of pistols and assault style weapons. He tells the man with the cart how many of each to include. Next we come to crates of bullets. Sam discusses what's needed with the men and they collect the necessary bins and crates, loading them onto the cart. Next we come to the armor. Helmets, vests, padding, everything an army could need.

"Enough of these for two hundred men," he tells the man with the cart.

"Impressive, isn't it?" George asks from next to me. I turn to find him pushing up his glasses with this index finger.

"It's too much I think," I tell him. Sam and the man with the cart wander further away. "I don't think we even have two hundred Volker in Phoenix."

"He's collecting enough for Crystal River," George reminds me.

"Oh, yeah." I push my hair out of my face. "I guess I'm a little distracted."

"About what?"

"Do you know why President Berkley is so afraid of Crane?" I ask.

"You don't need to refer to him as the President anymore," George says with a frown.

"Okay. Why is Berkley so afraid of Crane?"

"Berkley was safe. He was one of the original Funding Entities, one of the very first, the leader of the free world, even in all of its great depression. Crane approached him with this plan to create the Districts, to start over. And Berkley agreed."

"He just agreed? Crane didn't have to threaten him with anything?"

"No. There were no threats needed. He wasn't going to be President for another term and after what he did to this country there wasn't enough funding to keep his security detail up until he died. He knows that someone would have assassinated him. The promise of safety, of running his own District, that was enough."

"So what changed?"

"The Reformation was a secret to the rest of the world, to the population. Only a select few knew of us, knew what was about to happen and there were certain rules."

"No one talks?" I ask.

"Precisely. We didn't know who all the other Funding Entities were when this all started, we just knew that they were there and that they would work just as hard as we would to ensure the plan didn't fail."

"Failure is not an option," I parrot out the phrase

I've heard one too many times since I've become a part of this.

"Yes. I'm sure you've heard this before. Failure was not, and is still not, an option. We do what we can to keep the Districts running, to keep the Residents safe, to keep this new society humming along as a well-oiled machine. So all Berkley had to do was sit back and relax and wait for this all to unfold."

"Let me guess, he didn't sit back?"

"No. Berkeley went out and hired someone to figure out who else Crane was working with."

"Adam?" I guess with a whisper.

"Precisely."

"And that is how Adam knew Crane wanted me to help him."

"Precisely."

"This still doesn't explain why Berkley is still so afraid of him."

"Crane has one more surprise, one more detail to unleash in all of this."

"What is that?"

"I can't tell you."

"But you just told me you are on our side, that you'll help us get him out."

"Yes, but I'm not sure it's entirely true. Could just be a rumor between Entities."

I shake my head in disappointment. "You said that you're on our side, George."

"Don't worry, Andie, I am," he assures me with a smile, pushing his glasses back up on his nose.

"I don't like this," I tell George. "It feels like you're lying to me."

"I don't lie, Andie. This is just one fact Crane must bring to light on his own, that's all. Besides, if I wasn't on your side, I wouldn't have drawn up a plan to get you around the Tonopah District." He hands a piece of paper to me, a map of the intact train tracks, expertly drawn with a way to avoid even getting close to Tonopah.

"How do you know these tracks are secure?" I ask him, noticing the tracks veer off of our previous route, taking a separate set that cuts across the country.

"We've already checked them. I sent a team out when you left Phoenix. They flew the length of the tracks to make sure they are secure."

I take the map from him. "I hope you're right."

"I'm right. Go to Crystal River. Get them on board. And then go home."

"And if the Survivors attack?"

"Then you will have the perfect diversion to get Crane out."

"I suppose you're right."

George looks away from me. "I think Sam is done."

I look up and see Sam walking toward us, the other men behind him, pulling the cart loaded with supplies. "How will we get all of this back to the train?" I ask.

"We have vehicles and the workers here can help," he ensures me with a pat on my shoulder.

As I watch Sam walk toward us, I am reminded of the pact I made with Blithe.

"George?" I ask.

"Yes?"

"Why aren't you married?"

"Whoever said I wasn't?"

We return above ground to the Jeep. The Guardians sit, waiting and watching as we get in the vehicle. George pulls away, speeding across the sandy plain just as he did before. Sam turns around, his hair blowing wildly in the wind, and points behind us. I turn to see the Guardians running behind the Jeep at a steady pace. When I turn back around to face Sam he points at the speedometer. George is driving over eighty miles per hour. Sam smiles, a glimmer of wit in his eyes. He must be thinking the same thing I am: I've never known a dog that could run eighty miles per hour.

CHAPTER SEVENTEEN
Crystal River

The route George Crossbender mapped out for us was tiresomely uneventful. We saw nothing. Not a single person, or house, or demolished city. The tracks were spread across some obsolete stretch of land that held only emptiness. The sweltering Florida air was almost a welcome change among the monotony of the cross country trek.

"Horses won't last long in this heat," Tim warns us as Sam slows the train to enter the Crystal River District. There is movement in the surrounding tropical vegetation, the random movement of a heavy branch, the blur of a dark figure moving between the trees.

"We won't be here long," Sam replies.

"Someone's watching us out there," Tim says as he steps out of view of the engine car windows.

The now heavily guarded gate to Crystal River opens, allowing us inside. We slowly pass the grassy open area between the electrified fence and wall encompassing this District.

"Something's wrong," Sam says. The train lurches a bit as he slows it further.

"What's going on?" I walk up next to him. Sam points ahead of us. There is a row of Volker standing in our path, guns drawn. I notice that we aren't even inside the cement wall, we aren't close to the train platform. No, we are in the same location where we interviewed the Survivors, just far enough away to control problems and force the problem outside the walls. Now we are the ones looking down the barrels of twenty semi-automatic weapons.

Sam stops the train.

"What should we do?" I ask.

"I'm not sure." He moves to reach behind one of the benches, pulling out a duffel bag.

"What's that?" I ask.

He opens the bag, pulling out two pistols. He hands one to me and one to Tim. By the time he's done, the Volker outside have moved closer. I recognize Colonel Ramirez outside the window. There is the sound of a fist rapping on the door. I look to Sam.

"What do you think is going on?"

"Andie?" I hear Ramirez shout from outside the door. "Sam?"

"What do we do?" I ask Sam, my heart racing.

"Stay where you are," he says as he steps toward the door.

There is another sharp rapping on the door. "Andie?" Ramirez shouts.

Sam whips the door open. "What's this all about, Ramirez?"

The stern look seems to melt off of Ramirez's face. "You're all okay?" he asks.

"Why wouldn't we be?" Sam asks him.

"You missed your stop in Tonopah. We were afraid the train was intercepted."

"We had a change of plans," Sam tells him.

Ramirez leans into the engine car and looks around. He glances at Tim before his eyes stop on me. "You sure?" he asks. I nod.

"Okay, you can pull the rest of the way in." Ramirez steps away, signaling to the Volker to move off of the tracks. Sam pulls the train the rest of the way into Crystal River, stopping at the platform.

Emanuel is waiting for us when we exit the train. "Crane called," he snaps at us. "You were supposed to stop in Tonopah yesterday evening and pick up troops, what happened?" He looks from me to Sam.

"We had a change of plans," I tell him as Colonel Ramirez jogs up behind Emanuel, his weapon slung over his shoulder. I turn around noticing he's alone. "Where's the rest of the Volker that were with you?"

"Guarding the fence," he says as Ramirez wipes the sweat off of his forehead.

I look at Emanuel. "The Survivors are watching us," he says. "They are always at the fence, day and night. We've had to keep Volker out there to guard the entrance. Now, what's this about changing your plans?"

"I had to go to the Districts where I had the greatest possibility of getting everyone on board," I tell him.

"What do you mean?"

"We couldn't stop in Tonopah," Sam tells them. "Sakima would never side with us on this."

"You're planning something, aren't you?" Emanuel asks me.

"We want Crane out," I tell him. "He's a loose

cannon. I have most of the other Funding Entities on board."

"Who else?" Emanuel asks.

"Wolf Creek, Hanford and the other Sovereign in Phoenix," I tell him.

"What about Galena?" Emanuel asks. "Did you speak with Berkley?"

"I don't have time to go all the way to Galena. But from the sound of it, Berkley doesn't much care for Crane."

"What's in it for us?" Emanuel asks. "If we side with you?"

"We have weapons for you," I tell him.

"And horses," Sam speaks up.

"I don't have orders to leave horses here," Tim interrupts from behind us. I almost forgot he was here, listening this entire time.

I hold my hand up, silencing him. "The original plans of the Funding Entities remain the same," I tell Emanuel. "The only change is that Crane is out of the picture."

"What are you going to do to him?" Ramirez asks.

"Exile him, imprison him. We're not sure," I tell them.

"Well," Ramirez looks to Emanuel. "That would explain why we lost communications."

"You lost communications with Crane?" I ask.

"Yes," Emanuel tells us. "This morning I've been unable to contact Crane. This is unlike him."

This is too early for Crane to be disappearing. Elvis and Ian agreed to wait until we made it back or if the Survivors attacked while we were gone. This change of events is unplanned, unexpected and it worries me. "We need to get home then," I tell Sam.

243

"Why didn't you stop in Tonopah and get them on board? You were supposed to bring troops to help us," Emanuel asks.

I shake my head at them. "Sakima keeps everyone in the Tonopah District medicated, so they will listen to him. Do you really think it's a good idea having armed Volker from Tonopah in our Districts, following the orders of Sakima?"

"I've never been fond of Sakima," Emanuel replies with an itch of his chin.

"We will leave you horses and weapons," I tell them.

"Are you trying to bribe us?" Emanuel asks.

"Hell yes. And having Crane gone should be an adequate bribe. The horses and weapons are the icing on the cake," Sam tells them. "They are for you to defend yourselves from the Survivors until we get a chance to deal with them ourselves."

Emanuel shifts on his feet. "Ramirez, go get the others. Andie can fill them in while you help unload what they've brought us."

Ramirez leaves, walking toward their District Headquarters which is just across the parking lot from the train platform. The heat rises off of the cracked blacktop in waves and swirls around his legs as he walks.

"Tim." I turn to find him glaring at me. "I need you to leave half of the horses here."

"Them horses ain't ready," he says in an angry country drawl.

"Then leave the ones that are closest to ready. I'm sure you know the ones," I tell him. "I have to call home."

I step away from the men as they walk toward the

244

cars holding the cargo. The horses whinny and stomp, eagerly awaiting their release from the stuffy train. I open the cell phone, noticing that the battery is less that twenty-five percent but there's a full signal. I press redial and wait. The phone rings. It rings and rings and no one answers. I end the call and dial the number again, my heart rate picking up, my mind running a mile a minute. This can't be good.

I turn to find Ramirez leading Richard Ruiz to where I am standing. I see the gleam of Richard's fancy watch and I can barely believe he's wearing a dark gray suit in this heat.

"So," Richard starts as he gets within earshot of me. "I hear you're planning a revolution. I knew you were trouble when I met you." He gives a sly smile.

"I'm not planning a revolution, Richard," I tell him. "I didn't plan anything. I was just asked to help rally the other Entities. Where are Javier and Mateo?"

"They aren't Entities, therefore they don't get to hear this," Richard replies.

"I assumed that didn't matter here since Ramirez has been present for all of our conversations."

"That is because Goyo Ramirez is one of us."

I look behind Richard, at Ramirez, who shrugs his shoulders at me. "Of course he is."

"Did he fill you in then? Are you on board?"

"Details, my dear," Richard says. "What are the details?"

"We are bribing you with guns, horses and Crane's removal from the Funding Entities. Are you with us?"

"How do you know Tonopah wouldn't like to join in?" he asks. "I heard you never stopped to ask them."

"If you know anything about Tonopah, Richard, then you know Sakima is just like Crane; he would never agree, he would side with Crane. And if we exile Crane I'm sure he will run straight for Tonopah."

Richard looks toward the blue sky, contemplating. After a moment he turns back to me. "I suppose you're right."

Feeling the sweat trickle down my back, I ask him, "Aren't you dying in that suit?"

"I'm used to it," he smiles. "I'm originally from Rio de Janeiro." His accent suddenly turns thicker, his voice dropping a few octaves as though he's just revealed a deep secret.

I blink at him. "Aren't you dying in that suit?" I ask again.

Richard laughs. "I'm used to the heat." He wipes his hand across his brow. "See, I'm not even sweating."

"That's great. You want to help unload?" I point to where Tim and Sam are unloading the horses by leading them down a wooden ramp and off of the train. Emanuel takes the reins from Tim and, talking gently to the horses, he leads them away.

As Richard and Ramirez leave to help unload, I open the cell phone and try calling home again. I count the rings: fifteen. There's still no answer.

Sam and Tim slide closed the door to the train car that holds the horses. Then they move on to the car holding the weapons. I walk over to them as Sam pulls crates of securely packed weapons, bullets and armor to the edge of the opening. The other men lift the crates in pairs, carrying them to the shaded area of the train platform.

"Sam," I interrupt him. "No one is answering the phone in Phoenix."

He stands, sweat dripping down the side of his face, saturating his Volker uniform. "We'll leave as soon as we're done."

Richard and Emanuel stand at the opening to the train car, next to me. "Survivors are getting brave," Emanuel tells us. "We've had a few try to jump the fence."

"How is that possible?" I ask him. Their electrified fence is over twenty feet high.

"There are some young ones, they climb the trees, try to swing themselves over."

"What did you do to them?" I ask.

"Nothing." Emanuel reaches for the next crate that Sam sets down. "The fence took care of them."

And by that I know he means it fried them to a crisp.

We leave half of the horses and almost half of the weapons and armor. "We'll be in contact," I tell Emanuel and Ramirez as I step on the train to leave. Tim paces the engine car, stopping only to look nervously out the windows at the horses we've left behind.

Sam starts the engine and, driving forward, turns the train around on the loop track ahead of us. I wave at Emanuel out the window as we pass them again. As we get closer to their fence, the Volker walk closer to the entrance, readying their weapons.

"I think it might be best to get up to speed as soon as possible," I tell Sam, noticing the movement in the nearby vegetation. Just like before, branches quiver and shadows move within the tropical forest.

"Yup," he replies, pushing the gear forward.

--

As the evening darkens, Tim leaves the engine car to

head for the sleeping bunks. I flip open the cell phone, the battery icon is red and there is only one bar of signal. I dial home. There's still no answer.

"You're going to kill that battery," Sam warns me from the helm.

"It's almost dead already," I tell him.

"We'll be home soon. Just a few more hours, probably make it home by dawn."

I nod at him, my head heavy with exhaustion and anticipation. My body isn't sure if it should sleep or pace. "I don't like traveling," I admit to Sam.

"I know," he replies. I can almost see his face with the soft glow from the single bulb that is attached to the wall behind him. "Sis?" he asks.

"Yeah."

"Do you ever remember what it was like before all of this?"

"Every day."

"You remember when we were kids?"

"Um hmm." I remember his tall, gangly arms and legs. Everyone called him my big brother even though I was almost six years older than him. I remember living in a time when the only worries we had were what we would get for Christmas or what brand of backpack we would pick out for school.

"Do you remember when Mom and Dad used to take us to the lake, to that fish place?" He looks out the window quickly. "We would have dinner and ice cream and then throw rocks into the water. I can't remember the name of it. Do you remember?" he asks me.

I close my eyes, trying to remember. I can see us standing on the shoreline, the shadows of the seagulls circling overhead. The smell of dried lake weeds mixed with the heavy scent of fried food. Sam holds a giant rock over his head and tosses it into the lake water with all of his might. I see the white clapboard building, weather worn and facing the lake.

"Rudy's," I tell him. "I think it was called Rudy's."

"Yes!" he exclaims. "Rudy's, that's the name of it. They had the best chicken nuggets. Oh, I can taste them now. I miss that food."

"Oh my God, Sam," I laugh a little. "You were just talking about this great fish shop and then you say you loved their chicken nuggets."

"I guess I just miss it all." He moves to sit next to me.

"I do too," I tell him, leaning against his shoulder.

"Do you think this will work?" he asks.

"It's kind of late to be asking that, isn't it, Sam?"

"Probably. I just worry what else will happen when we get back."

"Me too. Things will never go back to normal, I know, but I would just like them to remain at a constant."

He stretches his arm behind me and gives me a brotherly hug. "That would be great," he says.

We sit in silence for a moment, listening to the hum of the train.

"Do you remember that girl I was dating in High School? She had red hair. Jessica?"

"Yeah," I tell him. "I think that was the longest relationship you were ever in."

He pinches my shoulder. "Stop!" I swat at his hand. "Admit it. You went through girls faster than Lina went through diapers."

"I know," he says with a smile. "I just wonder where she is, what she's doing now." He stops. We both know what question comes next. I wonder if she's still alive, if she survived the bombings.

"You lonely, Sam?"

As I feel him shrug next to me, I remember the promise I made Blithe.

"I have a secret to tell you, Sam."

"Hmm. That's not really a surprise."

"Blithe has a crush on you," I tell him bluntly. I feel him stiffen a little. "And there's more."

"Okay."

"Blithe has been writing reports on the children and sending them to Crane. She's the one writing to Crane about Raven not meeting his milestones. I asked her to change them."

"What did she say?"

"She said she would, but in return she wants me to pair you two together."

I feel his body soften this time. "So you're going to pimp me out, is that it?"

"I kinda told her I would. You know what Crane said about Raven. So what do you think? She's pretty, and smart, and tall, like you."

"Don't you have to double-check our genetic makeup in your computer programs?"

"Not anymore. Not with Crane out of the picture. Actually, I guess none of this matters with Crane out of the picture. I just wanted you to know."

"Well–" Sam is interrupted by the lurching of the train, the kind of forcing lurch that is only made when something moving at a high speed makes impact with something else that is standing still.

Sam grabs my arm as the force knocks me out of my seat. But since he's being tossed out of the seat too, he doesn't stop me. We both land on the floor with a heavy thud. There's another thud from the sleeping bunks, combined with the sharp squeal of the train pushing against something. Sam crawls forward to the controls and pulls the train to a stop.

"What just happened?" I ask, pulling myself to my feet.

"I think we hit something." Sam walks toward a bench on the other side of the car and, lifting the bench seat, he pulls out a shotgun and a fully loaded magazine for the handgun on his hip.

I hear Tim's footsteps as he stumbles out of the sleeping area. Even in the dim light I can see he's holding his hand to his head and a trickle of blood streams down his face. "Think y'all hit something," he mumbles.

"Take care of him, Andie." Sam says in a hurry. "I'll go see what happened."

Sam heads for the door, one of the Guardians at his heels, following him outside. The others stay and watch the door as Sam closes it.

I guide Tim toward the light. "What did you hit your head on?"

"Not sure," he mumbles, pulling his palm away from his temple. Blood streams down his face.

I take Tim's hand and move it back to his head. "Sit down and keep pressure on that. I'll be right back."

I run to the bunks, pushing the door open to the first one I come to. I grab a pillow off of the bed and strip the pillowcase off of it. Next I grab the sheet, rolling it into a ball and shoving it under my arm. The fabric is thin enough to rip into bandages. Running back to where Tim is sitting, I rip the seams of the fabric. I kneel down, ripping the sheet to make a bandage to soak up the blood.

"Here," I pull Tim's hand away from his head to

place the folded fabric in his hand. He stares at his palm, dripping in blood. His face pales. "It looks worse than it is. Head wounds bleed like crazy." I tell him, moving his arm to press clean fabric to the gash on his temple.

"Should check on them horses," Tim mumbles to me.

"I'm sure they're fine," I tell him as I move his hand and replace the saturated strip of sheet with a fresh one. I take one of the long strips and fashion it around his head, holding the makeshift bandage in place.

Wiping my hands off, I look at the door. The three Guardians stare at the exit. I pull the cell phone out of my pocket, my arms shaking, and flip it open, wishing I could call for help. The screen is black. If there was anyone I could call, the phone is dead and it's no use to me now. I set it on the bench and walk toward the door.

"Stay here," I tell Tim. "I'm going to check on Sam."

"You sure that's a good idea?" he asks, squinting to look out the windows in the dark.

"Probably not."

I step out of the door and into the night.

CHAPTER EIGHTEEN

"Sam?" I ask, stepping out of the train. The Guardians push their way ahead of me. I lock Tim inside and wait a moment for my eyes to focus in the darkness.

The Guardian that followed Sam barks. I head toward the sound, the three remaining Guardians walk by my side, each emitting a low growl. Hearing a rustle from in front of the tracks, my heartbeat picks up, and the hairs rise on my arms. Just as the rustling stops, I notice Sam's Guardian standing a hundred feet from me on the tracks, facing the dark woods, growling.

"Sam?" I ask louder, picking up my pace to investigate what the Guardian is growling at.

There is a loud popping sound followed by the whine of the Guardian in front of me. I rush toward it, bending down as the Guardian slinks to the ground.

"What's wrong?" I whisper to the dog, rubbing my hand over the Guardian's thick coat. When I get to its shoulder I feel something wet and sticky. Just as I pull my hand away, focusing in the moonlight, I realize the substance is blood.

Something is wrong, terribly wrong.

Three more popping sounds rip through the night, followed by the *thud* of the three Guardians near me dropping to the ground. A hard shiver runs down my back, an internal warning to get the heck out of here. But I can't go without my brother.

"Sam!" I shout into the night, standing to my feet. "Sam, where are y–"

Before I can finish, I hear the crunch of gravel under a boot. The soft settling of a thoughtfully placed foot on the ground behind me quiets me, and before I get a chance to turn around, or think to run, I'm pushed down, and a boot is placed firmly in the middle of my back holding me forcefully against the ground. A rough, musty smelling fabric is placed over my head as I try to look around. A rough hand draws my wrists together behind my back and I can feel them winding a rough rope around my left wrist.

They pause before tying my right wrist, twisting it to get a better look at the mark there. The click of a flashlight and a rough finger running over the skin of my wrist comes next.

"Holy shit," I hear.

"What?" a forceful voice asks.

"It's her."

"Who?"

"That Sovereign one from Phoenix. Be a pity when they find out she's lost."

"How do you know?"

"Look at her wrist. She's the only female one in that Phoenix District."

A rough hand twists my arm. "That's a damn prize. Let's go."

I hear the groans of men as they pull me up by my

254

arms. Twisting at the waist, I try to pull my shoulders out of their grasp. Large hands settle on my shoulders, holding me in place.

"Let me go," I shout through the fabric.

One of them laughs. "This one's feisty," another voice says from behind me.

"Sam!" I yell through the fabric. "Tim!"

"That's enough," a deep, soft voice says.

"What are you doing? What do you want?" I ask.

That voice doesn't respond. Instead, hands move my shoulders and give a gentle push, or maybe a pull, either way, I walk. It's not long before I hear the excited whinny from the horses. They've brought me back to the train.

"Don't open that door," the deep voice next to me instructs.

"They have horses," one of the other men states.

"What else is on the train?" the deep voice next to me asks.

I think to lie. I don't want them to know that the train is fully loaded with an arsenal of weapons. That would be valuable to these people. But maybe, maybe they would let me go if I told them.

The large hand squeezes my shoulder, promising pain if I don't answer. "There's horses," I say, feeling my voice shake.

"What else?" Fingertips press crudely into the sensitive area between my clavicle and shoulder.

I pause, biting my lip in an effort to calm myself and focus. "You can take it," I tell him. "Take it all, just... just let us go," I plead.

"What else?" he asks, his voice gaining an edge.

"Let me go. Let us go. You can have it all," I beg, knowing that giving up the horses and the weapons would put Phoenix at an extreme disadvantage should the Survivors make it past our walls.

"I can make her talk," one of the other men says. I can almost hear him smiling as he speaks.

"She's not to be damaged," the deep voice says as his fingertips sink deeper into my skin. I bite my lip harder. My knee seems to bend on its own, trying to draw my shoulder away from his painful pressure. It doesn't work.

"There's horses," I finally tell them. "And... and guns."

The hand leaves my shoulder and I can feel the cool night air blow around me as the warm bodies of the men walk away. The doors of the train cars slide open. The horses stomp. A crate is being dragged. I move my feet, testing my limits. No one stops me. There is the scraping sound of another crate, followed by the sound of wood being stressed and cracked. They must be trying to pry open the crates.

Stepping to the side, my feet hit something hard. I tap around with my toes feeling what can only be the metal rails of the train track, knowing that the forest is behind me, I back up until I hear something, the sound of someone breathing heavily near me. Not right next to me, but close enough for me to hear them. Knowing that the men are sifting through our guns, it can only be one person.

"Sam?" I ask.

"Andie?" I hear Sam's muffled voice.

"Where are you?" I ask over the sound of the men dragging the crates. Shaking my head, I try to loosen the bag.

"I don't know. I can't see," Sam replies.

"Me either. What do we do, Sam? They killed the

Guardians. All of them."

"Run, Andie." Sam says firmly. "Get out of here. Did you see who they are?"

"No. I didn't see anything. It was dark, they knocked me down from behind."

"It's a group of Survivors. You need to run. They'll kill us!"

"But... They tied my wrists. Sam, I can't–"

"Go hide in the woods. It's dark enough, they won't find you. Run and hide."

I can't think of anything worse than being in the woods at night with my head covered and my wrists bound, alone. "I can't leave you, Sam."

"Go. Now. Before they are done pilfering the weapons. When you get yourself free just follow the tracks back to Phoenix."

"How far away are we?" I hear Sam moving closer to me.

"Probably somewhere near Pennsylvania."

It will take me forever to get home from here. And with no supplies I might just die trying. Especially if I run into any more Survivors.

"Go, Andie!" Sam urges, knocking his shoulder into me. It's enough to almost knock me off of my feet.

"No. I can't leave you."

"You have to. Now go!"

"Sam..."

"Go. That's an order." He bumps into me again, harder this time.

"Okay... okay."

I turn and walk at a hesitant pace, afraid to run since my balance is off having my arms secured behind me. I'm also afraid that I'll run face first into a tree and knock myself out. Shrubs catch on my ankles, my shoulder scrapes against a tree trunk. The sound of the gun crates scraping across the floor of the train car lessen behind me.

I count the trees as I brush by them or smack into them. When I pass seven trees the scraping sound stops. It's followed by shouting. They must be yelling at Sam. I walk faster, a near-running pace. A low branch slaps my face. If I could just see, I need this bag off my head. I shake my head trying to loosen the fabric. The men yell louder. Then the worst sound fills the night, the popping sound of one of the handguns. I drop to the ground. After a few moments of silence and rapid heartbeats, I roll slightly, trying to get further away or find something to hide behind. Feeling a tree at my feet, I scoot down and prop myself against it.

I wait, crouched on the ground behind the tree trunk. The base of the tree poking at my back sharply gives me an idea. Using the sharp nub of the tree trunk I rub my head until I feel it catch on the fabric that's covering my face. Lowering myself until I'm flat on the ground again, I work the bag off my head. And then, just like that, it's off. I take a deep breath, letting my eyes adjust to the night. There are a few slivers of moonlight filtering down between the leaves of the trees. Sitting up, I look around, seeing the stretch of forest in front of me. I turn, peeking around the side of the tree trunk that's barely thick enough to conceal me. I can see motion and it looks like I'm barely ten yards from them. I can hear Sam's voice but not what he's saying. I also hear the voices of the others. My heart is pounding, my head thudding right along. Sam told me to run and now I need to.

I push myself up, using the tree as a support until I'm standing. And then, taking one last glance behind me, I run deeper into the woods. Twigs snap under my boots. Branches scratch at my arms and legs. Having the bag off of my head isn't much better considering the dark night. And since my wrists are still bound, my balance is still off.

When I'm far enough away that I can't hear them any longer, I slow myself, afraid of getting too far from the tracks, knowing that they can help me get home. Veering to the right, I start running again at a slower pace. More twigs break. The leaves rustle and crunch under my feet. My breathing is too heavy and I'm making too much noise. I slow myself to a stop, twist my wrists trying to loosen the rope. The movement makes the rough ties dig into my skin harder. I walk, twisting and pulling the rope, trying to break free. As I'm standing there, struggling to free myself, I feel a sharp *ping* on the side of my head. The object hits me so hard that I'm certain I hear a hollow knock when it connects with my skull. This is followed by a bright explosion of light behind my eyes and pain and the feeling of my body dropping to the forest floor.

--

My world has shifted.

It is daytime and I am no longer standing in the dark forest but hanging over something incredibly warm, covered in rough hair, and moving. I can still feel the rope around my wrists. But instead of being tied behind me, they are now hanging over my head, which throbs. I slowly open my eyes to find myself staring at the flank of a horse.

This is an uncomfortable position.

I move my arms, propping myself up on my elbows

and trying to stop my body from bouncing off of the horse's side with each step it takes. I soon realize that up is nothing more than parallel to the ground. My stomach churns.

"Hold up," I hear a deep male voice shout.

A pair of dirty boots step into my view. I look up, following the height of the form in front of me, stopping at his face. He frowns at me. His hair is dark blonde and long enough that it's pulled into a ponytail. He has gray eyes and a thick beard that covers his face. "You ready to behave?" he asks with the same deep, soft voice I've heard in the dark.

Since I don't have many other options, I nod my head yes.

He reaches forward and, grabbing me under my shoulders, he pulls me off the horse's back. Before I know it, I'm standing in front of him. He's tall. But then, so are most people compared to me. He wears relatively clean clothes: jeans, boots, a T-shirt with a light jacket over it. He doesn't look like the vicious Survivors described to me. He looks...normal.

"You're Andromeda?" he asks me.

I nod to him.

"I'm Mack." He raises his hand to point behind us, down a path lined with tall grass. "We have someone who wants to meet you."

"What did you do with my brother and Tim?" I ask the man named Mack.

"We let them go. They started their train and left."

"You're lying to me. What did you do with them?"

"I have no reason to lie to you." Mack scowls down at me.

I stare at him, still waiting for an answer.

"What do you think we are, barbarians?" he asks

with a smile that shows a deep dimple in his chin even through the beard.

"You didn't let me go," I glare at him.

"Can't do that. You're important to them."

"What about the horses and the weapons?" I ask.

"Stashed them. We'll send a team back to get them later."

"So where are you taking me?" I ask, looking around. We are stopped on a path that cuts through a field of tall grass. Further away a forest surrounds us. There's no sign of the train tracks I was supposed to follow home. I can barely control the tremble that rolls through my body as I begin to understand the predicament I am in. Crane will not be happy with this. And most likely he will make Sam pay for losing me.

"You don't need to know," Mack says.

"You don't understand," I tell him. "Crane will kill them for losing me." I shake my bound arms, feeling the tears swelling behind my eyes. I have no control over this situation at all. Nothing to bargain with and no visible escape. This feeling is terrible. I begin to take short stuttered breaths. "I can't be here," I tell Mack, panicking. "I can't be here. I have children, a husband. I can't do this. You can't do this to me. You don't know what he'll do to us!'"

Suddenly the tears are streaming down my face. I make no attempt to stop them. Part of me hopes that they will see that I am nothing more than a weak sobbing woman, and maybe, just maybe, they will have pity on me and let me go.

"I have to go home." I hold my hands out, twisting my wrists at him. "You don't understand what they're like. He'll hurt my family." Just the thought of Crane punishing Sam for losing me makes my stomach churn harder. The side of my head throbs.

Mack looks at me with a blank stare. He must be expecting this. Or maybe he wasn't expecting it to be this bad.

"You're one of their Sovereign. You are one of the ones in charge," Mack says, pointing a thick index finger in my face.

"No." I shake my head at him. "You don't understand what it's like. I'm not in charge of anything."

Feeling a large tear run down my neck, I move my hands to wipe at it. When I move my hands back in front of me, they are not wet with tears, but with streaks of blood. I panic at the sight, probing the side of my face until I touch the goose-egg at my temple. It's then I remember standing in the night and feeling something echo off of my skull. My hair is matted to the area and I can feel warm blood trickling down my face from the wound. Moving my hands, I stare at all the blood.

"I think you need to settle down," I hear Mack say with his deep soothing voice.

But I can't settle down. I wipe at the side of my head again, breathing faster. More blood coats my hands. More tears pour out of my eyes. I feel the flush of saliva fill my mouth, which can only mean one thing: I'm going to puke.

Mack must sense this, as he steps aside just as I throw myself into the tall grass and let my stomach empty itself. When I am done, I stay there on my knees, crying into the tall grass.

"She's crazy," I hear one of the younger men whisper behind me.

"Shut it," Mack warns him.

I take a deep breath, trying to calm myself. I don't turn when I hear the footsteps behind me.

"You done now?" Mack asks.

"I think you gave me a concussion when you hit me in the head."

"Sorry about that, he wasn't supposed to hit you in the head, but it was dark."

"I don't usually act like this," I tell him between breaths.

He doesn't say anything to me, but he doesn't need to, I can feel him judging me with his eyes.

"It must be the head injury," I mumble to the grass.

Mack still doesn't respond. Instead, he stands there, waiting for me to get up. Eventually I do and then I wish I were still sitting. My knees are weak and I feel the blood drain from my head.

"Think you shouldn't be walking right now," Mack says as he observes me. He takes my elbow and leads me back to the horse I was slung over. Before I can say a word he grasps me around the waist and lifts me onto the horse as if I weighed nothing. "Have you ever ridden a horse before?" he asks me.

"Never."

"Swing your leg over the side and hold onto her mane. Chuck there will lead her." Mack waits as I adjust myself and grip the horse's thick, black mane. He pats the horse hard on its shoulder before walking ahead of me and waving to Chuck and the other man.

They walk.

"You're pretty stupid," the young one named Chuck says as he walks beside me, leading the horse. He has the same voice as the person who said they could make me talk. I notice a sling-shot hanging out of his back pocket and my head throbs at the sight of it. He must be quite the shot to hit me in the head in the dark. Even if he wasn't supposed to hit me in the head, I get the feeling that he meant to.

I don't talk back. Instead, I grip the horse's mane tighter between my bloodstained fingers. It was stupid, trying to run away at night. I should have stayed with Sam. I should have tried to do something other than save my own skin. Now I'm trekking through the Virginia mountainside with a group of Survivors. They stopped our train. They stole our horses and our weapons. And now I'm their prisoner.

--

We walk all day, stopping only once at a forest stream.

The horses drink. The men relieve themselves. Mack unties the rope from around my wrists and allows me a moment of privacy behind a bush. When I step out, finished, he holds the rope out. I sigh, and holding my hands out for him I notice the red marks around my wrists from the rope rubbing. I focus on the imprint of the Phoenix on my inner wrist. *We are your Sovereign.* I remember telling the room full of Residents. *We will take care of you.* But here I am taking care of no one. I wonder if I'll ever be able to go back there, if I will ever see my children again. Maybe I could get them to untie me and then I could run again. In the daylight, without the ties, I could be faster.

Mack stares at the mark too. "If you promise not to run, I'll leave them off for a bit," he says, as though he knows what I'm thinking.

"I promise," I tell him.

"Go get a drink from the stream." He begins coiling the rope around his hand as I walk away.

I stretch my arms on my walk, loosening the tense muscles before crouching at the stream. It's shallow, crystal clear and fast-moving. I rub my hands in the water to clean them. Cupping my hands, I bring some of the water to my face and smell it. It smells like nothing, just crisp, fresh water. In the calmness of the water I hold in my cupped hands, I get a glimpse at my reflection. My face is streaked with blood and dirt. I drop the water, unable to look at myself.

When we left Florida I had put a button down shirt over my tank-style blouse. Now, I unbutton it and submerge the corner of the shirt in the water. Ringing it out, I scrub my face with the shirt, try to rub the blood and dirt off. I bend down, scrubbing my neck and face until it feels clean. I lift the dry end of the shirt and dry my face on it. Then, cupping my hands, I drink.

As I drink, there is one thought that consumes my mind: I cannot stay here with these men; I cannot go wherever they are taking me.

When I am done, I stand and turn to the men. They busy themselves with the horses; talking in soothing voices, patting them, adjusting their rope harnesses. I thought Tim said they weren't ready for riding, but these ones seem pretty tame.

The third guy—they never said what his name is—he stands with another horse. This one has sacks hanging off each side and guns tied together and slung over each side of the horse.

"Ready?" Mack asks. He's less than a hundred yards from me.

I nod at him. Now's my chance.

I bend to pick up my wet shirt and as I stand, I glance toward Mack, then across the stream.

One heartbeat, that's all it took for me to decide

265

which direction to run in. And three steps, that's all it took for me to cross the cool crystal clear stream where I had just washed my face.

CHAPTER NINETEEN

I wouldn't recommend planning an escape with a concussion, and then actually carrying it out. I'm pretty sure I only made it five hundred yards before Chuck caught up with me. He grabbed onto the back of my shirt, effectively bringing my escape to a halt.

Swinging around, I raise one arm and smack him in the side of the neck, then I kick him in the balls. "That's for knocking me in the skull with the slingshot, jerk!"

As Chuck groans and grabs himself, I take off running with the sound of Mack yelling. Running around trees and over the debris of the forest floor, I don't have to turn around to know that they are following me. I can hear them, even over my labored breaths and the ringing in my ears.

A tiny bit of joy takes over the fear flooding my chest as I focus on the forest before me and see what looks like a narrow clearing filled with bright sunlight.

The tracks! It has to be the tracks.

Not even sure that I could keep running like this, or

what I would do once I make it to the clearing, I continue on with hope being the only thing keeping me moving.

I can tell by the sound of hollow pings hitting the nearby trees that they are shooting at me. Three hit my back. I weave side-to-side as I run, afraid that one more shot to the head and I'll be too damaged to do much for Crane any longer.

As the bright light of the clearing draws nearer, I reach out with one hand, wanting to pull myself toward it, toward home. But all that hope is dashed as a hard object pings off of the back of my head.

--

This time when I wake, I can feel that they strapped me to the horse. A tight rope digs into my back. Blinking to clear my blurry eyes, I can see that it extends around the horse's body.

I take in my surroundings.

This time Mack takes my horse's reins as we walk. I stare at the back of his head, noticing that his hair reaches almost to his shoulders. It's strange for a man. But then, I'm sure it's not easy getting a haircut these days. I haven't had one in years.

"What are those marks on your back?" Mack asks me. He turns, his gray eyes looking into mine.

He must have seen the marks when I was washing myself in the stream. I don't answer. I don't know how much he knows about the Districts and I'm definitely not going to be the one to tell him where they are. I don't want him knowing how much I know. And I'm pissed that they hit me in the head again. So I just stare back at him.

"You put them there or someone else?" he asks.

Someone else put every single one of them there but, "I didn't," is all I tell him.

He nods. It's a deliberately slow nod. One that says he understands my words and the tone of my voice, someone else put those marks on my back, the marks of each District, so I would never forget what I learned during my tour. Well, it looks like what I learned no longer matters, seeing how Crane no longer has control over me. Now the Survivors do.

"Where are we going?" I ask.

"Just up here a bit. Won't be long now."

I stare straight ahead, watching Chuck walk in front of us. The slingshot sways in his back pocket. Maybe if I could get a gun, or the slingshot, any weapon, maybe I could get myself out of here.

Even with all the thoughts of escape, I don't make a move. The horse is too high for me to easily get down, plus they've strapped me to the animal. And I'm sure I'm not much of a match for three men. I sigh to myself in defeat. It's a pathetic sigh, collected from deep inside my lungs. I inhale loud and blow it all back out. It doesn't help me feel any better.

Mack must hear me. "Give up with yourself?" he asks. It's almost like he's been listening to me talk in my head the whole time.

I decide to change the subject. "What state are we in?" I ask him. Sam had mentioned we were almost to Pennsylvania so that leads me to believe we are in the Virginias.

"West Virginia," he says with a nod. "One of the safest places you could be out here. Surrounded by state parks."

"So we're going to a state park?" I ask.

"Nope, sleepy little town in the middle of the state parks. Romney is what they call it, what the sign says anyway. There was no one left here when we came about."

"How long have you been here?"

"Long enough."

Hearing our conversation, Chuck turns and glares in our direction. Must be Mack isn't supposed to tell me these things.

"What do you want with me?" I ask Mack.

"I told you. Someone wants to meet with you."

"I don't know anyone out here," I tell him. "Who is it?"

"You'll find out. Soon enough." Mack swings his arm down and plucks a tall piece of grass from the ground, breaks it, and begins chewing on the end.

The walk continues for a few more miles until I see the break in the forest, the bright daylight shining in from a clearing. Mack stops my horse and begins untying the rope that tethers me in place.

I sit up, grasping the horse's mane as my head spins.

"We're almost there," he says as he pulls the coil of rope out of his pocket. "Hold your hands out." I do and watch as he coils the rope around my wrists. From another pocket I watch as he pulls out a piece of fabric and shakes it open. I recognize it, even though I never saw it in the daylight. Knowing what comes next, I bend down. He places the stiff cloth over my head and then we start moving again.

The horses' footsteps change from the soft steps of walking on the forest floor to the hollow clomps of them walking on pavement. It's not long before the motion stops. "Time to get down," Mack says. He grips me by my upper arms and pulls me down from the horse. Although he is tall and obviously strong enough to be placing me up on the horse and lifting me off, I still don't take kindly to being manhandled. Or maybe it's that we've come to our final destination and I fear what comes next. Either way, I wretch my shoulders from his grasp. It seems he just takes the rope that binds my hands and pulls me in the direction we are going.

"Step up," he says as my toes hit something hard. I stumble, trying to walk up the steps, unable to see. I must have made him angry, pulling away from him. Now he makes no attempt to help. He doesn't tell me that the steps stop and I wind up taking a step onto air and stumble. Mack just pulls me along. There is the sound of a door opening and I notice the difference in flooring and smell. Wherever we are, it's a place that hasn't been used for a long time. No longer feeling my arms being pulled along, I stop. Someone clears their throat.

"It's her," I hear Chuck's young voice announce proudly. "We've captured that Sovereign woman from Phoenix."

It's as if they've found someone so important, or the missing link, or a unicorn. I want to tell them that I am no one special. Nothing more than a prisoner, forced to do things I never wanted to do. I feel my wrist being twisted and inspected just like before.

"Thought she'd be bigger." I feel someone poke at my shoulder. "More regal or something. Short. She looks like a teenager."

I want to shout at them that I am an adult and I've finally reached the grand age of thirty. I have children at home waiting for me and a husband. But I don't say any of those things, I keep my mouth shut. I feel someone brush my hair away from my neck. They grasp the chain around my neck. My necklace. The one Adam gave me, the one I hung my wedding band on. He tugs hard, pulling it off. "Take her to the penthouse."

I turn my head, his voice suddenly sounding slightly familiar but hard to place with the disruption from the bag and the sounds of footsteps around me. Unable to place the voice, I am led away by a tight grasp on my elbow. We walk, up stairs and down long hallways. I hear a door open. The ties across my wrists are undone.

"Don't try anything stupid," I hear Mack's voice.

The cloth is pulled off my head. Someone shoves my shoulder, hard. I stumble and as the door slams I open my eyes.

This is not a penthouse.

This is a windowless room with a bare bulb hanging from the ceiling. There is a cot in the corner, a small sink, a toilet. And that's it. I turn around, running toward the door. There's no handle, no window, no bars. I bang on the door with my fist.

"Hey!" I yell. "Let me out!" I pound on the door with all my might. "Mack! Mack! Let me out of here!"

My shouts are only answered with silence. I walk across the room and, running, I slam my body into the door. It doesn't budge. It doesn't even move. I do it again and again, until my shoulder aches from the impact. Finally, I hear footsteps and voices. I watch the door, waiting for it to open, noticing a small hinge at the bottom of the door. The hinged portion pushes forward, hitting my foot. Someone has pushed through a tray with a bottle of water and a piece of bread.

Prisoner food.

CHAPTER TWENTY

Time passes. Too much time. Much more time than I am comfortable with. They turn the light off. They turn the light on. This is my only judgment of time since I have no clock and no window to see the light. I wash the blood out of my hair in the rust-stained sink. I spend my days yelling at the door, trying to get someone to let me out. No one does. Sometimes, when I hear the footsteps of people walking down the hall I shout at them. I bang on the door. I shout for Mack and Chuck to let me out. I wish I knew that other guy's name just so I would have another name to yell.

"Thought she was something special to them?" I hear a voice say on my fifth day. "They haven't sent anyone for her."

"That's because she's crazy," I hear Chuck's voice. "They were probably happy to get rid of her."

I stop my pacing and slouch against the wall just as a tray is pushed under the door. This time it's a boiled potato and a small bruised apple.

As I eat, I rub my fingers across the lump on my

arm where Crane injected the transmitter after I completed my final task and Morris died. Crane can track me and yet, he has sent no one. With the speed of that train Sam should have been home by the next morning after the night they took me, unless something happened to him.

They turn the light off. I finish my meal in the darkness. Feeling the rough door, I move my hands until I find the hinged area at the bottom and push the tray through before I make my way to the cot in the darkness.

I don't like this prison and all of its loneliness. I miss my old prison, The Pasture. I miss my home, my children, my husband, my long walks in the fields. That prison was much more tolerable than this one, even if I did have to deal with Crane. At least I had my family with me. At least I knew they were safe. Right now, I know nothing and it makes me think about how little I have known since The Reformation occurred.

--

Sometimes they give me what tastes like bread crumbled in some kind of milk, goat milk I think. Its thick consistency clogs my throat. It makes me wonder if they have a farm here. They must be growing their own food. This must be a settlement of some sort.

Today I get a spoon. I use the spoon to mark the wall. There are ten lines, ten days I think I've been here. I stare at the bottle of water, wishing it were coffee. I guess I was really quite spoiled having a coffee maker in my house. I'm not sure where they got the coffee beans from. I never asked. Thinking about it now, I realize that was quite stupid of me to never ask Morris where those products came from.

I open the bottle of water and take a sip. It tastes sweet today, as though they've added a bit of sugar. I stare at the wall. I pace the room. I hold my ear to the door, listening. Only footsteps, no voices. This is how I spend my day.

"Let me out!" I yell and bang on the door. "Mack! Chuck!"

Nothing.

The light is switched off. I lie down and close my eyes. The nightmares start. I've been so long without them I almost forgot how bad they were, how bad they are. They must hear me screaming in my sleep, whoever is standing guard outside my door. They wake me by pounding on the door. But the light stays off. It must still be night. Eventually I keep my eyes open, afraid to close them, afraid of what I will see. I lay there drenched in sweat, my throat dry, waiting until they turn the light back on.

When they push the tray into my room, I get up and sit by the door. More crusted stale bread and a bottle of water. My throat is so dry from the sweating nightmares. I open the water and take long gulps of it. When half of the bottle is gone, I stop and give myself a chance to breathe.

The water is sweet again today. I stare at it, with the feeling that there is something not quite right. I hold it up to the bare bulb that illuminates my room and notice small particles floating in the water. They aren't small translucent sugar particles, these ones are solid. I get that dropping feeling in my gut. Something is in this water.

I push it away, along with the bread. I push it all the way under the door and away from me so it can't tempt me. I turn on the water from the small sink. It's tinted a rusted red, the same with the toilet water. The same way it's been since the first day I got here. I can't drink this water.

Sitting on the edge of my bed, focusing on the newly worn hole in my sock, I have just one thought: I have to get out of here.

When the light goes off, I don't close my eyes. I keep them open. I envision the starry night sky from the Pasture. It's a perfect picture with tiny dots. I start counting them.

Two days of this. I don't eat their food. I don't drink their spiked water. My stomach grumbles. My lips are dry, cracked, and sore.

I can feel it starting again, like when I was first banished to the Pasture. Except this time there's nothing to distract me, just white walls and a cot. There's no water tower to climb. No forests to wander. I never thought this would happen, but I suddenly crave the Phoenix District. I miss my home, the people. I miss my children. God help me, I miss Ian and all his smothering goodness.

I have to get out of here.

They turn the light off. I don't close my eyes. At least I didn't think I did, but somehow I am transported to the Pasture. I've had this dream before, I remember it. *Wake up!* I stare at the house before me. The small farmhouse. I can see them. Lina, Sam, Ian, even Blithe and the boys are all trapped in the house, pounding on the windows, screaming for help. I can see the bomb whistling through the sky. It looks like one of those atomic bombs from the old cartoons, large and bulbous, headed straight for the house. I run, screaming, pulling on the door, trying to break the windows. But it's no use. I can't get them out. I stay on the porch as the bomb whistles down, crashing through the house, exploding. I was hoping it would kill me too, but all it does is throw me away from the house so I can watch it go up in flames, consuming everyone I love.

Then I am screaming, trying to run back to them so I can pull their bodies from the wreckage, so I can be a nurse again and fight to save them. But I can't. Something is holding me back, pulling me by the hair. Even in my dream state I remember it was Crane before, holding me back. This time when I turn it's nothing more than a faceless man. A ghost.

"Let go of me!" I scream at the ghost.

He reaches his bony skinless phalanges and, grasping the skin of my upper arm, he twists it, hard. My eyes open. The burning house, the faceless ghost, they are gone. I take a deep breath. Someone is shaking me. The light flicks on. A face comes into focus before me.

"Andie, wake up," it says.

I recognize the voice. I focus on the man in front of me. His hair is long, his beard thick, but his eyes, those are the same light blue.

I'm still dreaming. I have to be dreaming because Adam's ghost is right in front of my face.

"No!" I feel myself freeze. I don't know what they put in that water, but it's making me hallucinate, I'm sure of it.

"Andie?" it asks.

"No! No!" I pull back. "You're dead! You died!" I pull harder, trying to get away from it. His hands are cold, freezing.

"I'm here," the ghost says, its voice calm and

soothing.

"Get away from me!"

"It's me, Andie," the ghost says again.

"No!" I scream, pulling. The ghost grips my arms tighter. "You're dead." I close my eyes hard. *Wake up, wake up, wake up!* I pull myself harder, I wretch my shoulders. He won't let me go. I pull my knees up, tipping myself back and I kick him square in the chest with the soles of both of my feet. He stumbles back. Ghosts don't feel like that. I'm sure they aren't that solid, like kicking a brick wall. The ghost regains its balance, staring at me as though it's surprised.

I should be surprised. I'm the one seeing a ghost. I've never seen a ghost before. I must be stuck in some horrible dream, or somewhere in the middle, is there a place between dreaming and awake? They definitely put something in the food or in that water.

"Go away," I tell it.

"I won't. I'm here."

"No, you are dead!" I scream at the ghost. I push my tangled hair away from my face. I'm losing it.

The ghost paces, just like I've been doing for days. Every few steps it stops and looks at me, its eyes sunken, almost hollow. I pull my legs up, burying my face in my knees, trembling. I can't look at it anymore. He's dead. Adam is dead. He died years ago to save me and Raven. I buried him. I buried his T-shirt that smelled so good, just like he did, so I could forget him. I mourned him and then I hated him for leaving us and for lying to me about who he was. I can't think straight. I need to wake up.

"Go away!" I tell the ghost.

"I'm not going anywhere."

"You lied to me," I tell the ghost. "I went to the

house. That was not your family. Waters is not your last name."

The ghost sighs. I lift my head. He's still there, standing across from me, leaning back, his shoulders resting on the wall.

"Leave me alone!" I yell at it.

I rock myself and count. *One, two, three, four, five...* I have to focus. I have to wake up. When I reach one hundred I raise my head. Adam's ghost pushes off the wall. It stalks toward the door and knocks three times. The door opens, he leaves.

Ghosts don't use doors. They walk through them. They can walk through walls. I'm sure of it. All the ghost stories I heard as a child or watched on television, ghosts don't use doors.

I crawl to the door and knock three times just like the ghost did. Nothing happens. I stare at the door longer, waiting for the ghost to return. I knock three times again. Nothing. I crawl back to my cot. I resume my position of my forehead on my knees. I rock. I count. I try to remember the smell of Lina's hair, the feel of Raven's chubby fingers on my cheek. I sniff, holding back the burn of impending tears.

The light goes off and since I never woke up, I just continue on dreaming.

--

We sit at the dinner table just as a normal family would. Not a family that has been saddled with the tasks that we have. The promises of the future. One child destined to run this District with her peers, the other whose destiny is uncertain because he has never spoken a word. My Lina. My Raven. Even though I'm sleeping, I can feel the wrenching in my chest. I miss them so much.

Just a few years ago, when I took the tour of the Districts, there was a time that I feared I would die. I told Adam so. And that fear of death, of uncertainty in my future, it gave me fear in life. I see now that I was afraid that from the grave I could not protect my children. I could not ensure that Crane wouldn't steal Lina way from me. I look at her now. Almost ten years old, smarter and stronger than I ever expected her to be. She is caring and attentive toward her little brother, a brother I never thought I could give her. Yes. I was afraid of death. I was afraid of their future without me. But now Ian is strong. Sam and Elvis are ready. And while I may fear the Survivors descending upon this place, I no longer fear for the safety of my children. I am certain that Ian will protect them. He will find a way, now that he knows a fraction of what he is up against.

Somehow as I sleep the realization comes to me: I no longer fear death. I know it will bring me one thing: peace. This new awareness comforts me.

"You okay?" my dream Ian asks from across the table. I look into his scrutinizing eyes and see a flash of concern. Perhaps I was making some type of a face. I smile, relishing in the fact that I can see his dark brown eyes one last time.

"Fine," I tell him.

My stomach grumbles and I look down at the plate in front of me. It's spaghetti and I am hungry. Starved from two days of denying the food my keepers have slid under my door. But this is not real food. This is dream food, it will not give me comfort. Seeing my family will though.

I look up at Ian. His face is so perfect in this dream. He reaches across the table and squeezes my wrist, the wrist that has the imprint of the Phoenix District. "You sure?" he asks again.

Lina and Raven look up from their meal, Astrid too.

"Perfect, actually," I tell him.

"You sure?" He squeezes my wrist again.

The children look between us. I smile at them. "Yeah, I'm sure," I tell them all. "I love you."

When I open my eyes it's still dark. I remember the dream. It wasn't like the others. I wasn't scared, or worried. This dream was my soul divulging one true fact: I'm not afraid to die, not anymore. At this point I could almost welcome it. Dr. Drake was right when he told me I was weak. Only a weak person could totally give up right now.

Lying on the cot, defeated, I can feel it before it hits me; the heavy shallow breaths, the soda-bubble burn in the back of my nasal cavity. I press my lips together, trying to hold it in, trying to swallow the tears that are threatening. A small squeak gets out. I roll over and press my face into the mattress with the realization that I am sure I will not make it home ever again. I cry.

--

The light comes on. The door opens. Still lying on my stomach, my face pressed into the damp mattress, I turn my head to the side, looking to see who has entered the room. It's the ghost again. I stare at him from the cot. I should move to a more defensive position, but I just don't care anymore. The ghost stares back as it sits on the floor across from me.

"Want something to eat?" the ghost asks.

"No," I whisper to the ghost.

"You look hungry." The ghost itches its now neatly trimmed beard on its chin.

"I'm not hungry and I don't want the food, it's poisoned." My stomach growls loudly.

The ghost makes a face. "You're obviously hungry."

"I'm not hungry. I'm dreaming and dream food doesn't fill a stomach."

"You are still a particularly bad liar," the ghost replies. "And you're not dreaming."

"Then how am I talking to a dead man?" I blink at the ghost, my eyes feeling like sandpaper. "I am dreaming."

"I'm not dead."

"Yes, you are. And this is a dream, a terrible horrible dream, just like I used to have." I glare at the ghost before pressing my face back into the soggy mattress. "They stopped when you died," I mumble out into the mattress. "And now they're back."

"Mine never stopped," the ghost says.

I turn my head to look at him. "Ghosts don't dream."

He shakes his head, frustrated. "I'm not a ghost."

"Yes, you are. It's the only way, the only explanation." I move to sit up, ignoring the quivering of my limbs. "My God, they've had me in here so long I've lost it. I've gone mad. I have to wake up. I have to do something to wake up!" I hear my voice in my ears. But it doesn't sound like me. I sound crazy. I slap my cheeks.

"You are awake," the ghost says with a calm voice.

I point at the ghost with a trembling arm. "Shut up, Ghost!" I let my feet drop to the floor and walk to the door, the ghost watching me as I move. I knock three times. I hear footsteps.

"Don't answer the door!" the ghost hollers.

The footsteps stop and then walk away.

"What the hell!" I turn back to the ghost.

"You are awake," it says again.

"You are a ghost!" I point angrily at the figure on the floor. I look at my hand, it still shakes.

"No. I'm not." He stands. This ghost is tall. I don't remember Adam being this tall. But then, it was years ago that I last saw him or stood next to him. Maybe we get taller when we become ghosts. That would be nice, gaining a little height. I drop to a crouch as the ghost takes a step toward me. Creeping along the wall, pressing myself against it as though it may protect me, I scoot away from him until I reach the comfort of my cot.

"Get away from me, Ghost," I warn it.

He starts walking toward me slowly, as though he is trying to calm a feral animal. His eyes are boring into mine, his palms face-up. "I'm not a ghost," he repeats.

He has to be; his eyes are sunken, his face thin, but... his skin seems darker, tan from the sun. Maybe my vision is going, from not seeing daylight in so long. "You're a ghost. And I've lost my shit. Now go away so I can wake up."

"I'm not a ghost." He stands in front of me now, his arms crossed.

I pull my knees up and close my eyes. I squeeze them shut as hard as I can, pressing my face into my knees. The mattress gives as he sits on the cot next to me. I feel him scoot closer.

"Go away, Ghost."

He smoothes my tangled hair back, tucking it behind my ear. "I'm not a ghost," he replies softly. I feel him reach under me and pull me onto his lap.

"Stop it, Ghost," I tell him numbly.

"Still not a ghost." He wraps his arms around me and pulls me into his chest.

Oh God. I remember this smell. It's just like the shirt I buried in the ground, a woodsy spice and bergamot. Ghosts don't smell like this. They can't. I am certain. This is a dream. It has to be. I raise my head. He looks pale now. *Crap*, he could still be a ghost. Or I could be losing my vision.

"They took my necklace," I tell him.

"I'll get it back."

"You're dead."

"No. I'm right here, Andie."

"I'm talking to a ghost."

"It's ok." He rubs my back.

"*I'm fucked up*," I think.

"It's ok," the ghost says.

It must be able to read my thoughts. Unless… I touch my lips, maybe I was talking. "*I'm dying in here*," I think. My lips move. I must be talking.

"I'll get you out." He kisses the top of my head.

"You can't. You're a ghost."

"God damn it, Andie." He pushes my shoulders away from him and stares into my eyes. They're still the same light blue, tropical ocean water blue. Just like Raven's. "I am not a ghost. I am here."

"You are dead, Adam! You died. And I haven't been the same. I've been sad ever since you left us."

"Did you cry?" The ghost asks oddly, tipping his head to the side.

"No. Not for you." I never cried for him. I've only cried for my children.

The ghost frowns. "Maybe you should. Maybe it

284

would help."

This ghost is pissing me off. He just won't go away and he's killing me, making me it worse. I can't handle this. "Fuck you," I tell him.

"That's not nice." His eyes emit a glimmer of amusement.

"Neither is tormenting me."

"I'm trying to help you."

I push at him, wanting to get away, but his hands are clasped behind my back. Each time I struggle he just pulls me closer. Finally, I reach up and slap him as hard as I can. I'm expecting my palm to pass through him, just like the ghosts of the movies. But instead of feeling cold ghost air I feel something else: there is skin and bone and red that seeps from his lip.

Oh shit. Ghosts don't bleed.

He lets go, his hands releasing my back the instant I make this realization. Ghosts definitely don't bleed. I scramble off his lap, my eyes wide and panicked. I am not sleeping, this is not a dream.

"Oh my God," I tell the ghost. No, I tell *Adam*. "You're alive."

CHAPTER TWENTY-ONE

Adam has escaped death once already. When the world was different and he was in the Middle East being tortured for information. He escaped his death then, when they decided they were done with him. He has the scars to prove it. But this survival, there was no military to fix his battered body, if what Crane told me was what really happened. The only things out here are the Survivors. Still, he somehow survived. I have never known a person who has escaped death twice.

"You're not dead." I back up to the wall, feeling comfort in its solidity, hoping that the sensation of pressing my bones against the hard wall might ground me for this moment.

It seems we have switched places.

"No. I'm not. I told you that already."

"Why?" I ask him, shaking my head. "How?"

"Long story."

"But... you're supposed to be dead, Adam."

"I'm not. I never died. I may have come close a few times, but it didn't happen."

"Where have you been?" I ask.

"I was in Colorado. I came as soon as I heard they had you."

"What's in Colorado?"

"It's where I live now."

I stare at him. They let him in here, whoever is keeping me in this room. That means he might be able to get me out of here.

"Get me out if here," I tell him.

"I can't."

"I haven't seen my children in days, weeks. I don't know how long it's been. This place is making me crazy. I'm losing it."

"I can tell." He takes a step toward me, pressing his sleeve to his bleeding mouth.

"Get me out of here, Adam."

"I'm trying." He winces as he presses on his damaged lip.

"I'm begging you." I stop myself from falling to my knees and raising my hands to him. That would make me look more pathetic than I already do. Still, I consider the act.

His expression tightens and he seems to forget about his lip. "You should never beg for anything, ever."

"I have to," I argue with him. "I need to go home."

"I'll figure something out." He glances toward the door. "Come here." He looks toward me again and holds his hand out. I look at it, trying to figure out how I should feel right now. I know that if I take his hand he will pull me to him, and I can't have that. I am familiar with the feelings that his closeness brings. "Come here," he beckons me again.

"I... I can't," I tell him.

"Why?" A deep crease appears between his eyes.

"You lied to me. You left us."

"I know." He drops his hand, the one he was holding out to me.

"Do you know we buried you, Adam? I buried you. Every day I visited your grave. I brought your son there. We mourned you and here you've been the entire time." I pause, trying to lick my dry lips so I can talk more. "He looks just like you. Blue eyes, dark hair. Lina named him Raven." He smiles a small bit. "I could never forget you even if I tried because every time he looks at me, I see you." He smiles again. "Don't smile about it, Adam. Things aren't all perfect. Crane is trying to get rid of him, your son, because he's quiet. He's never spoken a word. He's never uttered a sound. Crane thinks Raven is handicapped in some manner."

"I know," Adam bows his head.

"No, you don't," I tell him. "You don't know anything. Morris died. I've replaced him. I had to reunite with Ian. District rules, they didn't want me tarnishing their family image, their guidelines. Do you understand what that means? I had to move on. If I had known all the time that you were alive, you're alive, Adam! And you didn't think to come back to us? Why?"

"Because," he spits out. "Because Crane left me to die on that rooftop. After all I've done for him. For the Districts. For the Reformation. I'm going to ruin him. If it's the last thing I do."

"We are already working on getting him ejected. Elvis and Ian and me. That's what I was doing out here. I met with the other District leaders, a few are on board but it's hard, they're all afraid of him. Then there's Tonopah. I don't know if Sakima will ever be on board.

Either way, they're all on board, they're siding with us."

"I'm going to do more than get him booted."

"What?"

"I'm going to kill him." Adam looks away from me.

"Is that all you care about?" I ask. "Getting revenge on Crane?"

"You would too, if he had shot you and left you to die."

"He told me that the Survivors shot you."

"He lied. He always lies. You know that."

"Crane shot you…"

"Yes." He presses his finger to his chest, just to the left of his heart. "Right here. Point blank with the pistol in his hand."

My jaw drops slightly. "How did that not kill you?"

The corner of Adam's lip tips up. "Bulletproof vest. Not Volker issue, of course. My own. Thinner, less noticeable. Didn't stop the shock, still knocked me out for a few minutes."

"And then?"

He takes a step away from me, thumbs hanging on the belt-loops of his waistband. "You don't want to know the rest."

I swallow hard, trying not to imagine all of the horrible things the Survivors could have put him through. "So you're going to kill Crane, and then what? What will you do after you kill him?"

"Something."

"You have no desire to come back to us?"

"You already told me, you have Ian. You replaced me." He looks into my eyes and, dropping his voice barely above a whisper, he says, "I never replaced you, Andie."

I don't know what to say.

He walks toward the door.

"Where are you going?" I ask, not wanting him to leave me.

"I have to go barter."

He knocks three times. The door opens. He leaves. I let my body slide to the floor. I wish I could say my mind was numb. Instead, it's reeling.

I sit for an unknown amount of time, my thoughts interrupted when a tray slides under the door. There are two bottles of water this time, two pieces of bread, a brown banana, and a little sad potato. I take the tray, hesitant to eat. My stomach growls louder. It's been over two days. I have to eat this. I pick up the bottles of water and hold them to the light. This time nothing floats. I open the first bottle and sip. There is no sweetness. I eat the meal.

--

I sit on the floor, eating my breakfast of bread soaked in goat milk. The door opens without a knock and Adam enters my cell.

"Why are you eating on the floor?" he asks, his face twisted in confusion.

I look around the room, chewing. "I don't see a table anywhere."

"You could sit on the bed."

I shake my head. "I don't want crumbs on it."

He sits across from me, crossing his legs and leaning back on his hands.

"You said you were going to get me out," I remind him.

"I am. I just need a few more days."

"I can't wait any longer. It's getting worse. I haven't

seen the sun in weeks. I haven't felt the air on my skin. I'm not some war criminal. I don't know who these people are. One minute I'm traveling with Sam and the next we are being ambushed. I didn't do anything. I don't deserve this. I want to go home. I want to see my children."

"Why were you traveling with a load of horses and guns?" he asks me.

"We were preparing for an attack. Survivors at the fence in Phoenix and Crystal River. We were preparing to defend ourselves."

"Why didn't you pick up troops in Tonopah?" he asks me.

I tilt my head and narrow my eyes at him. "Why are you asking me that?"

"Just tell me. I'll explain later." He moves to rest his elbows on his knees and folding his hands together, he sets his chin on them. Waiting.

"George Crossbender pointed out that the people of Tonopah are all medicated. All of them. You remember? They won't follow our orders. They will only follow the orders of Sakima. We didn't want those troops within our walls. They can't be trusted."

Adam nods. "How were you going to get rid of Crane?"

"I'm not sure."

"How could you not be sure?" he asks, annoyed.

"Are you trying to get information out of me?" I ask him, thinking that maybe this is how he's going to barter. Trade me for information.

"Yes."

"I've never lied to you, Adam. I've always told you everything."

"Yes, you did. And that's why Crane tried to kill me.

He said that I knew too much. Now tell me how you were going to get rid of him?"

"I don't know. Elvis and Sam and Ian had some plan. Alexander said he was in but only if he could go back to Hanford to be with his family. We weren't going to decide until I got back with the supplies. I was hoping there would be a diversion with the attack from the Survivors and we could force him out and let the Survivors have him."

Adam nods, digesting what I've told him.

"You weren't like this before, Adam."

"Things are different now." He narrows his eyes at me, his mood shifting. "You're one of them."

"What's that supposed to mean?"

"You're an Entity now. I know the pedestal Crane keeps you on."

"Did you forget, Adam, if that is even your real name?" I reach forward and jerk his wrist out. "You were Sovereign too. We share the same mark!" I look down to see his wrist covered with a thick leather band. I feel him tense under my hand. His pulse increases to a fast beat under my fingertips. I shouldn't have touched him. "You know that I had no choice in the matter. You brought me to them, Adam! You know what they did to me!"

"I have a plan." He stares at my hand on his wrist. I drop it and move away from him.

"I don't know what's wrong with you," I tell him. "One minute you're telling me you're going to get me out of here, the next you're prodding me for information and labeling me as being one of *them*. I had no choice. You know this."

"You shouldn't worry about it. You have Ian."

I lean back, confused by his response. It doesn't

292

make sense. He doesn't make sense. But then, not much of this does.

"Don't be a dick, Adam. I don't understand what's going on with you right now. Yes, Ian is there, he's still not the same. It's never been the same since you showed up."

"You have Ian," he says again. As he stands, he opens his hand and reveals my necklace. I take it from him. Then he walks for the door, stopping before he knocks. "They want to trade you for Crane," he says.

Adam knocks three times, then turns to see me staring with my mouth open. He knows exactly what I know: Crane will never trade himself for me. I catch a gleam of this in Adam's eyes right before he walks out of my cell.

--

"It's been a few days." I stand in the middle of my room as Adam enters.

"I know."

"What's taking so long?"

"I just need you to do one thing." He pauses, pondering, with his hands shoved deep in the pockets of his jeans and his shirt stretched tight across his shoulders, his face takes on a brooding stare.

"What?"

"Kiss me."

"Don't you dare."

"You have to."

"No, I don't."

"They're watching. I told them we were together. That I want you back. They don't believe me. They said if you kiss me, then you can go. We can go. I'll take you back to Phoenix."

"I thought they wanted Crane?"

"They do, but we have to go get him. A swap at the gates. Are you ready?" he asks. "Are you ready to go home?"

I stare at his lips, remembering how they felt. How good it felt. What it was like to be in his arms. I made that mistake before. I can't do it again. I can't bear to see what it would do to Ian.

"I can't."

"Why?"

"You're lying to me."

"Then you stay," he threatens.

"No! I can't stay here any longer."

He looks at me with a steely gaze. "Don't look at me like that."

"Like what?" he asks, his voice gruff.

"Like you're a porn star or something. Actually, don't ever look at me like that again. Period. I hate you, Adam. I hate that you left us. I hate that you lied to me. Every single chance you got you lied to me. And here you are, lying again."

He smiles. Standing, he walks closer to me. I walk backward until my back presses firmly against the wall. I am in an unfortunate position. Adam stops, his toes millimeters from mine.

Lowering his voice, "They're watching," he says, his eyes flitting toward the door.

I turn my head just slightly, seeing shadows pass from a small crack in the door that I never noticed before. I look back to Adam. He licks his lips.

"Kiss me now and we walk out that door," he whispers as his eyes gaze down to the necklace around my neck. The one he retrieved for me.

"You're lying," I tell him, my heart thumping faster in my chest.

"Try me." He leans forward, the tip of his nose trails across my cheekbone, to the sensitive skin of my ear, down my neck. I feel his warm breath there, caressing my collarbone. Trying not to shiver or groan or anything is too difficult with him so close, doing what he's doing.

I close my eyes, trying to think straight. Of all of my options I can't think of a worse one. Ian already forgave me for everything else that happened, but this, if he found this out, Adam offering to save me in exchange for a kiss. I'm confident Ian will kill him if he ever finds him or maybe Ian will finally give up on me.

It's nothing, I tell myself. *Just a kiss*. Just a quick kiss. It would mean nothing. Just my freedom. It could mean nothing. Or it could bring me more trouble. Loads of trouble.

I open my eyes to find Adam staring down at me still. He raises his eyebrows.

"I hate you for this," I tell him.

"Good," he replies, resting his hands on the wall behind me.

"I buried you once already. This is unfair."

"Life is unfair," he replies in a whisper.

"This will never happen again."

His lip twitches at the corner.

"This will *never* happen again," I repeat, more for me than him.

I take a breath in and, moving up on my toes, I press my lips to his. I kiss the dead man, the dead man who saved my life multiple times. And I take that tingling feeling in my gut and push it to somewhere dark and far away. That feeling is reserved for Ian, not Adam.

He is dead to me and I can never feel that way about him again. *One-one thousand, two-one thousand, three-one thousand*, I count in my head. Then I pull away, the soles of my feet planted firmly on the floor, my back against the wall. When I look back up to Adam he is staring at me with a thoughtful gaze.

"Was that so hard?" he asks.

"You have no idea how hard that was," I tell him before fixing my eyes on the empty space behind his shoulder.

He nods. "Let's get you out of here."

Taking my hand, he turns and walks toward the door. He knocks three times. The door opens and I recognize Chuck with a smug look on his face. He thinks I'm crazy. He's right.

We step into the hallway. It's dark, the only light coming from the ends of the hallway where large windows stream in daylight. I notice the long hallway with doors every few yards. There is colorful tile on the wall. Short lockers line the walls. I know where we are. We are in a school. I turn, looking at the room we have exited, seeing the faded area on the wall where it looks like a sign was once attached. Judging from the size of the room and the presence of the toilet and the sink, I'm quite confident that they were holding me in none other than a large handicapped bathroom.

Suddenly I feel filthy. Filthier than the days I spent in there without a shower. A small noise of disgust escapes my throat.

"Want a hot shower?" Adam asks.

He must have heard me. "That would be great."

"Come on then."

I follow him down the hallway. He turns, headed for a bright stairwell. There are more large windows here. I follow him down the two flights. He turns left. We pass a few men in the hall who stop talking and watch as we walk by them.

"Where are we going?" I ask Adam.

"To the locker rooms. You said you wanted a shower."

We pass classrooms and a double-door labeled *Gymnasium*. "Just up here," Adam says. He stops at the end of the hallway in front of the door that has a plaque with the figure of a woman in a dress. I look across the hall and see another door with the figure of a man on it. Adam pushes on the women's door, holding it open for me. I duck under his arm, stopping when I hear him following me.

"You can't come in here," I tell him, holding my hand up to stop his advance into the room.

"Why not?"

"Because it's for women. Didn't you read the sign on the door?"

"Get over it, Andie. You're the only woman here right now and I'm not leaving you in here alone."

"Fine," I tell him. "Just don't get any ideas. Remember, I hate you."

I start down a row of lockers, finding a row of bathroom stalls and curtained shower stalls at the end of the room. I stop, looking down at myself. I have no change of clothes or soap or towels. "This is going to be a cold shower, isn't it?" I ask Adam.

"No. They have some power here," he says as he starts opening the lockers. "Just not a lot. So don't go crazy. We don't want to piss them off by draining the hot water tank."

"What are you doing?" I ask.

"They said there were towels and soap in one of

these lockers."

"What about a change of clothes?"

"There are still old gym clothes in here." He pulls out a dark pair of sweatpants and shakes them out. "Might fit you."

I move to open the locker behind him and find a folded towel and bottle of liquid soap. "Jackpot!" I whisper as I take them and head for the shower.

I kick off my boots outside of the shower and hang the towel on the hook. Stepping into the stall fully clothed, I start the water. At first it's cold, then freezing, then it begins to warm. I strip my dirty clothes off, squeezing the soap onto them and washing them as I go.

Lastly, I wash my body. When I think I've finally rinsed the last of the soap out of my hair, I wrap myself in the towel and hang my wet clothes on the towel hooks. Taking my now clean underwear, I head for the row of hand dryers attached to the wall, noticing Adam sitting on the benches near the lockers, a stack of folded clothes next to him. On the top of the pile is a pair of brightly colored lacy underwear and a sports bra. I cringe.

"What?" Adam asks innocently.

"Those underwear look a little small and slutty." I point at the pile of clothes.

"Then free-ball," he suggests with a shrug. "Dryers don't work."

I sigh and collect the stack of clothes from the bench. Returning to one of the dry shower stalls I dress myself in privacy. Removing the towel, I use it to dry my hair, twisting it into a turban on top of my head. Adam has found a pair of fitted black sweatpants, a T-shirt with the high school logo of a bear printed on the front, and a hooded sweatshirt. The pants are a little loose, the shirt way too tight. It's a good thing the sweatshirt is just baggy enough to cover it all up. The clothes smell like stale dust. I leave the stall to look in one of the mirrors attached to the wall. The disappointment must be evident on my face.

"What's wrong?" Adam asks as he stands.

"I look like I'm in high school in this getup." I turn back to my wet clothes that are hanging on the hook. "Maybe I can change when those are dry."

Adam hands me a pair of running sneakers. I check the tag and see they are about a half-size bigger than what I normally wear. He moves to the shower and taking my wet clothes and boots he throws them in the garbage.

"Hey!" I start.

"You can't wear them again," he says as he walks toward me. "It's better that you look like a teenager. Give me your wrist." I look down to see him holding a strip of cloth in his hand. "Your wrist with the mark." His voice has the hint of impatience.

I pull the sleeve up on the sweatshirt and hold my wrist out to him. He wraps the cloth around my arm and knots it, covering the image of the phoenix. "I don't want anyone else finding out who you are."

"Why?" I ask.

"These Survivors were pretty happy to find you. And to think all I had to do was promise to trade you for Crane and let them keep the horses and guns. If others found out that you were loose, others who know what a value you are to Crane, we'd be in a load of trouble. It only took a few days for word to travel to me. I'm sure others will be looking for you soon enough." He looks at my feet. "Put the sneakers on.

We need to get out of here."

I look down at the brightly colored shoes. "We're at least two states away, Adam. I don't think sneakers are the best shoes. I'd rather have my boots."

"Too bad." He shakes his head at me. "Let's go."

I bend to put the shoes on.

"Are you planning on bringing Crane back here?" I ask him as I tie the shoelaces.

"That's the plan." He looks toward the door as I untwist the towel from my hair.

"And you think Crane will come?" I ask running my fingers through the curls and tangles.

"Probably not without a fight. But since you already started a resistance group in Phoenix, it should be easier to get him out of there."

"I didn't start the group," I tell him defensively. "I don't want to be held responsible for starting the resistance from within Phoenix. Elvis started the group. I was one of the last ones asked to be involved. Elvis brought on Sam and Ian before he even spoke to me."

"Then why did they send you out to speak with everyone?"

"Because Elvis said the other Entities trust me, that they would listen to me."

"Hmm." Adam looks around the empty locker room.

"Do you have more of that cloth?" I ask.

"For what?"

"So I can put my hair up." I motion to the mass of hair cascading down my back.

His gaze falls over me. "You should leave it down," he suggests.

"You shouldn't have died, and then maybe I'd listen

300

to your suggestions on how I should dress or do my hair."

He reaches into his pocket, retrieving something and holding his hand out to me, I see a rubber hair-tie resting in his palm. I grab at it and twist my wet hair into a bun. "Jerk."

"Are you ready yet?" Adam asks me impatiently. "Those men are going to think something else is going on in here if you take much longer."

"Shut up." I throw the towel in his face and march toward the door.

Adam grabs my arm before I get there. "You don't leave my side," he says, his face turning serious.

"Why?"

"What part of *you're the only woman here* did you not understand?"

Without giving me a chance to answer, Adam opens the door and we walk out of the locker room together. I follow him down the hallway, past the gymnasium and the stairs. The same men stand in the hall, again they stop talking and watch as we walk past them. I notice Adam walking toward the front doors of the building.

"Don't you need to speak to anyone?" I ask. "Let them know you are leaving?"

"Definitely not," he replies, pushing on the door at the entrance of the school.

"Hey!" I hear a familiar voice shout down the hallway. Adam grabs my arm and turns. Mack walks swiftly toward us. He looks at me then back at Adam. "You sure you want to take her alone?" he asks.

Adam nods. "Yeah. I can handle her and it'll be faster this way."

Mack leans to look out the door. "You know, if you

don't come back Christian will be looking for you. Won't be good," he warns, his eyes settle on me. "She put up a fight. Tried to run twice—"

"About that, Mack," I interrupt. "Tell Chuck thanks for the brain damage."

Mack smirks. "I warned you not to run." He turns to Adam. "You sure?"

"I told you. I can handle her," Adam replies with confidence. "You tell Christian I'll be back in a few days."

"Would love to," Mack says. "But I've never seen the soul."

"I'll be back. See you in a few days, Mack." Adam nods.

We step out of the building and walk down the front steps. For the first time in a long time I am filled with a sense of relief at my current freedom. Happy that I didn't die in that bathroom, relieved that I can go home. Finally.

And then something strikes me as odd, the fact that Mack is letting Adam walk out of here with me alone. I stop, turning to Adam. "They wouldn't have let you walk out of here with me alone if they had known we were together before."

Adam just stares at me, a smile starting.

"I didn't have to kiss you back there. Did I? No one was watching." His smile just grows wider. "You're an ass."

"Just think of it as a farewell kiss," he says. "I never kissed you goodbye before I left to find you the medicine. I regret that every day."

"You didn't have to lie to me, again," I tell him. "How are we getting back?" I ask, looking up and down the street.

"Well, I thought we could walk." I cringe remembering the walk we took home after the bombings. "But then I figured, why walk when I have a truck?"

"What?" I ask shocked.

He starts walking across the street toward an old black truck, no, it's not old. It's a classic, with rounded corners. I run after him. "How do you have a truck? Does it even run?"

"Why wouldn't it?"

"Because Crane bombed the entire country and there is no more fuel."

"There's some fuel. And a lot of people still have running vehicles. Fuel is just in very short supply."

"You have enough to make it home?"

"We'll see. I have enough to get us pretty far."

"What about the roads?"

"Some are good and some are bad. These guys let me know what the local roads are like, the ones that are passable. We'll just go as far as we can and then if we have to we'll walk the rest of the way. It's not like we haven't done it before, Andie."

He opens the passenger side door. I get in and watch as he makes his way to the driver's side and gets in. He starts the truck and, shifting it into gear, he pulls away.

"Say good-bye to Romney, West Virginia," Adam says as he drives down the street.

--

"Who's Christian?" I ask as Adam drives down a bumpy country road.

"Someone who thinks he's in charge of the

Survivors."

"Like their President or something?"

"Or something," he murmurs as he stops at an intersection. Pulling forward, he leans, looking down the roads, deciding which one he should take. They both look clear to me. Adam turns the truck left and continues to drive.

"What's it like in Colorado?" I ask.

"Why do you ask?"

"Because based on what Crane told us and what I heard from Dr. Drake, and what we've seen at the gates in Crystal River, it's not safe and it's not good."

"Colorado is okay," he says with a shrug.

"It's safe?" I ask. "I mean... you're safe there?"

"I have freedom." He looks at me. "I don't have someone telling me what to do. Colorado isn't so bad. But there are other areas that are terrible. The east coast is being overrun with some pretty dangerous people right now. That's why I came for you."

"You're not coming back to Phoenix are you?"

He turns to look at me. "Don't you want me to come back?"

"I don't think that's a good idea." I stare straight ahead and watch the trees pass by us.

"Why not?"

"Because everyone thinks you're dead. Including Lina and Raven." Bringing him back would only cause trouble.

He slows the truck to a stop and throws the gear into park. Turning toward me, with his arm stretched across the back of the seat, he asks, "Would you go back, now that you're out?"

"Would I go back?" It seems like such an absurd question I can't help but repeat it. "Of course. That's where my family is."

"Would you take them out of there if you had the chance?"

"They're safe there, even with Crane. I can keep them safe now. We may not have freedoms, but I don't have to worry about something terrible happening to them. We have food, electricity, a system that seems to work," I tell him.

"And then there's that little part where you altered the genome and created an entire sub-breed of humans." He doesn't even look at me when he says it.

"I didn't have much of a choice in that." I look away from him.

"You don't feel responsible for it?" he asks as he shifts the truck into gear and starts driving again.

"Of course I do. But what was I suppose to do, Adam? You were there. You saw what was going on."

"You don't want to take responsibility for what you've created?"

"I was forced to, Adam."

"You could have lied," he suggests.

I shake my head. "No. Crane would have figured that out. He's smart. Smarter than we think."

He drives in silence and the silence makes me feel like he's judging me, holding me responsible for altering the Residents. I don't like it.

"I tried to leave." I start again after we'd driven about a mile or so. "Remember? I took Lina and tried to run away from there. You remember what happened, even though you weren't there? You saw me afterwards." I move my hand, running my finger over the bump in my nose. "I couldn't very well keep Lina safe if I were dead. What would you have done in my position?"

Adam stares straight ahead. I can see the muscle twitch in his jaw. "I would have killed him."

"I wasn't trained to kill people like you."

"Training doesn't matter, Andie. I've seen plenty of people kill out here. And most haven't had any training. I guess it just comes down to what kind of a person you are."

"I've had enough of death, Adam. That's the kind of person I am. And I think I'm done with this conversation." I turn my body away from him, facing the passenger side window. And curling up on the seat, I lay my head against the headrest and close my eyes.

--

Somehow I slept. The anger boiling through my veins had the opposite effect of keeping me awake, instead it lulled me into a deep sleep. Or, maybe it was the effects of a full stomach, a hot shower, and finally feeling safe with Adam at my side, knowing that I was going home.

I wake with a stiff neck and the realization that we are no longer moving. I sit up in a panicked rush, looking around the truck cab. Adam is no longer at the wheel. I look out the windows, turning full around until I find him standing at the rear of the vehicle. He's filling the gas tank with cans from the back of the truck. Paying no attention to me, he looks up and down the long country road as he unscrews another gas can and pours its contents into the truck's gas tank.

My legs tingle from being in the same position for so long. I open the door and slide out of the passenger seat until my feet hit the ground. Adam watches as I walk to the back of the truck, running my fingers across the paint. It's a smooth black finish. Not a spot of rust or damage. It seems out of place here.

"How long did I sleep for?" I ask him as I reach the tailgate.

"About four hours." He tips the gas can, draining the last few drops into the truck.

"How much further?"

"Maybe another four," he says as he looks up to the sky.

I look up too. The day is fading, the moon already present in the evening sky, the sun headed for the horizon. "Do we travel at night?" I ask.

"That depends how long you want to be stuck in this truck with me."

"What if you run out of gas?"

"Then we walk."

"Great." I look around us at the surrounding forests. "Haven't run into anyone yet?" I ask.

Adam shrugs. "Passed a few people. Nothing exciting though."

"I thought you said it was dangerous on the east coast?"

He looks down at me. "It is. That's why we're sticking to the back roads."

I stare into the woods. My bladder spasms. "I have to pee."

"Go for it," he says, wiping his hands on a towel.

"You think it's safe in there?" I ask, leaning toward the trees.

"Well, you could just do it behind the truck," he shrugs at me and tosses the towel in the back of the truck.

I decide to relieve myself in the cover of the forest. Walking away from the truck, stepping over the tall grass and brush, I find a concealed area behind a thick bush. When I am done, I stand, adjusting my clothes. Then, hearing the rustling of leaves and snap of a stick, I run out of the forest as fast as I can.

Adam looks at me with wide, amused eyes. "Chupacabra?"

"I don't know," I tell him out of breath. "There were these people in Crystal River, they tried to climb the fence and get in. Ramirez said they were from the swamps of Louisiana. They spoke this Creole language. It was creepy."

"Swamp people, huh?"

"Yeah. They were really strange."

"I doubt they'd make it up this far."

"They made it to Phoenix."

"It was probably just a deer." He looks behind me. "Ready?" he asks.

I walk to the passenger side door and climb into the truck. Adam slides into the driver's seat and starts the engine.

"How's Lina?" he asks as he drives.

"She's going to be ten this fall," I tell him.

"That was fast." His hands grip the steering wheel tighter. "She named the baby Raven?" he asks.

"Yes." I smile at the memory of her deciding in the hospital.

"Why did she choose that name?"

"She said Ms. Black told her ravens were really smart, smarter than humans, and she said she knew he was a smart baby."

Adam smiles to himself and then frowns. "What's wrong with him?" he asks.

"Nothing. He's just really quiet."

"Is that normal?"

"Not really. But he's there, always observing. He

308

makes these faces when I bring him to school. I think he doesn't like Blithe."

"What kind of faces?"

"I don't know how to describe it. He just looks like he's pissed and bored to death."

Adam lets out a light laugh. "When I was a kid, the school district told my parents that I wasn't right."

"I think I'd have to agree with them."

Adam laughs again.

"Okay, in all seriousness, why?" I ask.

"Because I was quiet," he replies with a smile. "And then when I was a little older they made me take this placement exam so they would know what classes to put me in. So they could judge where I needed extra help. I aced it."

"What happened then?"

"My parents pulled me out of school. My mother quit her job at the salon, and taught me at home. I completed my high school work early and went to West Point. Graduated top of my class."

"But you told me you went to my High School. You knew everything about that place."

"I went there for filler classes. A few things my parents couldn't teach me at home. But I was never a full-time student there."

I stare at him, shocked. "You never told me this before."

"You never asked."

He drives in silence.

"Stevie died," I tell him.

Adam stares straight ahead as he drives. "How'd Lina take it?"

"Broke her heart." I swallow hard remembering that night and the days after, how hard it was for all of us. "Stevie was her best friend."

"How'd you take it?" he asks.

"Hard." I blink back a tear at the memories of our beloved family dog. "We buried her next to your grave. Yours and Morris's. Had a ceremony one day. Lina and Astrid picked wild flowers and laid them all out."

"I'm sorry I died," he whispers so low I can barely hear it.

"You're not dead anymore."

"There's still time," he says. "There's still time for me to die today."

"Why would you say that?"

"Because in a few hours I'm sure I'm going to come face-to-face with Ian. And since Crane has already had his shot at killing me I'm expecting Ian's next."

"He's not going to try and kill you."

"Sure about that?"

"He's not a violent person. He forgave me."

"Some men become violent when their family is threatened."

"He has no reason to be violent. You're bringing me home. You're not threatening anyone."

"So you think I'll stay alive then?" He sounds almost disappointed.

"Yes, I think you'll stay alive. But I will still hate you. Remember that. My dislike for you will keep you alive today."

That shuts him up. There's no more speaking. No more banter. No more stories or filling in on lost time. Instead, Adam drives, his jaw locked in irritation. I turn my back to him and watch the wind blow the trees. Leaves that have barely turned, still mostly green, litter the ground and blow across the road. There's a storm coming.

CHAPTER TWENTY-TWO

We pass only two other vehicles; a dusty red sedan pulled over on the side of the road and another truck, loaded down with men sitting along the edge of the truck-bed. I tense, expecting them to turn around and follow us.

"We're fine," Adam says as though he's sensing my apprehension to the truckload of men passing us.

"Will they come after us?" I ask.

"Nope." He grips the steering wheel a little tighter. "They looked like they were headed home for the night."

"How do you know?" I ask.

"They looked tired."

I wait, half expecting to see the truck spin around and come speeding after us. After all, they are Survivors. But it never happens. Instead, Adam continues driving for hours along the winding country roads. It's not long before the scenery starts looking familiar. Even on the back roads I recognize the forests of New York. The roadsides are thick with evergreens and inter-dispersed with maple and oak trees. I can even feel it in my body. I am almost home.

Adam continues north. The wind howling around the truck, the branches of the trees shaking as we pass, and just as the last of the evening sun begins to dip behind the tree-line, I feel the truck take a steep incline. Adam doesn't need to tell me where we are. I know. We are passing the city. I remember this drive, from when I used to commute back and forth from work. I know once the hill crests, if we drive at a steady sixty-five miles an hour I will be home in forty-five minutes. The anticipation tingles throughout my body, and then, Adam takes a sharp right turn in the wrong direction.

"What are you doing?" My voice sounds louder than it should, filling the truck cabin. "You're going in the wrong direction."

He taps a finger on the gas gauge. "Too close to empty. I have to get some gas."

I look out all of the windows and behind us. "Where? There's nothing here."

"There's a small settlement up here."

"How do you know?"

"Just trust me."

I might trust him, a little, I just don't trust the weather. Looking to the early darkening sky, thick gray clouds roll over, dousing out the last of the evening light. The wind blows harder.

Adam takes another right, then a left. As he slows, I focus on the road ahead of us. It's barricaded with cars parked perpendicular across the road. Then, I see movement. People with guns. Survivors.

"Adam!" I twist in my seat, uneasy. "What are you doing? They have guns!"

"I can see that." His voice has no concern.

"Then why are you continuing on? Stop and turn around."

"I asked you to trust me, Andie."

"But they have guns."

"It's okay. Just settle down." He stops the truck and reaches for the door handle. Two of the people at the barricade walk toward us, a man and a woman, weapons drawn. "Stay in the truck," Adam orders.

Adam gets out and walks toward the two people, palms up, speaking. I can't hear what he says, but whatever he tells them, they lower their guns, nod, look at me and then turn and motion for the others to open the barricade.

The wind whips at Adam's jacket and his hair. As he opens the door to the truck a cold wind blows in.

"What was that all about?" I ask.

"Not all the Survivors are terrible people. They have gas for us."

"Are you sure?" I eye them as Adam drives past the barricade.

"Yeah."

Adam drives down a road lined with small houses, trailers, campers and tents.

"What is this place?"

Adam shrugs. "Just a community. People who protect each other, get along for the greater good."

"But it's so close to Phoenix. How did they not find us? How did Crane not find them?"

Adam parks the truck next to a convenience store. "What makes you think one doesn't know about the other?" He reaches for the door handle. "You're coming with me. Get out of the truck and don't leave my side." He gets out, pushes the driver's seat forward and pulls out a black bag.

313

"What's that?"

"None of your business. Let's go." He closes the door and heads around to the passenger side. Getting out, the cold wind blows through my sweatshirt and I immediately wish I had something warmer to wear. "Come on," Adam says as I close the door.

I follow him as he heads toward the convenience store. As Adam reaches for the door, I notice a sign taped at eye level. It says, *Buy, Barter, Trade*.

A man and a woman stand behind the counter, both looking middle aged and unafraid of us. The man tips his head.

"Hello, Steven." Adam walks to the counter at a quick pace and holds his hand out to shake.

"Sir," the man named Steven replies. The woman at the counter looks between the men, before focusing on me. "What can I do for you?"

"Need a few gallons of gas. Then we'll be on our way."

"Barter or trade?" Steven asks.

"Trade." Adam holds up the bag in his hand. "You have a private place to talk?"

Steven points at a door in the rear of the store. "We can go back there. Betsy can run the place while we talk."

Steven walks around the counter, motioning for Adam to follow.

"Stay right here," he whispers to me as he passes, following Steven toward the door.

I nod, watch them as the door closes, then wander around the store. There are a few pre-packaged snacks, medical supplies, gallons of bleach, a few jugs of water, tools, rope, empty containers. Walking toward the cashier counter, I notice the most valuable things are kept there. Batteries, cigarettes, bullets and guns for sale.

I reach forward to pick up a package of lip balm that's hanging next to the counter. The cashier, Betsy, watches and I notice she's focused on the strap tied across my wrist, covering up my Sovereign mark. I pull my hand back and retract it into my sleeve.

"Want to trade?" Betsy asks. "For the lip balm?"

I lick my lips and back up. "No."

"You want it."

"No. I'm fine. It's just been so long since I've seen stuff like that."

"You sure you don't want it?" Her eyes narrow on me, specifically the arm I've drawn up into my sleeve. "You look like you want it."

"No. Really. Besides, I have no way to pay for it. I was just looking." My eyes flick toward the closed door where Adam went with the man.

Betsy rounds the counter. "Sometimes we take payment in the form of information." She takes a few steps toward me. I head for the door, but she moves fast, running around me and blocking me from reaching the door. "I get the feeling you know a lot of important information."

"No." I take a few steps back. "I don't know anything."

"You sure, Hon?" She crosses her arms. "Why you got that tie around your wrist? That man in there hurt you or something?"

I take a few steps back, wondering if I might be able to circle around the store and get away from her. "No," I respond.

"Not at all? Big, scary looking guy like that didn't harm one hair on your pretty little head?" She looks me up and down. "You're a little young for him, aren't you? What are you, like, eighteen or something? Not right, a grown man like that dragging you around. I've seen a lot of that lately."

Eighteen, what a compliment. I shake my head. "No. It's fine. We're fine."

"You sure now?" She presses on.

"Yes." I raise my voice to a near shout. "Adam would NEVER HURT ME."

Betsy tips her head and narrows her eyes at me. "Adam—"

Before she can finish, the door whips open and Adam is standing in the doorway. "What's wrong?" he asks.

Betsy moves to her place behind the register, focusing on something under the counter.

"Uh... nothing," I finally respond.

Adam looks around the store before turning to Steven.

"It's a deal," Steven says from inside the room. "Let's get your gas."

Adam moves and through the open door I can see three handguns and a box of bullets on the table. Adam avoids my eyes for the remainder of the time we are there; while we walk through the store to the garage behind the building where he drives the truck and Steven pours ten gallons of gasoline into the truck's gas tank.

It's when the men at the barricade let us through and we are finally driving down the highway in the dark that I finally ask him, "Where did the guns come from, Adam?"

"Don't worry about it." His jaw twitches when he closes his mouth.

"Why?"

"Just don't."

He accelerates into the darkness and before he can turn north, a heavy rain starts pelting the windshield. Adam turns on the windshield wipers and the heat. It's not long before the rain thickens and turns into a pelting hail storm. I grip the door, barely able to see the sides of the road. The cabin cools further until Adam has the heat on its highest setting. Then, it starts snowing, so bad that the road is covered and Adam can't drive any further.

I want to ask Adam about the guns, I want answers from him. But this is the kind of storm you don't argue in, not with the driver. When Adam slows the truck to a crawl, disappointment hits me in the bottom of the gut like a lead ball. We are so close to home.

"It's too dangerous to drive any further than this," Adam says as he stops the truck and puts it in park. Leaving the engine running, he presses his fingers to the heat vents. "We'll just have to wait it out."

"I don't want to wait it out," I tell him. "This could last for hours or days."

He shakes his head. "Every storm ends in time, Andie."

"Unless it turns to snow, *Adam*. Unless it's snowing and summer is almost here."

Adam looks out the window at the large snowflakes settling all around us.

"The the weather is so unpredictable. This is probably going to ruin our crops," I point out.

"Thought the Entities reformed everything to stop this sort of thing from happening."

"They did. But then Norman Eckstein seeded the ocean with iron, and there was a massive population die-off. The atmosphere must have overcorrected or something. I'm not sure. You could ask the brains in Hanford, I'm sure they have a meteorologist there. Weather patterns are not my specialty." My breath fogs the window as I look out the passenger side. I reach up and wipe it away. "I can't believe we are so close."

"You can walk the rest of the way."

"I would like to." Actually, I think I'd like to run the rest of the way.

"Well, we can wait until morning. I think that's the best thing to do."

I stare longingly out the window into the night. The wind blows stronger, snow and ice pelts the truck. I jump as a flash of lightning brightens the night sky.

"Wasn't expecting that," I mumble, turning back to Adam. He's looking at me, strangely. "What?" I ask.

"What if…" he starts, his face taking on some expression I am not familiar with. He sighs, closes his eyes and then looks at me again with his striking blue eyes. "What if I never see you like this again?" he asks.

"Like what? Waiting to go home?" I unclip my seatbelt and pull my legs up to my chest.

"No. All trusting and eager and, just a tiny bit, still… innocent."

I laugh a little. "I think you have me confused with someone else," I tell him flatly.

"I don't." The strange expression continues.

"I'm sure you do. Because right now I may be trusting you for five minutes while you bring me home, but I hate you. Remember that, Adam. I may have really enjoyed your company at one point, but now I hate you now. You lied, you died, you lied some more. You will never see me like this again because you will never see me again. Ever."

318

"Yeah. I was hoping that would make this easier." He turns to look out his window as another crack of thunder erupts, followed by another flash of lightening. At that instant he looks back to me and my stomach growls loudly, at what seems to be the most inappropriate time; it seems Adam has something to tell me.

"You hungry? I have some rations here." He reaches behind his seat and pulls out a bag. He takes out two aluminum bottles and a container filled with what looks like dried meat.

"What's that?" I ask him.

"Deer jerky." He hands me one of the bottles. "Water." He motions to the shiny bottle. I take a piece of jerky from the container and bite into it. At first, the flavor is mild, not too dry, and then the salt hits me. I set the jerky on my lap and swallow, my mouth puckered. Hurriedly opening the bottle of water, I catch a glimpse of Adam watching me from across the seat. I drink, washing the strong taste of salt out of my mouth. When my mouth has been thoroughly rinsed I catch the hint of an aftertaste in the water. Looking at the metal container I wonder if it's from the aluminum and wherever the water came from. I look up to find Adam staring at me, a frown on his face.

"What?" I ask, feeling my tongue slur a bit, and I wonder if it's from the strong salt.

"I'm sorry," he says, putting his water back into the bag along with his portion of the jerky.

"That was really salty," I tell him as I take another long pull from the bottle. This time when I stop drinking, I recognize the aftertaste. It's sweet, just like someone added a little sugar, just like what I tasted in the water the Survivors gave me.

Oh no.

"You asshole!" I yell at Adam as I throw the bottle it at him. He catches it with a magnificent finesse, as though I merely tossed it to him and didn't chuck it with all the energy left in my body.

"I'm sorry," he repeats.

"I trusted you!"

"I know."

"What was in there?"

"Just something to help you sleep." He reaches out, tucking a loose strand of hair behind my ear.

"Don' touch meh," I slur at him and wave my hand, missing his arm by a mile. He smiles. This time, though, it's not his mischievous smile that I once loved. It's sad. "Who 'r you?" I ask.

He clears his throat. "My real name is Christian Whitmarsh."

CHAPTER TWENTY-THREE

Christian, the one who is running the East Coast, the one who wants Crane, and the one using me to get him. I should have known something was odd when we were not interrupted, not even once, on our drive here, even though we passed a truck of men. They must've known who he was as they looked at us through the windshield.

I raise my hand to point at him but my finger barely stretches out from a relaxed curve. Whatever he gave me is hitting me hard. "Lied, again."

"I may have lied about a few things but never about how I felt about you."

"Why?" I ask, feeling a sudden surge of coherence. "Why'd you do this now?"

"I have family, too."

"No you don't. They died. I've already seen the Whitmarsh grave. I figured that much out."

"All except for one person. I have a sister. And like you've protected your family, I have to protect mine."

"Where?"

"In Phoenix."

"Who?"

"Blithe."

I reach for the door handle and hear it click as Adam locks the door from his side of the truck. "You should get some rest," he suggests.

"I hate you for this," I remind him as my eyes seem

to close on their own.

The last thing I hear is Adam, or Christian, let out a heavy sigh as he responds, "Me too."

--

There are people talking. The murmuring of male voices. I can smell something familiar. It's sweet and musky, makes my stomach churn. My eyes flutter open, still feeling heavy from whatever Adam gave me to help me sleep. Someone is close to me, too close.

"She's awake," I hear Adam's irritated voice.

"Ah, Andromeda." The body turns toward me and as I lift my head, I see it is none other than Burton Crane sitting terribly too close to me. I throw myself back, feeling the cold glass of the truck window on the back of my head. Looking between Adam and Crane, I wonder if perhaps I am still dreaming.

"Why?" I ask. It's the only word I can seem to get out.

"Because you needed to deal with Adam's death. Your relationship with him was a loose string. I let you flutter about for two years. It had to end."

"He's not dead."

"Oh, but he is," Crane replies as Adam simply watches from the seat next to him. "He is dead to you now. After this betrayal. That string is cut. Now you can move on from him. He is no longer a distraction."

"Is this another one of your lessons?"

"In a sense. You need to be of sound mind."

"My initiation is done. I completed all of your tasks in each of the Districts."

"No, it's not. You need to be of sound mind." Crane reaches forward with one speckled finger and taps me on the top of the head. "You are too soft. You contemplate too much. You need to be able to react quickly. You can't have things like love and family swaying your choices. They will get in the way of your judgment."

"I sort genes. That's all Crane."

"Yes, a very important task in this time. But you will do much more."

"What are you saying?"

"I might die soon."

"What?"

"I'm afraid your friend here is going to kill me."

"He is no longer my friend. And how does that affect me? You've been trying to kill me for years."

"I was merely adding to your strengths. It is a great possibility that there is a war coming between the Phoenix District and the Survivors now that Adam, or Christian as you now know him, has control of them. There are things within those walls that he desires very much and I need to be certain that you can defend us and what we've created."

"If I don't want to?"

"Oh, my dear Andromeda, tell me you don't want to keep your children safe from harm. I'll have a very hard time believing you."

My gaze flicks to Adam, who is simply staring at me, his eyes dark and angry.

"You have your hand in every single candy dish, don't you?" I ask Crane.

"I have to. I have plans for this new world."

"What about the other Funding Entities? Are they involved?"

"No," he gives a slight laugh. "I am done with the Funding Entities. It's time for the *Founding* Entities to

323

take charge."

"And where do I come in?"

"Oh, Andromeda," he says with laughter on his tongue. "That's simple, you choose to protect me or your family."

"I will never choose you. You know this. I will only protect my family."

He smiles. "That's what I was hoping to hear. Now close your eyes and go back to sleep."

And even though I hate him and I never follow his orders, my body feels overwhelmed with fatigue. I close my eyes and find myself thrust into darkness.

--

I wake, stiff and sore and cold. There is a thin layer of snow covering the windshield of the truck. The sun seems to be just rising. I exhale and a fog of my breath floats in front of me. Focusing, I sit up straight. I am alone. There is no Adam, no Crane, just me and a parka lying in the seat where Adam sat last night.

That's thoughtful.

I look around and orient myself. The truck is parked in the middle of the road on the main highway that leads straight into Phoenix. I know if I follow this I will run into the electrified fence that cuts across the highway, and then it's another fifteen miles until I get to town.

I get out of the truck, my sneakers squishing into the thin layer of watery snow that covers the road. There are no other footprints or tire tracks. I begin to wonder if Adam and Crane were even in the truck with me last night or if it was a dream. Feeling the cool morning air, I take the parka, push my arms into it, then walk.

Perhaps this should be a walk of shame, or one of stupidity and regret. But instead it's a walk of fury. Each step brings forth a memory and a sharp realization that I have trusted the wrong people–the wrong person. And Chuck was correct not so long ago when he turned to me and told me that I was stupid.

Seeing the chain-link fence in front of me, I pick up my pace to a near jog. I can hear its strange buzzing, even from the few hundred yards away that I am.

I can see one of the Volker standing stiff, watching me. His hand moves toward his pistol. I walk faster. He pulls the pistol from its holster and aims it at me.

"Stop," I hear him yell at me.

I move faster. "I am Andromeda Somers!" I shout to him. "Phoenix District Sovereign."

"Stop!" he yells at me.

But I walk closer to the fence. The buzzing gets louder. Too loud. It makes my head hurt and I feel something trickle from my nose. I reach up to wipe it away, finding a bit of blood.

"Back up," the Volker yells to me.

"Let me in!" I yell to him. "I am Andromeda–"

"Back away from the fence," he yells with urgency in his voice. I do and feel the buzzing sensation lessen in my head. "Show me your wrist," he yells across the fence.

Without thinking I pull up my sleeve and thrust my arm into the air for him. He makes a face and looking up I see that the cloth is still wrapped over the mark. I pull on the cloth, and show the Volker the mark that Dr. Akiyama burned into my skin.

"I am Andromeda–"

"I know who you are!" He shouts as he re-holsters

his weapon. "Stay there." He holds his hand out, signaling for me to stay where I am. Reaching for the radio on his shoulder, he speaks into it. When he is done, he turns back toward me. "I'm sorry about this, Mrs. Somers, have to shut down the fence to let you in here." He points at the gate in the fence and I notice that there is no keypad like at the other entrances to the District. "No way to stop it at this entrance." I nod at him. "It will be just a few minutes, stay there."

I stay where I am, pacing, the sneakers leaving imprints on the snowy road. I pace and I wait. More Volker collect at the gate. They talk into their radios. They watch me and the road behind me. It feels strange being stuck on this side of the gate, wanting to be let in so badly.

After a few minutes I hear the fence begin to power down, the buzzing lessens. "About ten more minutes!" The Volker yells to me. I nod and continue my pacing. I stop and turn to the forest, hearing the heavy plops of the night snow falling off of the trees as the sun warms the air. I guess that by afternoon all of the snow will have melted. I hear the buzzing of the fence lessen again and then completely dissipate.

I walk toward the fence. The Volker shakes his head. "What?" I ask impatiently.

One of the other Volker speaks into his radio. "Someone has to bring the key." He points at the lock on the gate.

The radio on his shoulder squawks to life. "Ten minutes out," a voice says.

I continue my pacing, this time closer to the fence since I don't have to fear its nose bleeding buzzing. Soon enough the Volker turn as an SUV speeds down the road toward us. The vehicle makes a hard stop, the tires skidding. People barrel out of the SUV, running toward the gate. I recognize Elvis, Sam, Alexander, and Ian.

"Andie!" I hear Sam's voice.

"Sam told us what happened," Elvis says as he pulls a ring of keys from his pocket and reaches for the now harmless fence. "How did you get free?"

"It's a long story," I tell him, looking at Ian. His face is a mixture of hope and worry. And I know that the entire time I was gone, he relived his worst fears.

Finally Elvis gets the gate unlocked and swings it open. I rush past them and throw my arms around Ian. Squeezing me to himself, he grips me so hard I can barely breathe. "I thought I lost you," he whispers into my ear. I pull back and look into his brown eyes, gleaming with the threat of tears. I've never seen Ian cry. I press my lips to his. After a few moments I hear Elvis clear his throat loudly from behind us. I pull away from Ian and step back as his arms loosen from around me.

"What happened out there?" Elvis asks.

"The Survivors had me," I start to say. "And–"

"Come here, boy," I hear Sam's voice. I look behind Elvis and see Sam standing at the gate I just ran through. "Come here," he repeats. I move to the side to see who Sam is talking to. There is a Guardian outside the gates, standing in the road where I just was.

"Crane is gone," Ian says.

"I know. Did you make the deal with the Survivors?" I ask.

Ian looks at Elvis. Elvis shakes his head. "We heard nothing from the Survivors. Crane wouldn't allow a search and rescue team to find you. We confronted him during a Committee meeting, forced him out."

"You just tossed him out into the wilderness?" I ask.

"We aren't assassins," Ian says. "What did you want us to do, kill him?"

"You could have imprisoned him or shot him in the head," I say.

Sam gives up on coaxing the Guardian back inside the gates, and taking note of our conversation he walks toward us. "We weren't going to kill him in cold blood," he says.

"Why not?" I ask. "He would have done it to any one of us."

"We'll let the Survivors take care of him. They're ruthless enough."

We all turn toward the road as the Guardian barks.

"Adam is still alive," I tell them.

"What?" All three of them respond in unison.

"Adam is alive, he's... his real name is Christian and he's leading the Survivors. He brought me here. Last night and..." I touch my head remembering the strange conversation with Crane in the truck. "He had Crane with him and then they were gone this morning."

Ian grabs my arm. "What did they do to you?" he asks.

The Guardian barks again. I turn, my memory feeling a bit foggy as I try and piece everything together.

"Why is that Guardian outside the fence?" I ask.

"Don't know," Sam shrugs off my question.

"What did they do to you?" Ian urges.

"I'm not sure..." I look at Elvis, Sam and then back to the Guardian. "Where are the children? Where's Lina and Raven?"

"They're at home," Ian says.

"With who? Why didn't you bring them?"

"We didn't think it was good for them to see you like this. Or if there was a problem we didn't want them stuck in the middle of it," Sam says.

"Who are they with?" I ask again.

"Blithe. Who else would we leave them with?" Ian says.

A moment of panic flashes through me. "We have to go. Now!" I start toward the SUV.

"Why?" Ian grabs my arm. "What's wrong?"

"Blithe is Adam's sister. Adam, who is really Christian, who is leading the Survivors. Who was with Crane last night–" I pause, focusing on the quiet fence. "How long has the fence been off for?"

"Maybe thirty minutes," Sam says.

From the look on Elvis's face I can tell he understands what just clicked together in my head. "Lock it up," Elvis instructs the Volker as he starts running toward the vehicle. He pulls a radio off of the dash and shouts something into it. Almost immediately the fence starts to hum. Everyone backs up.

I continue my run to the SUV. Elvis grabs my shoulder to stop me. "I'll drive." He opens the passenger door for me.

Sam, Alexander, and Ian get in on the other side as I buckle my seatbelt.

The ride is fast and tense.

"I'm sure they're fine," Ian says with a nervous tone.

"Tell me you knew nothing of this, Elvis?" I ask as he drives.

"I swear." He glances at me in the rearview mirror. "I didn't know. I would have never allowed this, Andie."

"Alexander?" I ask.

He shakes his head.

Elvis speeds through the streets, careens through the country roads that lead to the Pasture. Sam jumps out to open the gate. Elvis speeds through the opening, leaving Sam to run behind us. He skids to a stop near the barn. There is a collection of Guardians standing in the courtyard.

Leaping out of the SUV, I run for the schoolhouse, my sneakers sliding on the snowy grass. The door is open. The desks empty. The coatrack clear of child-sized jackets.

"NO!" I scream at the empty schoolhouse, my insides filling with a gut-wrenching horrible feeling. I've felt this before, except now it's twofold.

CHAPTER TWENTY-FOUR

"Why didn't the Guardians stop them?" Sam asks as I leave the main room of the school house and step out onto the porch.

"Because they weren't harming the children, just moving them. The Guardians protect all of us. Crane, Adam, and Blithe included," I tell him.

"I can't believe this," Sam replies.

"Did any of the weapons make it back with you?" I ask Sam.

He shakes his head. "The only thing I brought back was Tim, and he's not happy. Set him up in one of the Volker housing units until we figure out what to do with him."

"I have to find my children." I look around the courtyard, contemplating a plan. "You, Alexander, and Elvis need to stay here. You need to protect the Residents."

"What about you?" he argues.

"I'm leaving."

"I'm going with you," Ian says with a curt tone.

I glance at him. Judging by how he looks right now I know that there is no arguing with him. He's blaming himself for the children missing. I correct myself; they're not missing, they've been kidnapped.

Suddenly everyone is moving. Sam runs off to the barn with Elvis and Alexander. Ian follows me to the house. I strip off the borrowed sweats as I walk through the house, for once not caring that Ian is following me. I search my room for warm clothes. Clothes that I think might be useful in this journey that I am about to go on. Heavy jeans, layered shirts. I find an old pair of boots in the closet. Next to the boots sits a backpack. I take it, throw in a fleece blanket and head for the kitchen. I take a loaf of bread from the freezer and fill two water bottles. Then I head for the front door with Ian on my heels, picking up the parka I discarded on the floor when I walked in the door. He holds it out for me.

"Are you going to change?" I ask him as I slip my arms into the parka and zip it.

He's already wearing boots, jeans and a thick sweater. "I just need my coat." He reaches for the peg that his winter coat is hanging on.

I press my hand to his arm. "I don't blame you. I want you to know that."

He nods, removing the coat from the peg and putting it on.

Slipping my arms into the backpack, I run down the porch steps, headed for the courtyard. We meet the others at the barn.

"What are you taking?" Elvis asks. "The train?"

"Won't they be expecting the train?" I ask. "It wasn't hard for them to sabotage our route before."

"Where do you think he took them?" Sam asks.

"They had me in this small town called Romney, West Virginia. And Adam, or Christian, told them that he would be back there with Crane. But that was before I knew who he really is."

"That's two states away, we can't walk that far. I doubt they did," Ian speaks up.

"There's the truck Adam left on the highway last night," I tell them. "It has less than ten gallons of gas in the tank."

"You could take one of the Volker SUVs," Elvis suggests.

"Until we run out of gas. And then what?" I ask. "How do we make it home with a group of children and adults?"

"If Blithe even wants to come back," Sam whispers.

"What's that?" Elvis asks.

Sam shakes his head. "I can leave later with the train. Pick everyone up and bring them back." Sam suggests.

"How would we know when they're ready?" Elvis asks.

"We have a cell phone. One that Andie had before. She can call us," Sam says.

Thank God for the last cell phone on earth.

"We have to call Crystal River," I suggest. "They have satellites. Remember, Sam? They can search the roads leading away from here and see what type of vehicle they are traveling in and let us know."

"I'll get ahold of them," Alexander offers. "Actually, if it's all right with you, I think I'll go now so I can get them looking before you leave."

"I think that's good," I tell Alexander.

"Good luck," he tells us as he rushes out of the barn.

Elvis opens the gun case. He removes a handgun and gives it to Ian. He hesitates before handing one to me.

"Give it to me, Elvis."

"Just don't want you to lose your head, Andie. I know how Crane likes to push your buttons."

"Yeah." I reach for the weapon and pull it from his hand. "This won't be the first time I've pointed a gun at his head."

"Make sure you're pointing it at the right person," he suggests.

"She's not going to kill anyone," Sam says as he loads bullets into extra magazines. "She's just going to get the children. Andie would never actually shoot someone."

I look at Elvis. He knows what I did in Wolf Creek. I killed that imposter. I wonder if I could do it again. If Crane were standing in front of me, or Adam, could I pull that trigger again? I take the gun from Elvis and put it in my bag, along with the spare magazines from Sam.

"Here," Sam holds out his hand. In it is the cell phone I left on the train. "It's been charging since I found it. Full battery. I have the number so we can contact you."

I shove the phone in my pocket. "Ready?" I ask Ian. He nods.

We walk toward the SUVs. "Take the first one," Sam tells us. "It has a double tank and I just filled it."

Ian walks toward the driver's seat. I pause before opening the door, feeling the cold stare from the collection of Guardians waiting in the courtyard. I whistle for them.

"What are you doing?" Ian asks me.

"I think they should come with us. Some of them at least."

"Andie, those things are huge, we could only fit three of them in here if we are lucky."

I open the back hatch of the SUV and motion to the group of dogs. Three jump in. A fourth paces as though it's looking for room to fit. "You're going to have to run," I tell it, remembering how they ran after the Jeep in Hanford.

I get in the passenger side as Ian starts the vehicle.

--

We wait at the fence, the one I just walked through a few hours ago, the day still damp from the night's snow and cold. Elvis radios the nuclear plant to have the electricity diverted. Ian and I both pace as we wait for the loud purring of the fence to dissipate. When it finally does, Elvis moves to unlock the gate, pulling it open far enough for the SUV to fit through.

"I'm glad to see you're not going alone." Sam motions behind the SUV where a collection of Guardians waits.

"What are they going to do?" Ian asks.

"They'll follow us. Keep us safe," I tell him.

Elvis hollers for us to pass.

"Andie," Sam stops me. "Bring them back."

"I will," I tell him as I stand on my toes to hug him tightly. "I'll bring Blithe too, if she wants." I feel him nodding. "You two already had something, didn't you?"

"Yeah," he whispers. "I wasn't expecting this from her."

"She may not have known, Sam. If she went, it was

for the children. You have to know that about her."

"Andie?" Ian urges. "Let's go."

"You better go see what Alexander found out. Talk you soon, Sam." I leave him standing on the side of the road and get in the SUV with Ian.

Ian starts the vehicle. "Take the back roads," I tell him. "Stay off of the main highways."

"Okay," he replies, looking in the rearview mirror. I turn around to see the collection of Guardians running after us.

--

"Why the hell is it snowing?" Ian asks, flipping on the windshield wipers. "It's supposed to be summer."

"Sam says there's a bad storm coming in from the west. Emanuel can see it on the satellite images."

"Great," Ian exclaims as he slows the vehicle.

"Andie?" Sam asks into the phone.

"Yeah?"

"Emanuel says they are a few hours ahead of you. He can see a large vehicle, like a van. They are headed straight for Romney. But that storm is headed straight for you."

"Wonderful," I tell him.

"If you can get into Southern Pennsylvania you'll miss the worst of it. He says West Virginia looks to be in the clear."

"Okay," I tell Sam. "I'm getting off the phone. Call me if there are any changes." I end the call. "One good thing about the snow is it will keep the Survivors inside," I tell Ian. "At least we won't have to worry about trouble from them."

"This couldn't be falling on a worse day."

"Sam says that if we make it to Southern Pennsylvania we'll miss the worst of it."

"If we have that much gas."

I lean over and look at the gauges. "Sam said this thing has a double tank. That's all we used to get here. Two tanks and Adam stopped the truck just a short walk from the gates."

I wait for Ian to ask me about what happened, but he doesn't.

"They have to know we're following them." Ian shakes his head and sighs.

"I'm sure that's what Crane wants."

"I don't understand why he would take the children."

"Because Crane wants me to go get him. Adam wants to kill him. And Crane knows that I had no intention of saving him. So he took my children."

"Our children," Ian corrects me.

"Our children," I repeat. I don't argue that Raven is actually Adam's child, but I guess he's not much of a parent. Raven has known Ian his entire life. "I'm guessing Adam wanted to get Blithe away from Crane but she wouldn't leave the boys."

"Still," Ian scratches his chin. "There has to be something else."

"I'm sure you're right. There's always something else. We'll just have to wait until we get there to find out what it is."

--

By mid-afternoon it starts to snow. Ian drives. It's a white-knuckled-speeding-through-the-snow drive. The kind that we are used to in the north. Ian drives and drives, until the day passes and the snow lessens. We both watch anxiously as the gas tank gauge moves closer and closer to empty.

When I am sure it is the middle of the night, and there is nothing more than a thin coating of snow on the ground, the SUV sputters to a stop. With an expletive, Ian turns the wheel to ease the vehicle onto the side of the road before putting it in park and turning it off.

Moments later the cell phone rings.

"Andie?" Sam's voice asks.

"Yeah, Sam?"

"Emanuel just called and said your truck stopped."

"We're out of gas," I tell him.

"It seems Crane and Adam brought the children to an old school. It's in that town you mentioned. Romney. You're about ten miles away."

"It's still snowing here."

"The snow should stop overnight. But Emanuel says it's going to get really cold."

I look at the windshield, noticing the tiny spiderwebs of ice forming as he speaks. "So we should wait until morning?"

"Yeah," Sam replies. "We'll watch from the satellites and let you know if anything changes."

"Okay," I tell him before hanging up. "Thanks, Sam."

Ian looks at me expectantly. I fill him in on everything Sam just told me.

Ian turns to look out his window. "I don't see the other Guardians. Do you think they made it?" he asks.

"I don't know. I hope they did." I turn looking at the ones that are sleeping in the cargo area of our SUV. "We should get some sleep," I suggest.

I reach for my bag and pull out the bread and water. We eat in silence, only a small meal in case we need to make it last. It's not long before the heat of the vehicle dissipates and we can see our breath. I shiver, wishing I had put an extra layer of clothes on.

Ian moves toward me. "It's getting colder. I was hoping the heat would last a little longer in here," he says as he pulls me toward him. "At least we can keep each other warm."

I pull the fleece blanket out of my bag and lay it over us as we huddle together.

Ian sighs.

"What's wrong?" I ask.

"I just can't believe I let this happen again."

"Stop it," I tell him as I tuck my head under his chin, trying to quell my own worry for my children. "You didn't do anything."

"That's the problem, Andie. It's happening all over again. Crane takes our child and then you."

"Shush," I tell him. "We'll get the children and I'm not going anywhere."

I feel a shudder run through him. "I hope they're warm."

"I'm sure they are. The building they held me in had electricity and water."

"What did they do with you?" Ian asks.

I tell him every single detail, except the part where Adam tricked me into kissing him.

"This isn't working," Ian says when I'm done.

"What?"

"I'm freezing."

I feel him shudder again. "Maybe you shouldn't have lost so much weight," I tell him as I pinch his stomach. I turn around, seeing the Guardians in the back. "The dogs look warm," I tell him. "We could move in the back with them.

"Okay," he agrees through his chattering teeth.

We climb over the seats and Ian adjusts the back bench seat so it's lying down and we have one large cargo area. We lie between two of the dogs, with the third one laying at our feet. I look up at Ian, our noses almost touching. Feeling the heat radiating off of the large dogs, "We'll be sweating by morning," I tell him.

Ian smiles as he reaches out to wrap his arm around me and pull me closer. I lean into him and press my lips to his. "Thank you," I tell him.

"For what?"

"For not giving up on us."

"I couldn't give up on you, not even if I tried," he responds, his dark eyes penetrating mine.

--

I can't say I slept much between the three dogs. But being curled up, with my back pressed tight against Ian's chest and his arm wrapped tightly around my waist, kept me plenty warm.

The shrill ring of the cell phone causes us both to stir.

"Hello?" I answer.

Sam's voice responds. "Andie, the storm's over." I look out the foggy window and see the morning light start to fill the sky. "You've got about ten miles to walk. We've been watching the area all night. There's no movement in the forest, no patrols at all. It's like they're just sitting there, waiting for you to show up."

"Of course." I move to sit up. Ian sits and starts putting his boots on. "What's it like out there?"

"Looks like a mild day. Most of the snow should melt by the afternoon and it should warm up. It's a straight shot south if you follow the road you're parked on. We will keep an eye in the sky and call if there's a problem."

"Okay, thanks, Sam."

After ending the call I start pulling on my boots.

"Sam says the way there is quiet," I tell Ian. "They'll call if there's a problem."

Ian starts folding the fleece blanket. "Better get moving then." He crawls through the SUV, gets out and releases the trunk hatch.

The three Guardians jump out, followed by me. I adjust the backpack on my back and look up and down the road. The road is damp, the shoulder coated with snow, and the air seems to get warmer by the minute.

Just before we head south, Ian catches movement in the forest. He reaches for me, pushing me behind the vehicle. I hear the rustling of footsteps. Ian exhales.

"Holy crap."

"What?" I ask.

"There's a ton of them."

"A ton of what?"

Ian pulls on my sleeve until I am standing right next to him and points toward the forest. As my eyes focus on the shadowed woods, I make out the figures of more Guardians standing in the cover of the trees, as though they are waiting for us to make the first move.

"Wow," I reply. "It's like all of them followed us."

We walk south, staying on the road. Since I haven't heard from Sam, I check the phone. The battery is half-full and there's four bars of service. I remind myself to ask Alexander or George who else is connected to the lone cell phone service.

We walk in silence for over an hour until Ian asks, "Why did Elvis give you that look, when Sam said that you weren't going to actually shoot anyone?"

I skip a step. "What do you mean?"

"I watched Elvis give you this look, like he knows something Sam doesn't."

"I don't think you want to know, Ian."

"Why wouldn't I want to know?"

I can feel him watching me as we walk. "I don't want to make this any harder for you."

"What?"

"Accepting me back into your life. The past two years have been hard enough. If anything else–"

"Just tell me, Andie." I stop walking. Ian stops and turns toward me. "Andie," he urges, "tell me."

"Elvis gave me that look because… because I killed a man."

Ian's body stills and his jaw slackens.

"I warned you," I say. "I warned you that this wouldn't make it easier. I know you. I know your beliefs. This is why I never told you. This is why I didn't want to tell you."

He takes a step toward me. "Wh–"

I take two steps backward, raising my hands to keep him away from me. "I warned you, Ian. I had to do things I'm not proud of. Plenty of things I'm not proud of. You know most of them."

Ian grabs my wrist before I can take another step backward and pulls me into him, hard, wrapping both of his arms around my back in a tight embrace.

"My beliefs have changed. As soon as the Reformation occurred, it all changed. I can't hold those things against you. I won't."

"Ian–"

He presses his lips to mine, halting my words. "Now, what else are you keeping from me?" he asks when he breaks the kiss. "I'm not talking about the Entities. I'm talking about where you've been the past few weeks. What happened between you and Adam? I can tell there's something else you're keeping from me."

He squeezes me tighter and an emotion, a fear, wells up from my chest. I don't want to disappoint him, not again. I'm sure what I'm about to say could end us for good. But he wants to know, he's demanding it and I only want truth between us.

"I kissed him." I look away from Ian's face. "They had me locked up for over a week, they drugged me, and he said the only way he could get me out was if I kissed him."

"And," Ian asks, his voice thick.

"I just did it, but it didn't mean anything, you have to believe me, Ian. It was just a kiss. It was the only way I could get back to you."

"Did you enjoy it?"

I finally look into his eyes. "No."

He nods and releases me from his embrace. We resume our walk, the pack of Guardians following us softly, Ian's relaxed demeanor now gone. He's fuming and by the time we reach the rusted sign that says *Welcome to Romney*, I'm pretty sure he's ready to burst. I nervously check the cell phone to make sure we have service and Sam can reach us if there's a problem.

As we follow the road into town, it ends in a three-way stop and the school the Survivors kept me in is a few hundred yards to our left.

We run for the school.

A familiar figure is simply sitting on the front steps

343

of the school. It's Mack. He stands as we get closer.

"Thought you'd be here sooner," he tells us.

"Where are my children?" I ask him, slowing to a stop.

He leans to the side, taking in the pack of Guardians which stand behind us. "That orange-haired guy," Mack swirls his hand near the side of his head. "He wanted to speak with you first." He points at me. "Said it was important."

"The children," Ian demands.

"They're fine," Mack says. "Wasn't expecting a load of kids to show up, nor that pretty lady. Either way, they're playing in the gym." He thumbs toward the door. "You ready to talk to that Crane guy?"

"And Adam?" I ask.

"With Crane," Mack says.

"I'm not leaving you with them," Ian steps in front of me.

I press my hand to his back. He can do this. "I can handle Crane and Adam." I slide the cell phone into his pocket. And lowering my voice, I whisper, "Get the children and if you need to, get them out of here." I slide the backpack off and hand it to him. "There are train tracks not far from here. They walked me here in a few hours. Call Sam when you need to."

Ian reaches behind himself and squeezes my hand, hard. I take that as an agreement. We walk up the steps, the Guardians following us.

"Leave those outside," Mack tells us.

I glance at the large dogs. "They don't take commands," I tell him. "You keep them out if you don't like them."

Mack frowns before turning around and entering the school.

344

We walk into the familiar hallway of the school, the Guardians trailing behind us. The gymnasium is to the left. Ian's head snaps in that direction at the sound of a basketball hitting the floor. There is giggling and laughter from the double doors.

"Go," I tell Ian.

He walks toward the gymnasium as Mack stops in the middle of the long hallway. "They're in here," he says, pointing to the door labeled *Principal's Office*.

"How appropriate," I mumble to myself.

Mack knocks and pushes the door open. Crane and Adam are both there, positioned on opposite sides of the room. Crane sits in an office chair. Adam stands near the corner.

"I didn't come for you," I tell Crane as I enter the room. "I came for my children, not you. I don't care what this liar does with your speckled carcass." I point at Adam. "I'm not saving it."

I walk over to Adam, not even breaking my stride and slap him across the face as hard as I can. "What the hell were you thinking?" I yell at him.

He turns back to me with a grimace. "Deserved that."

"You're right. You did!" I back up before I give in to the urge to hit him again. "And you're lucky I didn't let Ian in here. I'm sure if he sees you, he'll kill you." I turn back to Crane, who sits behind the principal's desk apparently enjoying the display before him. "What are you doing, taking my children? Of all the bullshit you've pulled this has got to be the worst kind."

"I had to make you come back here. And you already told me that you wouldn't come for me, only your children."

"Why haven't you killed him yet?" I ask Adam.

He rubs the side of his reddened face. "Because you need to listen to what he has to say."

"I don't want to listen to him!" I glare at Crane. "I just want to go home. I just want peace from all of this. I did what he asked me. I did everything. He promised me peace. That is all I want." I shake my head and swallow hard, trying to control the trembling in my voice. "It's bad enough he planned the Reformation. He changed the world."

"Is it so bad now?" Crane asks as he folds his hands together. "All humanity needed was a little tweak to set things right. Did you take a breath outside? There's almost no pollution."

"Yeah, and no one seems to know what season it is anymore," I snap at him.

"It will settle out," Crane tries to soothe my speculation. "There's more wildlife. The forests are starting to regrow. What we did was right, Andromeda, the planet would not have survived if things kept going the way they were."

"And what are you going to do when the population starts increasing again and when the Sovereign stray from their vows to protect the Residents and turn corrupt, just like it was before? Except this time, you made me create those people. The Residents won't care what they do. They will listen to the ones in charge. They will do whatever they are told."

"That is exactly why I need you, Andromeda. I need you to help keep things on track."

"I've done all I can for you. I just want peace now."

"You can have your peace and you can have your children back, on one condition."

"I don't want to hear this." I start for the door.

"It seems your friend here has agreed to help me,"

he tips his head toward Adam.

Adam gives me a look. One that I've seen before, when I knew his face as simply Adam, the one that says there's more to this story.

"He's not my friend," I inform Crane. "He's nothing more than a liar."

"Listen," Adam says, his voice a baritone of reason.

I cross my arms. "What?"

"You agree," Crane pauses to clear his throat as though he's practiced this speech but now he is unable to find the words. "You agree, Andromeda Somers, to live forever."

"What are you talking about?"

"Live forever."

"Why would I want to live forever?"

"Everyone is afraid of death; everyone wants to avoid that fear. I'm offering you that chance. I need you."

"That's impossible," I dismiss him, reaching for the door.

"Not anymore. I made it possible." Crane taps his fingertips together in front of his chest. "A long time ago, I made it very possible."

I drop my arm, the slightest bit intrigued. "What do you mean?"

Crane clears his throat. "A very long time ago I invested in a lot of research. Genetic research, robotics, you name it, we did it. And Nanobiotechnology was a major field. We created nanocytes, tiny little robots that can be injected into the human body and they repair all the damage associated with age, illness, and injury. The end result is that the biological specimen injected with the nanocytes gets to live forever." Crane adjusts his tie as I digest this information.

"I don't believe you," I tell him.

"Hmm. You don't?"

"No."

"Ah yes, it must be the scientist in you. Would you like some proof? Some numbers and data to mull about in your brain. Here's one: Did you ever wonder why the Guardians just keep multiplying? After all these years living outdoors, many of them should have died. I know how you work, Andromeda. You count things and I know you've counted them. I know you've noticed there are more. That is because they don't die."

"I still don't believe you."

"Well, we have time for you to see that I'm telling the truth."

"No," I take a step closer toward the door. "I'm not listening to this garbage."

"Agree." His voice gets louder, almost a warning. "This new world needs you, forever. There is no one else who can do what you do. No one else has the attachment to the Residents that you do. And the Residents trust you, the Sovereign trust you."

"No," I tell him again. I look at Adam. His face is placid as he stares at me. He believes this propaganda that Crane is spewing.

"You want your children freed? You want to go back to the serenity of the Pasture? Agree."

For a moment I think if I agree it might just get us out of here. If I just agree to his lies, no matter how incomprehensible they seem. If I say yes, he'll just let us go. "And my family?" I ask him.

"I am only offering this to you." Crane stands from his seat.

"Definitely no," I tell him, taking another step toward the door.

"You don't worry about your fragility, Andromeda? Why Baillie almost crushed you a few years ago. I'm sure you recognized it then."

"I don't care, Crane. I'm not afraid to die. I realized that a long time ago. I thought I needed to be alive to protect my children from you, but now I have a lot more people on my side. People who will take care of them. I am not afraid to die trying to get them out of here. But I'm definitely not going to live forever without my family at my side."

"It's your decision. Immortality, everlasting life, or your family. They'll move on without you. And you will get over their deaths when the time comes."

"And if I kill you now? Then it won't matter, then I can do whatever I want."

"Sure, that would be one scenario. But the nanocytes are already waiting within your body. All I have to do is press a button to release them. You kill me, you get blessed with an immortal life."

"You're full of shit."

"Try me. They've been there since you returned from Crystal River and Morris died."

Pushing up my sleeve, I rub my fingers over the small scar where Crane injected the tracking device in my forearm. "You're not even giving me a choice." I look to Adam, who remains standing still on the other side of the room. "I don't want this," I whisper. "I don't want this," I repeat louder looking at Crane and Adam to make sure they heard me.

"I know," Crane replies. "But many others do. It's a gift. One that I've only offered to a few. Those with strong principles, those who no longer fear their own death."

"You don't fit that description," I tell him.

He laughs. "I did once. A long time ago. But that's what watching the same cycle of contamination and corruption repeat itself over and over again will do to a person."

"Then why are you doing this?" I ask.

"Because we are creating a new world. Instilling old morals that most have forgotten, and now this new world needs deities to guide them, deities to fear."

I step closer toward the door. From the first Committee meeting I speculated that he was playing God, but this, to actually hear it from his mouth, floors me.

Crane continues his speech, "For hundreds of years humans speculated in a divinity, each arguing that their idea of God was correct. They prayed and worshipped and sacrificed, and guess what? Nothing happened. Because there were no gods, just stories. Humanity continued in their downward spiral of wickedness and corruption. We can give them what they've always prayed for. Real gods, real responses to their prayers."

"So this is why everyone appeases you? This is why they all fear you and do what you say?"

He nods. "They just want a piece of the pie. They want this gift that I have offered you."

"This is why Dr. Drake wanted to be on my team, because he knew, didn't he?"

He nods, smiling.

"I can't live without them," I tell him.

"Imagine it. A life forever. You could have a thousand new families."

I close my eyes, envisioning Lina and Raven growing into adulthood, finding their own pairs and having their own families. Standing beside them, I see Ian, his hair graying, his skin wrinkling, while I stay the

350

same. I can see their children. My grandchildren. Ian's grave. Lina's grave. Raven's grave. But there will never be a grave for me, not with this future. My static existence next to them seems so wrong. A heavy, hot tear slides down my cheek. I don't wipe it away. I let them see it. I let them see what this will make me become. This will ruin me.

I open my eyes, pulling myself back from this heartbreaking future and ask, "Who else?"

"What do you mean?" Crane asks sweetly.

"Who else are you offering this option to?"

"Well, there's you. Me, of course. I tested the nanocytes on myself and here I am, the epitome of health."

"When?"

He smiles a sly smile. "When did I test them on myself? A long time ago. Long before you were born."

"Who else then?" I demand.

"Sakima, George Crossbender, and a few other of the original Funding Entities are on my list if they fulfill my wishes, if they pass the right tests." He stands and begins walking toward me.

"This is so wrong, Crane. You chose the most extreme members of the group. The absolute worst and best."

"No." he reaches forwards, grasping my hands, squeezing them. "It is so right. The earth will be forever taken care of. There will be no shifting of power, no alteration of laws, just the same few to watch over and keep everything right. They will keep a balance, a yin and a yang, opposites; they will balance it and keep it right."

I try to pull my hands out of his grasp. "I don't want this."

"You made those people, Andromeda." He lets go of my hands. "You made those Residents, you altered them genetically and now you need to watch over them. Nobody will watch over them better than you will."

"Find someone else, Crane. There are plenty of brains in Hanford. You don't need me for this."

"Ah, but we do."

I hear the loud laughter of the children down the hall as they play in the gymnasium.

"Why are we doing this here?" I ask Crane. "In the middle of nowhere West Virginia?"

"There are ears everywhere in the Districts. And if the other Entities knew that you have been given this gift, they would be very jealous of you. And now that this little Resistance has formed against me, you'll see. You'll see what those Entities will do for a chance to live forever. But they don't know what I've just told you. They still fear their death. It is obvious that you do not."

"You don't think they'll find out? With each year they'll notice I'm not aging."

"Don't fret, Andromeda. I will ensure your safety."

"What happens after?" I ask. "After you've done this to me, then what?"

"You go home. You live your long life and resume your duties. You watch over generations of Residents. You decide with the other Entities on changes."

"I don't want you in Phoenix." I tell him.

"That's fine. There are other places I can go. Although, Phoenix is my hometown, the place where I grew up a long time ago."

"What are you talking about?"

"I'm sure when you last visited the family grave you

didn't pay attention to the old, crumbled gravestone near the tree line?"

I think back to the day I was there with Raven, telling him stories about the relatives he will never know. He did, at one point, place his hand on an old gravestone outside of our family plot. That one strange stone with the name *B. C. Bertrand*.

"A grave would mean that someone is dead."

"Or presumed dead," he offers.

"That's impossible, we are not related," I tell him with disgust. "I would have seen it. I would have seen it in our data!"

"It's not a blood relation."

"Then what is it?"

I look at Adam, who shrugs and rubs the stubble on his chin.

"Let me tell you a story," Crane smiles. "Once upon a time there was a young man, a very intelligent young man—"

"I don't want to hear your life story," I interrupt him.

"This is not a story of my life. So this young man was very intelligent, his name was Arthur. He graduated at the top of his class, attended Stanford University on a full scholarship and then moved on to Johns Hopkins University to pursue his post-doctoral work. This young man had a very promising future, working on the cutting edge of cancer research and all. You see, cancer research was a major topic in those days. The chance of a cancer diagnosis among the general population was astronomical and everyone wanted a cure. The race to find a cure was a competition. Scientists were often pitted against each other, always in pairs, working on the same type of cancer research. We had the same cells, the same samples, the same equipment."

"Now that you're saying *we*, I'm guessing you've come into the picture?" I ask.

"Yes. So Arthur and I were paired together, both of us working ourselves to death trying to find a cure for a specific form of bone cancer. Now the rules were you were not to speak or collaborate with the team you were working against. The Cancer Institute founders didn't want a contamination of theories. One team worked during the day, the other at night. We were not to cross paths. But one day, we did. Both of us sitting in the park outside of our government funded housing development. We were walking our dogs and realizing that we had the same breed, we stopped to talk. When it came to the topic of work... we realized we were on opposing teams. Arthur and I were really working against each other.

"Arthur and I knew that we had a better chance of finding a cure if we worked together. So we did. Meeting secretly, collaborating. We spent all of this time cutting out tumors, irradiating body parts, injecting dangerous medications into the bodies of these sick people only to have another cancer spring up, a secondary diagnosis. For years we did this, until one day we came to a conclusion. This was an unwinnable fight, this race for a cure, these cancers that were consuming humans. So we looked elsewhere. We looked at the food we ate, the chemicals we were exposed to, the toxic wastes leaching into our systems from years of abusing the earth. All the while the population was exploding, the ozone depleted, and soon the skies over the busiest cities were thick with smog. Arthur and I knew we had determined the cause,

354

the whole time the real cancer was the human race.

"So as the government was shifting monies from research and development to better the human race, to food and housing to care for the population, it wasn't long before our funding was cut. Both of us were without a job. But I had a secret. One that not many knew. I had a wealthy family trust and being the only inheritor I was able to better our lives. I bought a little island, built a little lab, hired a few scientists and crew. Having no means to support himself, Arthur joined me immediately. And instead of searching for a cure for cancer, we searched for a way to cure the human race from its cancerous ways.

"The money didn't last for long. So we had to outsource ourselves. This was a time when people wanted to choose the gender of their children, their eye color, their hair color, and we could do that. We were solicited by the richest members of society; celebrities, kings, queens, rulers of the free world, you name it, they came to us. And so we made money, and contacts. Are you listening, Andromeda?" he asks in the middle of his story.

I'm listening. I've been listening, so intently that I find my mouth hanging open. I close it slowly and swallow hard. What an information dump.

"Because this is where it gets good. This is the important part. One week Arthur was attending a genomics conference. While I had instructed him to only bring back a few of the brightest minds to help us, he brought back one person: a biomedical engineer. She was a very beautiful woman with blonde curly hair and green eyes, much like our Catalina. At first I was very wary of his selection, not only because of her beauty, but she was so quiet and I was sure Arthur was not thinking with his head when he brought her back. But I was wrong. Andrea turned out to be one of our best scientists. She was the one to suggest we branch off into the field of Nanobiotechnology. We had come to the conclusion that there needed to be a larger change to society and we all feared that finding others to continue on with this plan would be hard. So we were searching for a way to continue on ourselves."

"And you made the nanocytes so you three could live forever and do this. This Reformation was your plan, wasn't it?" I ask.

"Yes, it was. It didn't take long for us to figure it out."

Crane smoothes his hand over his tie. "Soon, something began to change in Arthur. It seems he fell in love with our biomedical engineer. But then, living on a tropical island surrounded by the beauty of nature can do that to a person."

"Let me guess," I interrupt him again. "You loved her too."

"No," he says with a small smile. "I was too intent on this plan we were creating. I had no time for love, or marriage, or children, as Arthur did. It wasn't long before Andrea became pregnant. They did it the natural way, you see, there was no playing with the genome of Andrea and Arthur. I worried for them, but I was wrong. Andrea delivered a beautiful baby girl and they named her Selene." He stops for a moment to clear his throat. "While I never wanted children I found myself very fond of Selene. Especially when she called me Uncle Burton. It was… very sweet." He looks away from me for the first time since he started this story.

"So back to the adults. Being involved with the leaders of the world, tweaking their genetic data, meant that we were also involved with the high criminals of the world. And this made our job very dangerous. We created our own security detail, the Volker. And furthered that security detail to include the Guardians. But we also had to travel a lot, which made that danger uncomfortably close at times. This became apparent as Arthur and Andrea traveled back to the states to solicit a very prominent scientist and bring him back. It seems there was a drug lord in Rio de Janeiro who was rather unhappy with the intellect of his son whom we genetically altered for him. This drug lord wanted a smart son, someone to take over the family business, but what we gave him was a genius brain and drug lords have no time for a child with book smarts, they want the street smarts kind. If only we had realized this before. Sadly enough Arthur and Andrea never made it back from their last trip. They were murdered in their hotel room as they packed to leave."

"What about their child?" I ask.

"Ah, Andromeda." He smiles. "That is a very good question, indeed. They must have had some intuition about their mortality, or maybe there was some warning. Either way, after their bodies were discovered so was a child, hiding in the back of the hotel closet. Selene was alive and well, albeit she had just witnessed the murder of her parents, my greatest friends and collaborators."

"Let me guess, you raised her as your own and everything was unicorns and rainbows?"

"No. I was–I am," he corrects himself, "a very selfish person. And Arthur and Andrea and I had a plan. We promised each other that we would continue to carry it out even if something happened to one of us. So because of my selfishness, I allowed Selene to go to a foster family. Being an orphan myself, despite having been placed in a poorer example of a family when my parents died, I hand-picked a couple whom I thought embodied the ideas and beliefs of her parents. I have missed them terribly, but I know that I have been able to keep my promise to them."

He stops, looking at me expectantly. Perhaps he does have a heart.

"I don't understand, how does this relate to me?"

"You haven't figured it out yet?" he asks.

I stare at him, my brain spinning, trying to make some connection here. But the sound of the children laughing down the hall is distracting and so are the eyes of Crane and Adam on me.

"Your grandmother was an orphan. Did your mother never tell you?"

"Yes, she did, but my grandmother's name was–"

"Constance *Selene* Salk," Crane says. "The women on your mother's side of the family have a habit of not changing their last names once they are married. I'm guessing it has something to do with not wanting to forget the past. Not wanting to forget that loving family that adopted Selene. Except for you, you're the first to take on your husband's surname."

"So you are my great-grandfather's best friend?"

"Yes," he smiles proudly.

"That means you should be dead."

"And here I am. Another example for you that the nanocytes work."

"And you've been keeping an eye on me this entire time? My whole life you've been keeping tabs on me."

"Yes."

"I can't believe this."

"You should. You need to. It will help you come to

terms with your legacy."

"I don't want it."

"I promised your great-grandfather."

"I didn't know him!" I yell.

"This is your birthright."

"You've done nothing but play with my head this entire time." I point at Crane. "You ruined my family, you threatened me, you wanted me to pair us together. What if I had agreed to your proposition back then? If I had paired us–" I hold down the bile rising in the back of my throat.

"I would have let Baillie kill you and waited for Catalina to grow up," Crane says before I have a chance to finish my thought. "It would have meant that you were weak, not strong like your great-grandmother was. She fought for you to live. She hid your grandmother in that closet and fought to protect Selene. I had to make sure that you had these same traits."

I don't want this.

"Just think, Andromeda, you can keep them safe for forever. Generations of your family members."

I don't want this.

"No harm will become of them. And if someone else should meet the requirements, they may inherit the same gift I am about to bestow upon you. You can make a difference."

I don't want this.

"Andromeda, you want this. You need this. I need you."

I don't want this.

But... if he can get them into me, then he can get them out of me. And if I say yes now, then that will give me time to find a cure, to retract the nanocytes and live in peace. I've done it before with his creations. I removed the transmitter from Adam's arm. I can find a way to remove the nanocytes. If I say yes, I get them back, and Crane will believe that I'm on board with this plan of his, this plan of my ancestors.

I don't want this.

"Andromeda?" Crane asks one more time.

"Okay," I say with a hesitant voice.

"You're ready?" he asks.

I don't want this.

"I... I think so." I close my eyes. *No!* "Yes."

Opening my eyes, I watch as Crane reaches into his pocket and removes a small metallic disk, no bigger than a half-dollar. "They've been inside you this entire time," he says as he places the disc between his index finger and thumb. "Waiting for me to release them. The pain will only be momentary as they attach to your cells and familiarize themselves with your DNA." He pinches the disc between his fingers. "Forgive me, Andromeda, for the path to becoming a leader of men is not without pain."

I feel a sharp pain in my arm, throbbing from where Crane injected my tracking device. I press my hand to the area. It does nothing to stop the throbbing. The feeling intensifies into a burning sensation deep within my arm and then moving up, toward my shoulder.

"Just give it a moment," Crane says.

I swallow a groan of discomfort, dropping down onto one knee, pulling my arm close to my body. It stings and burns as though I submerged my arm in a pot of boiling water. Adam starts to walk toward me, holding his hands out to help me.

"Get away from me!" I warn him.

He stands up straight and does nothing but watch.

After a few minutes in this position, it seems, the pain dissipates until I can feel it no more. I move to stand once again.

"Ah," Crane smiles with accomplishment. "It is done. Congratulations on your immortality."

"I'm not thanking you for this," I tell him.

"I expected that," he replies. "So this is where we part. I will give you some time to come to terms with your new mission, Andromeda. But I will call on you again. There are things that need to be discussed."

"Where are you going?" I ask.

"I think I'll go to Hanford first. I have to have a discussion with George Crossbender. Then I will visit Sakima."

"What about the Residents, the Survivors?" I ask, remembering the war we were planning on defending ourselves against.

"There will be no war," he says as he walks toward the door. "You have control of the Residents of Phoenix. And Adam, or dare I say Christian, has control of the Survivors. All is well." He pulls the door open and walks through. "Tootles." He waves.

I follow him and watch as he walks down the hallway and out the front door of the building as though he had not a care in the world. I feel Adam's presence next to me.

"What does he have on you?" I ask, turning to Adam.

He shakes his head from side-to-side, refusing to answer.

"How could you do this, Adam? How could you agree to this and pull me into it? You're so selfish." I start walking toward the gymnasium.

"No more selfish than you." He grabs my arm,

stopping me. "All this time you've been fighting to keep your family safe. This started with *your* family."

"Don't turn this on me."

"I've escaped death twice. What happens if there's a third time? I succeeded in keeping Blithe out of trouble, keeping her safe within Phoenix. And now there's Raven and Lina, and you."

"Don't include my family. Ian and I can take care of ourselves."

"You'd like to think so wouldn't you?"

"I'm done, Adam, or Christian. I don't even know what to call you anymore."

"Call me Adam."

"Whatever. I don't ever plan on seeing you again, so it doesn't matter."

"And if I want to see Raven? He is my son, after all."

"Yet you've never been there for him."

"I met him when we brought them here."

"And that's the last time. I'll be dead before I let you near him again."

Just then I hear the door crash open, slamming against the wall. It seems it's only a second before Ian is running toward Adam. He doesn't stop or slow or anything. Instead he runs at full speed, stopping only when his fist makes contact with Adam's face, and it's a bone crunching sound. A grunt of pain erupts from both of them.

"Stop!" I yell to Ian. "Stop!"

"Who the hell do you think you are?" Ian spits out as he punches Adam from the other side. Adam backs up. I notice he's not fighting back and barely defending himself. Perhaps he thinks he deserves this.

"Ian!" I scream at him. "Stop!"

"Don't ever come near my family again!" Ian threatens him, twisting the neck of his shirt tight across Adam's throat. Adam glances in my direction. "Don't!" Ian warns pulling the handgun from the back of his pants. He presses it to Adam's lower jaw, his finger twitching near the trigger. "Don't you dare look at her or the children," Ian warns with a voice so low and angry it scares me.

Adam says nothing, he just nods his head slightly, the barrel of the handgun pressing so hard it tips his head to the side. One of the Guardians that has been waiting in the hallway begins a low growl.

"You're lucky the Guardians are standing here right now, because if they weren't, you'd be dead. Which is what will happen if I ever see your face again." Ian releases Adam's shirt with a hard shove. Neither of them looks at me.

"Ian, let's go, we have to go," I tell him, pulling at his arm.

Adam leaves, walking down the hallway toward the locker rooms at the end. I rush to the gymnasium to find the children and Blithe staring in the direction of the doors. They must have heard the commotion. I run to Lina and Raven, crushing them to me, kissing their cheeks and hair. "Are you okay?" I ask them.

"Mom, you're back!" Lina answers. Raven stares. "What happened out there?" She leans to the side of me, looking toward the door.

"Nothing." I run my hands over the children feeling for injuries. "Just an argument. Come on." I pick up Raven and take Lina's hand. "Let's go home."

"But Adam's out there." She looks toward the door. "He's not dead mom," she whispers, eyes wide. "It's a miracle."

"No, sweetie, it's not a miracle. Adam lied to us. Come on. We need to get out of here."

"But, Mom," Lina stalls.

"I'm sorry, but he's not coming back with us. Adam lied. We don't trust people who lie."

Moving her eyes to the floor, Lina says, "But he's alive."

There are so many things I want to explain to Lina about love and trust, but this is not the time or the place. Hopefully seeing someone who she thought was dead didn't ruin her too much.

I turn to Blithe, who is standing there wide-eyed. "I want to go," she says. "I told Ian already. I didn't know what they had planned. Adam showed up and said that there was an emergency. I just wanted to keep the children safe."

"I know," I tell her. "But you're going to leave Adam? You're going to leave your brother and come back with us?"

"Everyone at the Pasture is the closest thing I've ever had to a family since my parents died and Adam disappeared. He came back after I was recruited by Crane, but... but I barely know him anymore. And..." Blithe looks more out of sorts than I've ever seen her, her blonde hair pulling from her bun to fall on her neck and shoulders.

"Sam?" I ask.

She smiles a little. "And there's Sam."

"Okay, let's go."

Ian is on the phone with Sam as we step into the hallway. I hear him getting directions to the closest area of train tracks.

Picking up Raven and taking Lina's hand, I lead Blithe and the children out of the school. Ian follows, repeating directions into the phone. As we reach the front door, I notice Mack standing near the entrance.

"See ya, Mack!" one of the boys shouts as we walk by him.

"Later, gator," Mack replies. He looks up as we pass and gives us a nod. "Just follow the trail back to the tracks," he tells us.

We walk the trail that Mack and Chuck brought me to Romney on.

"Do you want me to carry Raven?" Ian asks when we reach the field where I remember throwing up and turning hysterical.

"No." I shift Raven onto my opposite hip. "I'm not tired yet."

--

When we reach the edge of the forest and the train tracks are visible in a narrow clearing, Ian takes out the cell phone and dials a number.

"Alexander?" he asks. "We're at the tracks–" He pulls the phone away and stares at the screen, his brow wrinkled.

"What's wrong?" I ask.

"The line went dead." The corner of his mouth downturns as he tries to call again. I see a notification pop up on the screen.

"What's it say?" I ask.

"No service," he replies.

"No service?" Blithe asks from next to me.

"Great, whatever secure tower the phone was connected to is out of service," I say.

"Or that they shut off service to this phone," Ian points out.

"What do we do now?" Blithe asks as she turns and looks toward the children.

"Sam is already on his way," Ian says. "I guess we just wait."

We pass the time by playing games and singing songs with the children, sitting in the clearing near the tracks.

"If we have to play *Eye Spy* one more time, I'm pretty sure my eyes are going to bleed," Ian grumbles as he leans toward me.

"Nice," I tell him.

Blithe laughs. She's sitting across from us. And then, stopping abruptly, her face pales and I notice she is no longer focused on us, but behind us. The back of my neck tingles. The Guardians stand and begin a low growl. I stand and turn, looking across the tracks where Blithe is focused.

There is a man, his eyes black and hollow, greasy shoulder length hair, and a scar from his left eye to the corner of his mouth.

"Shit." Ian moves to his feet before I finish saying the word.

"Who the hell is that?" he asks, reaching for the handgun that is secured in his waistband.

Four more of the men slither out of the forest. I gasp, their long greasy hair is familiar, as well as the mud caked to their clothing and exposed skin. They each hold some type of weapon; a machete, an ax, or a strange sword-like thing. They don't speak; their eyes are black, hollow, and fiery. And fixed on us.

"Get the children, Blithe." I turn, pushing Lina and Raven toward her as she reaches for them. "Go back into the forest."

"What are you going to do?" She whispers through

her teeth. "They have weapons."

"I know," I tell her realizing how vulnerable we are at the moment. We have no Volker with us, just Ian. The oldest of the children, Marcus, is only twelve, and Cashel eleven.

"Who are they?" Ian asks.

"Swamp people, from Crystal River."

The man with the scar smiles, his mouth curving up just like an alligator's mouth for an attack. He takes a step toward us.

"Stay back!" Ian shouts to them.

The man with the scar says something in their Creole language that I cannot understand. I hear a scream from behind us. Turning, I see that it is Astrid. Blithe tries to soothe her.

"Take them back!" I tell Blithe. "Follow the trail back to the school." I reach for my bag, pull the handgun out that Elvis gave me. I hand it to Lina. "You know what to do, Lina. Just like in target practice."

"Mom!" Lina cries.

"Go, Lina. Take Raven and go with Blithe." I look at the older boys, their faces pale and sweating. Marcus takes Ira's hand, Cashel takes Lex's, Lina takes Astrid's. A small whimper escapes Lina. Blithe picks up Raven and directs the children to the trail we came on.

"Run!" I tell her. "Run as fast as you can!"

I watch for a moment as they run into the forest, hand in hand, following the trail that led us to the tracks. The cluster of Guardians runs with the children, only two remain with us.

Turning, I see that more of the Swamp people have emerged from the tree line. There are now ten of them. Ian flicks the safety off of the handgun.

"Stay back or I will shoot you!" he yells to them.

The man takes another step forward. "We hungry," he says in a thick southern accent.

"We have no food for you," I shout to the man.

He smiles, showing a row of crooked, rotten teeth. "Looks like plenty o' food hiya."

"What the hell is he talking about?" Ian asks.

"I think they're cannibals," I tell him.

"Shit." Ian corrects his stance and fires a bullet at the feet of the man with the scar. He laughs. Another row of people slinks out of the tree line. The man with the scar takes another step forward. The Guardians growl louder, flanking each side of us.

"I only have fourteen bullets left," Ian whispers to me.

The man with the scar laughs loudly as though he heard. I reach down, pulling a rock and a stick from the ground.

"Go!" Ian says. "Go after the children."

"No." I grip the heavy stick in my hand. "I'm not sacrificing you to them."

"A stick and a stone aren't going to do shit," he argues. "Get out of here!"

"No."

The man with the scar stops laughing; gripping the machete in his hand, he lowers himself to a spread-legged, bent-knee stance. And as though I'm watching a pack of wild animals, the rest of the men follow, gripping their weapons, settling themselves into a similar stance, readying for attack.

"Shoot them," I whisper to Ian.

"I'm waiting for them to make the first move."

He's hesitating, he can't hesitate. I want to take the gun from his hands and shoot these people so he doesn't have to, so he doesn't have their deaths weighing upon his soul. I don't want that for him, but there's no time for that. I can't save him from this.

"Don't wait, shoot them!"

On key, as soon as the words come out of my mouth, the man with the scar lunges. Ian fires a shot, hitting the dirt at the man's feet. He stops at the tracks, but the rest of the Swamp people continue moving, leaping over the train tracks right toward us.

"Run, Andie!" Ian yells to me.

The Guardians growl and snarl before leaping into the row of men that run at us. I watch as one lunges for the neck of one of the swamp people, tearing out a bloodied chunk of skin. The man drops to the ground, lifeless. The Guardians continue, leaping and attacking. One gives a loud yelp as it is cut by one of the attackers. I hear Ian shoot and watch as two of the men go down. I take a few steps back, and notice one of the men headed straight for me. I reach back and throw the rock at him as hard as I can. It makes contact with his shoulder, skimming off the man's clothing and barely stopping him. He slows, but doesn't stop. I grip the stick, thinking that maybe I could jab it in his eye. As I get ready, another gunshot rings through the crowd, leaving a hole in the head of the man who was running at me. I turn to Ian, who lets out the last of his bullets.

The Guardians growl at a cluster of the Swamp people who remain on the other side of the tracks, apparently afraid of the large dogs. There are at least five bodies and the man with the scar has yet to move.

"Yer outta bullets," the man with the scar taunts.

Ian flips the handgun in his hand, grasping the barrel. The man with the scar starts running toward Ian. And without thinking, I run at them both, throwing myself onto the man. Ian reaches out, hitting

369

him in the side of the head with the butt of the gun. Someone pulls me off of the man with the scar. I can tell by the smell, pungent and sour like rotting meat, it's one of the Swamp people, either escaped from the Guardians or his injuries were slight enough for him to get off the ground.

I kick at him as he grips me around the waist, dragging me across the tracks, the whole time watching the scene of Ian fighting with the man with the scar. Ian hits him with the butt of the gun, until the man slaps it out of his hand. And then there is scuffling, the dirt by the tracks fills the air. I hear the sounds of punching, groans, bone hitting bone. Ian yells. The man with the scar fights with an eerie muteness.

The man behind me moves his arm across my neck. He talks into my ear, his rotten breath sliding over my face, "Don' have much ladies in our company." He laughs as I try to elbow him in the sides, unsuccessfully. "Oh! Oh, wait!" The man tightens his grip on my neck, and squeezing my face, he turns me to watch across the tracks from where he has just dragged me. "Dis de best part."

When the dust clears, I scream as loud as I can, fighting to get myself away from the man holding me. Ian is on the ground, the man with the scar on top of him, holding the machete over his head. I can see the blood on Ian's face, his shirt is ripped, and there is a long slice in his arm, blood streaming out of it. He struggles to get loose, but the way the man is perched on him—a foot on his neck, his knee across Ian's pelvis—Ian can barely move.

"Ian!" I scream as the man with the scar starts to bring the machete down.

"No, no," the man holding me warns, adjusting his

grip on my face and neck. "Jus' wach."

My heart beats so hard in my chest, watching, knowing that I'm going to see Ian die right in front of me. "No!" I shout through my teeth which are currently pressed together by the man's grip.

Then, the man with the scar stops midair. The machete drops from his hands, falling next to Ian's head. Ian moves his arms, pushing the man off of him and as he rolls, I notice an arrow sticking out of his chest.

I look in the only direction it could have come from, the tree line. There is movement above the ground and I see Adam, perched on a branch, an arrow aimed at me.

"Aw, shit," the man holding me calls out. His grip loosens. Ian stands, running in my direction. I look up to Adam as his arm moves back, he squints to aim. I close my eyes, holding my body as stiff as I can. Something rushes by my face. The man groans and drops to the ground.

"Andie," Ian reaches me, pulling me toward him.

I turn to see the Swamp people that the Guardians have corralled start to slither back into the forest, the one that was holding me now lying on the ground, an arrow sticking out of his eye.

Adam jumps down from the tree and stalks toward us. Looking at Ian, his eyes dark, he says, "Looks like you might still need me."

Ian glares back, pushing me behind him. Adam doesn't look at me, but I look at him, and I can see that his face which was once bloodied and bruised from Ian's assault is fully healed.

Impossible.

I take off my jacket, wrap it around my waist, then

remove one of my layered shirts and begin wrapping it around the wound on Ian's arm.

"Where are the children?" Ian asks.

"Mack is watching over them," Adam stares at Ian. "Let's get you cleaned up before Sam shows. Kids don't need to see you like this."

We retreat to the narrow trail. Ian shakes me off as I try to help him walk.

"Not that bad," he waves a bloodied-knuckle hand at me and moves an arm length away so he's walking in the tall grass.

"Did you know this would happen?" I ask Adam.

Adam, walking in front of us, simply turns his head so I can see the corner of his eye as he looks at me, without responding. But that's all I need. He must've known, or had some sense or warning that the Swamp People were near, and used the situation to promote himself, teach us a lesson.

Adam veers off of the path, into the forest. I can hear the bubbling of the stream. I follow Ian to the water. He bends, unties the shirt I wrapped around the wound on his arm and submerges it in the cold water.

"Let me help you." I reach for the shirt.

Ian moves away. "No. I don't need help."

"Ian." I grab his uninjured arm, squeezing it. "Let me help you." He's pale, much paler than he should be. The nurse in me realizes it must be a bit of shock, of relief, anger. Maybe all three combined. I push him back. "Sit. Now, Ian. I will do this." After all that has happened to us, I will not let this one incident be the final straw that tears us apart. I take the shirt from his hands, wring the cold water out, and use it to wipe his face. When the dirt and grime and blood are gone, and the only thing left are fresh cuts and swollen points threatening to bruise, Ian's eyes meet mine. There is a glimmer there, a wateriness for just an instant, and then as quickly as I see it, it disappears, replaced with a blank stare, focused on the forest across the stream.

As I rinse the blood off of the shirt in the cold stream, my fingertips turning blue, the realization comes to me that Ian just killed a handful of men. I squeeze the shirt, rip a sleeve off, take a large cold rock from the bottom of the stream and wrap it in the remaining fabric of the shirt.

"Here. Hold this." I press the wrapped rock to a knot on the side of Ian's head that's starting to turn purple. Using the sleeve, I begin wrapping around the cut on his arm. "You did what you had to do, Ian. No one will judge you for fighting for your family. Not me, not Lina, not even God. You kept us safe, you did well." I tie the bandage around his arm, jerking him a bit to make him focus on me and not off in the forest. "We would have died if it weren't for you."

His face is blank. I look up to find Adam watching us, his bow gripped tightly in his left hand.

I grasp Ian's face on both sides; move his head so he has nowhere else to focus but on my face directly in front of his. "Be here," I whisper. "Now, Ian. Be here now. I am here, our children are here. I will not let this ruin you." And just to prove that to him, I lean in and press my lips firmly to his.

When I pull away, he's changed, now focused and aware. Ian stands, the wrapped rock still pressed to his face. "I'm not going to thank you, Christian." Ian tells Adam. "If it wasn't for you, we wouldn't have gotten into this mess in the first place."

"Fine with me." Adam crosses his arms over his chest. "Just do me one favor," Adam stares at Ian.

"Call me Adam Waters in front of my men."

Ian laughs. "That is the only and last favor I will ever do for you."

"Fine. Let's get the children and get you all out of here."

Adam turns abruptly and lets out a loud whistle, a trill of notes. He turns his head to the right, holds his hand up for us to stop. Somewhere from within the forest the whistle returns. "Come on." Adam waves. "They're close."

As we follow him back to the trail, Ian leans toward me. "Why am I holding a rock to my face?" he asks.

"It's cold."

"And?"

"You know, like an ice pack." I explain.

"Oh."

"What did you think it was for?" I ask.

"I thought you wanted me to throw it at him."

We break the cover of the forest and find Mack walking toward us, Blithe and children in tow, surrounded by the remaining Guardians. I run for Lina and Raven, picking them up and holding them close to me.

"What happened to Daddy?" Lina asks as Ian walks toward us, a slight limp noticeable in his gait.

"He's okay, honey. He got a little hurt." I tuck a loose lock of curls behind her ear. "It's safe now. We're going to go home."

We return to the tracks, escorted by Adam and Mack, standing there in an awkward silence until we hear the vibrations of the train tracks. Blithe herds the children to the protection of the forest cover and wait. The train pulls up slowly. I can see Sam through the front window, searching the side of the tracks for us.

Ian steps out of the cover of the forest and waves him down.

When the train stops, Sam opens the door and steps out. Ian and I help the children into the engine car.

Blithe stops, waiting for us to get in.

Sam steps up next to her and takes her hand.

"Decided to come back?" he asks her as he helps her into the engine car.

"I didn't want to leave," she tells him softly before turning to the children and settling them on the benches.

We wait for Sam to climb up, but he never does.

"What's he doing?" Ian asks.

"I'm not sure." I walk to the door, down the steps, jump off and land on the solid ground near the tracks.

I find Sam talking to Adam near the tree line. They turn to look at me, stopping their conversation.

"Sam!" I shout to him. "Let's get out of here."

He waves, says one more sentence to Adam, then jogs toward the engine car. I stop him before he gets in. "What was that? Why are you talking to Adam?"

"It was nothing–"

"Nothing?"

"I was just thanking him for getting you guys safely to the tracks."

"Really, Sam. He kidnapped the children, made us all come out here, and you're thanking him?"

"It wasn't just him, Andie." Sam tips his head at me. "You have to know, there's always something else going on."

I shake my head in exasperation. "Can we just get the hell out of here?"

We board the train. Ian gives me a questioning look when my eyes meet his.

"Ready?" Sam asks.

"Let's go home," I tell him.

Sam eases the train into full gear. "Next stop, the Phoenix District."

I look out the window and see Adam and Mack watching from the tree line as the train pulls away.

--

By the time we make it back to Phoenix it is night. A row of Volker, as well as Alexander and Elvis, are waiting to drive us back to the Pasture.

"Where's Crane?" Alexander asks as we carry the sleeping children off of the train.

"He said he was going to see George Crossbender," I tell him. "I need you to send for Dr. Akiyama, Ian is injured."

Elvis frowns. "He's not coming back here?"

"I hope not," I tell him.

"Crane's not coming back?" Sam asks as he carries Astrid, she is sleeping on his shoulder.

"No," I tell him. "We made a deal. He won't be back for a while."

"Where did he go?" Sam asks.

"I think he's going to Tonopah. But as long as he's not here, I couldn't care less where he goes."

We make the quick drive to the Pasture. And the feeling of the comfort of home envelopes me as we pass the gates.

Dr. Akiyama tends to Ian's wounds, stitching and bandaging the cuts. Sam escorts Blithe and the boys back to her house. Once the children are settled and tucked in together in the same bed having fallen asleep after Lina began reading a story to Raven and Astrid, I retreat to my room. Ian follows.

"What did they do to you?" Ian asks.

"I don't think you would believe me if I told you," I tell him looking around the room. Something is different here.

"Tell me."

"Crane only gave me the children back on one condition."

"What's that?"

"He wanted to inject me with nanocytes."

"What are nanocytes? Is that some more of his genetic engineering bullshit?"

"Yes."

"Did you tell him no?"

"Ian, you don't understand. He wouldn't give them back to me."

"Andie, what did you do?" He takes a step toward me. "You didn't let him, did you?"

"I had no choice."

"You always say that! You always say that you had no choice. Everyone has choices, Andie. You could have done something, fought back…"

"I don't want to fight, Ian! I've done enough fighting. I've seen enough fighting."

"So, you just laid down and took it?"

"No, not exactly."

"Then what happened?" He stares at me while I remain silent, until he starts pacing near the doorway. "Okay then, what do these nanocytes do? What is their function?"

"They fix errors and damage in the DNA. They reconstruct cellular breakdown so the body doesn't get sick, so it will heal, so I can't… so I'll never…"

Ian stops pacing, steps back, staring at me in

disbelief. "So you won't ever die."

"Yes." I break down in tears. And when I can calm myself, I tell him the story that Crane told me.

"So you'll be like this, forever?" he asks.

"Unless I can get them out of my body."

"Will you?"

"I'm going to try. I don't want this. I don't want to stay like this while everyone else around me ages and dies. I got you back. All I ever wanted was to grow old with you, like we promised to do together. I don't want to live on, alone..." Suddenly, I realize what's different about the room. "Where's Raven's crib?" I ask Ian.

"It was supposed to be a surprise." He walks over to the empty space along the wall that once held the crib. "I moved him into my old room."

I stare at him, letting it sink in. Husband and wife. That is what we are, and while we made strides getting back there, knowing what I know now, I can accept it. I walk over to him and wrap my arms around his neck. "I love you, Ian," I tell him. "I'm so sorry I let this happen. I don't know how right now, but I'm going to fix this. I'm going to make this right."

"Well, it looks like you have all the time in the world, now that you're going to live forever. Will you still love me when I'm old and wrinkled? Will you still love me and my old wrinkly balls?" He asks with a furtive smile.

"Shut up!" I smack his shoulder. "This is no time for jokes. Don't you see what he just did? Crane just took it to the next level. You know what he told me, that the Residents, these sheep Residents, need new Gods to fear. He thinks he's rewriting history. Rewriting faith, religion, and these people will believe him."

378

He releases me and steps back. "So, he's creating his own deities?"

"No. I don't know. I don't know what he's doing. All I know is that I am nothing more than a single person trying to keep my family safe."

Ian steps toward me, placing his hands on each of my arms. "Maybe you were, but I don't think you are anymore."

"I'm no different. I'll prove it to you."

I leave the bedroom and head for the kitchen. Flicking the stove burner on, I reach for a knife from the butcher block and hold it over the flame, sterilizing it.

"What are you doing?" Ian asks, having followed me.

"Something I should have done a long time ago."

I rest my arm on the sink and using my index finger I feel for the small lump that Crane injected into my skin. Finding it, I adjust the knife in my hand and press it to my forearm.

"Andie!"

"Be quiet!" I scold Ian. "You'll wake the children."

I press, suppressing the noise of pain in my throat. Bright red blood flows down my arm and into the sink. When I feel the tip of the blade hit something hard I stop. Setting the knife in the sink and using my fingers, I reach into the wound, grasp the transmitter between my fingernails, and pull it out. Holding it up to the light I inspect the small piece of metal. Crane told me it was a transmitter, and then he told me it housed the nanocytes. Whatever it really is, I throw it down into the sink drain and turn the water on.

"Oh my God," I hear Ian whisper as he grasps my arm and twists it toward him.

"What's wrong?"

I look down to find the gash I just cut into my arm has closed and the only thing left of my self-inflicted wound is a light pink line and the blood drying on my arm.

EPILOGUE

"Things are well?"

"Things are well," I repeat to Dr. Akiyama from his dark blue sofa. Ian squeezes my hand.

"I'm assuming you're speaking to each other on regular terms now?" he asks.

"Yes–" I start.

"I don't know, Doc," Ian lets go of my hand and stretches his arm along the couch behind me, "sometimes we do things that don't involve speaking."

"Ian!" I swat at his chest and feel my face becoming an increasingly darker shade of red.

"That answers that," Dr. Akiyama mumbles with a smile and makes a mark on his notebook. "Things seem good, there's progress, finally." He looks between us.

"It's good," Ian replies as he rubs his fingers over the wedding rings. I've taken to wearing them again instead of hanging them off my necklace. The necklace that Adam gave me, I had to hide that, I'm not sure I can ever look at it again without remembering every single lie he's ever told me.

"Have you spoken about the most recent turn of events, the outing to..." He flips through his papers. "Ah! Romney, West Virginia. It's beautiful country there I hear."

"I think so," I reply. I look at Ian and squeeze his hand.

"Ian, have you come to terms with what you've done?" Dr. Akiyama drops the tone of his voice.

I grip Ian's hand harder and watch as the color leaves his face. He's suddenly pasty, white, and against the light blonde of his hair it makes him look ill.

"How many men did you kill, Ian?" Dr. Akiyama asks.

"Seven," he responds.

"No." I squeeze his arm. "Six, there were only six." Adam killed the seventh and eight men; put an arrow through one's heart and the other's eye, the Swamp People.

"It doesn't matter how many," Ian mumbles as he moves his eyes to the dull gray carpet and releases my hand. I grasp it back, hoping that Dr. Akiyama didn't see the movement, which would be a demerit against our progress.

"Ian, do not let this weigh heavy on your heart," the doctor suggests. "There were abnormal circumstances and you were fighting to save your family. Something Andromeda has also experienced."

"That's different."

"Not by much, just by numbers and, well, you weren't being attacked, Andromeda, but the act was the same." Dr. Akiyama turns a page in his notebook.

Ian whips his head toward me. "What is he talking about?" he asks, his eyes turning an impossible shade of darker brown, almost black.

There is an uncomfortable silence as I stare and the doctor watches us. I never told him the details of my deep dark secret, the one I knew he would hate me for, but promised he wouldn't. Now it seems we share this sin, but mine feels a little darker. "The man I killed, he was unarmed," I whisper to him.

Ian doesn't respond, he just stares, his pupils widening as he takes in the image of his murdering wife sitting before him.

After a few moments Dr. Akiyama says, "You see, you both share this quandary. It is just another topic of discussion from which you can continue to work on your relationship."

We say nothing, both still looking at each other.

Dr. Akiyama clears his throat. "And how are things now that you know Adam is still alive?"

"Adam is dead to me. I never want to see him again, ever." As I say the words, I can still feel Ian's stinging gaze on me. I pluck at the edge of my shirt, nervously. Now, all of my children's parents are killers.

"I see," Dr. Akiyama replies. He closes his notebook and stands, moving toward his desk.

I move to stand, pulling Ian up with me.

"Crane will be happy with your progress, both of yours, well, now that he has left the District in your care for the time being."

"You talk to Crane still?" I ask.

"Of course I do. I would have thought that you would have realized this."

"I guess I just thought that when he left, we wouldn't hear from him."

"Quite the contrary, Andie. Either way, he will be pleased."

"So are we done?"

"For today." Dr. Akiyama opens a drawer on his desk and places the notebook inside.

"No, I mean forever. You said we could be done when progress was made, and it has been made."

Dr. Akiyama looks at Ian, who stands near the couch, then back at me as I've migrated toward his desk. "If you think you are ready," he replies. "But there are other events which are about to occur which you may need my counsel for."

"What events?"

Dr. Akiyama raises his brows, forming a thin white line across his forehead. "Ian's son will be coming to live with you at The Pasture. He has been chosen, showed promise as Sovereign. And since he is old enough, he will commence his training immediately."

--

"What's his name?" I ask Ian as we head to our vehicle.

Ian shrugs. "I have no clue. Shouldn't you know?"

"No. I don't keep track of him and...her."

Sliding into the passenger side of the SUV, to say the friction in the air is painful would be an understatement.

Ian starts the vehicle and heads for home, silent the entire way. I should have known, he said he forgave me for the infidelity, for the killing, for it all. But when Dr. Akiyama spilled the specifics of how I killed that man, that he was unarmed, Ian's face changed just like I knew it would. He doesn't forgive me, and he never will.

-The End-

384

CPSIA information can be obtained
at www.ICGtesting.com
Printed in the USA
BVHW032244291222
655301BV00001B/65